MW01129399

Coast

JAY McLEAN

Published by Jay McLean

Published: Jay McLean June 2016
Cover Design: Jay McLean

To Warwick McLean.
There are no wounds you cannot heal.
Transit umbra, baby.

PART I

JOURNAL

I woke up in a pool of sweat, my mind racing and my heart hammering in my chest. My heart—my poor, sad, broken heart.

I dreamt about him—the version of him that had me thrashing against the sheets and my fingers gripping tightly to the covers surrounding me, suffocating me in my own thoughts. My own fears.

I hated it.

I loved it.

Which pretty much describes everything I feel for him.

My heart loves him.

My head hates him.

Even now, over a year later.

The first thing I did when my eyes snapped open was clutch a hand to my chest wondering how my heart was still beating after the painful onslaught the visions my dream had created. Only they weren't just visions, they were memories.

True, life, memories.

He stood over me, his eyes glazed from tears mixed with rage. "I hate you the most, Becca," he'd said, and I'd stood still, afraid of him.

Him.

The boy with the dark eyes and shaggy dark hair whose smile had once lit up my entire world.

And in that moment, I ***feared*** *him.*

It's an overwhelming feeling, one I can't put down onto paper like Linda had suggested I do, yet here I am, trying to justify it.

If there was a single word to describe it, it would be ***torn****.*

My head.

My heart.

The two parts of myself ripping my being in two.

I should be used to it by now, right? How many times have I woken up in fear, my nightmares grounding me to my spot?

Fear.

Love.

Hate.

Caused by two entirely different people and circumstances.

One is dead.

One is Joshua Warden.

PROLOGUE

BECCA

A knock sounds on my bedroom door and a second later, the now familiar male voice speaks. His voice is quiet, barely a whisper. "Are you ready, Becca?"

I shut my laptop and slowly get up, turning to him as I do. His eyes are gentle, yet wary.

I nod, even though we both know it's a lie.

I'm not ready. *How can I be?*

But I made a promise to him that I'd *try.*

Just like I'd try to drive; another item on my list.

It didn't go well, but at least, I *tried.*

He'd sat in the passenger's seat and shown me what everything was, and then asked me to ease onto the accelerator. I'd done it. But as soon as we were on the road, I'd panicked and hit the brake at the same time. The screeching sound of the wheels spinning but the car not moving had set off something inside me. It also set me back three months of therapy. I'd blacked out apparently—like I was living in the nightmare—and I'd just screamed. He'd held me until it was over and then he drove home, where I'd spent the next three days in bed, awake and alive but completely dead inside.

Dead.

Dead.

Dead.

Just like my mother.

He'd kept my bedroom door open, and at night I'd see him there watching me, coffee in his hand, his shoulder against the doorframe and he'd cry.

He hadn't known I'd seen him.

I'd never tell him.

He'd sat on the seat in the corner of my room and had continued to watch me. I'd thought about Henry Warden, the man who died with regrets, and I didn't want that for him, so I'd agreed when my therapist had suggested the bucket list... but on one condition. I wanted him with me when I ticked off every one.

Which I guess is why a half hour later he's standing by my side, twenty feet away from a tour bus with the giant Globe Shoes logo on the side.

"Is that him?" he asks, and I can feel everything inside me move faster, beat harder, and then *drop.*

My heart.

My stomach.

Everything drops when I look at the bus, at the open door and the kid in his father's arms, as he gets handed over to his mother.

Tommy laughs, and Natalie smiles as she takes him from Josh, who steps out of the bus and wraps his arms around both of them. He kisses his son first, on the cheek.

And then he kisses *her.*

On the forehead.

They laugh together—this beautiful family.

Natalie places Tommy on the ground, her hand holding his and they turn and walk away.

"Is it?" Dad asks.

I nod once, tears pricking my eyes as I try to hold it together.

I watch Josh.

He watches his family.

Time stands still.

After a while, he drops his gaze and shoves his hands in his pockets, his broad shoulders lifting as he kicks the toe of his shoe on the ground.

I close my eyes, trying to find some relief from the pain. Pain I was not at all expecting.

Finally, I look up. Up. UP.

And everything stops.

Everything.

My breath.

His foot.

My heart.

His mouth.

My world.

Everything.

Stops.

Then he takes a step forward.

And everything starts again.

Only now, it's all amplified.

He comes closer and closer, all while I stand still, *afraid*—not of him—but of the devastating love I still feel for him.

"He *sees* you, Becca."

CHAPTER 1

---

sense

/sɛns/

noun

1. any of the faculties, as sight, hearing, smell, taste, or touch, by which humans and animals perceive stimuli originating from outside or inside the body.

He stands two feet in front of me, his eyes as intense as his stare. He looks the same as the image I have of him forever burned behind my eyes, eyes that have wept for him.

His hands are in the pockets of his shorts, his T-shirt stretched across his chest. Physically, he hasn't changed a lot in the year since I've seen him. But it's his presence that has my feet glued to the ground beneath me.

He's no longer the sad, beautiful, mourning boy who had needed me like the last time we were together. Now, he stands a little taller, a little more confident. I guess when you work hard to make your dreams a reality, you have every reason to walk with your head held high.

My gaze drifts to the faded gray *Globe* logo printed across his chest, and I don't know how long I stare at it, my heart thumping harshly in the walls of my chest before I realize the image is still.

Frozen.

My brow bunches as I look down at my top, watching the rise and fall of my chest created by my heavy breaths before looking back at his.

Still frozen.

I inhale sharply, my eyes snapping to his, and I blink once, twice, forcing back the tears threatening to escape.

He's holding his breath.

Slowly, I raise my hand, my mouth parting, his name—silent—forces its way out on my exhale.

Then he does the same, his lips spread, his shoulders dropping with his outtake of breath. It's loud, forceful even. But his single exhale doesn't just release the breath he held within him, it releases a jumbled mess of memories. Hundreds, thousands of them. All of *us*.

Josh takes a step forward at the same time my dad's hand lands on my back. He *knows* I want to run.

Josh takes another step.

And then two.

Three.

He's close, almost *too* close, as he bends at the knees, his nose level with mine.

My hands fist at my sides.

Then his lips curve, his eyes widening. *"Emerald Eyes."*

The two words are a prayer as they fall from his lips, his voice like a symphony teasing my ears, ears that have roused for him.

He's so close, I can feel his breaths on my forehead, smell the slight scent of cologne mixed with everything Josh. My head spins, my mind becomes lost in the thousand memories of us. From the first time he knocked on my door, wearing the same exact cologne, to the first time I sat in his car wanting nothing more than to breathe him in. I told him I loved the way he smelled. And now, just like then, I want to get lost in it. In the way it wraps itself around me, making me dizzy, making me needy for him.

I kissed him that day, his lips warm and soft across my mouth. The taste of his kiss forever scarred on my lips—lips that have longed for him.

His mouth moves, and I know he's speaking, but the thumping in my eardrums has turned the world silent. My dad's touch is gentle, urging me forward, and I force the chaos out of my mind. Josh raises his eyebrows waiting for my response, but I don't have one. Dad, however, clears his throat and steps forward, half blocking me from Josh's view—something Josh senses right away because he straightens to full height, his chest rising with his intake of breath.

"We're here to see Josh Warden," Dad says, even though he knows he's speaking *to* Josh Warden.

Josh Warden, *Josh Warden*, ***Josh Warden***. His name replays in my mind, over and over, while his shoulders slump, his gaze switching to me quickly before going back to my dad, taking in all 6'4" of him. "That's me, sir," Josh murmurs, the confidence he exuded only minutes ago no longer visible.

I step away from behind my dad's protection and lift the tag from the lanyard hanging around my neck. I tap it twice and then look up, waiting for his response.

His eyebrows bunch and he reaches for the tag, his fingers brushing mine.

His touch is like fire. Sweet, torturous flames setting off too many emotions. I struggle, and I fight, and I fight some more, to not move away, to not fear his touch.

But I *fail*.

Because I'm Becca Owens—a broken girl.
And he's Josh Warden—the boy who broke me.

CHAPTER 2

JOSHUA

I can hear them following behind me as I lead them to my bus, their footsteps crunching on the gravel now the soundtrack to my fear.

Every day I thought about her, missed her, *craved her,* and now she's here, and her presence has me struggling for air.

Chris's eyes widen when I open the door and Becca comes into view, his mouth opening, closing, opening again. He pushes off the table he's leaning on and taps away at his phone. After a while, he looks up, first at me, then at her, and then her dad behind her. "Becca Owens," Chris says into the thick, tension-filled air. "You're doing the interview for *Student Life*?"

Becca nods, her gaze everywhere but on me.

"Right." Chris returns her nod before looking over at me, his demeanor changing from being my agent to being my friend. "You good?"

I hesitate to answer because I don't know if I am. That's a lie. I *know* I'm not good.

"Why don't you guys set up?" Chris says, pointing to the couch. "We just need a minute."

He's trying to save me, and I appreciate it. But all the

minutes in the world couldn't save me right now. I wipe my sweaty palms on my shorts and swallow hard. "I'm good, man," I tell Chris, then to Becca, "Do you need anything? Water or..."

Her head shakes as she points to the table behind Chris.

I move out of her way so she can get past. Her dad follows, and I wonder for a moment if he goes to all her interviews or if he's just here because it's *me*. Because I'm the reason she is the way she is, the reason she can no longer speak.

Becca sets up on one side of the table, her dad standing next to her, his arms crossed over his massive frame, doing everything he can to elicit the fear inside me. But it's not him that has my heart hammering, making it impossible to breathe.

It's *Her*.

It's *always* been Her.

I take a step forward and offer her dad my hand. "I'm Josh Warden, sir. It's a pleasure to meet you."

He takes it, shaking it harder than necessary. "Martin," he grunts, and it's that moment I know he *knows*. About as much as I know that there's not a damn thing I can do about it now, so I suck it up and take the seat opposite his daughter. I wait, watching her set up her phone, iPad, and computer on the table. Then she sits back, her hands on her lap, and she looks right at me, her eyes searing mine. After a moment, her lips curve into a smile, and I die. A thousand deaths. Over and over. Because while on the outside, I'm living the life, living my dream, it had never felt real and I had never felt worthy. And for that split second when her eyes were on mine, and her smile was directed at me, she gave value to my existence.

Her smile fades when she leans forward, her fingers frantic as they press down on key after key of her computer. She hits one, then pauses and looks up at me, waiting for the mechanical voice to sound. *"I should probably start by introducing myself.*

I'm Becca Owens, and I'm a student at Washington University here in St. Louis. I'll be interviewing you for Student Life newspaper. The interview will run a little different than what you're probably used to because I'm speech impaired. I'll be communicating via my trusted old friend Cordy. If this is going to be a problem, please let me know now."

I stare, unblinking, feeling my worth, my value, being sucked into a black hole along with the rest of me.

"I'll be using my computer to speak with you. My iPad is for recording, and my phone has my notes. Again, if this is a problem, please let me know."

Wiping my palms on my shorts again, I glance up at her dad before leaning forward, my forearms on the table. "It's no problem, Becs. Whatever you need."

Her dad sighs, and Becca's gaze drops.

"Sir?" Chris says, his voice loud as he shoves his phone in his pocket. "What size feet you got?"

"Excuse me?" Martin asks.

Chris points behind him. "I got a bunch of shoes out back. The sponsor likes it when we hand 'em out. You interested?"

For the first time since I saw him, Martin seems to relax. "I got big feet…"

Chris smiles. "I got plenty of sizes. Plenty of styles." He motions to where we keep the shoes. "Take your pick."

Martin places his hand on Becca's shoulder. She doesn't flinch, unafraid of his touch. "You good, kid?" he asks her.

She smiles up at him and nods once, then shoos him away with a wave of her hand.

We both wait until they're in the back part of the bus, the door closed behind them, before she types and I speak. "You look good, Becs," I say, the same time "Cordy" says, *"Sorry about my dad."*

I laugh.

She frowns.

Then her fingers are moving again. *"I haven't been following your success, so I had to have someone else on the newspaper write up the questions. He was supposed to be here, but he had a family emergency come up, so you're stuck with me."*

I clear my throat and push aside my disappointment.

"Ready?"

"Not really," I mumble.

Her frown deepens, her fingers tapping. *"You took quite the hiatus for a few years there, and you've made it known in previous interviews the reason you did—your son Tommy—but you've never been clear on why you came back. Feel like giving a small time college newspaper an exclusive?"*

Her chest rises and falls as she keeps her head lowered, waiting for my response. "You want an exclusive?" I ask.

She chews on her lip, her gaze dropping. She hesitates a beat before her fingers move again. *"I'm sorry. He'd e-mailed the questions to me a few minutes before I arrived and I didn't get a chance to read them. I'm not looking for an exclusive, I swear. I don't want you to feel like I expect more because of our history or whatever."*

Her eyes are on mine now, wide and filled with fear. And my memories, my visions, my dreams of her do not do her justice because she's so much more.

I'm about to speak, but a knock on the door cuts me off. A moment later, Chris is back, Martin—holding three shoe boxes —following behind him. "I got it," Chris says, the door already half open. Justin's on the other side, his hands in his pockets. "Oh, I'm sorry." He eyes Becca before switching to me. "I didn't know you were still working."

"It's cool, man. What's up?"

"We're trying to get Tommy to head to the hotel, but he won't go without—"

"I got it," I cut in, not wanting Becca to hear. I get up and move to Tommy's room in the bus and grab what Justin needs.

"Here you go," I tell him, back at the door. He pulls his gaze away from Becca and looks down at the skateboard, the camera, and the framed drawing of Tommy's "family." He focuses on the drawing, and then up at Becca, then back down, again and again, while my heart thumps in my chest and my eyes drift shut because I know he *knows*. His thumb swipes over the glass of the frame, over the bright green crayon eyes, and he gasps, his mouth dropping, his eyes wide as he looks back up at Becca. "You're—"

"Is that it?" I ask, cutting him off. But I'm too late because Becca's already seen his reaction and now she's on her feet, moving closer and closer to me. She takes the frame from Justin's hands, her eyes as wide as his were while her thumb skims from the green crayon eyes to the bandage on her stick figure chest.

"Because you had a boo-boo," I whisper. Then clear my throat. "Becca, this is Justin, Nat's fiancé. Justin, Becca."

The fear in Becca's eyes is replaced with something else, and she hands back the frame before turning quickly and sitting back at the table, her hands on her lap and her focus on her computer.

"Thanks for this," Justin says, and I nod and shut the door.

"Interview done?" Martin asks.

Becca shakes her head, glaring at her screen like it's somehow going to give her answers to the thousands of questions a year apart has created.

Sitting back down, I watch the sadness take over, watch the tears fill her eyes. "Becs..." I start to reach over, but her eyes narrow, her lips pressed tight when she slams a finger down on a key.

"You took quite the hiatus for a few years there, and you've made it known in previous interviews the reason you did—your son Tommy —but you've never been clear on why you came back. Feel like giving a small time college newspaper an exclusive?"

I suck in a breath and keep it there while I hold her gaze. The seconds tick by, one after the other until my mind begins to spin, and my heart begins to race, and I know, deep down, that the only thing I can offer her is the pain that comes with the truth. "I met a girl with raven dark hair and eyes the color of emeralds..."

CHAPTER 3

BECCA

"I met a *girl with raven dark hair and eyes the color of emeralds. I came into her life with an insecure past, and she came into mine with a tortured one. My future was set, and hers was uncertain, but at the time, it didn't matter. We filled our days with porch-step kisses, filled our ears with three-year-old laughter, and filled our hearts with love. Deep, soul-aching, desperate love. She believed in me in ways only my father ever had, and I wanted to prove that I was worthy of that. So I agreed to SK8F8. For her. But then one day my future became as uncertain as hers, and I crumbled. I was so afraid of the destruction she'd cause when her life would no longer be filled with those things—kisses, laughter, and love—and so my fear pushed me to destroy the things I loved. Physically. Metaphorically. Every way possible. And when the dust of my demolition settled, she re-appeared, like sunshine between two buildings, and she gave me a chance to validate her belief in me. So I did. With her by my side or her following behind me, I skated my heart out. And as I stood on that pipe on the day of my so-called 'come back,' my heart hanging in the balance, just like my board on the edge of the coping, I looked down at the girl, a girl I knew I had lost, a girl whose emerald eyes were blocked by her*

camera, and I felt the same thing I felt the moment I fell in love with skating. The moment I fell in love with her. She made me feel weightless, feel free, feel airborne. So I kicked, and I pushed, and for the past year, that's all I've been doing because it didn't feel the same, and I knew in my heart that without her, I'd never be able to coast."

JOURNAL

I dipped in his words.
Bathed in his declarations.
Submerged myself in the tale of his love.
His one true love.
It was perfect.
Too perfect.
Every sentence.
Every word.
Every damn syllable.
Perfect.
Until the last word was spoken.
And I drowned in his lies.
And I realized...
That the world was full of perfect things.
And broken, faulty people.

CHAPTER 4

BECCA

I pull the earphones out of my ear and turn to my door where Dad is standing, calling my name. I spent the rest of last night thinking about Josh, and when I awoke, I thought about him some more. So I listened to his interview, over and over, until I had his words memorized, and then I became angry. Unjustifiably angry. And when the anger faded, I became sad. Miserable, even. And I had no idea why. So I wrote down my feelings in the stupid journal and stared at my words until they, too, were memorized. Seared into my brain for all of eternity as a reminder that no matter how good he looked, how good he smelled, how good I *felt* when his eyes were on mine—that I could never go back there. *We* could never go back there. Because as much as he told me he loved me, that I was everything to him, my mother had said the same things. And I'd spent the past year, three days a week, in some form of therapy trying to force myself to believe that it was *not* love. It couldn't be.

"How you doing, sweetheart?" Dad asks.

I nod and smile.

"You working on that article?"

Another nod. Another smile.

"Listen," he says, stepping forward, his hands in the pockets of his sweats. His eyes—green just like mine—drop to the floor, and I know he's nervous. It's the exact way he'd approached me the first few months I'd moved in with him. "That Warden boy is at the door."

I stand quickly, knowing—*praying*—he's wrong, and rush to the door because there's absolutely no way in hell that Josh is standing outside *my* house on the morning of a day when he should be competing. Yet here he is, looking as disheveled as I feel. My mouth forms an *O* as I stop in front of him, half hiding behind the door when he looks up at me. I feel the same way I did when he looked at me last night, *exposed*, as if he could see all my secrets and hear all my thoughts and sense all my fears.

"Hey," he says quietly, one hand in the air, the other rubbing the back of his neck.

I close my mouth and square my shoulders, feeling Dad's presence behind me. He's here to protect me, and knowing that creates an ache in my chest. Two years ago, I'd laid down in the middle of a basketball court, holding hands with the boy in front of me, a boy who declared that he'd never let anyone hurt me. That I'd never have to be afraid of him. But here I am...

Josh looks over my shoulder. "I'm sorry for coming over unannounced like this—"

"How'd you get my address?" Dad asks, his voice deep, intimidating.

Josh steps back, his demeanor proof he felt the threat in each word. I turn to my dad, pleading with my eyes for him to back off, just enough so I can *breathe.* So I can sort through the havoc in my head. Dad rolls his eyes. "He could've at least brought us coffee." Then he spins on his heels and walks away.

I look over at Josh, his eyes wide as he points his thumb over his shoulder. "I can go get him a coffee."

I smile. I can't help it. Shaking my head, I mouth, "It's fine," and step out onto the porch, closing the door behind me. I raise my eyebrows. He rubs the back of his neck again. “Do you—I mean—can we go for a walk, maybe?” He grins the same crooked grin that used to give me butterflies, and I’d be lying to myself if I said it didn’t have the same effect now. “Honestly, Becs, I thought your grams was scary, but she’s got nothing on your dad.”

I laugh, and even though he doesn’t hear it, he *sees* it.

He *sees* me.

CHAPTER 5

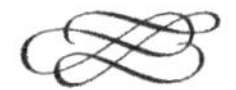

JOSHUA

I have no idea what I'm doing here, walking side by side next to the girl I've spent endless nights dreaming about. But after she left last night, I couldn't get her out of my head. Not that I expected to. Every moment seemed to replay in my mind, and I questioned everything. *Everything.* Not just about our pasts or the decisions we made, but even the small things that shouldn't matter. I examined every word I spoke, every movement I made, and I wondered how it was she could so easily walk away with nothing but a computerized "Thanks for your time" and leave my sorry ass standing there in a pool of my regrets.

I woke up this morning and looked out of the hotel room window and saw the sun rising, letting me know it was a new day, and I gathered all the courage, all the confidence I had, and decided I wanted a do-over. And then her dad answered the door and asked me what the hell I wanted, and the only thing I could think to say was, "Becca."

I wanted *Becca.*

And now I had her. Even if the few minutes we'd been walking were spent in silence, her feet following mine, her long jet-black hair whipping across my arm, I still *had* her.

I just need to come up with something to say to start my do-over. "So you're on the school paper?" *God, I'm pathetic.* I look over at her and wait for her response, but there isn't much of one, just a slight nod of her head followed by an unsure shifting of her eyes. I kick myself for suggesting we walk because it makes it difficult to read her, to *see* her. And so I walk a few more steps until we reach a bus stop, and I sit down and hope she does the same. She hesitates, just for a moment, but then she joins me. I face her. She looks straight ahead. "Are you enjoying it?" I ask. "I mean college. Classes. All that stuff?"

She nods again, palming her unruly hair away from her face.

"And do you like St. Louis?"

Another nod.

"And your dad?"

She inhales deeply, her hands gripping the edge of the bench, and turns to me, her head tilted to the side. "You?" she mouths.

"Me?" I shrug. "I think I'm still adjusting to everything, to be honest. Things kind of took off insanely fast and I still don't think I'm ready for it. It's a lot of travel and a lot of meetings and phone calls and, like, putting up a front on social media and stuff."

Becca turns to me now, one leg bent on the bench, the other outstretched, her foot on the ground an inch from mine. She waves a hand in the air, asking me to continue, so I do. "I guess I'm kind of blessed," I tell her, and I don't know why I'm saying all this stuff, especially to her, but she's here and she's listening and it's more than I ever thought I'd get. "I'm lucky I get to do it all before Tommy has to start school, so he can travel with me, and Nat and Justin are beyond helpful when it comes to doing the whole co-parenting thing around my schedule. They're gone three months at a time, so when they do come back, they make sure to be wherever we are, even if it means staying at hotels with Tommy when I'm at tournaments."

Her features soften as she listens to my words.

"Chris and my mom handle everything and I get told where to be and when to be there, and I get to skate." I choke on a breath and look away from her eyes, because watching her watch me feels like a knife piercing my heart over and over, or maybe it's the guilt of giving her lie after lie after goddamn lie. Each one rehearsed in the car on the way to her house. I thought it would be easier to give her the same version of me as everyone else gets. I told myself if I gave her that, then I could walk away—not happy—but not as miserable as I felt when she left me last night. I was wrong. But what was I supposed to say? That the only part of my life I loved anymore was Tommy and skating? The truth is, I'm not even sure if I love skating anymore or if I do it for Tommy and for his future and to make two certain people proud of me. One of those people is dead. The other is staring at me, her eyes, her lips, her entire body void of any emotion. She lifts her hand and forms the sign for "phone," so I reach into my pocket and hand it to her. I scoot closer so I can see her thumbs working over the screen. She taps on the Notes app, types away on the keys, and I read the words she's written: *What are you doing here, Josh?*

I clear my throat. "I have a comp," I mumble.

Her thumbs move again. *Not here in St. Louis. HERE. With me. Why did you come to my house?*

I drop my gaze and cut the bullshit. "I don't know, Becs. Maybe for the same reason you came to interview me yesterday." I feel her shift next to me, both her feet on the ground now. "I looked you up online and on your college newspaper. You got a lot of photographs there. Really good ones, too. But all art based. None for sports. And you've definitely never done any interviews—"

She stands up before I get a chance to finish, and I know

I've blown it. Whatever the hell *it* is. She's looking down at the ground, her head moving from side to side. Then she hands me my phone and starts to walk back to her house. I follow after her, because I can't not, and I rush my steps until I'm in front of her, walking backward, giving her no option but to deal with me. "I'm sorry, Becca."

She might be looking at me, but I can't tell because her hair's flying everywhere, and for a second, I get lost in the scent of it, lost in the memories of how the strands felt between my fingertips and on my chest, and I want nothing more in the entire fire-trucking world than to go back there, back to a place and time where we existed only for each other.

I sigh when her steps hasten and mine do the same. "I'm sorry, okay? I don't care *why* you came to see me and I don't know why I'm here, but the fact that *you did* and *I am* has to mean something. Doesn't it?"

She pauses, just for a moment, before moving ahead, her steps faster than before.

"Stop," I tell her, but I don't dare touch her. "We need to talk about this." As the words leave my mouth, the mistake like acid on my tongue, I freeze. So does she. Then she holds her hair behind her neck, and I see her eyes, bright behind the layer of tears. "Fuck."

She starts to walk again, only now it's slow, as if the thoughts in her head are preventing her pace. And again, I follow. Because I'd follow her to the end of the fucking earth, even when she's pissed, if it meant being with her. Or being *around* her. Or just breathing the same damn air as her. We make it halfway up her porch steps, my mind racing, trying to find a way to say goodbye without saying *goodbye*. But then her front door opens and a guy wearing a Washington University Basketball jacket, a stupid *C* on the chest, steps out of the house, his glare directed at me.

Next to me, Becca covers her mouth with her hands. She

looks from him, to her dad standing behind him, and then over at me. The air turns thick, the silence palpable, and the knives are back, stabbing my heart over and over and over.

I wish for death.

As stupid as it sounds, I almost beg for it.

Anything would be better than what I'm experiencing.

Her steps are rushed now, moving toward him, and he tears his glare away from me to look down at her. Her hands are moving between them, fingers switching positions, and his focus isn't on her face like when I look at her, it's on her hands.

"Okay," he says, and she drops her arms to her sides, her shoulders relaxing with her exhale. Then she's gone, past her dad and through her front door, closing it after her. This time, I don't follow her, because she's no longer mine to pursue. And as the knives twist and prod and poke at my battered heart, I look up at the guy whose hand is out, waiting for me to shake, and I succumb to the pain, to the loss, to the *grief*. "I'm Aaron," he says. "You must be Josh."

I shake his hand, my fingers numb caused by my dead, non-beating heart, and I murmur a "Hey."

Before he can respond, the front door opens again and the cause of my grief walks through it. She'd changed into a dress that shows off the tanned legs and arms and curves I've craved. After going through her bag, she looks up at Aaron, her hands and fingers a blur as they move in front of him.

He nods.

Swear, I actually hear the clicking of the pieces in my head.

One by one.

Click.

Click.

Click.

She's *signing*.

And *he* understands her.

"Becca wants me to tell you that it was good seeing you

again, Josh," Aaron says. "We're running late, so we have to go. But she's glad she got to catch up with you."

Becca's hands move again.

"She says to take care of yourself, and of Tommy."

Becca waves a goodbye, her eyes blazing against the morning sun. But she's not looking at me. She's looking past me, hoping to find a way to make me and the entire situation disappear.

I stand and I watch, unwilling to say goodbye, as they walk down the steps and toward his car. He opens the door for her, and she settles into the seat, like it's something they've done a thousand times before. She doesn't look up. Not once in the time it takes him to close the door, make his way to the driver's side, start the car, and drive away does she look at me.

"They met in group therapy..." Martin says from behind me, "that's where they're going now."

I face him, but the racing of my mind and the lump in my throat prevent my thoughts from forming into words.

He steps closer, his arms crossed. "It's a group for young adults who've overcome some form of tragedy. She says it helps her."

I'm not exactly sure why he feels the need to tell me any of this but I take it in, as much as I physically and mentally can. "Is um... Aaron—is he deaf or...?"

Martin shakes his head. "No. His ex-girlfriend was, though. That's why he learned to sign. And that's how he was able to teach Becca and it's how they communicate." He exhales loudly. "She passed away in a car accident. He was driving. Hence the therapy."

I nod, not knowing how else to react.

He steps closer again, his threatening demeanor relaxing a little. "I've thought about this moment a lot since Becca moved in—what I would say to you if I ever got the chance. Truth is, I don't know how to deal with any of this, Josh. I can look at you as a punk kid who hurt my daughter, and that side of me makes me want to punch you in the face and tell you not to contact her again because I can guarantee you she didn't sleep a wink last night. Then I see you as a dad, and that part of me hopes I can reach out to you and you'll understand what I say next..." He takes a breath. And then another. All while I pray for the ground to swallow me whole. "She's doing better. A lot better than when she moved in. The therapy helps. She seems to like college and likes this area, and I think she even likes me. As a father, you should know what it feels like—this need to protect your child—so I'm telling you this because she's gone through enough in her life that I couldn't protect her from, and now I *need* to do that, Josh. I *need* to make sure that she keeps taking steps forward." He gives me a once over before saying, "Unfortunately, I don't think that you being in her life is going to allow that."

I shove my hands in my pockets, his words clearing my mind, each one seared into my memory.

"I don't exactly know what happened to you guys," he adds. "But I do know the reason she went to see you yesterday is because it's on The List."

Looking up, I raise my eyebrows. "What? Like a bucket list?"

"Yeah, Josh. A bucket list of *fears.*"

CHAPTER 6

BECCA

"I'm just going to make an assumption here and tell me if I'm wrong, Becca," Aaron says, glancing at me quickly from the driver's seat. "Your interview with Josh last night didn't go well, or something happened, and you had to do it again?"

I look down at my hands and stay silent. Because silence is all I can give him.

"It's just that I'm finding it hard to come up with any other reason as to why you were with him this morning."

I grab my phone from my bag and type away, then hit *speak* and wait for the speech to come through his car speakers. *"He just showed up at my door. I wasn't going to tell him to go away. It would've been rude."*

"Rude?" he asks incredulously. "What's rude is showing up at your house when he has no business to do so."

I watch him a moment, surprised by his tone. He's never spoken to me like this before. My shoulders drop with my silent sigh. I lower my gaze and focus on my phone. *"I don't know what you want me to say, but I don't deserve the way you're talking to me right now. You're trying to make me feel guilty or apologize for something, when I haven't done anything wrong."*

Aaron pulls into a spot in the church parking lot, then turns to me, his bright blue eyes on mine. "You're right," he says, his face clear of a definable emotion.

I wait for him to continue and when he doesn't, I have Cordy say, *"I've been open with you throughout this entire experience."*

"Experience?" he asks, his face scrunched in annoyance.

I roll my eyes and tap away at my phone. *"You know what I mean. Don't be an ass. I gave you plenty of chances to tell me you were against it, and you never did."*

"You don't need my permission, Becca," he says softly.

"But I wanted it, Aaron. Not your permission but your support, and I thought we were in the same place with this."

"We are," he says, reaching over and gently taking my hand. He leans forward, his lips soft against my forehead. "I'm sorry." Then he dips his head, his nose touching mine and I know what he wants, I'm just not ready to give it to him. I pull away and point to the church where the group therapy sessions are held. I mouth, "Late."

It's hard to watch the disappointment and frustration take over him, but I'm not willing to succumb to the pressure of what he wants versus what I *need*. And right now, I need to sit in a room with people whose lives are just as fucked up as mine had once been.

Once out of the car, my phone chimes with a text.

Unknown: Why didn't you tell me about him?

My feet falter, just for a moment, before I gain the courage to write back, my thumbs sweaty from the sudden panic I feel.

Becca: Because it's not relevant. Besides, you never asked.

His reply is immediate.

> **Unknown:** You're right. I should've asked. I thought maybe you'd be stuck, like I am, spending the past year unable to move on. But I'm glad you have someone who sees you, Becs.

I read his words, over and over, the panic I'd felt turning to pain. I blink hard, pushing away the tears threatening to fall.

> **Unknown:** And you have my new number now. So let me know if he breaks your heart, I'll fly right over and break his legs. ;)

A smile spreads across my face, completely unexpected. But also not. Because that's the thing about Josh, he makes me *feel.* In two simple texts he managed to break me and heal me.

"You coming?" Aaron asks, standing by the door of the church.

I'm one foot in the building when my phone sounds with an e-mail and I'm reminded of the lie I'd told Josh about not following his success. Because as I look down at my phone, at the now open e-mail alert for none other than Josh Warden, my heart shatters and the world around me turns black.

"Josh Warden, favorite to take out St. Louis Skate Tour, withdraws from event unexpectedly."

CHAPTER 7

JOSHUA

My best friend Hunter answers his door in nothing but sweats, holding a baseball bat. He's never played baseball in his life, but it's a valid reaction to someone knocking on your door at three in the morning without so much as a text. I'd switched off my phone right after I called Chris to tell him I was leaving. I didn't want to deal with what I knew was coming.

Hunter lowers the bat when he sees me with Tommy asleep in my arms, and steps aside to let us in. Chloe comes down the stairs, her hair a mess. Without a word, she takes Tommy from me, kisses my cheek, and then goes back upstairs. "Aunt Chloe?" Tommy whispers, his head resting on her shoulder.

"Yeah, baby, it's me," she answers. Hunter closes the door and leads me to his kitchen, switching on the lights as he does. He doesn't speak as he opens the cupboard and pulls out two glasses, then reaches into his freezer and grabs a bottle of vodka. After filling the glasses, he pushes one across the counter to where I'm now sitting. His gaze searches mine, and I can already tell he *knows*. He's aware of where I've come from, and he also knows who else lives there. He lifts his glass, his eyes apologetic. "To broken hearts and mended souls."

I down my drink. He refills it. We repeat this twice before he says, "Whenever you're ready, man."

I focus on the empty glass in front of me. "I broke her, dude. And it's not even her heart I'm worried about... I'm pretty sure it's healed because she's moved on with some other guy. *Aaron*." I spit his name, hating its presence on my tongue.

"I'm assuming you saw her?"

With a nod, I push the glass away and drop my head on my arms. "She interviewed me for her school newspaper." I wipe my lips on my sleeve and look up at him. "You should've seen her, man. She had to have all these things to help her communicate. She types and her laptop relays what she's written and her..."—I push down the puke—"her boyfriend—he taught her sign language so now—"

"He's deaf?" Hunter cuts in.

I shake my head. "His ex-girlfriend was, or something. I don't really know. You should've seen this kid, man. I guess he's some kind of athlete at their college and they met during *group therapy*. I fucking caused her to go to therapy and—"

"Becca's past was pretty fucked up, Warden," he says quickly. "And I'm almost positive she *needed* therapy even before you came along."

I ignore him and continue. "The kid's like a perfect poster-child Abercrombie model looking douche-tool—"

"And you're jealous of his perfection?"

"—and I'm just some punk skater," I finish, and tap my glass.

He refills it. "*Pro* skater," he says, quirking an eyebrow.

"Irrelevant." I practically inhale the vodka. "And no, I'm not jealous of his perfection. I'm jealous that he's perfect for *her*."

Hunter nods once. "Right."

I tap my glass again. And again, he refills it.

"And that's why you left the comp?"

I stay silent.

"Does she seem happy?" he asks, and I sit up straighter, the truth in my answer hitting me hard.

"Yes."

He lifts his glass. "To perfect poster-child Abercrombie model looking douche-tools."

"So you're toasting *you*?"

He laughs once. "Fuck you, skater punk."

I tap his glass with mine. "To the girl who chose to be happy..."

JOURNAL

I'd never been to church, not until Grams had asked me to go with her when I first moved in. It was everything I expected it to be, but also nothing like I had hoped. I thought I'd walk in and God would know who I was and everything I'd been through. He'd look down on me, and I'd look up at Him and a calm would wash over me. I hoped that He'd somehow make me understand why it was this life had been chosen for ***me.*** *No such thing happened, at least not from Him.*

But when Grams pulled into the driveway and Josh looked up from yet another hole he was digging and he smiled, I felt the calm I'd been searching for. I also felt something else—like the beginning of turbulence. I shouldn't have ignored that feeling, but I did. Maybe if I chose to grasp on to that instead of the calm, he wouldn't have taken me on a ride that had me gripping my armrest and struggling for breath.

JOURNAL

I've been having these nightmares lately. We're in a small plane—Josh and me. The plane starts to shake and I hold on to the edge of the armrest, my knuckles white from my grasp. "I got you," Josh whispers in my ear, his breath warming my neck—relaxing me enough so he can take my hand. "I'll always have you." He uses his free hand to secure my seat belt. "You'll always belong to me, Becca."

That's the last thing he says before the plane nosedives and crashes into a field.

I always wake up at the point in the dream when I get my camera out and take pictures of Josh's dead body.

"Morbid" was the word Dawn, my therapist, used to define my dream.

"Morbid" wasn't really what I was hoping for and I told her that.

She looked at me for a long time and then finally said, "Guilt."

Guilt was the cause of my constant nightmares. It made sense, I guess, considering I'd spent the two weeks after the competition on the Internet, frantically searching for a reason for his sudden withdrawal. Maybe there was a family emergency, or an injury, or... anything that wasn't me. Nothing came up. He disappeared. No one could get in contact with him, but his manager—his mother—and his agent had come out and said that he was fine physically. It was all I could talk about during my sessions with Dawn. Until one day, she "strongly suggested" that I cancel the e-mail alerts and stay offline. So I did what she said, and I took her advice to focus on classes, focus on building my strength instead of trying to find reasons to excuse my weakness. And Josh, as she said, was my excuse, not my weakness. Whatever that meant.

JOURNAL

I spent a good portion of group therapy today listening to Aaron talk about Brandi, his ex-girlfriend, and all the guilt he felt for her death. All I could think about was whether my mother felt guilty for all the shit she put me through, or if she was pissed she didn't succeed in taking me with her. When it became my turn to "speak," I typed on my phone and let the words echo off the walls in the small room.

"I hate you.

I love you.

I hate that I love you."

I was speaking about my mother. I saved the text as ***Josh.***

JOURNAL

A couple weeks ago, Dawn found this app and she made me download it. She has the same one on her iPad. It shows her what I'm writing in real time so I can't delete my thoughts and provide her with something safer. She's mastered differentiating my truths from my lies based on how long it takes me to respond. I hate the stupid app. I hate it so much that I came home and defied her by looking up all things Josh Warden. Now I hate myself. Good job, World.

JOURNAL

My mother took me to get ice cream on my tenth birthday. She didn't yell. She didn't hit me. We smiled and we talked and we loved. It was one of the happiest days of my life. The next day, she asked if I'd stolen money from her purse. I told her I hadn't. She said money was missing and that she hadn't been anywhere in days. I reminded her of the ice cream. She didn't believe me. I worked out later that she was drunk during our little outing and legitimately had no memory of it.

I wonder if she remembers her hand wrapped around my throat or the pillow she tried to suffocate me with.

Earlier, Dad bought five tubs of ice cream. We threw one against a brick wall, chucked one off a bridge, took a baseball bat to another, and then ran over one with the car.

"You know it's your grams's birthday in two weeks," he said, watching me from across the kitchen table.

I dropped my spoon into the now empty fifth tub of ice cream and looked up at him.

"Should we go and surprise her?"

Whatever look I had on my face made him laugh—this deep, gruff chuckle that warmed my heart. I reached over to him and grasped his hand, causing his smile to spread. Then I grabbed the worn piece of paper sitting between us and picked up a pen and handed them both to him.

Today, we marked "Ice Cream" off my list of fears.

JOURNAL

My dad invited Aaron to come to North Carolina to visit Grams with us. I don't know why he did this. But of course Aaron said yes and now all three of us are going. I guess Dad assumes Aaron is more to me than he is and I can't fault him for that. He probably believes Aaron is saving me in some way, and to a degree, maybe he is.

I probably shouldn't feel as angry as I do about it. Okay, so angry might be too strong of a word, but that's how I feel. And trapped. I don't know. But I feel like what he assumed was a kind gesture is having the opposite effect. I feel forced, like I'm being pushed into something I'm not at all ready for.

Or maybe I'm just reading way too much into it.

Either way. Aaron is meeting Grams. Yay.

CHAPTER 8

BECCA

"How long has it been since you've seen Josh?" Dawn asks, her gaze dropping to the iPad on her lap.

Just over three months, I type.

"And you think you're ready to see him again?"

I'm not really sure, but I want to be there for Grams's birthday. Besides, he's traveling so much with his skating, he probably won't even be there.

"Do you want him to be there?" she asks.

I pause, my fingers hovering over the screen.

"Okay, let me rephrase that. Do you think three months is long enough to change how you'll feel when you see him again?"

I look up at her and shrug.

"I'm concerned," she says, setting the iPad to the side. "I'm worried that seeing him will have the same effect it had when he was in town last. It broke you, Becca, maybe not completely, but it still broke you. And I know feelings were still there, even if you refuse to tell me that. It caused problems for you and Aaron and—"

Anger builds in the pit of my stomach and her iPad sounds, alerting her to the words I've begun to type:

You do realize that I'm not here because of Josh, right? I don't know why everything always comes back to him. He was just a boy.

"Becca, look at me," she says, her voice soft.

I wipe at my eyes, not wanting her to see the tears. I hate when she does this—when she talks about Josh like he's poison in my veins.

"Don't deny yourself the feelings you had for him. All of them. The good and the bad. Because we both know he wasn't *just a boy.* He was a boy who at one stage loved you beyond your unspoken words. You deserve to feel that love. And denying that means you're denying you ever felt worthy of that love. I know you're here because of the hell your mother put you through, but your mother's dead, Becca, and nothing we say or do will change that. Josh, on the other hand… he alone has the power to change *everything.* So I'll ask you again. Do you want him to be there?"

I stare at her. Right into her eyes, and I try to find a reason to fight her because fighting would be so much easier than hurting. But there's nothing there. Nothing but sincere concern. So I let the anger fade and welcome the truth that keeps me hostage.

Yes. I want him to be there.

~

"Good session?" Aaron asks, leaning against Dad's car.

I sign, "Same old."

He smiles as he opens his arms for me. I step into his embrace, but I don't return it. "I'm really excited to meet your grams," he says, his mouth so close to my ear, his voice grates on my eardrums. "You ready to go? Your dad and I packed your bags in the trunk when I dropped off my car at your house."

I pull back and nod up at him.

"Good," he says, unconvinced. Then he kisses me, again and again, and I let him. For the same reasons I let every other boy besides Josh Warden kiss me. Because he makes me feel *safe*, and at the same time, he makes me feel *nothing*.

CHAPTER 9

JOSHUA

After dropping Tommy off at my uncle Robby's, I drive to my house, my excitement building. As soon as I step out of my car, I run up the porch steps and knock harshly on her door. Chazarae takes a while to answer, but when she does, I wrap her in my arms and lift her in the air. "I missed you so much!"

She giggles into my chest and squeals when I spin her around before setting her back on the ground. But I don't let her go yet. She feels too much like *home*.

"Joshua!" She pushes my chest and rears back, her dark, wrinkled eyes squinting against the sun behind me. "I love you and everything and I'm glad you're home, but boy, you need a shower," Chazarae says.

I laugh, my head throwing back with the force of it. "I know. I've been in car after car, plane after plane, and I just couldn't wait to see you!"

She rolls her eyes. "Of all the women you see in your travels, you can't wait to come home to me?"

"You'll always be my number one girl," I joke, and her eyes roll higher.

I clap and rub my hands together. "So tomorrow. The big 6-5!"

"Oh, Joshua, I hope you didn't come home just for my birthday."

I lean against the porch rail and cross my arms, inconspicuously smelling my armpits. She's right. I need a fucking shower. And a shave. And maybe five days' worth of sleep. "I wouldn't have missed it for the world," I tell her truthfully. The past year of my life has changed beyond what I'd ever imagined. I barely see my friends, my family, besides my mom—who has a hard time switching from mom to manager. But it keeps her busy and takes her mind off Dad's passing, so I let the moments of confusion slide. The one constant through it all has been Chazarae. Regardless of where I was and what I was doing, I'd always come home to her. And through it all, she hasn't changed the way she treats me. She'll always be my savior, and I'll always be the kid who needed saving.

"You're a good boy, sweetheart," she says, her smile soft. Then her gaze shifts to the cast on my arm, and I already know what's coming.

Gasp. *Tick.*

Inspection. *Tick.*

Hand on my cheek. *Tick.*

"Oh, Josh..." Concern. *Tick.* "What did you do to yourself now?"

"Broke my elbow."

"Again?"

"Yep."

She eyes me sideways. "You didn't even compete since I last saw you."

"Chris wanted a demo video for Check and Deck. It was just street skating."

She shakes her head. "Why couldn't you have pursued a

different career? Something safe. Something like... I don't know... washing cars?"

I chuckle under my breath.

"I guarantee no one's broken four—now *five*—bones in a year washing cars. You're lucky God is on your side."

"Well, I don't know about God," I tell her, pushing off the rail. "I'm lucky I have *you* on my side, Ma'am." I give her a face-splitting grin. "Now go dress pretty! Lunch date. You and me. And then we'll go pick out those flowers you asked me to plant three months ago."

I turn to leave but she grasps my cast. "You can't plant the flowers with this on your arm."

I kiss her forehead. "Watch me."

After taking a breath, she grips my arm tighter. "It's good to have you home," she says. "I was getting a little lonely out here."

"I know." I chew my lip. "You know the invite's always there for you to travel with me."

Her nose scrunches. "And be around boys as smelly as you? I'd rather be lonely."

I can't help but laugh, but it dies quickly when her hands are no longer on me and she's halfway to her door. "Ma'am." I wait until she's looking at me before speaking. "My final goal hasn't changed. Wherever I end up, I'm taking you with me. You have no choice."

I take the longest shower in the history of showers and wait by my car for her. After a few minutes of checking e-mails and Facebook and all the things Chris forces me to do, a car pulls into the driveway. The windows are tinted, so I can't see who's inside, but as soon as the car door opens and I see one tanned leg step out, followed by another, my heart races, beating harshly against my chest, and then it stops, just long enough for it to drop to the ground because she's stepping out of the passenger's side. And as bad as it sounds, considering the last time we spoke, I hope and I pray that it's her dad driving, not Aaron. But my prayers go unanswered, and my stomach joins my heart, as well as the joy I'd felt only minutes ago—all on the ground, where I'm currently staring, refusing to look away. They're *all* here. Becca, her dad, and *Aaron*.

I hear the front door open, and I still don't lift my gaze. Even when I hear Chaz squeal as she runs past me and toward her *real* family. Chaz laughs and in my head, Becca does, too, her voice raspy and ridiculously hot and I almost look up. *Almost.* But then I hear Chaz say *his* name and I keep my head lowered and shove my hands in my pockets, waiting for the world to stop spinning so fast. It doesn't. And when enough time passes and all I can hear is *his* voice saying all the *right* things, I turn on my heels and head back to my apartment.

I'm halfway there when Chaz calls my name, and it takes everything in me to stop. To not let my pride overshadow her wants. I turn slowly, making sure to focus on her and only her, but Becca's here. She's *here* and no matter how hard I try to fight it, I'm drawn to her. Right to her eyes—eyes that seem to see straight through me. "Are you able to change the reservation to five?" Chaz whispers.

I tear my gaze away from Becca and look down at her. Her lips press together, her face pleading. "How about I call and make it for four? You go spend time with them." I reach into my pocket and pull out some cash, but she covers my hand to stop me.

"Josh. I'm not going to go—"

I turn my back on all of them, but she follows and stands in front of me, blocking my path. Squaring my shoulders, I try to keep it together. "I'm not going with *them*," I say, my voice low, my words meant only for her.

"Why not?"

I sigh. "Please don't make this awkward. You *know* why." I push the cash into her hands, and she opens her mouth to speak, but I cut her off. "Please," I beg. "You know I would if I could, but I can't be around *them*."

A frown pulls on her lips, and I hate myself for causing it.

"I'm sorry," I tell her.

She nods, pushes off her toes and kisses my cheek. "I know."

I hide out in my apartment until they're gone and as soon as they are, I head back out, grab a board from my truck, and I bail. I skate the streets until I'm at my uncle Robby's house, and when I hear Tommy's laughter coming from their back yard, it takes away some of the ache in my chest.

"What's up?" Robby says when I come into view. "Aren't you supposed to be out to lunch with Chaz?"

I sit down on the chair next to him and focus on Tommy, like I do whenever I feel like things are getting to be too much. He's standing in front of my aunt Kim, his arm out in front of him while she wraps soggy strips of newspaper around his elbow. "What the hell are you doing to my kid?" I ask Kim.

She eyes me sideways while Tommy bursts out laughing. "I'm like you, Daddy!"

"You've already had one broken arm, you don't need another one," I mumble.

Robby says, "Imagine if he ends up a skater like you. You'd flip your shit with the amount of broken bones your mom and dad had to go through."

"Flip your shit," Tommy repeats.

"That's a bad word, sweetheart, don't listen to your uncle," Kim coos, her eyes narrowed at Robby.

"I wasn't that bad," I tell Robby.

"Bullshit," he replies.

"Bullshit!" Tommy yells.

I turn to Robby. "You gotta quit cussing around him. You know what he said to me after I placed second in my last comp?"

Robby rolls his eyes. "What'd he say?"

"He told me it was okay because the other guy was an *asshole*."

Robby laughs.

"It's not funny!" I punch his arm.

Tommy punches Kim's shoulder.

"And I'm the bad influence?" Robby asks, and I just shake my head. "So why aren't you with Chaz right now?"

"Change of plans." I drop my board and set my feet on it, rocking it from side to side, my shoulders slumped. "Becca's here."

"She's *here*?" he almost shouts.

"*My* Becca's home?" Tommy yells, his grin from ear to ear.

"No, bud," I lie. "Not *your* Becca. A different one."

Tommy drops his gaze, his frown instant. "Oh," he says, at the same time Robby stands. "Let's walk."

We sit on top of the half-pipe in his backyard. The one he made me to celebrate when I signed a deal with Red Bull. It was supposed to be a place for me to train when I came home. Honestly, though, I think it was just a way for him to make sure I *came* home. "So Becca's home?"

"Yep. Becca, her dad, and *Aaron*."

"I take it we don't like Aaron."

"No, we don't like Aaron. In fact, we *hate* Aaron. To the point where just hearing his name makes me want to stab my ears." I look over at the horizon, an insane view that can only be seen from this exact spot, and the ache in my chest rebuilds itself. "I guess they came in to surprise Chaz."

"Are you pissed?"

I sigh. "I'm trying not to be, because I don't really have the right, you know? It's been a long time since we broke up, and she's moved on."

"And you haven't?"

"I can't, dude," I tell him truthfully. "I've tried. And it's not like the opportunity hasn't presented itself—"

Robby blows out a breath, cutting me off. "I can't even imagine what it's like for you on tour. I've read the shit online, watched the videos of all those girls throwing themselves at you. You must have the strength of a thousand men, Josh."

I look at him, my heart in my throat. "Or the weakness of one."

CHAPTER 10

BECCA

His truck was here when we got back from lunch, the same truck which held memories of a sand-stealing night at the beach, of first kisses, and of first loves. Grams had taken a piece of cake from the restaurant he'd booked and as soon as we got home, the first thing she did was march up his stairs and knock on his door. He wasn't home. And he hasn't been home since. I know, because I'm in my old bedroom, staring out the window with my thumb between my teeth, the curtains spread, watching and waiting for him. Just like I'd done during the first two weeks I'd moved here. But I don't just want to see him. I want to talk to him, or at least my version of talking, and I want to apologize for ruining his plans. I'd spent the entire lunch feeling horrible about it, all while Aaron sat next to me, his hand holding mine on the table, charming the absolute crap out of Grams.

I give up hope at around midnight and get into bed, but I don't sleep. I can't. My mind reels with absurd assumptions. Not absurd in a way that they can't possibly be true, but absurd in that I have no right to be feeling how I feel *because* of those assumptions. After a half hour of tossing and turning, I'm convinced Josh is with a girl. And I get mad at myself that it's so much easier to convince myself of that than it is to remind myself that it shouldn't matter, because I'm here with a boy, a boy who has been so excited to meet my grandmother—and he's sleeping in the room next door.

I silently moan into the pillow, frustrated, then punch it a few times, because over a year of therapy has taught me that it's better to hurt the pillow than it is to hurt myself, because hurting myself gets me nowhere (besides over a year of therapy). And that's how my thoughts go for the next hour, around and around and around some more, circles of insanity flipping over and over in my mind. Then I hear a sound that has me sitting up and reaching for my phone. A sound I've never admitted to missing: four wheels spinning on concrete.

I jump out of bed and switch on my lamp before parting the curtains and looking down into the driveway. He rolls in, both feet on the board, and stops by his truck. After throwing the board into the back seat, he shuts the door and just stands there, his head lowered. A moment later he starts to move, one foot in front of the other, until he's halfway to his stairs and suddenly, his feet falter and he looks up. Up. UP. I quickly shut my curtains and look at the wallpaper, my phone held tight in my hands. My eyes shut as I try to level my breathing, and when the beating of my heart slows enough so I can actually think, I open my eyes and look down at my phone.

Becca: Can you meet me outside?

The seconds feel like minutes while I wait for a response.

Josh: Will you be alone?
Becca: Yes.

Josh: ok.

I dress quickly and as quietly as possible, rush down the stairs, my nerves building. I pause for a moment with my hand on the knob and try to steady my thoughts. When I open the door, Josh is the only thing I see. Visible only by the moonlight, he sits at the bottom of the stairs, hat in his hands and his head lowered. He looks up when he must hear me approaching. I wave. He does the same. Then he motions to the spot next to him. I hesitate, because standing in front of him is one thing. Sitting next to him, possibly touching him, is another. But when he looks at me, his eyes tired and his smile forced, I push aside my fears and give in to his request.

"What goes on?" he murmurs.

I pull my phone from the pocket of my hoodie and type, *I'm sorry for ruining your plans with Grams.*

"It's fine," he says, his voice sharp, when I show him the screen.

The silence that passes is awkward, filled with tension—tension I try to relieve.

So, you weren't even going to say hello to me? I type, forcing my own smile when he looks up at me.

He laughs. It's quiet. But I hear it. I see it. And I let myself get completely lost in it. "Yeah," he says, looking up at the stars. "I'm sorry about that. I guess seeing you just..." He faces me now, his eyes searching mine. "You kind of knocked the wind out of me, you know?"

I exhale slowly, feeling the effects of his words, and I do everything I can to tear my gaze away from him and look down between us. I tap his cast, something I knew would be there because an e-mail alerted me to it three days ago. After looking back up at him, I raise my eyebrows. "It's fine," he says with a shrug.

He's leaning in to me now, his arm touching mine, his leg

doing the same as he reads my message. *And Tommy's? Is his okay?*

"He's all good," Josh says as I stare down at my phone. "He healed like a pro."

That's good, I type, my thumbs trembling. *Where is he now?*

"Robby and Kim's. I just left there."

I hide my grin, glad he wasn't with a girl, and nod as I look up at the sky, trying to ignore the effect he has on me.

"So." He pushes my leg with his, breaking the silence. "I kind of planned this surprise party for your grams tomorrow, but I can cancel," he says, replacing his hat on his head. "If you wanted to do something with her or whatever. Just let me know now so I can make the calls first thing."

"No," I mouth, shaking my head, my smile wide. My thumbs move across the phone again. *That's really sweet of you to do that. She's going to love it, Josh. Thank you.*

He doesn't respond for a while, so I turn to him, to his eyes set right on mine, and I try to read him, try to feel something more than the nerves and the tension building between us.

His eyes narrow as he licks his lips, lips chapped from all the outdoor skateboarding he does. "You don't need to thank me. She means a lot to me. Even before *you* came along."

I'm not exactly sure why his words hurt, but they do, so I reach into my pocket and pull out the cash that he'd given my grams. It wasn't the reason I came out here, why I'd waited all night to see him, but it was my saving grace, and right now I'm weakening—by his presence, by his words, by our pain. I hold out the money for him and wait for him to take it.

Aaron paid for lunch. He said thanks for the offer and for booking it all. He really enjoyed the meal, I type, not knowing what else to say.

Josh shoves the money in his pocket and leans forward, his arms resting on his knees. He lets out a moan from deep in his throat and looks at the darkness in front of him. "I'm glad you're here, Becs. It means a lot to your grams that you are. But do me a favor..." He faces me. "Don't talk to me about him, okay?" I open my mouth, my words on the tip of my tongue, but he beats me to it. "It's bad enough that I have to be around him, in my own fucking house, but it kills me to have you sit here and talk about him."

Crossing my arms, I narrow my eyes at him, my mind reeling with a response. As soon as one comes, I type frantically on my phone. *You're being mean.*

He reads the message and then drops his head in his hands, another frustrated grunt leaving him. I watch the rise and fall of his shoulders, wide and nothing but muscle, pulling against the fabric of his shirt. After removing his hat, he runs a hand through his hair, tugging at the ends. "I'm not being mean," he mutters. "I'm just being honest, Becca." He sighs loudly, still refusing to look at me. "You know," he starts, his voice low. "When things didn't work out between us, I thought about how it would feel when you moved on. What it would be like to know that it was some other guy lying next to you at night, some other guy who got to see you in ways that I've spent the past year and half dreaming about. I hate that he gets to touch you, and hold you, and get lost in your eyes, and feel everything I felt and *still* feel. And for a long time it was okay..." He sniffs once and wipes his eyes against his sleeve, keeping his head lowered. There's no anger in his voice, no insult in his words. Just pure heartbreak. His *and* mine. "It was fine because I was never jealous of a specific person. I was jealous of everyone and everything around you. I was jealous of the air you breathed, the paths you walked, even the hearts you'd crush. Because they all got to be around you and I couldn't." He finally looks up, his glazed eyes doing nothing to cover his torment. "But then I met him, and now he has a face and a name, and I *hate* him. And I told you I would. I told you I'd smile and I'd nod and I'd be amicable toward him. For your sake and for your grams. But I fucking *hate* him. And you can't blame me for that." He chokes on a breath and stands quickly. "You can't be hurt and you can't be upset that it makes me sick to my stomach having to sit here and listen to you talk about him. Listen to another guy's name fall from your lips. Lips *I've* craved and *he's* tasted. You just can't, Becca."

CHAPTER 11

JOSHUA

The pounding on the door matches the throbbing in my head, and my first thought is that it's Aaron knocking. That Becca had gone back to her bed and back in his arms, crying about the way I'd left her on my steps. But then I remember it's Chaz's birthday, and I curse myself for staying out so late last night and forgetting my plans. I put on some pants and tear open the plastic around a new Globe T-shirt sitting in my suitcase before shrugging it on. Then I rub my eyes and inhale deeply, hoping to make it through today. For Chaz, and maybe for my own goddamn sanity.

A middle-aged man looks up from the clipboard in his hand when I answer the door. "You Josh Warden?" he asks.

"Yes, sir."

He hands me a stack of papers. "Here are the non-disclosures and insurance papers you requested. All my workers signed them." I can tell he's holding back an eye roll, and to be honest, I understand why. But Chris makes everyone who does work for me fill out the stupid papers. "What are you anyway? One of those reality stars or something?" he asks, looking into my two-bedroom garage apartment.

I drop the forms on the entry table. "Or something."

"That's cool." He shrugs, already bored with the notion. "Where do you want us to set up?"

I step out, shutting the door behind me, and lead him to the backyard. The driveway is already filled with catering vans and decorators, and even though it's just a small party with Chaz's church lady friends, I wanted to do something nice for her. I owe her that much. "So you guys will be done by 1? It's a surprise, so I'd like it ready before she gets back from church," I tell him.

He grins. "You had the funds, I got the manpower." And with that, he gets to work.

I watch, making sure they don't do any damage to Chaz's garden. A few minutes later Robby shows up, his truck loud as it reverses down the driveway. I walk over and inspect the timber loaded in the bed. "It looks good," I shout while he jumps down from his seat.

He closes the door. "Of course it does. You seem to forget I taught you everything you know," he says, stopping beside me. "It's to the exact specifications you wanted, Josh. I went over it fifty times. Even had Kim out with the measuring tape just to be sure. I know how important it is to you."

"I appreciate it. I just wish I had the time to do it myself."

"We can say you did. She doesn't have to know."

"And live the rest of my life under God's watchful eye knowing I lied to her? Nah, man. I'm good."

He laughs at that before motioning to my cast. "Are you going to be able to help me put it together, or you want me to call one of the guys?"

As if right on cue, the front door opens and Aaron and Martin walk out, Becca following behind them. "You guys need a hand?" Aaron asks.

I look over his shoulder at Becca, who's looking down at her feet.

Then I nod.

I smile.

And I act *amicable* toward him, just like I said I'd be. "That would be *swell*."

"*Swell?*" Robby whispers.

I turn to him, baring my teeth with the fakest of all fake grins. "Just fucking *swell*, Rob."

With Aaron's help, it doesn't take long for us to put together the arbor I'd had Robby build. For the past six months, Chaz had been hinting about it. Talking about it. Showing me pictures of it. Asking to go on trips to the lumber yard to pick out the material. Even going as far as making copies of the picture and wallpapering my bedroom with it while I was out of town. "*I got jokes,*" she'd said when I confronted her. But I don't think it was about the arbor itself. I think she did it for the same reasons Robby built the half pipe in his yard. It was a reminder that I had a family and a home, and they were all here waiting for me.

I sit on the grass and compare the picture in my hand to the arbor itself and smile a genuine smile for the first time today. "It looks really good, man," Aaron says, sitting down next to me.

Taking a breath, I try to ignore the anger and jealousy building in my chest. "Yeah, it turned out amazing." I don't know what he's doing—sitting next to me trying to drum up conversation like we're old friends. I stare down at my shoes and clench my fists, mentally picturing them smashing his face. Over and over. Right in his perfect poster-child Abercrombie model looking douche-tool teeth.

"So Grams tells me you're home from a media tour or something?"

I hate that he calls her Grams. I *hate* him. Still, I smile, my hands now fisted in the grass beside me. I'm about to answer, but something cold, something *wet,* is placed on my arm, and I know what it is without looking. My eyes drift shut, memories of a scorching summer day with the exact same sensation filling my mind. Blindly, I reach for the glass next to my arm and take a sip of the ice-cold water. I don't look at Becca when I mumble, "Thanks," but it doesn't matter because she's walking in front of me now, her legs only inches away, and it takes everything in me to not reach out, to not touch her. But *he* does. He wraps his hand around her ankle as she passes him his own glass. "Thanks, baby," he tells her, and I puke. In my mouth. Just a little. I wait for her to leave because I can handle her, I can even handle him, but I can't handle them together. She doesn't leave, though. Instead, she sits down opposite us, not in front of me, but not in front of him, either. She crosses her long, perfect legs, and I blink hard, pushing away the reminder of what it felt like to be between them. Her hands settle on her lap and she chews her lip, her gaze moving between Aaron and me. Then she pauses on me, her eyes pleading. For what? I have no idea.

I have absolutely no fucking clue what she could possibly want from me. It should be enough that I haven't broken a skateboard on her boyfriend's face, but now she's looking at me, wanting more, and I have nothing more to give.

I've given her everything I am.

"Thanks for your help, man," I tell Aaron, standing up and taking my glass with me.

I spend the next half hour pretending like I give a shit about balloons and flower arrangements and cheese fucking platters. It was a lot easier to pretend I cared about those things than to pretend like I *didn't* care that Becca and Aaron's existence was crushing my heart, stomping on it, shredding it to pieces. "You good?" Robby asks, standing next to me.

I pick up a flower from a vase and replace it in the exact same spot. "I'm fine."

"So… Becca just asked me to ask you if she could help with anything."

I turn to him before looking for her in the yard. I scoff when I don't see her. "She can ask me herself."

"She said she would if she didn't think you hated her."

"I don't hate her," I snap.

"*I* know that," he says, leaning against the catering table. "But she doesn't, and you speaking to her boyfriend but acting like she's invisible isn't helping."

I blow out a breath, my shoulders dropping with the force of it.

"Maybe just talk to her, man."

"No."

"Josh."

"What?!"

Rob shakes his head. "Don't be an asshole, okay? You're not the only one who went through what you guys did. In fact, she had it worse. Have you even stopped to think how brave it is for her to be here right now? She's come back to a place that's caused her pain and grief and enough suffering to last a lifetime. Maybe try *not* making it about you this time and—"

"What the fuck is that supposed to mean?"

He raises his hands in surrender. "I didn't mean it like that. I just…" He sighs. "I like Becca. She's a good girl. And she was good to *you* and she loved Tommy—"

"Don't," I cut in, my tone flat.

"Just talk to her. She's out in the driveway."

Two years ago, I'd stood in this exact same spot beside her, watching her do the exact same thing… holding a camera to her eye, one hand gripping the body, the other twisting the lens. I remember looking at her profile, her dark skin and high cheekbones beneath eyes I wanted nothing more than to get lost in. I'd asked her why she was taking photographs of a dying flower. She'd turned to me, my breath catching when her eyes caught mine. And I'll never forget what she said: "*Some things will always be beautiful, even in the face of death.*"

I'd wanted to ask her what she meant. I didn't. Maybe I should have. Maybe that simple question could've saved us.

Now, she's holding a different camera.

But she's still the same Becca.

And I'm still so miserably in love with her.

She snaps away a few more times before lowering the camera and turning to me, her free hand pointing to herself, and then to the yard. She begins putting the camera back in its bag, and without meaning to I reach out and stop her, my hand covering hers. "I'm sorry," I rush out. "I've been acting like an asshole—"

Her mouth opens, but nothing comes out, and I feel the stabbing pain of the knife in my heart, over and over, because *I* caused that. Regardless of how many times people have told me that it wasn't my fault, that a lifetime's worth of torture and turmoil led to her actions, they're wrong. And I know that, because with every single click of a shutter I hear, every piece of elation I feel when I land a trick, every time my name's shouted from the stands, I think of her. And I know that it's because of her I get to have all that. And I wonder if every time she opens her mouth and silence falls from her lips, every time she types on her laptop to communicate, every time she shows a message on her phone because her voice no longer works—she thinks of me. Because I'm the one who *made* her that.

"It's hard for me to have you both here," I continue, my voice cracking. "But that's on me, not you. I'm sorry I keep hurting you, Becs. It's the last thing I want."

She looks up, a perfect frown on her beautiful mouth, and I force myself to not reach out and run my thumb across her lips. After putting the camera away, she grabs her phone from the back pocket of her denim shorts and starts to type, moving closer so I can read it. *Friends?*

No single word in the history of unrequited love has ever caused more pain than the word *friends*. Not that I'd know. I had Nat, and then I had her. I smile. I nod. "Sure."

Her grin is instant, and for some pathetic reason it causes more pain than that single word. But I remember Robby's speech and remind myself that it isn't about me, so I return her smile and throw in another nod, because it's what I promised I'd do, but in my mind, I'm already picking out the boards I plan to smash the second she leaves. But then she steps closer, and closer again and her arms start to rise and a part of me wants to run, wants to push her away, because I know she's about to touch me… and when she finally does, her arms around my neck, I feel the burst of life kick in… the exact same moment I feel a part of me die.

Her cheek presses against my chest and my arms go around her waist and I die a little more, and the longer we stand there, my arms wrapped around the only person who's ever truly *seen* me, I can feel myself sinking, drowning, begging for air. I force myself to pull away, but she holds me to her, her head lifting and her eyes locked on mine. Her smile's gone now, the frown back in place, and I get lost in her gaze, a place that holds all my secrets, my fears, my desires. Then she rises to her toes, her mouth against my ear, and her breath warm against my skin. "Thank you," she *whispers*.

My eyes widen in shock, my heart… I have no idea what it's doing, but apparently she finds my reaction amusing because she laughs, or at least her version of a laugh, and seeing it gives me the same feeling of life *and* death. I'm about to speak but my name being called cuts me off. Chris walks up the driveway, his look of shock matching mine from only seconds ago. "Becca." There's distaste in the way he says her name, and I know why, I just don't want *her* to know why. So, I release her quickly and turn to Chris, squaring my shoulders as I move her behind me.

"Thanks for coming," I tell him.

"It's no problem. In fact, I'm glad I showed up. Who knows—"

"We'll talk about it later."

"No, Warden," he says. "I think we should talk about it now."

Shaking my head, I narrow my eyes at him. Then I give in to the inevitable and turn to Becca. "I'll see you later, okay?"

Her bottom lip traps between her teeth, her eyes worried as she looks between Chris and me.

"It's fine," I assure her, then face Chris and motion toward my apartment.

The second we're behind closed doors, he lets me have it. "What the hell are you doing, Warden?" he yells.

"I'm not doing anything! Jesus Christ."

"Oh yeah?" he asks, his eye roll adding punch to his sarcasm. "I can totally see that."

"Not here. Not now," I grind out. "Give me a fucking break!"

"A break? You had a break! You took two weeks off after the shit you pulled in St. Louis."

My head lowers, my hands at my hips. "So fucking what?"

"So fucking what?" he repeats. "This isn't a fucking game, Warden. You're a pro athlete now. You have people paying you big money and those people depend on you—"

"I don't want any of that shit! I told you that. I just want to skate."

His eyes narrow. "That *shit* is what allows you to skate for a living. It's what allows you to travel with your son everywhere so you don't have to miss a second of him growing up. You think I'm doing this for me? I *have* money, Josh. I couldn't care less about any of that."

"Get off your high horse. I'm the one who fucking earned it!"

"Exactly!" he shouts, his voice echoing in my ears. "You earned it, Josh, and you can't just throw it away over some girl!"

I step to him. "Watch your fucking mouth."

"This is bullshit," he murmurs.

"Why are you even here, then?"

"Because as much as you don't want to believe it right now, I'm your fucking friend."

"Yeah, well you're not being my friend right now. You're being my agent."

"No. Right now I'm being both."

I shove his chest. "What the fuck is your point, Chris?"

His jaw sets, but he doesn't push back. He seems to take a calming breath, or ten, all while the frustration and anger settle in the pit of my stomach. He says, "My point is that if her being here is going to push you off track again, then let me know. If I need to cancel your commitments for the next few weeks, then I'd rather do it now, so I can get us prepared to lose another major sponsor, maybe even drop a couple world ranks like last time."

"Fuck you." I don't wait for a response; I simply open the door and prepare to walk out on him. But I can't. I don't get further than a step because Becca's standing just outside the door, her eyes wide, and her hand raised in a fist, ready to knock. Her mouth opens, closes, and then opens again, and with each second that passes, her tears build, and I know she heard everything. *Everything*. "Becca," I say through a sigh.

She drops her gaze and points down the driveway where Chaz's friends are currently moving toward us.

"Becca," I say again, and she looks up. Not at me, but at Chris behind me.

"It's nothing personal," Chris tells her. "It's just business, Becca."

CHAPTER 12

BECCA

My dad spends hundreds of dollars a month on the best speech therapist in St. Louis. He and my therapist were the only people who'd been able to reap the rewards of his hard earned cash. Until I was in Josh's arms and for a moment, the safety in his touch outweighed my fear. I *whispered,* and in doing so, I gave him a piece of me I'd been saving for a moment worthy of it. And it was. The look on his face was completely worth it. Until Chris showed up and spat my name like I was trash. I was confused, at first, but then I saw Grams's friends show up, and when I went to knock on Josh's door, everything became clear. A little too clear. I guess the guilt Dawn had pushed me to rid myself of was justified. And, somehow, I had to find a way to spend not only my time here, but the rest of my life, dealing with it. I remind myself that seeing him when he was in St. Louis was on The List, and that it *had* to be done. Because at some point, or so Dad keeps telling me, I have to put myself first. But at what cost?

I did my best to keep my chin up and not let it bother me. Grams's reaction to her surprise party helped a lot, but the feeling was still there. Still in the back of my mind, in the ache of my chest, in the turning of my stomach, eating away at my thoughts. It wasn't until she and her friends were clearly drunk on what they called "Jesus Juice" that some of those thoughts faded. It helped that they did everything in their power to tease Josh in ways that had him blushing like I'd only seen when we first got together.

I'd watched interview after interview, promo tape after promo tape of him, and not once did he seem as embarrassed as he did when Mavis, one of Grams's oldest friends, asked him to take his shirt off so she could sell it on eBay. The teasing was relentless. At one point, Mavis asked Grams if she remembered all those times she'd come over here when Josh first moved in under the pretense she wanted to make sure the young punk wasn't taking advantage of Grams… turns out she was here just to watch Josh skate shirtless out in the driveway.

"I was seventeen!" Josh yelled, his eyes wide.

"Heck yeah, you were!" was Mavis's response, followed by a bunch of drunken old lady high fives and continued banter. The entire afternoon went on like that, until it got to the point where Mavis passed out drunk under the arbor with an empty cheese platter on her face. Josh, always the gentleman, offered to take her home and make sure she got in bed, to which Mavis responded, "You can take me to bed any time you want, handsome."

That was the last I heard from Josh. I assume that by the time he got home, the party was over.

As the day neared to an end and the joy from the party faded away, I was left with the weight of guilt pushing down on my shoulders. But not just that, I was left with a resounding amount of disappointment. I sat on the porch while Aaron caught up on his studies in his room, and Dad caught up with Grams inside, watching the sun set over the horizon, and I longed for a boy, a little boy whose smile was just like his father's.

It's not until dark clouds replace the sun, and I'm getting ready for bed that I hear a car door slam shut, followed by another, and then Josh's voice. Then a sound I'd spent the entire day listening out for. "Daddy!"

I grab the bag I'd brought with me, Tommy's present wrapped neatly inside it, and I don't think twice. I run downstairs and open the door, my anticipation building. By the time I'm on the driveway, Josh, his aunt Kim, and Tommy are climbing the stairs to his apartment, Tommy in Kim's arms. I call Tommy's name, but it's only audible in my mind, yet somehow Josh hears it, or at least senses it, because he turns to me, an unjustified fear in his eyes before practically pushing Kim and Tommy into his house. He closes the door behind them, and then he just stands there, one hand balled at his side, the other still on the knob.

I grip Tommy's present to my chest and watch as Josh finally turns around. With rushed steps, he makes his way down the stairs and stops in front of me. Through a sigh, he says, "What are you doing, Becca?"

I realize I'm still smiling.

I don't know why I'm smiling.

I guess the second he herded his family into the house and away from me, I froze.

Physically.

Mentally.

Inside.

Outside.

Everything.

Froze.

He takes a step forward, and I take a step back, and it's as if the anger that begins to boil inside me sets free the chills of my frozen state. He's acting like Tommy has a reason to *fear* me.

Like I'm the one who yelled and cursed at his son's mother and threw shit from the top of the stairs before trashing the crap out of his own truck. I'm not the danger here. *He* is.

I regret the thought the second it develops, but I don't regret the way I feel.

I hate him.

I love him.

I hate that I love him.

I throw the bag at his chest and turn around, but not before I see his eyes drift shut and his jaw tense in anger. He has no right to be angry, but he is, and the tone he uses to hiss my name is proof of that.

I'm one foot away when his hand circles my arm, my name falling from his lips, calmer and quieter than the last. "You can't do this," he says.

I gather my courage to face him. "What?" I mouth, harshly tugging out of his hold.

Instantly, the rage in his eyes disappears and is replaced with pity. I look up at his apartment and choke on a sob. I don't need his pity. I need my *best friend.*

A single drop of rain lands on my arm, and I stare down at it—a once single bead, now separated by the impact and I compare it to *us.* I wonder if it weren't for the circumstances that destroyed us, if Josh and I would still be one, or if life and distance would've ruined us anyway.

"I'm sorry, Becs," Josh says, his hand's on my arm again, soft and gentle and *safe.* "Tommy—he can't know you're here."

Swear, I try. I try so damn hard to keep it together, to not let him see the effects of his words, but I can't. And as my shoulders shake while sob after sob completely drain me, I look up at him and mouth, "Why?"

He releases me quickly and locks his fingers behind his head, and I can see his pain, see his struggle to say what he says next. "Tommy asks about you every day, Becca. When things didn't work out between us, it didn't just ruin me, it hurt him, too." He pauses a moment as he looks down at me, and I wonder if he can see the weight of his words pushing me down, making me feel beneath him. "He sleeps with a damn camera every night expecting you to come home, come back in our lives as if nothing has changed. He thinks you're out there, photographing these adventures, and he looks at me with those eyes… you *know* the ones… and I don't have the heart to tell him otherwise. But seeing you here and—"

I cover my face with my hands to hide my cries, unwilling to show him my weakness. It's pouring now, rain beating down on us. My tears, my pain, my fears getting lost with it.

"I'm sorry, Becca," he says, and I can hear the reflection of my ache in his words. I keep my eyes closed when I feel him step forward, his fingers gentle as they run up my arm. "I don't say this to hurt you. Look at me. *Please.*" There's an urgency in his words now, so strong it overpowers the hurt.

After dropping my hands, I glance up at him. And the second I do I regret it, because he's already looking at me, right into my eyes, and I feel the same thing I felt the first time he smiled at me. *Calm.* But he's not smiling now. And there's no reason for my calm. Especially when he wraps me in his strong, wet arms—arms that somehow warm my body, my heart. "I'm sorry," he whispers in my ear. "I can't seem to stop hurting you. I don't want this. You have to forgive me, Becs."

I try to force myself to move away, but I can't.

He's making me *feel.*

He rests his forehead on mine. "For *everything.*"

I return his embrace, and he holds on to me tighter, his cast now ruined, drenched by the rain. I surrender in his arms, and take a breath, and then another, watching the beads of water fall from his lashes with each blink. His gaze drops to my mouth quickly, then to my eyes, and down again, over and over. My heart's racing now, my fingers aching from their grip on his shirt. His chest rises and falls against mine, matching his gaze… from my eyes to my lips, up and down, and I can't take my eyes off his. He exhales slowly, his breath mixing with mine. I lick my lips, and his eyes drift shut. He moans when my shaky hands find his hair, tugging desperately. I push aside my fear, my confusion, just for a moment as I use his embrace to keep me upright. "Goddammit," he groans, his hesitation clear. I close my eyes and lean closer into him. Then I rise to my toes, my lips craving his. But he doesn't move. Not the slightest. I freeze, my lips an inch from his, waiting for him to make the first contact. He doesn't, though. Instead, his hand drifts to the small of my back, his touch like fire, burning flames igniting my soul. "You *know* me, Becca. You know my heart. And you know I'd never take another guy's girl. *Never.* But you're not just a girl to me and you never have been. If you need me to prove that to you, I will. If you want me to fight for you, I will. If you want me to go to war for you, I fucking will. You know that. Somewhere, deep in here"—he places his hand on my chest and my eyes snap open, meeting his—"you know I would. But you need to give me a sign so I know that it's not for nothing. You have to give me *something.* I can't go through that heartache again."

My breath gets lost in his words while I get lost in his eyes, eyes that completely expose me. So I do the only thing I can think to do…

I *ruin* us.

Then I rush up the stairs, my shame like heavy weights around my ankles. Through silent sobs and hurtful regrets, I reach for the doorknob, but it's not my room I go into, it's the room next door.

I stand at the edge of the bed and grab the phone on the nightstand, my hands shaking as I type out a text. I lower the sheets, and without a thought to my current soaking state, I welcome the warmth of the body next to me.

"Becca?" Grams says, sitting up. She switches on the lamp on her nightstand before facing me. "Oh, sweetheart. What happened?" She combs her fingers through my hair then looks down at the phone in my trembling hands.

I kissed Josh.

JOURNAL

He peels away the layers
Of fear and of pain
Leaving me exposed
From my heart to my veins
While I tiptoe the land mines
Of scene after scene
Waiting for the destruction
That left us unclean
But I worship the moments
That kept us bare
And I hold them there
With safe touches
And gentle words
And silent tears
And silent cries
Beneath silent stars
And when I close my eyes
I push down the hurt
Of a three-year-old smiling
His face covered in dirt

CHAPTER 13

JOSHUA

Five months ago I skated a comp that, if won, would rank me fourth in the world. I had one final trick up my sleeve and 11.3 seconds on the clock.

When I poured my heart out to Becca, begging her to forgive me, asking her to give me a sign that she still felt everything I felt, I had the same feeling. One last trick. One last chance.

I started my run up, board in my hand and my mind already three seconds ahead. Then I dropped the board, and I kicked and I pushed, focused on the grind rail in front of me. Focused on the prize.

World Ranking.

Becca.

There are two parts to completing a trick. The landing and the balance to continue. I found myself in the air, the clock ticking down, and my board flipping somewhere beneath me. The second my toes touched the grip tape, I knew I had the landing down.

When Becca's lips met mine, cold and wet and perfect, I knew I'd landed my last trick. Landed her.

A second later, the board tipped forward, throwing me

completely off balance. My foot came down an inch too close to the front of the deck, and I fell nose first on the ground. Blood poured everywhere, taking my pride with it.

Just like Becca when she walked away from me.

But there's a reason why skaters skate. Why we bust a trick fifty times just to nail it once. Why we suffer broken bones and bruises and scrapes over and over. It's all in our heads. We deceive our minds into believing that there is no pain. That's when the adrenaline kicks in. And the adrenaline is what we live for. We fall. We get back up. We kick. We push. Again and again. Because the joy of success is greater than the depression of failure.

It took me three weeks to get over the loss at that comp.

It took me three seconds to trick my mind into believing that the pain of Becca walking away didn't exist.

So I get into bed, my mind clear and my dad's final words replaying in my head.

"Time to coast, son."

CHAPTER 14

BECCA

It shouldn't have come as a surprise. The moment we pulled out of Grams's driveway to head to the airport, I knew something was wrong. Aaron barely spoke to me on the flight and he stayed that way on the drive home. As soon as we were out of Dad's car, Aaron asked if we could talk. That was the first time he actually looked at me. He was upset. It was obvious. And I was upset for him. We broke down, sitting in his car outside my house, and we released the truths to the lies we'd been living. But there was no yelling, no arguing. Just… understanding. And sadness. So much sadness. He confessed that he used the trip as a way to determine our true feelings for each other. The fact that I basically ignored him the entire time was proof that I didn't feel the way he'd hoped. I tried to argue with him in my own silent way, but he kept shaking his head and telling me that it was okay. It was okay because he realized that it didn't hurt him the way it should have. It was painful—to have him sit there and tell me that he thought we'd been using each other in the hopes that it would somehow help us forget our losses. There was a reason he was drawn to a girl who couldn't speak, a girl who he'd hoped would rely on him the way Brandi had, a girl who found comfort in his need to understand her. But like he said, I wasn't Brandi, and he didn't love me. Just like he wasn't Josh, and I didn't love him. Again, I tried to argue with him. Or maybe it wasn't him so much as it was myself. I didn't love Josh. I *couldn't* love Josh. But even through my silent cries and untrue declarations, he felt the weight of the truth as much as I did. He held me while I cried, and I did the same for him, and we promised each other that we'd remain friends. That we wouldn't let it change our relationship. As much as I wish that was going to happen, I knew it wouldn't. And as much as I didn't realize it while it was happening, he was wrong. Maybe I didn't rely on him the way he wanted, but I still did. In my own way. A way I'd feared.

I became sad, and then angry, and then desperate. I lay in bed, tears soaking my pillow, and I wished my mind to be as empty as the rest of me. I'm not exactly sure why I became so upset, why I took it so badly. It's not as if I'd planned to spend the rest of eternity with him. Maybe it wasn't so much the fact that he broke up with me as it was the reasons why. I tried to justify my actions over the course of our "relationship." Tried to convince myself that I wasn't a horrible person. I wasn't using him. Not really. But he'd said it himself. We were using each other. And that would make him just as horrible as me… only he wasn't. Not at all. And that made me feel worse.

So I became sadder.

Angrier.

More desperate.

I spent days in bed wallowing in my self-pity, ignoring Dad's constant concern. I didn't open up to him. I couldn't. I skipped classes, didn't show up to therapy, and on the fourth day of crying silent tears, I left my room, sat on the couch with Dad, and told him I was fine. Only I wasn't. Not at all. I was so *un*fine that all I could think about were the horrible things I'd done. Not just to Aaron, but to everyone around me. My dad relocated, took a lower paying job in a city he'd never been to just so he could take care of his daughter—a virtual stranger. My mother died. DIED. Because of me. I thought about everything I'd done, all the people I'd lost, and I became so lost in the depths of my loss that I could no longer think straight. I guess that's why I found myself walking to a mailbox at three in the morning in a night gown and mailing a letter that, up until that point, I had no intention of sending. I regretted it as soon as the envelope slipped through the crack, and I cursed myself the moment I heard it land amongst all the other ones. For a while, I just stood there, staring at the mailbox and wondering how many of those letters held pain and regret and hopes. Unjustified hopes. Then I started kicking it. Over and over. Until I felt my toes become numb and a wetness seeping through my socks. I knew it'd be blood, but at the time, it was better than my tears. The walk home felt like an eternity, and once behind the closed door of my bedroom, I continued my spiral into depression. Dad came in a few hours later, saw my emotional state, witnessed what I'd been failing to hide from him, and after holding me and assuring me that everything was going to be okay, found The List on my desk, hidden beneath a pile of used and discarded tissues. His eyes scanned the items, one after the other, and then he looked up, a smile pulling on his lips, and said, "How hard would it be to sell things online?"

My eyes widened, and I sat back against the headboard, my knees raised. "Now?" I mouthed.

He smiled. "Right now. Unless, you know, you want to get your ass to class."

I shook my head.

"But tomorrow, you will, right?"

Another head shake.

He sighed as he folded The List and placed it carefully back on my desk. Then he sat on the edge of the bed, his hand gentle as it settled on my arm. He gave me *that* look. The one that showed he had no idea what to do or what to say because he was in way over his head.

"Okay," I mouthed, and he smiled.

"Okay." Dad rubbed his hands together and said, "Lemonade, sweetheart."

My dad loves phrases, but would always say them wrong. He'd say things like, "I'm not here to give you the fifth degree," or "You're climbing up the wrong branch." So, "Lemonade, sweetheart," was his way of saying, "When life gives you lemons…" you know the rest.

So I turn the stupid lemons into lemonade.

I huff out a frustrated breath and pick at a worn spot on the kitchen table, the fear of what we're doing suddenly hitting me.

"You okay, kid?" Dad asks.

I nod—a lie.

Selling my work is the only item on The List that had nothing to do with my mother (or Josh). In fact, it has everything to do with me. I had planned my future based on my photography, yet I'd been too afraid to show the world what I could do. Besides teachers, some students, family (and Josh), no one had seen it. And the idea of throwing it out there for the world to judge was absolutely petrifying.

Dad shuts his laptop, pushes it to the side, and leans forward on his elbows. "It's overwhelming, huh?"

I shrug.

"Well, let's start with the first step. Have you thought of a name?"

I drop my head, another sigh leaving me. Then I pick up a notepad and pen, scribble down the name I'd chosen a year ago and slowly slide it toward him. His smile is instant. "Views Of Emeralds." He glances up at me with the eyes I'd inherited. "It's perfect, Becca."

I spend the next month going to classes, going to therapy with Dawn, and going to voice therapy. I don't go to group. I'm not ready, and Dad—he understands that and he leaves it alone, for now, but not forever. Dad and I work together to create an Instagram account to hopefully sell the images through there. Last week, I asked Pete, the editor at the school paper, if he could run a tiny story without giving away my identity. He agreed, and now I have forty-nine followers on Instagram and absolutely no interest from anyone wanting to buy the photographs. But like my dad keeps reminding me, it wasn't the prospect of money, or lack of, that had me wanting it on The List. It was purely getting it out there. Now, I had done that. And without even realizing, I slowly start picking up the pieces of my once not-so-broken life.

My phone sounds with an alert, and a smile begins to spread when I hear my dad's footsteps get louder until his huge frame crashes against my door. He knocks. Waits. And then enters the room. "Did you see it?" he shouts over the commentary of whatever game he's watching on the television.

I nod once, his excitement forcing the grin out of me.

"Fifty followers, Becs! That's amazing!" He throws his hands in the air. "We should celebrate."

I quirk an eyebrow.

"After group therapy."

My shoulders drop.

"Let's go. You don't want to be late."

Aaron's here. I assumed he would be, but still, watching him approach—his hands in his pockets while he chews his bottom lip—is so terrifying, I should've added it to The List.

"I was wondering if you'd ever come back," he says.

"I'm not here willingly," I sign.

He smiles. "Your dad?"

I'm about to nod, but the session starts and a minute later, we're sitting next to each other in a large circle. In the month I've been gone, a few people have left, replaced with newer, sadder faces. They release their hurt, some release their tears. The stories are the same, but different. The words are heavy, and the pain we share even heavier.

Aaron passes when it comes time for him to talk, which surprises me because he's always had something to say. It dawns on me now that he's been silent the entire time, his knee bouncing—something he does when he's nervous.

"Becca. Your turn," Cliff, the group leader, says.

I keep my eyes narrowed at Aaron, who's avoiding my gaze, and reach into my bag for my iPad. I pull up the speech I'd prepared last night, take a deep breath, and hit *speak*. My eyes lose focus the second Cordy starts to speak.

"I've been a little down lately which I guess is the reason why I haven't been coming to these sessions. It's probably counterproductive considering this is therapy, and we should be using it the most during those times. The truth is, I lost someone from my life who I loved dearly. Maybe not in the way I should've loved him, but still, I did. I think the part that hurt me the most is that I didn't show him that, and in turn, that hurt me. And it's that thought that had me spiraling down. I know what you're all thinking... Becca had her heart broken by a guy, boo-hoo. But the truth is, he wasn't just a guy. He was a guy who helped me through some of the toughest times of my life. He helped me heal, and he taught me that my biggest physical flaw was not at all an emotional one. And that it shouldn't stop me from at least attempting to reach my life goals.

"I guess it's because of him I chose to start showing more people my photography—my life goal. My dad encouraged me to set up an Instagram account and we have about fifty followers. No bites for sales yet, but that's not really the point. I know it may seem like a small step for most, but it's a giant leap for me. I think that regardless of common advice, sometimes it's important to fall and stay down for a while to appreciate why it's so important to get back up. I'm grateful to Aaron for helping me realize that. And I just want to thank him, even if he disappears from my life forever. I want him to know that he means so much more to me than I let on. And sometimes, the fear of losing someone important makes you push them away. And for that, I'm sorry."

Silence fills the room seconds after the last word, and I keep my eyes lowered, afraid of people's judgments. When I find the courage to glance up, no one's looking at me, they're all looking at Aaron—who's smiling. "What's your Instagram account?"

"Where's your car?" I sign to Aaron, using his body to shield me from the sun.

He rubs his jaw, his eyes shifting to the side. "Yeah… I kind of wanted to talk to you about something, but then the group started and well…" he trails off.

I grasp his arm and wait until he's looking at me before signing, "What's going on?"

He waits a beat, his cheeks darkening. "I kind of met someone…"

An emotion hits me. I'm not sure what yet, but I sign, "Is that what you were going to talk about in there? Because you could've."

Aaron shrugs. "I know. It just didn't seem appropriate. And then you started talking—"

My eye roll cuts him off.

He chuckles. "Of all the things I'll miss about you, Owens, your eye roll is extremely low on the list."

I shove his shoulder just as a car pulls up to the curb. A girl walks out, blonde and beautiful, her eyes only for Aaron. "Hey, babe," she says, and I look down at my feet.

"Hey," he responds, but I can feel his eyes on me.

I take a breath and look up at them, just in time to see her go in for a kiss and him back away. I fake an eye roll, causing Aaron to laugh, and his girlfriend's brow to bunch in confusion. Then she looks over at me, her eyes widening before her features straighten and a smile, although forced, curls on her lips. "You must be Becca?" she says, taking Aaron's hand when he puts his arm around her shoulders. "Aaron's told me so much about you. I'm Macy." There's sincerity in her words, and I hate myself for thinking she was anything but pleasant. I know Aaron, and I know the type of girl he'd fall for. I raise my hand in a wave and return her genuine smile.

Macy looks up at Aaron. "So Dex is in the driveway waiting for you. He's got the basketball hoop set up and everything."

"Dex is Macy's little brother," Aaron tells me.

"And Aaron's biggest fan," Macy adds.

They laugh together, this perfectly perfect couple.

Aaron removes his arm from around his girlfriend and spreads both of them wide, inviting me. "Can I get a hug?"

I hide my smile against his chest and hold him for longer than necessary, but he's not the first to let go, not the first to weaken. I am.

"I'll see you next week?" Aaron asks me.

I nod.

They get in the car, Macy driving away while Aaron waves from the passenger's seat. I wave back, my eyes drifting shut when an unexpected calm washes through me.

. . .

The next evening, I go to therapy and ignore Dawn's usual greeting. Instead, I type, *I want to do something.*

"Something?" she asks.

With a nod, I type, *The second to last item on the list. I want to do it.*

Silence pass for a beat before I look up at her. She's smiling —the same kind of smile Aaron gave me in group. "Are you sure you're ready?"

I've never been more prepared.

Her grin spreads as she opens a drawer on an end table. "I've been waiting for this moment." Then she reaches across, covering the space between us, and hands me a stack of papers:

Volunteer Application for Say Something.

I almost laugh at the irony of the name, then stop while I read on about the program. My eyes lock on Dawn when she asks one more time, "Are you sure you're ready?"

I wait for an emotion to hit me, anxiety, fear, panic. But nothing comes. Nothing but a peaceful calm.

Dad and I spend the entire night on the computer looking up anything and everything about Say Something. We learn that it's an extra-curricular non-profit organization. But after going through the information sheet Dawn had supplied, we find out that it isn't just a place for parents to drop off their kids and go on a lunch date. The Say Something project works closely with counselors in elementary schools within the district and recommends their services for "at risk" kids, which (for obvious reasons) is something not commonly known by the community. What "at risk" means, I don't know. But I sure as hell want to find out.

. . .

It takes me a week to send the application, most of that time spent writing an essay about why I want to volunteer. You'd think it would become easier to get the words down, to relive the moments of darkness, to explain my situation, my abuse, my constant hopes for someone or something to save me, hopes for a program just like Say Something. It doesn't, though. If anything, it gets harder the "stronger" I get. Dad thinks maybe it's a good sign, like I'm somehow getting more immune to my past. Personally, I think it's because I'm more aware of how my past can destroy my future.

Another two weeks passes before I get an e-mail from them asking me to come in for an interview. I reply, mention that I'm not great with interviews because I'm speech impaired, to which they respond, *It's just protocol. We have to do it with everyone. But trust me when I say, we would love to have you on the team. – Sandra.*

So a few days later, I enter the doors of an old warehouse, the Say Something logo printed on paper and stuck on the window. My hands grip my bag strap, soaking it in my sweat, while my heart races, nervous for my interview. A woman in her fifties with greying hair and gentle eyes greets me. "Are you Becca?"

I nod and reach for my phone to reply, but her movements have me glancing toward her. She walks around the desk and stops in front of me. Then she *signs*, an understanding smile curving her lips, "I'm Sandra. It's a pleasure to meet you. Welcome to Say Something. We're happy to have you on board."

We spend a good hour going through what everything is and how things run, and then we go through my class schedule to work out my future shifts. I leave the building filled with self-doubt and conflicted emotions. Fear and anticipation. There's something going on in my gut, like the early onset of butterflies. I could be wrong, but I think it might be excitement. And if it is, that excitement doubles when I get the first ever direct message on my Instagram account. Attached to the message is a picture I'd taken of the sunset from the roof of the arts building on campus.

Dear Ms. Owens, I would be honored to purchase this photograph so that I may carry it with me always. Sincerely, Aaron

And with that, I close a significant chapter in my life and prepare myself to write a whole damn book worthy of my existence.

PART II

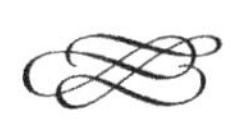

CHAPTER 15

BECCA

I finish my beer, listening to the laughter and cheers from the students around me—all celebrating the end of midterms at a bar near campus.

After the "break-up" with Aaron and starting the volunteer job at Say Something almost a year ago, I decided to throw everything I had into classes, work, and therapy. Not just to keep me busy and take my mind off things, but because I genuinely wanted to. I wanted to do better, not just mentally, but in every aspect of my life. I wanted to do well in class, not just float through unnoticed like I'd been doing. And I wanted to take the steps toward crossing off the second to last item on The List.

Leave a mark on that which has marked me.

Sandra offered me a position on the team that allowed me to work closely with some of the more "at risk" kids—the quiet and withdrawn ones who showed signs of physical or mental abuse. I teach an art and craft therapy class, a skill I'd learned from a three-day seminar that Say Something had paid for me to attend. It's perfect for me, and the kids seem to love it. It's amazing what you can learn from watching—through strokes of art, no words needed.

It was hard at first, trying to push aside my own history and not jump to conclusions every single time a kid walked in with a bruise or a broken bone, while at the same time, making sure I didn't ignore those signs. I spent a couple therapy sessions with Dawn telling her all this, fingers aching from typing so fast, while she sat and read everything I had to say. Then she looked up at me, smiled, and said that everything I was feeling was normal. *Good,* even. Because emotional attachment and empathy were imperative if I wanted to make a change in the world. I wasn't really planning on changing the world, and when I told her that, her smile widened. "But you *can,* Becca. The point is you *can.*" And with those simple words, I started looking at the world differently, started seeing things from all angles. My life no longer became about healing the pain of my past. Instead, it became about preventing the past from taking away my future. One *kick* at a time.

When Pete, the editor at *Student Life,* heard about what I'd been doing at Say Something through one of the "conversations" I was having with a journalism major on the team, he pulled me aside and asked if I would be interested in writing my own weekly column in the Human Interests section. Besides that one article I wrote on Josh (where I chose to leave out certain parts), I'd never written anything before. I mean, I wrote in my journal but that was about it. "But you have heart, Becca. And that's something most people lack these days," Pete said. So I agreed, and now my column gets the third most hits on the *Student Life* website, right under Sports and Entertainment.

I slip out of the stool and gather my coat and bag. "You're leaving?" Pete shouts from the other side of the table.

I begin to pull out my phone, only to realize it'd be useless to have Cordy relay my message over the sound of drunken celebration. Instead, I nod, and once my coat is on I wave goodbye.

"You're not driving, are you?"

I shake my head and mouth, "Cab."

"I'll share one."

I narrow my eyes at him, knowing he lives on campus—across the road—and I don't, so sharing a cab would be counterproductive. He laughs as he slips on his jacket. "Just entertain me, okay? You know the idea of you catching a cab alone at night gives me hives." It's true, it does, for absolutely no other reason than the fact that Pete was raised a gentleman. It'd be useless to decline his offer, so I wait until he's said his goodbyes, and we exit the bar arm-in-arm. "Your dad home?" he asks, opening the door of the waiting cab for me.

I shake my head.

"Sigh."

With a smile, I get in the back seat and watch him do the same. Once the door's closed and he's given the driver my address, he says, "Set the security alarm, and make sure to lock all the doors, okay?"

I pull out my phone, type out a message, and show it to him. *I already have one dad. I don't need another.*

He rolls his eyes. "Smart ass."

The moment I step foot in my house, I switch on the lights, lock all the doors, and set the alarm. Then I shoot off a text to my dad. A few months ago, he went back to working on the oil rigs—short contracts here and there to help cover the bills, but nothing that would keep him away from home for too long. I've offered to get a job, but he won't allow it. At least not until he's positive I'll be okay on my own.

Becca: Finished exams. Had a couple drinks at a bar to celebrate. Met a tattooed junkie. It was love at first sight. Got married at the 24-hour chapel. Had unprotected sex. Caught syphilis. Good news: You're going to be a grandpa!

Dad: That shit ain't funny, Becca.

Becca: Who's joking?

Dad: Well, I hope he has a job.

Becca: He's a male stripper. But OMG, Dad, he's soooooo dreamy.

Dad: Lock the damn doors and set the alarm. And STOP giving me anxiety.

Becca: Already done.

Dad: Congrats on killing the finals.

Becca: I don't know if I killed them.

Dad: I know you did, and I've never been wrong.

Becca: I miss you.

Dad: I miss you, too.

Dad: And I love you.

I stare at his message, my heart sinking at the image of him looking down at his phone, waiting, wanting to see the words I've kept to myself.

Dad: Good night, sweetheart.

Becca: Good night, Dad.

JOURNAL

My mother loved me.

But love means nothing.

It's an invisible, fleeting moment.

Somewhere between false adoration and pure hatred comes an emotion, a vulnerable need, a single desire.

It lives within the ones who miss it, who crave it, who know better than to expect it.

Love is relentless, even when the love turns to hate, turns to loathing, turns to death.

CHAPTER 16

BECCA

I wake up early the next morning, my head clear from the alcohol consumed the night before, and get ready for my shift at Say Something. It's a Saturday, which means it's going to be packed with kids and scheduled activities. Dad finally taught me to drive without having constant panic attacks, and I *barely* scraped through my driver's test. He celebrated *his* achievement by handing me keys to my very own car. It isn't anything fancy, a silver Honda Accord the same age as me, but it's enough to get me from A to B, and to me, it's perfect. I still catch the bus to WU because parking is a bitch, and so I really only use it to get to the center—a fifteen-minute drive away—and to get to therapy sessions when Dad's not home. When he is, he likes to drive me around. He says it makes him feel needed.

I pull into a spot, just as my phone sounds with a text and I smile, knowing it's either Pete or Dad checking in on me. My mind's already reeling with smart-ass responses when I grab my phone from my bag. My breath catches when I see Josh's name on the screen. I stare at the letters of his name, moving from one to the next, J, O... wondering what it is he could possibly have to say. He hasn't communicated with me once since Grams's birthday. Not a call. Not a text. Not a single e-mail. Nothing. And now… I inhale deeply, the cold air filling my lungs giving me the courage I need to open the message.

Josh: Hey Becs. I'm really sorry to bother you, but do you know where your grams is? I came home yesterday and knocked on her door, she wasn't home but her car was. I left her a present at the door and when I woke up this morning it was still there. She's still not home.

My heart skips, my thumbs shaking as I try to reply. I attempt to type the same word five times, failing each time, before I realize I'm holding my breath. I force an exhale and push back the panic creeping in my chest.

Becca: I don't know where she is. She sent me a text a week ago. That was the last I heard from her.
Josh: I'm sure it's nothing. She's probably with Mavis or something. Don't panic, okay?
Becca: You have a key, right? Go in the house.
Josh: I just did. She's not home. TV's on.
Becca: Did you try calling her?
Josh: Yeah. She left the phone on the kitchen counter.

I try to reply, but the shaking of my hands makes it impossible, so I run into the center, phone gripped tight in my hand. The second I see Sandra in her office, I call Josh's number, set it to speaker, and sign to Sandra to translate for me.

With wide eyes, she nods, all while the sound of the phone dialing fills the room. "What's going on?" Sandra asks, and all I can do is shake my head, tears filling my eyes. There's a lump in my throat, threatening to escape in a silent sob, and the panic escalates with each continuous ring. I feel like I'm back in the hospital, Tommy in a room with a broken arm, and me pacing the waiting room trying to call Josh. The call cuts off, and I hit redial, tears falling, streaking down my cheeks. Finally, the call connects, and I can hear his fear in a single word, "Becs."

"Uh. Hi," Sandra says, her eyes on my hands—hands too weak to move. "I'm Sandra. I work with Becca, and I guess I'm going to translate for her..."

Josh doesn't speak, but I can hear his rushed breaths, hear the sound of his footsteps as he moves around my grandmother's house. Doors open. Doors close. "Ma'am!" he shouts.

In the background, I hear Tommy call out, "Ma'am. Where are you?"

"Hey, buddy," Josh says. "It's okay. She's probably just playing hide-and-seek. Yeah. That's what she's doing." He exhales loudly. "You stay in the house in case she comes out, all right? I'm going to look in the yard for her."

What's happening? I sign, and Sandra repeats it.

"I don't know. I've searched the entire house. She's not home." The background noise changes, letting me know he's outside. I hear the creaking of the gate to the back yard.

"Is she there?" Sandra asks for me.

"No. Look, I'm sure it's nothing," Josh says, his voice cracking, revealing his fear.

Sandra's eyes focus on my hands before she says, "Josh, maybe you need to call the police, hospitals..."

"Yeah. Yeah, I'll do that. *Shit*. Hang on."

"What's happening? Did you find her?" Sandra asks without my prompting, her fear matching mine.

"A cop car just pulled up. Hang on."

The worst possible scenarios infiltrate my mind, and the

only thing I can do is stand here and listen, my heart aching, my pulse shattering every nerve.

"She's here," he breathes out. "She's in the car."

He seems to cover the phone, because all I can hear are muffled voices as he speaks to the cops. The seconds feel like an eternity before he says my name, his tone calmer. "So apparently they found her walking the streets. I'm going to take her to the hospital and get her checked out. I'll take care of everything, okay? I promise."

"Who are you talking to?" Grams asks him, her tone gentle.

"It's Becca," Josh tells her.

"Who?"

My eyes snap to Sandra's while Josh says, "We're going to take you to the hospital. Just to get you checked out and make sure you're okay."

"I'm fine, Joshua. You always worry too much."

His loud exhale crackles the speakers on my phone. "Then humor me, okay? Let me take care of you for once."

Sandra smiles.

I can't.

"Tell him I'm going to catch the next flight out," I sign, and Sandra relays it for me.

"I'll call you back in a few minutes. Don't go anywhere yet."

I shake my head and stomp my foot.

Sandra tells him, "She doesn't seem too happy about that."

"Two minutes," he says, and then he hangs up.

I watch the seconds of the clock in the office tick by. One minute turns to two while Sandra consoles me, her words meant to comfort only cause more pain. Two minutes turn to three. Four. Five. *Ten.* Finally, my phone rings, and I jump to answer it.

"Becca?" Josh says. I can tell he's in his car now, the wind whooshing in the background.

"She's here," Sandra tells him.

"A private plane will pick you up. The pilot's going to send through the details of which airport, and I'll forward them on to you. He says he can be there within five hours. There's a big Check and Deck logo on the side of the plane. You can't miss it. Just give the desk your name. Message me when you get here, okay?"

I nod.

"Okay," Sandra says.

"Good. Drive safe. And Becca, please don't worry. I'm not going to leave her side. I promise."

I let his words sink in while I wipe at my tears, my heart slowing just enough to stop the ache in my chest. I take the phone off speaker and hold it to my ear, my eyes drifting shut as I force a swallow and prepare my throat to whisper, "I'm scared."

CHAPTER 17

BECCA

The second I land in Wilmington I text Josh and let him know. He replies immediately, telling me there's a car waiting for me just outside the exit. When I find the driver, he asks if I have any bags, and I realize I don't. I don't have anything. I went straight from the Say Something warehouse to the airport without even stopping to think.

It seems to take forever to get to the hospital, and as soon as I see the signs from afar, the driver makes a call to Josh. "We're pulling in now, Mr. Warden."

Josh is already waiting outside when we arrive at the hospital entrance. I open the door, not bothering to wait for the car to come to a complete stop. Then I'm in his arms, my cheek pressed to his chest. "She's okay," he says, his hand rubbing my back. "She's okay," he repeats, and I sense his *need* in the tightness of his embrace. It's only now that I realize how hard this must've been for him. How being the one to find her missing must've made him feel. I pull away, just far enough to look him in his eyes—eyes red and worn—evidence of the tears he's shed. "She's being examined at the moment for any physical—" He chokes on a breath, and I guide him with one hand around his waist into the waiting room of the hospital. He sits on a chair and I do the same, our fears and panic merging into one. I feel the warmth of his hand on my leg, and I don't remove it. Instead, I cover it with mine and squeeze once. "It's my fault," he mumbles. "I shouldn't be leaving her alone for weeks at a time. I should've had Kim check in on her, but your grams hated it, you know? She hated me worrying about her and, God, what if something happened to her? What if she was hit by a car, or attacked, or..." His words are rushed, admissions of regret pouring out of him and I wish I could tell him that he's wrong, that none of this is his fault. But I can't say a word. So I do the only thing I know to do. I release his hand and cup his cheeks, forcing him to look at me. His eyes meet mine, then drop to my lips when I mouth, "Stop."

He shakes his head. "You don't understand, Becs. When she wasn't there, I thought she was—"

"Stop," I mouth again. "Please." I'm begging now, my head moving from side to side.

"I'm sorry. I'm making it worse." His hands lift to circle my wrists, holding me to him as his eyes drift shut. I watch his shoulders rise and fall while he takes a few calming breaths. He looks up, his eyes clear, his cheeks flushed. "Are you okay?"

I nod. "You?" I mouth.

He exhales loudly. "I am now." His lips twitch with a smile, though I know he's trying to hide it. "Hi. You look good. I mean... you know... under the circumstances and all."

I return his smile.

"Was the flight and the car and everything okay?"

I stare, unblinking, and wonder how almost two and a half years have passed since we've been a *we,* yet the feelings are still there, still filling my heart and making it weak.

He releases my wrists to cup my jaw, his thumb skimming my bottom lip. "I'm glad you're here, Becs."

His voice, his touch, his entire presence has my heart

hammering in my chest. I drop my hands and turn away quickly to look straight ahead, hoping he can't read my reaction to him. "Sorry," he mumbles, but I ignore him and reach for my phone.

Do you know anything?

He runs his hand through his hair, watching me with a look in his eyes I can't decipher. "The nurse came in about half an hour ago and said that they were probably going to run some tests for dementia. I guess it's common for people your grams's age and considering how the police found her..."

With another nod and another breath, I type, *So, we just wait for results?*

"I guess."

His breath is hot and heavy on my neck as he leans over me, reading as I type, *Where's Tommy?*

"My mom met us here and took him back to her place."

A solid minute passes, neither of us saying a word, even when my mind is racing with them.

He breaks the silence. "I hate this place so much."

The hospital?

"Yeah... it just reminds me of Tommy and my dad and *you*. It's so fucking miserable."

I frown.

He smiles. It's a sad one, though, one caused by pure pain and heartache. His hand runs down my arm, toward my fingers, where they lace through mine, gripping gently as he brings them to his mouth. He releases a shaky exhale, right before his lips, soft and wet, make contact with my skin. He kisses me once and then settles our joined hands on his lap. "I meant what I said," he murmurs, eyes focused on our hands. "I'm so glad you're here. I don't know what I'd do without you."

A nurse calls Grams's name, cutting off my response, and Josh and I stand, our hands still connected. We make our way over to her. "How is she?" Josh asks her.

"She's physically stable. There's a little build-up in her lungs, most likely from walking around in the cold."

Josh's grip on my hand loosens. "So that's good, right?"

"That's just based on the initial tests," the nurse says. "We need to admit her for a few days."

Now my hand squeezes his, and he looks down at the phone in my hand. *Days?*

"This is her granddaughter Becca Owens," Josh tells the nurse. "Do you know when it might be possible to see her?"

"She's back in her room, but she's still a little out of it." The nurse looks at what I assume is Grams's chart. "Does she have any other family?"

I let go of Josh's hand and start typing on my phone. *I messaged Dad when I was waiting for the plane. He's going to fly in as soon as possible but it might take a day or so.*

After reading my message, Josh shifts his gaze to the nurse. "Just her son, but he works offshore so he might take a couple days. We can take care of her until then, right?"

The nurse nods, but her eyes are on me, squinted and confused.

"Becca's speech impaired," Josh informs her, bouncing on his toes, his patience fading. "Can we see her now?"

"Sure." The nurse speaks to me this time. "I just… I feel like I should warn you that she may not react to you as you'd expect. She may not be the grandmother you know, and she may not remember certain things. And at this stage, it's best if you don't force her."

Grams is lying on her side sleeping peacefully, the covers bunched under her chin. The monitors beep, a steady rhythm echoing off the walls of the small, sterile room. Josh takes my hand and leads me toward her bed. We stand side by side, looking down at her for seconds, minutes, hours. I have no idea. Josh squeezes my hand, and I look up at him. "She looks so tiny," he whispers.

"Josh?" Grams calls out, and our focus darts to her.

She has one eye open, almost like a kid afraid of a horror movie. "Oh, thank God. I thought you were one of the nurses, poking and prodding..." She throws the covers off her. "You're here to take me home, right?"

Josh releases my hand to stop her from getting out of bed. "I can't yet, ma'am. Soon, though, okay?"

Grams rolls her eyes. "More poking and prodding?"

Josh gives her a half-hearted grin. "Just a little."

She gets back into bed, smiling fondly at Josh who covers her with the blankets. "Where's Tommy?" she asks, looking around the room. She doesn't see me standing behind Josh, my hands grasping his shirt. I don't know why I'm hiding from her, why I'm suddenly so afraid, but it's taking everything I have to not break down and right now, Josh is the only thing I have to prevent that.

He says, "Tommy's with my mom. He's fine."

Grams sighs, relieved. "I can't even imagine how scared you boys must've been. Oh, Joshua, I'm so sorry."

"Stop it, ma'am. I'm fine. You're fine." He runs a finger across her forehead, shifting the hair from her eyes. "Everything's good, okay?"

She grasps his hand with both of hers. "Did you win the tournament?"

"I did."

"Oh, I'm so proud of you."

"I know you are." He starts to step aside, but I fist his shirt tighter, so he reaches behind him, grasping my wrist gently and encouraging me forward. "I got a surprise for you," he tells her. He's talking to her like he talks to Tommy, a tone I was once so envious of. Josh tugs on my arm, and I finally find the courage to reveal myself.

Grams's eyes light up, her smile matching mine. Then I wave, and her grin spreads. She looks from me to Josh. "Oh my," she says to him. "It's about time you got yourself a lady. Who's this beautiful girl?"

CHAPTER 18

JOSHUA

---

try

trʌɪ/

verb

1. make an attempt or effort to do something.

I sit with Chaz, holding her hand until she falls asleep. When Becca left the room after Chazarae showed no signs of recognition, I was torn on whether to go after her or stay with Chaz. Obviously, I decided to stay. I didn't want to, but I felt it more important that Chaz not feel overwhelmed. Like the nurse said, it was best we not push her. But now I'm sitting here wondering how it's possible for her to remember my stupid skate tournament but not remember her own granddaughter.

I release her hand, making sure not to wake her, and kiss her forehead. Then I leave the room, phone in hand, ready to message Becca. But I don't need to. She's standing just outside the room, her back leaning against the wall.

"Hey…"

She fails at trying to force a smile. Then she's in my arms, her tears soaking my chest, her arms wrapped tightly around me. "I'm sorry," I tell her, because I don't know what else to say and I don't even really know what I'm apologizing for. For Chaz not knowing who she is? For not realizing something was wrong? For not finding her earlier? I don't know. All I know is I'm *sorry*. But it doesn't seem to matter because she's crying harder now, silent sobs wracking her entire body. "Becs..." I rear back and hold her face in my hands. Her cheeks are wet, her eyes wetter. "Tell me what to do, and I'll do it."

She chews on her lip to fight the trembling while her sad, desperate eyes meet mine. Then she shakes her head, her hand reaching for her phone. *There's nothing we can do. She has no idea who I am.*

I read her text, again and again, hoping it gives me time to come up with a response that will take away some of her pain. "I understand you're hurting. Trust me, I do. And she might not know you now, but it's just... she's been through a lot."

She knows you!

I swallow the knot in my throat and whisper, "She's just known me longer. That's all."

But she's my family.

Her eyes plead, begging for a response to somehow take away her pain, but the only thing I can think to say only elevates mine. "She's *my* family, too, Becs."

Her eyes drift shut, her hand covering her mouth.

I take a chance and step forward, tugging lightly on her top to get her attention. She opens her eyes, but she doesn't look at me. "I know it's hard," I whisper, my mouth an inch from her ear. She drops her arm to her side, allowing me to come closer. My hand's on her waist now, my thumb grazing the bare skin between her top and her jeans. I push aside the memories, the longing, the desire to have her this close always, and I swallow my nerves. "But as hard as it may be for us, it's worse for her.

She's not going to understand what's happening, so we need to be there for her, in any way we can."

We sit next to each other in the moonlit room on a small couch beneath a window—a couch similar to the one I slept in while my father lay in a bed just like the one Chazarae's in now. Chazarae—a woman who saved me when I needed saving. I try hard not to think about it, not to remember the moments of despair caused by a man who's no longer around. I try not to compare them—try not to choose which pain would be worse because she's not close to death. *She can't be.* And all of a sudden I'm crying. Again. Revealing tears I'd tried to keep hidden from Becca. It's all I've been doing since I found Chazarae missing—*trying. Trying* to keep it together, *trying* to say and do all the right things at all the right times. *Trying* to justify why she's here when she's the last person who deserves it. *Trying* to ignore my feelings for Becca—now a million times more painful because she's *here*. And no amount of *trying* in the past year since I've spoken to her has helped me shake my feelings for her. I try to keep my breaths even so she can't hear my pain. But her hand on my arm proves she can hear it. I don't acknowledge her touch because I'm supposed to be the strong one, and I don't want her to see me fading, to see me cracking under the weight. Becca's hand moves up my arm, the darkness hiding the motion, until she finds the back of my neck. "Josh," she whispers and my breath catches, her lack of voice only making it worse.

The guilt returns. The guilt of my actions, of hers, of the moments spent in this same hospital, my broken heart in her hands while time stood still, waiting to see her. And now Chaz is here, because—"I should've been there," I whisper, eyes snapping shut to fight back the tears. A second later, her lips are on my cheek, kissing away the tears, and God, *I'm pathetic*. Because the feel of her touch outweighs the shame of my emotions, and so I hold her to me. Even when her mouth's no longer there, still, I hold her, needing her close. She must know that, sense it somehow because her body seems to relax. We end up lying on the couch, her body molded against me, my hand on her waist, her emerald eyes on mine. And in the semi-darkness of the room, in the silence that surrounds us, and the pain that keeps us together, I manage to find a moment of bravery in my otherwise fearful existence. "I missed you so much, Becs."

At some point, Becca drifts off to sleep, her breaths warming my chest. I don't sleep. I *can't.* Night turns to morning, the occasional visit from a nurse breaking up the silence, bar the constant beeping of the monitors. Then Chaz stirs, moans escaping her before she's fully come to.

I peel Becca off of me, trying not to wake her, and move over to Chaz, hoping, *praying*, she's okay. Chaz blinks a few times, getting used to the morning light drifting through from the window. She smiles when she sees me. "I thought it was a nightmare," she whispers.

"It'll be over soon." She looks around the room as I ask, "Do you need anything, ma'am?"

She reaches for the pitcher of water on the nightstand, but I stop her, pour some into a plastic cup, and help her to sit up before handing it to her. She pauses, the straw halfway to her lips when she sees Becca on the couch, her body curled into a ball, wearing my hoodie I'd forced on her because I knew she was cold. She's always cold.

Chaz's eyes snap to mine, her smile barely contained. "I almost forgot about her," she whispers, placing the cup back on the tray. Chaz sits up higher, moving the pillows behind her before motioning to a chair next to her bed. I sit down, taking her offered hands, my heart swelling and squeezing at the pure joy on her face. "How long have you been together, and why did you hide it from me?"

My stomach drops, my gaze trailing from her to a still-sleeping Becca, and I don't respond.

"She's so beautiful, Joshua," Chaz whispers, her voice laced with excitement. "And those eyes..."

I don't know what to say. What to tell her that won't do any damage to her emotional state, so I press a button on the control attached to her bed and page a nurse, an action I'm all too familiar with.

CHAPTER 19

BECCA

Hands on my shoulders, shaking gently, wake me from my sleep. Josh's eyes are the first thing I see—dark and tired and full of sadness—the same way they've been every time he's looked at me since the night of my "incident." I miss the joy in them, the laughter, the love I used to get lost in. I miss *him*. I wanted to tell him that last night when he'd said it to me while his arms were wrapped around me. But my throat was worn, and reaching for my phone meant moving away from him, and neither of us wanted that. So I searched his gaze, while he searched mine, and I hoped that he'd be able to *see* it.

"Your grams is awake," he whispers.

I look over his shoulder to the nurse attending to Grams and then back at Josh, my lips parting, my silent question hanging heavy between us. He shakes his head, his gaze dropping. "I'm sorry. She still..." His voice fades, the truth in his answer left unspoken. *She still doesn't remember me.*

"I'm going to hang around here if you need to go home. I won't leave her side."

I sit up and reach for the phone in my bag. *I'm not going anywhere.*

"Okay."

Did you sleep at all?

He shakes his head again.

Maybe you should go get some rest.

He licks his lips before rubbing his eyes. "Even if I left, I couldn't sleep. Not until I know what's wrong with her."

I'll go find us some coffee, I type, offering a supportive smile.

He shoves his hand in his pocket and pulls out some cash just as the nurse says, "She's fallen asleep again. I have to monitor her for a while so why don't you both go? Get something to eat, too. I don't think either of you have left the room since you got here."

Josh raises his eyebrows. "It's probably not a bad idea."

Josh leads the way, hands in his pockets, head lowered. He doesn't look for signs or ask for directions. It's like he has the entire hospital mapped out. I wonder for a moment exactly how much time he's spent in here. As if reading my thoughts, he murmurs, "When my dad was still able to eat, he used to swear that the hospital food would end up being the cause of his death, so I spent a lot of time at the cafeteria here getting him what he wanted. Then he got sicker, and in my mind it was my fault because it's hospital food for a reason, right? It's healthy and it's what patients need to get better. So one day, I refused to get him the egg sandwich he wanted, and I practically shoved the hospital food down his throat. The next day, he was no longer able to swallow on his own." He laughs once, but it's sad, broken. "Sometimes I wonder if he did it just to spite me. Because he was that damn stubborn. He went three days without food before his body finally shut down." His steps falter before stopping completely. Then he turns to me. "This is so morbid, I'm sorry. Your grams isn't..."

"I know," I mouth, ignoring the heaviness of my heart at his words.

He starts moving again, his hands still in his pockets. "I spoke to the nurse while you were sleeping. There's a specialist on duty tomorrow. Dr. Richards. He'll be running all the tests and talking to your grams, so we won't know anything until he gets here. Right now, she's not in any pain. She has a slight cold, but her lungs are clearing. I guess it's just her memory." He glances at me quickly before looking away. "I'm sorry she doesn't remember you, Becs. Especially considering you're so damn hard to forget."

JOURNAL

I wonder if it's possible for time to stand still.

For the seconds of the clock to just STOP.

For minutes to slow to a pause and then nothing exists.

Nothing but two beating hearts.

Mine and his.

Through forced smiles and encouraged actions, I'd been moving forward.

One kick at a time.

Time after time.

Day after day.

Night after night.

But now I realize I'd been numb.

Because when he appeared,

My heart skipped a pulse,

reminding me that I was alive.

And now, I wish for the numb.

As much as I wish for the next joint heartbeat.

CHAPTER 20

BECCA

We spend the day in the hospital room with Grams who falls in and out of sleep. When she's awake, she speaks to Josh, mainly asking questions about the skate tournament he just competed in, asking about Tommy. Josh finds ways to avoid her questions about "our relationship," something Grams thinks is hilarious. But when she asks him about Natalie, I decide it's time to leave the room and get some fresh air. It hurts enough she doesn't remember me, but Grams remembers *her*. A girl who caused Josh nothing but hurt and anger.

I sit on a bench just outside the hospital doors and reply to my messages from Sandra, Pete, and Dad. The earliest Dad can get in is the day after next, so he asks me to stay until he arrives —as if I'd be doing anything else. Sandra assures me to take as much time as needed, and since it's winter break, she can get the other volunteers to cover my shifts. And Pete—he offers as much support as he can from a thousand miles away.

"Everything okay?" Josh asks, stopping in front of me.

I nod and point to my bag he's holding, my head tilting in confusion.

"So your grams kicked us out."

"What?" I mouth.

"Yeah. She said it was pointless that we be in there when nothing was actually happening and then she started to get riled up. Started yelling at me because I was spending my time off hanging in a hospital room when I should be with my *girlfriend*"—he points to me—"showing her a good time."

My jaw drops.

His laughter reaches his eyes. "Yeah. I don't think she meant *good time* the way we're probably thinking..."

"So what are we supposed to do?" Cordy asks for me.

He shrugs before handing me my stuff. "I guess we leave. Come back first thing tomorrow?"

A few months ago, Grams told me that Josh signed a huge sponsorship deal with Oakley sunglasses. She suspected it was seven figures, but she would never ask. Anyway, as soon as the contract was signed and the money was his, he paid off his parents' mortgage and went into partnership with his uncle Robby to expand the construction business. He also donated a bunch of money to Grams's church, breast cancer research, as well as the American Liver Foundation. It was also around the same time Say Something got a huge anonymous donation. So, with knowing all that, it doesn't at all surprise me he's still driving around in the same truck he had pre-pro-skater Josh. Nor does it surprise me that he still lives in Grams's garage apartment. "So my mom's at my house with Tommy. She's cooking dinner. She says she wants to meet you." He glances at me quickly, looking for a response before focusing on the road again. "You don't have to," he rushes out. "It's cool if you just want to be alone."

I've met his mom. She knows I've met her. She also knows I asked her never to tell Josh about it. I appreciate her keeping her word, but that's not what has my breath caught in my throat and my thumbs frozen, hovering above my phone. She's with *Tommy*—my best friend.

"Becs?" He pulls the car over and kills the engine, then turns to me. "You okay?"

My breaths are harsh, my chest rising and falling.

Josh sighs. "Look. I know last time you were here I said some stuff about Tommy—"

He doesn't get a chance to finish because I throw my arms around his neck, my excitement overpowering every other emotion.

"Becca," he whispers, hands on my arms pulling me off of him. He sits up straighter, his gaze on mine while I try to push back the disappointment. Then he clears his throat, his voice louder when he says, "I um… I've wanted to say something ever since you got here last night and I just… I haven't found the right time but the truth is, I'm struggling here, Becs. It's hard being this close to you when all I want to do is touch you. Honestly, I want to do more than touch you. Every time I look at you, all I can think about is kissing you and—" He breaks off when my eyes widen, throwing his hand up between us. "Don't worry. I won't. I just… I *want* to. I spent the entire night watching you sleep, letting my mind get lost in the memories of what we used to be and it felt so good to be back there again. Almost too good. And then morning hit, and so did reality, and now it almost hurts to be with you. So I've spent most of the day trying to stay away, trying to make it easier to the fight the urges. But it's tough. *Real tough*. Especially when you're looking at me the way you are…." I don't think I'm looking at him like anything, so I shake my head, but he ignores it and starts the engine again. "We should go."

He focuses on the road and nothing but the road for the rest of the drive home while I sit there, completely *un*focused, lost in the daze of his declaration. It's not until we near the house and I see Tommy and Josh's mom, Ella, out in the driveway, Tommy messing around on a skateboard while his grandmother watches over him, that I snap out of my daze. The second we pull up, Tommy jumps off the board and runs toward us, ignoring his grandmother's demands for him to stop. Josh hits the brakes, forcing me forward, his reflexes quick, his arm shooting to the side to protect me. "Sorry," he murmurs.

"It's okay," I mouth, unable to control my smile when I see Tommy at my door. His hands are frantic as he tries again and again to open it, but the truck is big—too big for him to pull on the handle, so I unbuckle my seat belt and open the door slowly, giving him enough time to move away. He screams—one I'm sure would match mine if I actually *could* scream. Then he says the words that settle the ache in my chest, but create a fear in my mind. "Becca's home!"

Tommy's hug is tight. Mine is tighter. Ella approaches me once Tommy and I have settled down. "You must be Becca," she says, her arms spread. I trust her enough to touch me, to hug me, to hold me, to keep our secret safe. "It's so nice to finally meet you. Tommy doesn't stop talking about you."

I look down at Tommy, his full set of baby teeth on show. He's grown so much. His baby fat is gone, replaced with boyish cheekbones. His hair is thicker now, just like his dad's and even though he still has his mother's eyes, bright blue and for sure the cause of future heartbreaks, it's his smile that captures all my attention—a smile just like his father's.

I squat down so we're eye-to-eye and hold up a finger. He nods enthusiastically, an uncontrollable burst of laughter filtering out of him. I point to him, then I rub his belly, making him laugh harder. He nods again, and I do the same when he points to mine.

Behind me, Josh says, "I think they're hungry, Ma." And just like that, we fall into step, Tommy by my side.

Ella says, peeking over her shoulder, "I made fried pickles, Becca. I heard they were you're favorite."

"Silly Nanni!" Tommy shouts. "Becca thinks fried pickles taste like poop!"

Josh chuckles as he stops at the bottom of the stairs, waiting for us to pass. Once we have, he walks next to us, his hand on the small of my back, mine wrapped around Tommy's, and for a second, just *one*, I almost let *love* mean something.

Josh and his mother speak throughout dinner. They talk about Grams for a while and then discuss business. Against his mom's wishes, Josh tells her to cancel his appearances for the next week. I shift uncomfortably when she mentions Chris and tells Josh that he won't be happy, that he won't understand, to which Josh tells her that he'll have to deal with it.

Tommy talks to himself, and sometimes his food, promising to save some of his pasta shells as pets. He names one Shelly, another one Doofus, and another one Poop. Occasionally, I see Josh watching me, but I don't make eye contact. I can't. So I sit and I listen to three generations of Wardens, and I ignore the fact that I'd never felt more at home, more accepted, more at peace than I do this very moment.

When dinner's done, Josh and his mom clean up while Tommy takes me to his room and shows me all his new things —things that weren't here two years ago. Toys, iPads, new clothes, an abundance of skateboards, and the holy grail of camera gear better than mine. My jaw drops as I practically fall to my knees, my eyes wide in shock. "Chris bought him all that for his birthday and Christmas. He spoils the shit out of him," Josh says, leaning against the doorframe.

"Naughty word, Daddy!" Tommy shouts.

"Sorry, bud." Josh moves to sit on Tommy's bed and looks

up at me. "He's only now starting to understand how to use it all."

I grab my phone out of my pocket and have Cordy say, *"He's into photography?"*

Josh laughs as Tommy removes the lens from the body and replaces it with another. "Yeah. More than he's into skating, actually."

Moments of silence pass while Tommy attaches an action-stabilizing handle to the camera. "Tommy doesn't travel to my comps with me anymore, but he goes to the demo video shoots. He gets right in there and films it all."

I sit down next to him and show him my phone. *Is he any good?*

Josh bites down on his bottom lip and shakes his head, his eyes wide. "Horrible," he mouths, and I laugh a silent laugh. Then he says, "It's getting late, Tommy. Time for bed."

"Noooooooooooooo!" Tommy yells, but he's already opening the drawers and picking out his pajamas. "Is Becca having a sleepover in your room like last time?"

Josh looks at me, his eyebrows raised in question, and the only thing I can do is stare back. "No. But you'll see Becca tomorrow, okay? Promise."

I leave the room while Josh helps Tommy change, noting that the house is empty which means Ella's left, and return only when Tommy calls for me. He's lying in his bed, his arms outstretched. "Good night, Becs!"

I give him a hug, smiling when he kisses my cheek. Then he starts to talk again, about anything and everything, doing whatever he can to prolong my stay. Josh's hands find my waist, pulling me back. "Okay, bud. Lights out. Good night."

Tommy yawns loudly. "Night, Daddy."

Josh guides me out of the room and starts closing the door behind us, but Tommy yells, "Daddy, you forgot to do it!"

Josh's shoulders tense, his eyes locked on mine. Then he

faces Tommy and touches his finger to his nose and then to his chest. "I love you."

"Love you, too, Daddy," Tommy says as Josh turns to me, his eyes distant while he mouths what must be Tommy's routine words, "And I love Nanni and Ma'am and Mommy and Justin and Aunt Kimmy and Uncle Robby and Aunt Chloe and Uncle Hunt,"—Tommy takes a breath as Josh steps closer to me—"And most of all, I love *My* Becca."

My stomach flips, my heart… I can't even explain it.

I don't know how long we stand there, a foot apart, his eyes never leaving mine. But it's too long. Or maybe not long enough. He's the first to break, looking away when he says, "You don't have any bags."

I don't know if it's a question or a statement, but I nod anyway.

"You um… you left some clothes here from…" His voice fades as he spins around and walks the few steps to his bedroom. I ignore the voices in my head telling me that I shouldn't follow, that I shouldn't let him close the door after me. "They're in my closet," he says, but he makes no move to get them. Instead, he just stands there, staring at me like he did outside Tommy's room. I can feel the heat creeping into my cheeks, the sweat forming on my palms, the beating of my heart crashing against my chest. The air is thick. My breaths are shallow as I finally get my feet to function and move around him to get to his closet. His bedroom's changed since I've been in it last, the floor covered with boxes stacked three or four high, filled with brand new t-shirts, all sealed in plastic, sponsors' logos printed on them.

"You can take whatever you want," he says, moving around me. He reaches over me to get a box from high in his closet and drops it on his bed. A few of my dresses are in there, along with tops, bras and panties. My cheeks flame while I silently question why he kept it all. I look over at him, but his eyes are fixed on the box, his cheeks as red as mine if not redder. "You can stay here," he says out of nowhere. "I mean, if you don't want to be alone tonight. But you're probably used to being alone, right? Because your dad and his job and all that... unless you're not alone..." He exhales loudly.

"I'm alone," Cordy says for me. *Stupid Traitor Cordy.*

His eyes lock on mine, then slowly drift down my body. "You can take the bed. I'll sleep on the couch. Or not. Whatever you want." He sits on the edge of the bed and looks up at me. Only now do I see the bags under his eyes, the struggle to keep them open, and I remember that he hasn't slept at all in two days. "The doctor's coming in at nine. Kim will be here at eight to take Tommy for the day. I want to be there before the doctor sees her, make sure she's up for it. Yeah... she'll probably hate that I'm there but... she's going to be okay, right?" His voice breaks. "She *has* to be okay."

I reach for him, but he stands quickly, avoiding my touch. "I'm going to shower." He opens a drawer in his dresser to grab a pair of boxer shorts, and without looking at me, he says, "I'll be back."

I sit on the edge of the bed, my mind racing with so many thoughts I can't focus on one. At some point, I hear the shower run, and I rummage through the box of my clothes for something to wear. There's nothing I can sleep in, so I grab a random shirt from one of his boxes and slip it over me, then I sit back down, and I wait. I don't know exactly what I'm waiting for. I recall him asking if I wanted to stay here but I haven't decided, so I spend the next few minutes trying to make up my mind. Before I know it, he's walking back into the room in nothing but his underwear, a towel in his hand, roughly drying his hair. He freezes when he sees me, and panic sets in. Is he so out of it that he doesn't remember asking me to stay? I start to get up at the same time he says, "I'll just grab a pillow." But the only part of him that moves are his eyes—eyes trailing from my bare legs, pausing at my waist, and then at my breasts before settling on my face. His eyes are no longer sad, no longer tired, and I struggle to breathe through the tension filling the air.

I reach for my phone on his nightstand and type: *I should go*. But without bothering to read what I've said, he takes the phone from me and throws it on the bed. Now he's close. Too close. His hand cups my jaw and tilts my head up, shifting my gaze from his abs to his eyes. "Please stay," he whispers. "*I* can't be alone."

CHAPTER 21

BECCA

I wake up, my body covered in sweat and an unfamiliar weight on my chest. Next to me, Josh is lying on his stomach, snoring lightly with his arm over me. He asked me to stay last night, for *him,* and I couldn't say no. So we lay in bed facing each other, the inches of space between may as well have been an entire country.

Within minutes he was asleep, and this time, I stayed up and watched him. I watched the rise and fall of his chest, the tremble of his lips matching his steady breaths. Unruly strays of hair had fallen over his brow—strays I wanted to touch, wanted to slip between my fingers. His chest was toned, his shoulders wide. I ended up shoving my hands under the pillow so I could fight the ache, the urge, the *need* to feel him.

As slowly as possible, I reach for my phone on the nightstand and check the time. It's 5:30 and still pitch black outside. With gentle hands, I remove his arm from my chest and free myself from beneath him. I get up, use the bathroom, then brush my teeth with my finger. When I return, Josh is sitting up, blankets bunched around him. He smiles sleepily. "What time is it?"

I get back into bed and show him my phone.

After a moan, he rubs his face and says, "Tommy will be up in an hour." Then he gets up and repeats my process: bathroom, brushes teeth, crawls back in bed.

I type on my phone and show it to him. *Did you sleep okay?*

With a nod, he takes the phone from me and places it under his pillow. Then he lies on his side, one hand under his head, the other resting on my stomach, releasing an entire kaleidoscope of butterflies. "Does it hurt?" he asks, his voice low. "When you whisper?"

I nod and look away from him, focusing instead on the ceiling—pretending to be fascinated by cracked white paint, and not the forbidden memories and reminders of moments spent lying on my back, my vision blurred from the pleasure he provided. We whispered endless promises in this room, revelations of love and admissions of pain. "Like a boo-boo?" he asks, running a single finger over my throat. "You know what fixes boo-boos?" From the corner of my eye, I see him lean up on his elbow, his eyes charged with adoration. I try to hide my smile, honestly I do, but it's impossible not to react to the way he's looking at me, the way he's making me *feel*. I freeze when he dips his head, his movements slow, giving me time to push him away. But I don't. I *can't*. My heart races while his hand moves back to my waist, his fingertips searing my skin. His lips—soft and sweet—make contact with my neck and he smiles against my throat. "Kisses make all boo-boos better."

Oh jeez. Josh Warden, world—the boy I fell insanely in love with.

Loud banging on his door forces us apart and as far away from each other as possible, as if we'd been busted doing something we shouldn't be doing. *Maybe we were.*

The banging sounds again, and Tommy cries from his bedroom. "Daddy!"

"Who the hell...?" Josh murmurs, standing at the side of his bed pulling on a pair of sweats.

"Daddy!"

"I'm coming, bud." He leaves the room and goes into Tommy's, his words soft and comforting. "It's okay. Someone's just at the door."

I meet Josh in the hallway, carrying a petrified Tommy. The banging is louder now, the entire house shaking with the force of it. Josh hands me Tommy, who cries harder. Then he marches to the door, protectively moving us behind him before opening it. I run my hand through Tommy's hair, kissing his tears, doing everything I can to calm him down. Then a familiar voice speaks, his tone turning my insides to stone. "Is my daughter here?"

I reveal myself from behind Josh, my gaze lowered as I place Tommy on the floor.

"I thought you weren't getting in until tomorrow," Josh says.

Dad doesn't reply. He simply steps to the side waiting for me to join him. We make it to the second to last step before Tommy yells, "You a butt sniffer, mister!"

CHAPTER 22

JOSHUA

The call connects on the third ring. "Shitstain," Chloe says in greeting. In the background, Hunter shouts, "Why the fire truck are you always calling my wife?"

"Because you always give horrible relationship advice," Chloe tells him.

"Have you boned her yet?" Hunter yells.

In my mind, Chloe's eyes roll so high she sees stars. "You're a Neanderthal," she says to him. To me, she says, "How's it going?"

"I'm failing."

"I told you not to kiss her!"

I laugh under my breath and set Tommy up with his breakfast. "I didn't kiss her."

"Okay? So..."

"But I told her I wanted to."

Silence passes a beat. "That's... kind of hot, to be honest."

"Yeah?"

"What else did you say?"

"I told her I spent the entire night watching her sleep, getting lost in the memories of her."

"Swoon. And then what?"

"Then I got scared and pretended like I hadn't said a thing."

Chloe laughs. "And how did she react?"

"I don't know. She sort of looked scared."

"Well…" She huffs out a breath. "Sometimes, it's good to be scared, you know? It means she's feeling *something*. And if you didn't make her cry, that something is probably a good thing."

"Maybe. At least now I've kicked, and it's her turn to push."

She laughs knowingly. "I hate to break it to you, Warden, but you're not the one who kicked. She did when she sent you that letter. Right now, you're doing the pushing. Just do me a favor, okay?"

"Anything."

"Don't push too hard."

Chloe hangs up before I get a chance to respond, so I dump my phone on the counter and look over at Tommy. "You didn't hear a word I just said. Got it?"

His eyes narrow in confusion. "But my ears are working."

"I know they are. But I meant, like, don't tell anyone what I said."

He tilts his head, looking even more confused. "But that's not what you said. You told me I didn't hear a word you said, but I did hear them. All of them. You said you told Becca you wanted to kiss her."

"I know that's what I said, but that's not what I meant."

"Is this another one of those finger of peaches?"

With a smile, I say, "Exactly."

Nodding slowly, Tommy's eyes shift around the room. Then he shrugs and bites down on a spoonful of cereal. "Who was that angry man?" he asks, milk trickling from the corner of his mouth.

"That was Becca's dad."

"Why was he banging on the door like that?"

I take a sip of my coffee and shrug. "I have no idea, buddy. He probably couldn't find Becca and got scared."

"Like you when you couldn't find Ma'am last time?" *Last time* are his new favorite words—the ones he overuses to the point of wanting to scrub my ears clean with steel wool. They change every couple of months, thank God. Last month it was *in your butt.*

I lean my forearms on the counter. "Yeah. Like that."

"When can I see Ma'am?"

"Soon."

"Is she going to be deaded, like Pa?"

"No, bud." I say quickly, shaking my head. I look him in the eyes—eyes refusing to meet mine. "What's going on? What are you thinking?"

"Everyone who goes in that hospital leaves. Pa deaded, Becca left, and now Ma'am will, too."

I try to come up with something to say to take away his fears, but nothing forms because I don't want to lie just to give him false hope. I'd done enough online research in the past forty-eight hours to know that if it is what the doctors suspect, Ma'am *will* be leaving. Maybe not physically, but her mind won't be the same, and Tommy loves her, understands her, at least well enough to recognize that she may not be the same woman we've always known and loved. "*I* go to the hospital all the time and nothing ever happens to me," I tell him, half joking, half hoping it'll erase his fears.

Tommy rolls his eyes, a goofy smile spreading across his lips. "That's because you're invisible, Daddy."

"You mean *invincible.*"

"No. *Invisible.*"

"If I'm invisible, then how can you see me?"

His eyes narrow, his mind deep in thought. "Silly Daddy. That's what I said. *Invincible.* Like Superman. You Superman, Daddy!"

"Helloooo," Aunt Kim calls, poking her head through the front door.

"Hey, did you know that I was Superman?" I ask her.

She rolls her eyes just like Tommy did. "Well, duh," she coos, making her way toward Tommy and ruffling his hair. "No broken bones can keep your daddy down."

Tommy smiles up at her. "There was a big scary man at the door last time."

"A big scary man?" Kim repeats, her eyes on mine.

"Later," I mouth, then focus on Tommy. "That reminds me… we need to talk about something, bud," I say, my voice stern.

"Uh oh."

"Yeah, *uh oh.*"

Tommy leans back in his chair and looks around the room. "I didn't dinosaur stomp on my iPad. I promise." He takes a mouthful of cereal, guilt written all over his face. *He totally dinosaur stomped on his iPad.*

I shake my head, trying not to laugh. "You can't call people butt sniffers, bud. It's not nice."

He spits out his cereal with his laugh. "But he is a butt sniffer!"

I wipe the milk off the counter with a cloth. "It's not funny."

"Butt sniffer. Butt sniffer. Butt sniffer."

"I have to get going. Be good to your aunt, okay?"

"Okay, butt sniffer in your butt last time!"

Becca answers the door to Chazarae's house, a shy smile on her beautiful face. "You left your phone in my bed," I tell her, holding it behind my back.

She throws her hand out between us, palm up.

I rock on my heels. "Yeah. No. I think I'm going to keep it."

Becca bites down on her lip, her emerald eyes penetrating

mine. She steps forward, closing the door with one hand, the other flattening on my stomach. "Please?" she mouths.

I shake my head and lean forward, my mouth to her ear. "You're going to have to work for it." I'm trying to flirt, though I'm almost positive I'm failing because both her hands are on my chest now, and all of a sudden I can't think. I can't see. I can't even breathe. I try to swallow but my throat's too dry, even though I'm pretty sure there's puke in there, and now my eyes are starting to water and there's some fucked-up acid shit in my nose and the air is thick and my vision blurs and dammit, *she pouts.*

"Don't pout," I breathe out.

She does it again. This time, batting her eyelids. Becca rises to her toes and presses her lips to mine. Just once. But enough for air to fill my lungs and for my vision to return to normal. I cave and hand her the phone just as her door opens, and her dad appears. She steps back, her arms falling to her side. "You ready, Becca?" her dad asks.

"Good morning, sir." I offer him my hand for a shake. "I need to apologize for my son this morning. He got a little rattled when he heard the banging on the door."

He looks down at my hand, ignores it, and then motions toward Chaz's car. "Let's go."

I get in my car, my thoughts running in circles as I drive the familiar streets to the hospital. I try to think back to all the encounters I've had with Becca's dad, every word I've spoken, and I try to justify why he's acting the way he is toward me. I understand, to a degree, but he wasn't this bad when he was here for Chaz's birthday, and I've had zero contact with him since. I push aside the concern—for now, but not forever—and instead, I focus on Chaz.

. . .

Chaz is awake when I enter the room, her nose scrunched in disgust as she prods her breakfast with her fork. She forces a smile when she looks at me, "Oh, Joshua, thank the Lord you're here. Go get me a chocolate bar, will you?"

With a sigh, I take the seat next to her bed. "Chocolate for breakfast, Ma'am? Who are you? Tommy?"

She laughs quietly—the exact reaction I was hoping for.

"How are you feeling?"

After pushing away the tray, she says, "I'm good. I just want to get out of here."

"I know. But a specialist is coming in soon, so hopefully we can find out more and get you back home as soon as possible."

Her smile reaches her eyes—eyes dark and aged and wrinkled, just like the rest of her. Her skin's dry, cracked from the hours upon hours she spends out in her garden doing the work I used to do before my skating took priority. Heaviness builds in my chest and I look down at my lap.

"What's wrong?" she asks.

"Nothing."

She shifts in her spot, moving the pillows to get more comfortable. "You know better than to lie to me, Joshua."

"I just wish I'd spent more time with you. That's all."

"Oh, hush!" She crosses her arms over her chest, her eyes narrowed at me. "I'm not dead. Not even dying. Now stop talking as if I am. It may be unfortunate for you, but I have plenty of years left. Now, let's talk about that girlfriend of yours. Where is she?"

I rub the three days of growth on my jaw with my knuckles and choose my words carefully, knowing it's important not to push her. "You know you've met Becca before..."

"I have?"

"Yeah. Your last birthday. She was there."

Chaz sighs, her shoulders dropping. "The nurse said I might have problems remembering things..."

"It's okay," I soothe. "It's not important."

Becca enters the room, her father following behind her. I turn to them, the same time Chaz gasps. "Dan, what are you doing here?"

I find out from Becca that Dan is her birth grandfather—information provided by her dad who's made an effort to openly ignore my presence. I sit with Chaz, he stands on the other side of the room, and Becca seems lost—floating between us.

We sit in silence, and we wait.

Dr. Richards arrives, introducing himself first to Chaz and then to the rest of us. She gets taken to a different room—a room only family members can access. And considering Chaz doesn't realize she actually *has* family here, she goes it alone, something I try to fight. But she calms me quickly, tells me to stop acting like she's on her deathbed. And so I sit in the room, the silence deafening, the walls closing in on me and I wait some more. Seconds. Minutes. Hours tick by.

Martin gets a phone call.

I get eight.

Becca's now refusing to make eye contact with either of us.

Mom shows up, papers in hand, asking me to sign contracts to things I can't even think about. She senses my mood, and now she's part of the silence.

Part of the wait.

Tommy calls.

Becca smiles.

I don't.

Because she's too far away, and I want her next to me. I

want her in my arms, and I want to go back to this morning when touching her didn't seem like a crime.

Mom says, "Maybe just look at the contracts, Josh. Get your mind off things."

"Stop." It comes out harsh, but I don't apologize. Right now, I don't need her here as my manager, I need her here as my mom.

Dr. Richards returns, no Chaz in sight. "We need to talk."

CHAPTER 23

BECCA

There's a ringing in my ears so loud it almost drowns out Dr. Richards's words. After what Josh had said, I was expecting the diagnosis. I guess I just hadn't prepared myself for it. And definitely not to this extent.

Frontal Lobe Dementia.

The three words replay in my head, over and over, while the ringing gets louder and louder.

Apparently, the CT scans they'd done showed signs of multiple strokes, ones that went undetected, most likely taking course in Grams's sleep. It could've been happening for months, but no one was around to see her decline. Dr. Richards continues to go through the results of the tests, speaking words that I've only read about since Josh mentioned *dementia.* My eyes sting, tears threatening to fall and I look over at my dad, a person who's been there through my ups and downs over the past two years. I search for comfort, for relief, but what I see is *nothing*. Not a damn thing.

"So cure it!" Josh yells, fist thumping on Grams's food tray.

I flinch at the sound, shocked at his response.

"Josh," his mom reprimands.

"There's currently no cure for dementia," the doctor says, grabbing a chair from the corner of the room and sitting opposite me.

Josh's fists ball, his jaw tense, and I close my eyes, preparing myself for a repeat of the anger I'd once witnessed. "So *find* one."

A sob escapes in an unfamiliar sound. *Sound.* I made a *sound.*

I choke on a gasp, my eyes snapping open to see everyone watching me, their bodies frozen, their eyes as wide as mine. Josh is the first to move, first to alter the still image my eyes alone had captured. He stands quickly, pulling me into his embrace. "It's okay," he whispers, his hands stroking my hair. "It's okay." He repeats the same words, the occasional apology thrown in, while I stifle my cries into his chest. His heart pounds against my cheek, his body trembling. Then he pulls back, holding my face in his hands while wiping my tears with his thumbs. "Look at me, Becs," he asks. So I do. Because right now, he's all I know. All I have. "We're going to get through this. You and me. Together, okay?"

I nod, choosing to believe his words, even if his words are lies.

He takes my hand and leads me to the chair he'd just vacated and squats next to me, his hands on mine hiding their trembles.

"I spoke with your grandmother, Becca," Dr. Richards says. "I needed to have the conversation with her while she was still coherent. Because of her mental state, we had to discuss a power of attorney. Do you know what that means?"

I nod at the same time Josh says, "It's someone to speak on her behalf and make decisions for her when she can't." He looks over my shoulder at his mother sitting in a chair next to me. "Like you were with Dad, right?"

Suddenly, his reaction, his anger, all of it makes sense. I see the fear in his eyes the moment they meet mine. A flashback of the past—of a scared, broken boy who thought he had to take on the world alone. But he didn't have to. Not then. *Not now.*

Dr. Richards speaks, forcing us to break our stare. "We're going to start Chazarae on some medication. It'll be ongoing. I'll need to keep seeing her on a routine basis, and because of how severe the dementia is, it'll be a good idea to look at alternative living arrangements for her."

"Like a home?" Dad asks, finding his voice for the first time since we left the house.

"She *has* a home," Josh says. "She's not going anywhere." I can hear the frustration in his tone, feel the anger simmering deep within him.

"We need to stay calm," says his mother. I know she's trying to help, but going by the tick in Josh's jaw, she's doing the opposite.

"Look." Dr. Richards sets Grams's chart aside and clasps his hands on his lap. "I know this is tough for you all. I often see family members of patients whose reactions are the same as yours. But there are a lot of facilities around, nice ones, that will look after her better than she can look after herself. She needs constant care and supervision."

Josh shakes his head. "I'll quit skating."

"You will not," his mom snaps.

My fingers work fast on my phone, my panic rising. *"I'll quit college."*

"No, you won't," Dad and Josh say in unison. *Great, at least they agree on something.*

I type again. *"You can't quit, Josh. You've worked too hard to give up skating."*

His eyes narrow at me. "Yeah, well you've *survived* too much to give up college!" The loudness of his voice makes me flinch. He takes a breath, trying to find a calm. "Becca, I've made enough money to support her. I'll do it." Josh turns back to the doctor. "What do I need to do? My dad—we had to do things around the house so his wheelchair..." His voice fades, his throat bobbing with his swallow. "Do I need to fix—"

"Josh..." Ella's hand lands on his arm. "You can't just stop everything you have going at the moment to look after Chaz. I know you want to—"

"Shut up!" he blurts. "You weren't there, okay? She was. *She* saved me! When you and dad turned your backs on me, *she* saved me! She practically raised Tommy, and *me*, because I had nothing. I *was* nothing. Nothing but a scared shitless little kid and she saved me. And now I need to do the same! Why don't you get that?!"

Dad stomps toward us, but I raise my hand to stop him. Then I hold up my finger at Dr. Richards, asking him to wait. He nods once, and that's when I stand quickly and grab Josh's arm, forcing him to his feet. I place my hands on his back and push him to the door. The second we're out of the room, he inhales deeply, his gaze on the ceiling and his fists in his hair. His eyes drop to mine, his lips trembling as he holds one hand over his heart, the other reaching for me. As soon as I'm in his arms, he breaks. "There's this build up in my chest, Becs. This ache so strong it's blurring my vision." He sniffs once. "Or maybe it's the guilt. Or the anger. I have no idea."

"It's okay," I try to whisper, but nothing comes out. *Nothing.* Not that it matters. I doubt he would've heard it over the heaviness of his breaths. His chest rises and falls as he struggles with the news, and once he's calm and his eyes are dry, he takes one more inhale through his nose. "Let's go," he says, taking my hand. Josh clears his throat a foot inside the room. "Just tell me what I need to do. *Please.*"

CHAPTER 24

JOSHUA

Dr. Richards makes an appointment for us at his office the next day, saying it's a lot more "tranquil" than the hospital. I know he directed the comment at me. I don't care. I don't need tranquil, I need solutions. Answers. He tells us Chaz is undergoing more tests, more prods, more pokes, and that she won't be back in the room until later that night.

The others leave. I don't.

I wait until she's returned and spend the entire night watching her sleep, and while I do, I wonder how it's possible that God can do this to a woman who's spent the majority of her life worshipping the words of the Bible.

With reluctance, I leave her mid-morning, my body aching from fatigue, and go home with just enough time to shower and change before the meeting at Dr. Richards's office.

Becca stands from her seated position on the porch steps when I pull into the driveway. Chaz's car is gone, meaning her dad probably is, too. And I try my hardest not to let his actions be the cause of my anger, because there's so much more happening right now that deserves my hurt than *him.*

"Did you spend all night with Grams?" Becca's phone asks as she falls into step beside me.

I head for my apartment and try not to look at her. "Yep."

"Did you sleep?"

"Nope."

She pulls on my arm, forcing me to face her, then looks down at her phone and types away. *"Are you mad at me?"*

"I don't know, Becs," I say through a heavy exhale. I glance at her eyes—a mixture of sadness and hope. "I don't know what I am right now." I shake my head. "Why does your dad hate me so much?"

Her frown is instant. Her thumbs, however, hesitate. *"He's just protective."*

"From me?"

She shrugs.

I take a moment to carefully select my words. "There has to be a reason why he feels the need to shelter you from me. The only thing he has to go by is whatever you've told him. So I guess that proves how you feel about me. Maybe the other night was a mistake. I should've never asked you to stay with me." Her mouth opens, no words come out, and I'm reminded again of why and how she is the way she is. "It's okay, Becs. Seriously. We got caught up in the moment and it's cool. I'm not mad."

She inhales deeply, her chest rising slowly and falling quickly. Then she uses two fingers and points to her eyes. I don't really understand why, but I keep my gaze on hers as it lowers so she can type on her phone. *"Please don't shut me out. Don't push me away."* She glances up at me, making sure I'm still watching her eyes—eyes I was drawn to from the moment I saw her. Then she taps her phone, her thoughts echoed through the digitized voice, *"Not again, Josh."*

My knees weaken at her words, words unintentionally destroying every thought process, every ounce of sense I'd spent the entire night trying to find, and before I get a chance to respond, she adds, *"I understand that Grams is important to you. But she's important to me, too. She's my grandmother. And everyone's treating me like they've forgotten that. It's bad enough that she has."*

"I know," I say quickly. I pull her into me, her hands trapped between us as she continues to write.

"And then there's this whole thing between you and Dad, and I don't know who to be near, who to comfort..."

"I'm sorry."

She returns my hug now, her tear-soaked eyes meeting mine. My lips meet hers, only for a second before the honking of a horn pulls us apart. Becca's arms drop, her gaze shifting between the car and me.

"Go with him, Becs. You need each other right now. You're her family."

Martin and Becca are waiting outside the office for me, along with the last person I thought would be here. Mom shuffles on her feet, her hands clasped in front of her and her discomfort evident. I feel like a kid—a kid who's disappointed his mother—which is exactly what I am. And all of a sudden, my heart's heavy, caused by the weight of my guilt. "I'm sorry, Ma."

"It's okay, Joshua. You're going through a lot."

"It doesn't excuse the way I spoke to you, though. Nothing does."

She smiles, but it's sad. "You know I love Chazarae, right?"

"I know. I was just being dumb."

She inhales deeply, before she rushes out, "Josh. Out there, in the skate world—"

"Stop. I don't want to think about it." *Especially with Becca and Martin right fucking here.*

"Just let me finish." She steps forward. "Out there, you're on your own. The pressure's on you and you alone to succeed, and you do an amazing job of that. There's not a single person out there who can say you struggle to do things on your own… but this doesn't have to be one of those moments. You have Becca, Martin, and you have your mamma."

I can't help but smile. "And I need my mamma."

She cups my cheek and pouts at me. "And I'm always going to be here, sweetheart."

Dr. Richards's office is small, or maybe it's Martin's behemoth frame. Add to that the giant elephant in the room and there's barely enough oxygen to cover us all. Becca and my mother sit on the chairs opposite the doctor. Martin paces. I stand by the closed door doing everything I can to focus on the reason we're here and nothing else.

"I spoke to Chazarae again after discussing her situation with you all yesterday," Dr. Richards says, his eyes scanning the room, making sure he's giving everyone the same level of attention. "In her case, time is a big issue, so I asked her again about who she wanted as her power of attorney. I mentioned that Martin was here, and so was Becca, and she understood, to a degree. But she still chose you, Joshua."

I nod, not at all surprised. "Okay."

"There's some paperwork to fill out, information we'll need from you… her PPO, HMO, life insurance—"

"I have no idea what any of that means. My son and I are covered through my team, but…"

Martin scoffs.

I glare at him.

Mom says, "I'll take care of all that. Don't worry."

"Look," Martin says, finally stopping his useless, mind-numbing, back and forth pacing. "She needs to go to a facility where they can take adequate care of her, right? That's what this is all about. So how much is this going to cost?"

I clear my throat and step behind Becca and Mom and speak directly to the doctor. "The cost does not matter. I'll cover it. But I really don't like the idea of her being in a home. It just doesn't sit right with me." I think about all the things that came to mind last night while I was watching Chaz sleep, her breaths even, her body peaceful. I thought of all the moments she's encouraged me, pushed me to be a better person, a better son, a better father. I swallow the lump in my throat and add, "She'll just be a patient there, not a person. And what about her garden? She loves her garden. And her TV shows. And church? Can she even still go to church?"

Silence falls, just for a moment before Mom surprises me by saying, "I agree with Josh. What about in-home care?"

"That's a possibility?" I ask the doctor, hope kicking in for the first time in days.

Dr. Richards leans back in his leather chair and crosses his legs. "It's a lot pricier."

"I don't care."

Martin scoffs. Again. And I crack. "What the hell is your problem?"

"Josh," Mom warns.

Becca stands, her hand on my chest, her back to her father. She shakes her head, another warning—only hers is silent. I inhale a calming breath and force myself to ignore him the way he's ignored me.

Dr. Richards answers, "I'm concerned. I think it's important for her to socialize and be around people who understand what's going on with her. As we all know, she's alone the majority of the time. In a facility, she'll be around—"

"Other people like her?" I interrupt. "She has friends. She has a life, and she'll continue to do so outside of this disease. I'll make sure of it." The words fall from my lips, rushed and unapologetic.

The doctor seems to concede. "A live-in nurse is an option. I can gather some files and résumés for you to go through."

"Yeah, let's do that." I turn to Becca. "Is that good with you, Becs?"

She nods.

"And immediate care until then? What does she need?" I'm glad Mom asks because all I seem to be doing is shoving my opinions and demands in people's faces.

"She can be discharged soon. A nurse will come by the house and make sure she has everything she needs. She'll also speak to you all so you can make sure she takes her meds on time, every day, until she's comfortable with the routine."

Martin clears his throat. I don't look at him when he says, "I have to be back at work in a couple days, so..."

So... *Good.*

"I can stay at the house, or drop by and check in on things. At least until Josh starts skating again and we're comfortable with whoever we choose," Mom says, lifting some weight off my shoulders.

Becca types away on her phone. "*I don't have classes for another week and a half. I'd be a lot more comfortable going back if we could get it done before then.*" And the weight returns, only now it's doubled, crushing my insides. Because she's leaving. I knew she would be—but not this soon, and having her actually say it makes the countdown real. She looks over at me before going back to her phone. "*Will that be okay, Josh? If we do it together, that should give us enough time, right?*"

And at her words, I remind myself that a week and a half with Becca is better than no Becca at all. "It's perfect, Becs."

CHAPTER 25

JOSHUA

My mom goes back home, back to work, back to making phone calls and excuses for me, while the rest of us go back to the hospital. None of us seem to know what to do, how to act, so we sit in silence and watch Chazarae sleep. She sleeps a lot. Apparently this is the new normal. At some point, I fall asleep, too, sitting on the chair next to her bed with her hand in mine. That's when Rob and Kim show up with Tommy, their quiet voices waking me. Becca introduces them to her dad while Tommy sits on my lap, a frown on his lips as he holds Chaz's fingers. "Is she going to be okay like last time?" he asks me.

I stare at my son and I try to think of the right words—words that will shelter him from the pain and the heartbreak of life. But he's older now than he was when I went through this with my dad, so I give him the truth, because he deserves nothing less. "She's not going to be the same, bud."

"But you said Ma'am wasn't going to be deaded like Pa."

"And she's not, but her memory is fading and she might not always act the same as you remember her. When she wakes up, she might not know you."

"But I'm Thomas Joshua," he says, beaming up at me. "Ma'am loves me. She'll remember."

I look over at Becs, her eyes as sad as I feel, and after a moment, she sits down on the couch next to her dad. She types something on her phone and he reads it, his eyes moving from side to side. Then he sighs, wraps an arm around her and brings her into him, kisses her forehead, making it impossible for me to dislike him as much as I had been.

The room fills with silence again, only for a few minutes before a nurse comes in, her eyes lighting up when she sees everybody in the room. "Young Chazarae must be very popular," she sings. It shouldn't annoy me that she's so happy, so immune to what's happening, but it does. "I just spoke to Dr. Richards. I have some good news and some bad news. Which would you like first?"

"This isn't a game," I mumble.

"Josh," Kim says, placing her hand on my shoulder. I'm getting real fucking tired of the way people say my name like I don't have a right to speak.

The nurse sits on the end of Chaz's bed, completely clueless to my reaction. "The good news is Chazarae can go home today."

"That's great," I say, at the same time Becca stands and moves toward me. "So what's the bad?"

"The bad news is that her body's taken quite a beating. She'll need some help moving around. She'll be able to walk, but not for extended periods of time, and she might need a wheelchair long term. She'll need rails in the bathroom, little visuals around the house that remind her of her routine, signs on walls, things like that. Stairs might be a problem, too, so I don't know what her house is like—"

"I'll take care of it. Give me a couple hours." I stand quickly and turn for the door, but Becca stops me. She types on her phone before showing it to me. *Do you need any help?*

I shake my head and point to Rob who's already saying goodbye to Kim. "I got it," I tell Becca. "Can you stay here until she wakes up and bring her home when she's ready. Just um..." I take a calming breath. "Just *please* make sure she knows I'm at home waiting for her, okay?"

~

Rob and I take measurements and create a list of supplies we'll need to build the ramp on the porch before he goes to the lumber yard and I start working on things in the house. Once my dad got too sick to walk, we had to convert the downstairs office at my parents' house to a bedroom. Chaz doesn't have any rooms on the first floor, so I make quick work of disassembling her bed upstairs to convert her living room into her bedroom until I can come up with a better plan or maybe make provisions for an extension.

I hear a car pull up in the driveway, and I look out the window to see Martin stepping out of Chaz's car. No Becca. I continue to watch as he leans against the hood and pulls out his phone. He taps a few buttons then holds it to his ear. A second later he's talking, lips moving, but I can't make out what he's saying. I give up trying and head back downstairs to start moving the furniture to make room for the bed. I try to push him out of my mind while I drag the couches in all directions, attempting to find the perfect position. But he's there, every interaction, every word spoken, every glare made my direction, he's there... until my mind gets lost in the hurricane of his anger and hate toward me, and before I know it, I'm stepping out of the house and walking over to him.

He says, "I'll call you back," when he sees me and hangs up the phone. "What do you want?"

"Will you at least tell me what your problem with me is?"

He laughs once—this arrogant, cocky laugh that has me

balling my fists. I forget for a moment who he is, as well as the fact that he's a fucking Goliath who could take me down in a single punch. "My problem with you is that my daughter contacts me, tells me her grandmother is sick, and that I need to come here. So I do. And what do I see? I see her in your apartment, practically naked, playing house as if nothing's changed between you two. Do you enjoy taking advantage of emotional girls, Josh? Is that your game?"

"Are you fucking serious right now?"

"Oh, I'm dead serious. Every fucking time you show up in her life this shit happens, and guess who has to pick up the pieces?"

I shake my head, my eyes wide in disbelief. "I don't even know what to say to you. I know I've hurt Becca in the past but—"

"And you'll continue to hurt her, because you can't seem to leave her alone!"

I start to walk away, because I can feel the anger rising, feel it burning a hole in my chest.

"What's your plan with her, anyway, Warden?"

I spin quickly. "What the hell are you talking about?"

"You're going to go off and skate around the world, different places, different *girls,* throwing around your money like it's nothing…" He steps closer, towering over me. "All while she's in college, going to classes, pining over the boy who once loved her?"

"That's not what this is, and what you *think* I *do,* isn't who I *am.*" The anger doubles, boils, bursts. "You don't know fuck-all about me!"

He fists my shirt, pulling me to him until I'm on my toes. His breath is harsh against my skin. Through gritted teeth and narrowed eyes, he fumes, "You're a punk who knocked up a girl when you were *sixteen!* And now you're going to do the same with Becca and ruin everything she's worked for! I've been in your shoes. I've made the same mistakes. You think I don't know you, Warden? I *was* you!"

I grasp his wrists, trying to get him off of me, but he won't budge. "Don't you *dare* bring my son into this."

His fists tighten, but he doesn't speak.

"You and me—we're nothing alike." The anger's gone now, replaced with bottled rage. "Because I'd never, *ever,* call my son a mistake."

Rob returns in my truck, the tires screeching as he comes to a stop. "Get your fucking hands off him!" he yells, running toward us.

I straighten my T-shirt when Martin releases me, and keep my eyes on his. "You want to come into her life and man up eighteen years too late, then good for you. But don't ever compare us again. Because I was there for my son through sleepless nights, and colic and teething and every bad thing imaginable. And I'd never let anyone or anything hurt him." I try to breathe through the agony, the burn, and take a calming breath so I can think. "Where the fuck were you all those times her mother abused her? Beat her to within an inch of her life? Where were you when she was crying, her nightmares a fucking reality? She wasn't the mistake. *You* were!"

Luckily, Martin leaves, giving me time to calm down. I can sense Robby watching me, wanting to ask questions he knows I won't answer, so instead, we focus on building the stupid ramp on the porch and moving the bed downstairs. As soon as we're done, Rob gets a call from Kim telling him they're on the way.

We wait for them outside, the tension between us building. "Don't you dare say a word to Becca about what you saw," I tell him.

"So I assume you will."

"She's going through enough, Rob. Please don't make this harder for her."

~

We settle Chaz in her new space while she tries to smile and nod through everything, but she's annoyed. Frustrated. I can tell. Six people surrounding her, all fussing over her? I would be, too.

Martin returns, refusing to make eye contact with anyone, and a moment later, a nurse I've never met before shows up. This one's here to make sure Chazarae has everything she needs at home, not just physically, but mentally as well. After making sure Becca and I understand what medications Chaz needs to take and when, she leaves, satisfied, with a promise to check in tomorrow. And as much as I love Chaz, as much as I want to be with her, it's just too damn much with Martin around.

"Are you guys all right for food?" I ask Becca, standing just outside their door. "You need me to go to the store?"

She shakes her head as she pulls on my shirt, wanting me closer. Over her shoulder, Martin stands with his arms crossed and I fight the urge to scream, to shout, to run like a baby and tell Becca everything he said and the way he treated me. Instead, I kiss her forehead and ignore the disappointment in her eyes when I tell her I'll see her in the morning.

I take Tommy's hand and lead him to the apartment where we pretend like everything is good and fine in the world, and that one of the most important people in our lives isn't a few feet away surrounded by people she doesn't know, lost in a mind that's no longer hers.

Mom comes by with food, and we all sit at the table continuing to pretend.

"Eat your broccoli, Tommy."

"Okay, Daddy."

I don't know if he actually does because I'm not looking at him. I'm staring down at my plate, my fork prodding my own broccoli.

"Remember when you used to call them little trees last time, Daddy?" Tommy asks.

I look up at him, my eyes tired. "Yeah."

"Why would I like to eat trees?"

I smile. I can't help it. Then I lean forward and push my plate aside, glancing at Mom quickly. "When I was little like you, I didn't eat my vegetables, either. So your Pa—he used to sit with me at the table until I'd eaten every single one on the plate." I point to Mom. "Nanni—she used to tell him to just let me go, that it was past my bedtime, but he wouldn't. And then one day, he came up with this idea to make up an entire land made of vegetables."

"And did you?" Tommy practically shouts.

"We did. We stayed up and made broccoli trees and carrot stick logs and a pea sea."

"Pee sea!" He cackles with laughter. "And then what happened, Daddy?"

Mom giggles.

"And then…" I say, my eyes wide. "He said I was a T-Rex and T-Rexes destroy land. And so I opened my mouth wide, and I ate everything on that plate!"

Tommy laughs, loud and free, and I watch, letting the sound of his joy overpower the misery of the past few days. "I want to be a T-Rex, Daddy!"

I stand and move toward him, but the breaking of glass from somewhere outside stops me. Chaz's screams fill my ears and dread kicks in. I look over at my mom. "Go!" she says.

I slip on my shoes and run to the house, cringing when I feel the glass crunching beneath my feet. The living room window's smashed, so is a ceramic vase now in pieces on the porch steps. “Get outta my house!” Chaz screams. “Get out! Get out! Get out!”

I push the door open with so much force, it hits the wall behind it. “What’s going on?” I take a second and look around the room. I look at Chaz standing there with her hands to her mouth, at Becca crying in the corner, and at Martin standing between them, his hands in his hair.

“She can’t…” Martin mumbles.

Becca cowers even more.

“Joshua,” Chaz cries, moving toward me. “Why are these people in my house?”

“It’s okay.” I hug her to me, but my eyes are on Becca.

“Who are they? They broke into *my* house and they’re… they’re…”

“It’s okay,” I repeat, slowly guiding her back to her bed. I look over at Martin and point to Becca. He seems to come to, quickly moving to comfort her.

“They’re trying to make me take these damn pills, Joshua. They’re trying to kill me!”

I settle the covers around her and sit on the bed.

There are tears in her eyes, fear in her voice matching the fear in my heart. “What’s happening?”

Behind me, Mom says, “Is everything okay?”

I turn to her, hoping she doesn’t have Tommy because I don’t want him seeing this. She must sense my unasked question because she says, “I set him up on his iPad. I video called Blake and Chloe. He’ll be occupied for a while.”

“Who is she?” Chaz asks. “Who are all these people?”

I take a calming breath, my eyes drifting shut from the sudden weight of the world. “Ma’am.” I take her hands in mine, and I pray to a God she so strongly believes in that I say and do the right things. “These people are your family.”

She shakes her head, her dark eyes focused on mine. “You’re

my only family, Joshua. I don't…" Her gaze drops, her tears ripping my heart in two. "I don't know them."

"I know. And that's okay. But I promise, Ma'am, they're not here to hurt you. They're here to help."

"I'm scared," she weeps, her hand squeezing mine. "I feel like I'm not real and this isn't real and you're the only thing that makes sense and that can't be right, can it? How…" Her gaze moves to the window, both hands covering her mouth. "Oh no! The window. What did I do?"

"Don't worry about the window. I'll fix it."

"You're always fixing things. Always taking care of me."

Martin clears his throat, his arms around Becca keeping her upright. "I read that it might be helpful if you talk about something she openly remembers…"

"Who is he?" Chaz whispers.

I sigh.

She cries harder.

I focus on Martin's words, and take a steady breath, trying to find the hope I felt earlier. "You remember me, right?" I ask.

She nods, freeing the tears from her cheeks. They land on the blankets bunched around her and for seconds, minutes, I watch them seep into the fabric.

I mumble, trying to find strength in my voice, "And you know my son, Tommy?"

She nods again. "Thomas Joshua. Such a beautiful boy."

"You met us at the store. Do you remember that?"

"Yes," she sobs, wiping at her eyes.

"I didn't know you were there watching—watching me with a baby in my arms, struggling to pay for his formula and his diapers and I was so afraid, ma'am. I was so scared because I felt like I couldn't take care of him the way I should. I was failing him, and I tried so hard not to let it show but you saw it, didn't you?"

Her lips tremble, her eyes filling again.

"And you followed me to that skate shop where I tried to sell my board, and then you followed me again into that alley. I was lost and alone, so alone, and I broke down. And you watched it all. You watched me look at my son, you heard me make promises I didn't think I could keep, and you *saved* me. You saved me that day, ma'am." Now I'm crying, too, our tears a mix of memories and heartache. "And then we went back to the store. Do you remember what you said?"

Chaz inhales deeply before blinking back even more tears. "I said my niece was coming to visit, and to get everything I needed for a newborn baby like Thomas."

"Right. And then you brought us here, led us to that garage apartment and we put away all the groceries you'd bought. Do you remember what you said to me? Because I'll never forget it, ma'am. Never."

She sniffs once, holding her breath to stop the cries from forming.

"You took my hand in yours and you said, 'It's not much of a house, but you and Tommy, you can make it your *home*.' You didn't just give Tommy and me a place to live. You didn't just save us. You gave us a family when we had none. And you gave us *you*. *You* are our home, Ma'am."

CHAPTER 26

BECCA

Loud hammering wakes me from my sleep, and I get up quickly and run downstairs to check on Grams. She's fast asleep, exactly the way I left her in the early hours of the morning. Josh is out on the porch with another guy replacing the window that Grams had thrown a vase—aimed at Dad—through the night before.

"Morning, sleepy head!" Tommy calls out, standing in the middle of the driveway with a skateboard in his arms.

I wave to him, just as Josh asks, "You sleep okay?" He's wearing work pants and work boots, the kind I'd seen him in often, back when we were together.

I nod. It's all I can do since I left my phone upstairs. Dad's voice from the other end of the porch grabs my attention. "How did you get a replacement so fast?" he asks Josh.

Josh ignores him, so the other guy—I now recognize as Michael from Josh's old job—answers. "Josh's uncle is my boss, and he called in a favor."

Dad's eyebrows rise. "A favor?"

"Yeah. Before Josh decided to make us all look bad by becoming a pro-athlete, he worked construction," he says slowly, like it's something Dad should know. He pats Josh on the shoulder as Josh hammers at the window frame. "My boss made a call to our supplier this morning and got it cut to size." Michael shrugs. "Josh can do the install on his own. I'm just here to deliver and get free shirts and shoes."

"The garage door's open," Josh mumbles, and without a second thought, Michael makes his way across the driveway toward the garage, cracking jokes with Tommy as he passes.

Josh faces me. "You better get some shoes on, Becs. I haven't swept the glass yet."

"I didn't know you could do this stuff," Dad says.

Josh scoffs and finally acknowledges him. "With all due respect, *sir.* There's a lot you don't know about me."

"What the hell *was that about?*" Cordy asks for me.

Dad rubs his hands across his face before sipping on his coffee. "What was what about?"

Grams woke just as Josh was finishing up on the window and he offered to take her for a walk. She's mobile enough to be able to eat on her own and go to the bathroom, but she still tires easily, so a walk meant him and Tommy on skateboards and her in her chair—something Tommy thought was hilarious. "The Really Wheely Team," he called them.

Cordy says, *"The way Josh spoke to you this morning. That's not like him. Did you say something to him?"*

Dad shrugs. "I may have a had a word with him and I don't really feel like repeating what all was said, if that's okay with you."

I stare incredulously.

"Sweetheart, I just worry about you. That's all."

My eyes narrow, and I become unreasonably angry. Not for me. But for Josh. *"I don't care what you said, but whatever it was, you're wrong. I care about him, Dad. And maybe that's not enough for you, but he's going through enough as it is. You need to apologize to him."*

Dad sighs. "Becca. Don't make a mound out of a molehill."

I tap my phone again, the words repeated. *"I don't care what you said, but whatever it was, you're wrong. I care about him, Dad. And maybe that's not enough for you, but he's going through enough as it is. You need to apologize to him."*

"You don't know him like I do. He's going to carry your words with him long after you leave, long after you realize you regret them. You have to apologize to him, Dad. And soon."

"What makes you think I regret it?" he asks.

"Because I know you. You're just like him. You're hot-headed and you don't think before you speak. You see everything in one dimension. You know everything. Until someone makes you realize that you don't."

He shakes his head as he looks down at me. "You're wrong, Becca. And he's right. I'm not like him at all."

CHAPTER 27

JOSHUA

I don't know why Martin's standing at my door, looking into my apartment like he has every right to. "I waited until the lights were out assuming your son was asleep. Is he?"

My jaw clenches, but I nod anyway.

He lifts a six-pack of beers between us. "You owe me nothing, but I'm asking anyway. Just hear me out."

I should wear a watch. That way I could at least tell you how long I sit at the bottom of the stairs, sipping on a beer offered by a man I might possibly hate. If he's waiting for me to speak, he'll be waiting forever. I don't have forever. Besides, he's the one who knocked on the door, and if silence is his way of hearing him out, then he has shit backwards.

"You think she could still be in love with you, Josh?"

My mouth opens, but the words are lost and I feel my heart sinking. "She sent me a letter," I murmur as if it's somehow going to be enough.

Martin quirks an eyebrow. "A letter?"

"Yeah."

"What did the letter say?"

I shrug and avoid his gaze. "It's irrelevant. I don't know why I said it."

He sighs. "Are you messing with Becca's head?"

"No!" I snap.

"*I* think you are, even if you don't realize it."

I suck in a breath and hold it there—in my chest—sitting right next to my battered heart.

After a while, he says, "Becca's stronger now, Josh. Stronger than she's ever been."

I speak quickly, not giving my mind time to think. "If you honestly believe that me existing is making her weak in any way, then I'll leave her alone." I roll my shoulders, trying to find courage in my words. "I think, at the end of the day, you and I both want the same things. We want Becca to be happy. Regardless of what Becca's probably told you, I do love her. I've always loved her. From the first moment I saw her until now, I haven't *stopped* loving her. I haven't been able to move on—"

"It's been—"

I laugh once, cutting him off. "Two years. Trust me. I know."

"And you haven't—"

"Not once," I interrupt. "Swear on my father's grave. I *can't.*"

He leans back, running a hand through his hair, but he doesn't speak, so I add, "I realize I've made mistakes, horrible ones, but I'm human. I'm flawed. I'm working on those flaws, but I'll never be perfect. I know that. So if it's those mistakes that prevent me from living the rest of my life without the person I'm insanely in love with, I'll wear that."

"I appreciate that, Josh. Really I do," he says, his voice soft. And I wonder what his angle is, what he could possibly expect from me. "But Becca's so fragile and…"

I ball my fists, and he must see it because his words die in the air, and he waits for me to speak, both of us knowing my words come from deep frustration and regret. "It's like you think I don't know that." I exhale loudly and try to keep my emotions in check. "She had these nightmares. She'd jerk in her sleep and wince like she was in actual physical pain. She'd cry, even when her eyes were shut tight, somehow tears would still come. And that was on a good night. Other times she'd scream, but it was silent, you know?" I turn to him, making sure he *sees* me. "Because even though she could speak before"—I swallow the pain of the past—"it didn't always work."

"You don't need to..."

I ignore him and keep going. "She'd bite down on her thumb so hard it would leave marks. She'd kick at me, hands covering her head, and she'd plead for it to stop, and the only way I could do it was physically." I disregard the knowledge of who I'm speaking to and tell him exactly how it is, exactly how I feel. "She wanted me to take away her emotional pain by replacing it with physical pleasure. And I'd do it. For her. I'd regret it as soon as it was done, but I wanted to make it stop just as much as she did. I didn't know any other way." My breath leaves me in a shudder, the ache in my chest making it almost impossible to inhale and painful to exhale. "And somewhere along the lines, she needed me and I wasn't there," I say, my voice lowering. "Truthfully, I wasn't anywhere. I was lost. She needed me and I was *lost*. She broke because of me. She tried to *kill* herself because of *me*. So you don't need to tell me how fragile she is. Believe me, I was there. I fucking know." I gasp for air, wishing the words back, but it's too damn late. "I used to walk around with a chip on my shoulder... poor me; single dad at seventeen, completely alone and forgotten. But then I'd look down at Tommy in my arms, a baby boy who was mine and mine alone, and I'd wake up every day grateful we had each other. Swear, I thought it was impossible to love anyone as much as I love my son." At the thought of Becca, air fills my lungs, slow and steady. "Then Becca showed up and she completed the gaps in my life that I didn't even know were missing. And I'd give anything to go back in time, back to even before we met. Because I know I'd *see* her in ways the others hadn't. I'd do anything to *fix* her. I'd take care of her the way she deserved to be taken care of. Not like how her—" I choke on a sob and push it down. "I don't understand how a parent can do that to their child. How *anyone* can do that to a kid… I look at my son and I see the way he looks at me, the way he relies on me to guide him through this world and—" I'm crying, tears falling fast and free. "Her mother should thank God she's dead, because if she wasn't, I'd fucking kill her myself. And I'd make her hurt a thousand times worse than she ever did with Becca."

I realize Martin's watching me with a look on his face I can't decipher. He takes a sip of his beer, and then another. And another. We go through an entire beer each, a comfortable silence somehow keeping us together until he finally says, "I'm lost, too."

I bite my tongue, confused by his words. "We're all lost here, sir."

"Yeah," he says through a sigh, kicking out his legs. "But I feel out of place. Like I have no purpose being here. Becca—she at least knows Chazarae. She lived with her for a while. You've been here for years. I only spoke to her a few times on the phone, met her once when I picked up Becca from that 'Personal Development' place and took her to St. Louis, and then again when we came here for her birthday. But I don't know her. I mean, yeah, she's my mother, but… I don't know her at all. And I see Becca getting all worked up, and you fighting her battles for her and I know I should be feeling something but I don't know what it is…" He takes a sip of his beer, his head dropping forward. "It's like Becca all over again."

I sit up straighter, light finally shining on my confusion of his actions. "What do you mean?"

He's quick to respond, as if he'd been waiting to tell someone, to lift the weight off his shoulders. "I mean, when I got her I had no idea what to do. I had a daughter who needed help, and so I tried to do everything a dad was meant to do. I gave her a home, gave her support, but she's not a little girl who needs her hand held to jump over puddles, you know? She was eighteen, a woman, and the majority of the time she was a strong one. Now, she's even stronger, so I don't really understand what my purpose in her life is. I feel like I should protect her from all the bad in the world, but you're right, I was eighteen years too late and she's already experienced them all."

"I didn't mean what I said. I was angry and this whole thing with Chazarae..." I trail off.

"No," he says, shaking his head. "I shouldn't have pushed the wrong buttons. I'm just having a hard time with everything. Add to that the guilt I feel because I should be working, making money, but if I'm at work, then I can't be here, and right now I don't know which one's more important. All that is going through my head, and then we get told that Chazarae needs medical support and all I can think about is how much it's all going to cost—"

"I said I'd take care of it," I cut in.

"I know," he says reassuringly. "And I appreciate it. I think with everything else going on, you being able to do that just added more fuel to my fire."

I don't know what to say, so I stay quiet.

He finishes his beer and starts another one. "Fifty years I've been around. Thirty of those I spent working the same job. I never thought I'd have a family, never really wanted one, to be honest. I blew my paycheck whenever I got it, never had a home, just crashed at friends' houses until I was back at work. Thirty years and I never really thought about anyone but myself. And then I get told about Becca and St. Louis and…" He swallows loudly, his beer almost empty again. "You ever feel like the world just stops, Warden?"

I stare ahead, letting his admission settle in my mind. "Yeah. All the time."

"That's how it felt when I saw her picture. I knew that she was mine, and I knew I had to do *something*. I couldn't turn her away. So I quit, gathered whatever savings I had, sold whatever I could, and rented that house near WU. I couldn't go back to work, not until I knew she was okay mentally. Even now I'm taking these small jobs because I don't want to be gone too long in case she needs me, which she hasn't for a while, but what if she does and I'm not around?" He's talking in circles, trying to justify every decision he's ever made. I know, because I do the same whenever it comes to Tommy. "College ain't cheap. Neither is all the camera equipment and computer stuff she needs, and the rent for the house—" He breaks off suddenly, his eyes widening. "I don't want you to think that I'm asking you for money, that's the last thing—"

"I know," I tell him, my mind spinning. "We're just talking, right?"

He laughs once. "I know this doesn't excuse the way I treated you."

"I get it, though." I find myself matching his position, legs kicked out, beer in hand, like it somehow makes this a man-to-man conversation. "You thought you were protecting her. And I know you probably don't want to hear it, especially from me, but I understand what it's like to be broke and to do everything you can for your kid. When Tommy's mother left, I went running to my parents. They slammed the door in my face—something they regret, and something I've forgiven them for. But I would've never gone to anyone else. Every man, even at seventeen, has a level of pride, and then it doubles when being a man comes second to being a father. But even though I never asked, help was offered. My best friend, Chazarae, my uncle—they all came through when I needed them the most. I guess what I'm trying to say is that I know it's hard to ask for help. But there's nothing wrong with accepting it when it's offered. Especially when your kid's involved."

CHAPTER 28

BECCA

I have no idea what Dad said to Josh that made Josh speak to him the way he had. But I do know they spoke, and the next morning right before Dad left, Josh stopped him in the driveway, handed him something and said, "You didn't ask." They hugged. Honestly, it was a little awkward for me to watch, so I can't even imagine how awkward it was for them to do it. Once the cab drove away with Dad, Josh turned to me and he smiled the same crooked smile that sets off all the butterflies and said, "Let's take care of your grams."

So that's what we do. We get the résumés for the in-home nurses and spend a couple days with Ella going through them all. We call the ones who seem like a good fit and organize interviews with them. Grams falls in and out of sleep constantly. She still doesn't know who I am, and I've accepted that. It hurts, but the hurt lessens with every look, every smile I gain just from being around her.

The next few days after that go by in a blur. We interview nurse after nurse until they all blend together in a sea of credentials and experience. Ella sits with us through all of them while his aunt stays with Tommy in the apartment. Josh finds it necessary to remind me constantly that even though he has the power of attorney, I'm as involved in making the decisions as he is. We struggle, a lot, overwhelmed with the importance of the choices we have to make, and aware of the time ticking by, getting closer and closer to the day I have to go back to St. Louis.

Grams has a lot of visitors, some she remembers, others she doesn't. Josh's aunt and uncle are a constant. Blake and Chloe come by once and take Tommy for the night. The one person I wasn't expecting, though, was Chris, and going by the look on Josh's face when he shows up, Josh wasn't expecting him either.

Chris steps out of his car, or truck, or something in between the two. Whatever it is, it's black and looks like it costs more than my dad's house. He reaches inside and pulls out a bouquet of flowers approximately the size of the ozone layer. So maybe I'm exaggerating, and I'm also being a judgy mcjudgepants, but it's not like I have a single reason to be happy to see him. He stops in his tracks when he sees me sitting on the porch with Tommy, then raises his free hand. "I'm just here to see Chaz," he says in his defense.

I realize I'm glaring at him, my brows knitted, and a snarl pulling on my lips.

Josh stands between us, looking from one to the other. He doesn't get a chance to speak before Tommy leaps off the porch steps and tackle hugs Chris, who smiles down at him. "Uncle Chris!" Tommy shouts, the happiness in his voice deflating my anger.

I stand, too, and slowly make my way to him, my pride being pushed away with each step I take. "I'm sorry about your grams," Chris says. He grabs ahold of the flowers, and only then do I realize there are two bouquets. "I got these for you," he says, handing me one. "I know it's not much, and it doesn't make up for the way I treated you last time—"

"Last time!" Tommy shouts.

Chris laughs at him, then goes back to me, a sincerity in his eyes that knocks me back a step. "My grandpa had dementia," he tells me. "Would it be okay if I visited your grams for a while?"

A knot forms in my throat at his admission, and I nod while accepting his gift. I turn on my heels and lead him toward the house, smiling sadly at Josh when I catch him watching me.

Grams doesn't recognize him, but Chris doesn't seem at all surprised by that. Still, he sits with her, and he talks about Josh; something Grams is familiar with. I set our flowers in vases—a new set Josh went out and bought the day after she threw one at Dad's head. Chris stays by her side until she tells me she's tired. He steps to the side and allows me to settle her into bed.

"Thanks for visiting..." Grams says, her voice tired. "What's your name again?"

"Chris."

"Right. I'm sorry. I'm so tired and it's hard to remember—"

"I understand," Chris cuts in. "Though, I'm pretty sure you don't need any *more* beauty sleep."

Grams giggles like a schoolgirl. "He's charming," she tells me. "Just like my Joshua." And then she's asleep, her breaths even and her mind at peace, no longer wandering through a life she's trying to piece back together.

"I really appreciate you letting me see her," Chris says from beside me, his fingers skimming Grams's hand.

I reach into my pocket and pull out my phone. *"Why wouldn't I?"*

He sighs. "Did Warden ever tell you about the time the team was here?"

I shake my head and look up at him. He deserves that much.

"Yeah, we were here for an appearance for the new storefront, and she invited us all over for dinner. First home-cooked meal the boys had had in a long time. She wouldn't let us stay in a hotel, said her guest bedrooms were fine. Four boys, two beds… but we couldn't say no. She had us going to church with her the next morning and then out with Warden working on her yard the rest of the day. She paid us with rose petals *in* lemonade. It was gross, but we took it like champs and downed it."

My eyes narrow in confusion.

He adds, "Looking back now, it was probably the beginning of her illness…"

I suck in a breath, my chest tight. "*You said your grandpa…*"

Nodding, Chris looks away and says, "My mom took care of him, had to watch his decline like you and Josh are doing now. I was young, so I didn't really understand it all. I think I was Tommy's age when he passed. I don't remember much of it, but I do know that it took a lot out of my mom. Almost ruined her." He clears his throat, his voice lowering to a whisper. "Your grams was like a grandmother to us all after that visit. She's important to the whole team. And so is Josh." He turns to me, his eyes right on mine. "Josh—he's kind of the soul of the team, Becca, and that makes you the *heart* of it."

Josh looks up when I step out of the house later in the day, closing the door behind me, but he doesn't say a word, just continues to land trick after trick on his skateboard. His hands, his legs, his entire body moving, outlined by the light inside the open garage. I sit down on the porch steps, now only half of what they used to be because of the ramp, and I watch him. I watch the grace, the skill, the passion he has in what he does. Occasionally, he'll land wrong, curse under his breath, and then try again. And again. And again. An hour goes by. Then two. Neither of us saying a word. Then he finally stops, grabs his board and takes it with him as he sits down next to me.

I type on my phone and show it to him. *Why'd you stop?*

He laughs. "Why'd you keep watching?"

I could watch you forever.

He looks up from the phone, his eyes meeting mine. I shrug, trying to play cool, but deep down, my heart's picked up pace—reacting to the way he's looking at me.

How do you know when Tommy wakes up? I type, pushing away the feelings creeping beneath the surface.

"He's so used to me being out here, he just opens his window and calls out to me."

Silence falls between us while I look up at the stars and get lost in his scent. He still wears the same cologne that drew me to him all those years ago. "You still wear that stupid ring?" he asks.

I frown and look down at my hand, at the ring he'd given me while we sat in this exact spot on my eighteenth birthday. "Not stupid," I whisper, then swallow the ache. Not just in my throat, but in my heart. I've never taken the ring off. Not once.

He sighs while I drop the phone on my lap and spin the ring around my finger, my thumb skimming over the words *I shoot like a girl*. I pick up my phone and angle it so he can see what I type, *It was one of the best nights of my life, Josh. Don't take that away from me.*

He blows out a breath, long and slow.

I change the subject. *Chris told me that Grams made you guys drink rose petals in lemonade?*

He laughs once, but it's sad. "You know, I was thinking about your grams... about all these things she'd done when I was home that I didn't pick up on at the time. That was one of them. Another time I came home and she was out in the garden in the back yard on her hands and knees. She said she was looking for her earrings. She doesn't even have her ears pierced. The next day, she was out there again, and when I asked her why, she said her toothbrush was missing. We found it in her fridge." He shakes his head, his mind lost in the memories. "I don't know why I didn't see things earlier, Becs. I'm sorry. I should've."

I stay quiet a beat, replaying his words in my head. *Where was her toothpaste?*

"That's what you got from that?" He laughs, his eyes narrowed and his head shaking in disbelief. *"Where was her toothpaste?"*

A giggle builds in my chest, then releases in silent laughter.

"Why are you laughing about this?"

I wait until I've settled, then type: *It's Grams—she was always a little nutty anyway, before any of this happened... so this just makes her more... eccentric? Besides, what would be the point of life if we couldn't find laughter and joy amongst the turmoil?*

Josh just stares, and stares, and then stares some more. Then he says, "I got your letter, Becs."

And just like that, there's no laughter, no joy. No logic to my actions. My eyes drift shut, my stomach dropping to the floor. It's not as if I didn't expect him to get it, but I'd hoped, prayed, that he wouldn't bring it up. Regrets are stupid, and just like that letter, I can't take either of them back.

He says, "I was only home for a few days before I had to travel again. Then I was gone three weeks. When I got back, it was there waiting for me. I knew it was from you, I could tell by the handwriting. But I couldn't force myself to open it because I knew whatever it was, it would either ruin me, or I'd somehow ruin us." He pauses a beat, his eyes distant, his hand rubbing his jaw. "For a week I carried that letter around, waiting for the right time, and it never seemed to come. It wasn't until I was on a plane to Brazil for a tournament that I finally got the balls to do it. I almost made Chris turn the plane around when I saw what was in there. I was going to call you, message you, tell you that I'd gotten it, but I wanted to wait until I saw you in person." He turns to me, his lips thinned to a line.

"And..." I type, my eyes never leaving his.

He breaks the stare. "And… six months passed before I finally got the nerve. I went to tell your grams that I was going to see you but before I got the chance, she started talking about you. She told me everything you were doing in college, working on the paper, working at Say Something, getting your *license.* I know how hard that would've been for you, so you must've been doing really well. And I…" His voice cracks, and he clears it before adding, "I didn't want to ruin everything, because I know me, and I knew that I would. Somehow, I'd fuck things up for you, and as much as I wanted to see you, as badly as I wanted to be near you, I couldn't do it."

There are so many words, so many responses flying through my mind and I want to say all of them. Want to *speak* every one. But my voice doesn't work, neither do my hands, because I can't even find it in me to give him the reply he deserves.

"Anyway…" he mumbles, probably sick of waiting for me to respond. He changes the subject, his voice lighter. "What was wrong with that one nurse I liked? She had experience with dementia patients and she seemed to get along well with your grams."

I pick up my phone and get Cordy to speak, grateful for the switch in conversation. *"Who? Sadie?"*

"Yeah. I thought she was perfect."

I roll my eyes.

"What?" he asks, clearly confused.

I joke, *"She is perfect. For you. Young, leggy, blonde."*

He laughs under his breath. "Are you serious? Becca, I didn't even look at her like that. Besides"—he shrugs and pulls on a strand of my hair—"I'm not into blondes."

I bite my lip to contain my smile. *"The mother of your son is blonde,"* Cordy reminds him.

He grimaces, his eyes shifting from the phone to me, over and over again. Then he looks away. "She doesn't count."

I scoff. It's silent. *"So maybe I just didn't like the way she was looking at you."*

His eyes light up with his smile. I squirm when he leans closer, his touch like fire on my bare leg. "Stay with me tonight?"

It would be easy, almost *too* easy, to fall into him again. To have the safety of his arms be the reason I wake up with my mind at ease regardless of what's going on around me. And I know it's wrong—and swear, I'm not messing with his head on purpose. I just don't know if I can handle wanting him the way I do. *"I leave in two days,"* Cordy says.

He leans closer again, his lips curving on my shoulder. "So stay with me for two nights." Then he pulls back to read my reaction.

He must see the battle playing behind my eyes because he smirks, knowing the effect he has on me.

I kiss his cheek softly, then stand and make my way to the front door.

Behind me, Josh chuckles. "Good night, *Emerald Eyes*."

I run inside, closing the door behind me, and up the stairs, away from my feelings. Away from Josh. Away from *my heart*. I pace my room, over and over, trying to make sense of the things I just ran away from. Then I bite down on my thumb, a thousand regrets—each a heavy weight—filling my chest. *I could watch you forever,* I told him. What the hell was I thinking?

I sent him the letter.

I sent him the truth.

And the truth is the one thing I can't escape.

I look out the window so I can watch him some more, because I can't not. I'm drawn, like a million moths to an inferno of flames. My teeth grind into my thumb and I push away the pain, and wait for the punishment. But it never comes. My bite loosens when a smile forms, caused by Josh's when he sees me watching him. He does a couple tricks on his board before he picks it up—his eyes never leaving me. Then he makes his way up to his apartment, and I wait with baited breath until the light comes on in his room. A second later, the curtains draw, and he's there, opposite me, his grin matching mine. I release my thumb completely and focus on my phone as I type out a message. I stare at the words, one letter at a time, until I finally find the courage to hit send.

Becca: Sweet dreams, Skater Boy.

CHAPTER 29

BECCA

I swallow my pride as I walk up Josh's stairs the next morning, Sadie's footsteps following behind me. "So is Josh home a lot?" she asks.

My shoulders lift with my shrug, but I don't make an effort to face her. Facing her would mean looking at her, and even though Josh was right—that she is the best suited for the live-in nurse's position—it took everything I had to send her the message this morning and offer her the job. She's pretty. No, that's a lie. She's insanely beautiful. And tomorrow, I'll be gone, and she'll be up close and personal with *my* boys. My stomach turns, jealousy swarming in my veins.

Tommy answers the door, still dressed in his camera-patterned pajamas with a bright green top hat. He looks like a sleepy leprechaun, only a thousand times more adorable. "Top of the mornin' to ya, madam," he says through a giggle, tipping the hat and taking my hand. He kisses it once, just as Josh calls out from somewhere in the house, "Tommy! I told you not to answer the door without me."

Tommy rolls his eyes—a trait Josh swears he learned from me. "It's just Becca and some lady," Tommy moans.

The door opens wider and Josh appears wearing nothing but a towel around his waist. His dark hair's wet, beads of water hanging off the ends, falling onto his shoulders, down his chest, past the dips of his abs and into—"Becs," he says, and my eyes move to his, but my mouth's hanging open, and I can't seem to shut it. "You want to borrow Tommy's camera? Take a picture? It'll last longer."

My mouth snaps shut, my brows knitting. I give him the most dramatic eye roll I can muster, then point over my shoulder.

His smile widens. "Hi, Sadie."

"Top of the mornin' to ya, Sadie," Tommy says.

Josh's gaze flicks between Sadie and me. "Who's watching Ma'am right now?"

Sadie answers, "She's with a nurse from the hospital. Don't worry. I sat in through all the important stuff. Everything's taken care of."

Josh straightens, his welcoming smile switching to an arrogant smirk. "We were just getting ready to have some breakfast. Would you like to join us?"

I step inside, not bothering to wait for a response, and march to the kitchen where I turn on the coffee pot and start pulling out things for Tommy's breakfast.

Josh says, "Why don't you have a seat, Sadie?"

I hate the way he says her name, like there's an ulterior motive behind it. *Sadie. Sadie. Sleep with me, Sadie?* "Morning," Josh whispers, his mouth to my ear and his hand on my waist as he stands behind me. I reach into my pocket, pull out my phone, and without looking at him, type: *Get some damn clothes on!!!*

He chuckles when he reads it, but he doesn't say anything else. He just steps to the side, tightening the towel around him. He makes quick work of pouring coffees and getting Tommy's cereal for him, all while walking around practically naked—no shame to his game. He says, "Tommy, doesn't Becca look beautiful today?"

Tommy smiles up at me. "Beautiful!" he repeats.

"In fact, I'd say she looks pretty damn hot."

"Pretty damn hot!" Tommy repeats again.

Sadie giggles.

Josh announces, "I'm going to get dressed." Then he moves toward me, a smirk still in place, right before he throws me over his shoulder. I'd scream. You know… if I actually could. But I fight. My fists thump on his bare back the entire way down the hallway and into his room. He lowers me slowly onto his bed and hovers over me, his weight held up by his outstretched arm. His eyebrows rise. "So you called Sadie?"

After shoving him out of the way, I stand quickly and move to his dresser where I pull out a pair of his boxer shorts and throw them at his head.

He laughs. "Sure you don't want to dress me?" he asks, already slipping them on under the towel. "I don't think I've ever seen you jealous, and I gotta be honest, I'm kinda really into it."

Wow. He got real cocky overnight.

I cross my arms. "Shut up," I mouth.

He laughs harder. "You know, I've always said green was your color."

I pull open another drawer, pick out the first T-shirt I see and throw that at his head, too. Then I do the same with a pair of sweatpants. He dresses himself, his stupid grin never leaving him. "Yo. What size do you think Sadie is?" he asks, moving around the cardboard boxes lining his wall. "I think I have some girls' clothes here." He rummages some more. "Here they are." He holds up a pair of bright pink shorts. "Red Bull *booty shorts*. You think she'd like them?" His nose is in the air now, like he'd just found a solution to world peace, not mastered the ability to push my buttons. As ashamed as I am to admit, it works, because something takes over me. I'm not sure what. But the next thing I know, I'm jumping on his bed, using it as leverage to leap up and grab the stupid shorts from him. He holds them behind his back just in time, and wraps his free arm around my waist, trapping me to him. He's laughing—an all-consuming laugh—and I fight the urge to do the same. He dips his head, his mouth to my ear again. He smells like soap and memories of mornings helping him get ready for work—back when work meant hanging dry-wall. "I like this game we're playing, Becs. I could do it all damn day."

I unpin my arms from his hold, and wrap them around his neck so I can see my phone. *"Why are you in such a good mood?"* Cordy asks for me.

He kisses my neck. Just once. But enough for my mind and body to spiral into an abyss. "I got this text from a girl last night—a girl I've been borderline obsessed with for years—and I dreamt about her. It felt so real, so raw, and when I woke up, I swore she'd be in my bed with me. She wasn't, though. But she will be tonight, and so I'm going to make the most of the day until night falls, and she'll be in my arms again, her breaths warming my skin, her fingers in my hair, taking away this ache, this longing I've had for too damn long."

My eyes drift shut, his voice *still* like a symphony playing in my ears.

He rears back, his hands on my shoulders. Then he nods, as if answering a question only he knows. "You should definitely kiss me now."

"What?" I mouth, pushing against his chest. So damn cocky.

"Fine. Be stubborn. I'll kiss you."

I turn and walk out of his room, hearing his chuckle all the way down the hall. In the kitchen, Sadie's sipping on her coffee, nodding as Tommy talks to her between mouthfuls of cereal. "My Becca taught me how to take photographs." *Chew*. "She has special eyes, and takes pictures of adventures all over the world." *Swallow.* "Daddy said *our* Becca is in college."

Sadie smiles when she sees me. "So you guys..." She points between me and Josh, now standing beside me.

He throws an arm over my shoulders. "Me and Becs? No." He shakes his head. "She won't even kiss me."

Tommy laughs. "Oooh shit!"

"Don't swear, Tommy!" Josh snaps.

The reverse beeping of a truck has Josh moving to the window. "Supplies are here," he says, before turning to Tommy. "You ready to dig some holes, bud?"

Josh helps unload the truck while I sit on the porch steps with Tommy like we've done so many times before. He shows me the pictures he's taken on his very own Instagram account. The kid's five and has over twenty thousand followers, and a bunch of blurry skate shots.

Sadie's back in the house helping Grams change for the outdoor temperature.

Grams was a little standoffish when Sadie came in first thing this morning, but once Sadie explained that Josh had chosen her to help out, Grams seemed to accept her fate.

With hand signals, I ask Tommy if we can use his camera to take pictures of all the new potted flowers that just arrived. He agrees and tells me to come with him to choose the lenses. When we come back out, Grams is outside, her body so weak she has to hold on to Josh's arm to help her stand. I stand behind them, smiling while Grams gives Josh orders about plant placement, and I remember the first time I saw them like this. I hadn't yet gotten the nerve to come out, so I watched from behind the curtains of my bedroom, my interest piqued, my mind lost in wonder about the boy who would later steal my heart. My soul. My very existence.

"The roses should line the porch. I've always liked them there, and they do well in the shade," Grams struggles to say. "You know who loves roses, Joshua?"

"Who, ma'am?"

"My grandbaby Becca. Oh, I miss her."

Josh turns to me, his eyes as wide as mine.

Grams adds, "Did I tell you she's in college? Over in St. Louis. She's going to take the world by storm with her photographs one day. Just you watch and see."

Josh faces her. "Ma'am, Becca's not in St. Louis right now." He releases a breath, causing his chest to fall. "She's *here.*"

There are currently over 1,025,000 words in the English language and not a single one of them could ever describe what I feel when Grams turns around and sees me. Not when her eyes fill with tears. Not when she steps forward, her palms cold against my cheeks. And not when her eyes drift shut after recognition fills them, and she whispers my name like it's a stolen memory. Not even when she repeats the words of a little boy who so easily became my best friend. "Becca's home."

CHAPTER 30

BECCA

---

should

ʃʊd/

verb

1. used to indicate obligation, duty, or correctness, typically when criticizing someone's actions.

I help Sadie with Grams to settle in for the night, and then take any personal things from my room to the spare one, making space for Sadie to move in. I say goodbye to the curtains, the window, the wallpaper I once loved/hated, my chest aching and swelling at the same time. Then I begin to pack what little things I'm bringing back to St. Louis, and shoot off a text to Dad, keeping him informed with all that's going on with Grams.

My phone beeps with a reply no more than a minute later, but it's not from Dad. It's from Josh.

Josh: Look. I'm just going to be honest here. I've

> been out in the driveway nailing trick after trick for over an hour trying to get your attention. I've even treated your grams's porch steps as if they were the gnarliest three-stair I've ever ripped. I know you're heading off early tomorrow, so I'm working against the clock, but are you planning on coming out and kissing me any time soon? Or should I just stab myself in the chest, rip out my heart, and leave it out in the open?

With a smile, I set the phone on the nightstand and shower, using the time to come up with a response. When I get out, more messages are waiting.

> **Josh:** Stupid autocorrect.
> **Josh:** What I meant to say was *hi.*
> **Josh:** So hi.

Josh halts to a stop when I step out on the porch wearing one of Grams's long nightgowns. He waits for me to get to him, eying me from head to toe, before saying, "You look insanely hot, Becs."

Shoving his chest, I roll my eyes at him.

He stifles his laugh, then says, "It's about fire-trucking time you came out. I'm pretty sure I've been out here so long, my toes are bleeding. I think I need a nurse. Hey! You know a nurse, right?"

I take his hand, and practically drag him toward his apartment using my fake annoyance to hide the fact that I'm actually terrified of what will happen the moment we're in there. As soon as we're in his house, we switch positions. I let him lead me down the hall, toward the semi-darkness of his room, and once we're inside, he closes the door after me. I lean against it, using it as my emergency escape. "Tommy's over at Nat's," he says, and the fear inside me escalates. I don't know what I expected when I met him outside, but I figured it couldn't be too bad if Tommy was in the house. But he's not. We're alone. Just me and him and a thousand unanswered questions.

"So…" He rocks on his heels, his hands in his pockets while I flatten mine against the door, my fingers scratching at the timber as if it's somehow going to create a hole wide enough for me to escape through. "Why do you look so scared right now?"

After swallowing my nerves, I type on my phone and let the electronic words fill the silence. *"Because I am."*

He sighs before stepping forward. "Why?"

I chew my lip as I type out the message, then lift my gaze and watch his response when I tap my phone. *"After tonight, nothing changes, okay? I go back to college, and you go back to skating. This doesn't mean anything. Got it?"*

His eyes are slow as they lift to mine, then he shakes his head. "You can play your games. I'll play mine. But you're wrong, Becs. This changes *everything.*"

"Why? It doesn't have to," Cordy says.

He takes a moment, gathering his thoughts into words. "Because I'm in love with you, Becs. I've never stopped loving you."

My eyes drift shut, his confession knocking all sense out of me. I blindly reach for him and find his chest, then move up to his neck, my heart thumping with the abundance of insecurities infiltrating my mind. But it doesn't stop me from kissing him.

I kiss him until the questions disappear, and we're nothing but tangled limbs and urgent emotions on a bed of memories. Our hands touch, tease, re-familiarize. I get lost in his taste, in his kiss, in his words. Somewhere far, far in the back of my mind, I know it *should* feel wrong. But it doesn't. I want him this close. I want his lips all over me, his breath warming my skin, his hands drifting, touching, feeling me in ways I've feared and craved at the same time. I remove his shirt and skim my nails up his back. He squirms, a light chuckle escaping him. "Good to know you remember how much I *hate* that," he mumbles, his legs between mine, and his weight on his forearms.

I fight against his attention, the same time I fall deep in his web. My fingers lace through his hair, tugging harshly to pull him away from me.

"Stop?" he asks. *I should say yes.* I should push him away. I should do a lot of other things *but* kiss him harder, begging, pleading for him *not* to stop. He groans when I pull back, my head landing on the pillow. He's still holding himself over me, his hands in my hair. He licks his lips, tasting the aftermath. "That's all I get?"

I laugh, silent but real, and he nuzzles my neck, his body pressing into mine. I can feel his excitement against my center, his slow kisses like pure agony toying with my need. Then he starts to move, gentle thrusts setting my entire body on fire. He pulls away from my neck and a moment later, we're kissing again, moving together, mouths and tongues franticly searching and quickly finding a familiar rhythm. He rears back, his eyes on mine. "I missed you every day, Becs."

He feels so right.

So perfect.

Our fingers lace together, his palms pressing down on either side of my head. He keeps the kisses relentless, breaking only to catch our breaths, and I feel myself fading, rising and falling with the constant pressure building inside me. "Let me touch you," he says, his voice rough. "Fuck, I *need* to touch you." He doesn't wait for a response, though. He simply shifts to the side, taking me with him. His fingers brush the space between my legs. I know he can feel it—how wet I am—and I know what he wants to do. His mouth finds mine just as he pushes my panties to the side. He slides a finger inside me. Slow. Soft. Painfully arousing. Each movement is measured, calculated, deliberately prolonging my release. His mouth, his hands, his every touch bringing me closer and closer to the edge. He knows what I like, what I want, what I *need*. Because he knows my body better than anyone. Better than myself.

He rolls onto his back, taking me with him while his fingers continue to pleasure me. Now I'm on top, my hands and knees keeping me upright. He sits up, forcing me to do the same just as his thumb finds my clit, halting my breath. "Take your clothes off, baby."

He's so bad.

So, so bad.

With a grin, I do as he asks. My breasts fall free, nipples hard and needy an inch from his lips. His eyes drift shut as he leans forward, lips warm and wet when he takes me in his mouth. He keeps the same pace between my legs, slow and steady, and in my head I'm cursing, over and over, while I breathe harshly through my release. My body trembles and, God, I needed this. Needed *him*. I hold his head to my chest, using his body to keep mine steady. "God, Becs," he rushes out, his breaths as sharp as mine. I reach over to his nightstand where I know he keeps condoms.

"You should check the expiration date," he says.

My lips part.

He laughs quietly. "It's been a while." He shrugs. "And I haven't had a need to buy any more."

After checking the date, he lies flat on his back, his hands linked behind his head and a devilish smile across his lips. I rip the packet open with my teeth and pull down his boxers and sweats at the same time. Then I roll the condom over him, something I know he loves to watch. He groans when he slides into me, his fingers digging into my hips. Then he reaches up to grasp my nape and pulls my mouth to his.

Swear, there's no physical pleasure greater than Josh Warden inside me, his tongue dancing with mine, his moans filling the air while his hands worship every inch of my body.

"Stop," he grunts, hands holding my hips in place. "Fuck." He blows out a heavy breath. "If I make it three more seconds, that's what? Five seconds more than the first time we did this, right?"

I laugh into his neck, my eyes closing when his hands find my hair. I pull back and reach for my phone.

But you made up for it the third and fourth time.

His eyebrows lift when he reads the text. "So this isn't a one-time thing?"

I'm here all night.

Somehow, we end up on the floor of his living room, in our underwear, sitting cross-legged opposite each other, in a fort made of blankets, eating ice cream out of the tub. This is after making love in his bed, the shower, and the kitchen. We treat time like it doesn't exist, like our joy and laughter is the remedy to prevent the sun from rising and delaying my imminent departure.

"Do you *have* to leave tomorrow?" Josh asks.

I nod.

"Why?"

I drop my spoon in the tub and get my phone. Cordy relays for me, *"I have to work."*

He scoffs, sprays of ice cream flying from his mouth and landing right on my face. Laughing, he uses the blanket to wipe it away. "Who the hell works the day before Christmas?"

I soften my scowl. *"I do. Obviously. And I'll be working Christmas Day, too."*

"Oh yeah?" He eyes me sideways. "Doing what?"

I find myself smiling. *"Visiting the families from the center."*

He returns my smile with a wider one. "Say Something, right?"

Nodding, I have Cordy say, *"Yeah. I take the family portraits, and this guy I work with—Joey—he's going to dress up as Santa."*

His gaze lowers. "Joey, huh?"

I pat his head teasingly. *"I should tell you all about Joey,"* Cordy says for me.

Josh shakes his head. "I don't want to know."

"What?"

After dropping his spoon in the now empty tub, he says, "If you're with some guy back in St. Louis, and you just cheated on him or whatever, I don't want to know."

I pick up the spoon and use it to thump his forehead. Then type, *"I'm not a hussy."*

With a chuckle, Josh says, "Hussy?" He picks up his phone and holds it to his ear. "Becca? Yeah. She's here… hang on." He hands it to me. "2001's on the phone, they want their word back."

I give him the finger, but I'm laughing with him. *"What I was going to say was: he's a big fan of yours. He talks about you all the time. He was at the St. Louis Skate Tour finals just to see you. Something about a 720 gazelle you did in Miami…?"*

Josh cringes, then somehow gets tangled in the sheets and trips over himself. Seriously, I've watched YouTube videos of him doing triple backflips from thirty-foot cliffs and he struggles with blankets?

What?

I stalk him, okay?

There.

I said it.

Finally settled on his side, he faces me. "Does he know about you and me?"

I shake my head, pretending to scoop out the melted ice cream from the tub.

"So I'm your dirty little secret?"

I drop the tub, my mind spinning. Then I lie down, leaning up on my elbow so I can look down at him—at his eyes—eyes a mixture of sadness and sorrow. His gaze searches mine as Cordy says for me, *"Sometimes I want to tell him that I know you…"*

"I want to tell him about everything. But then I begin to type the words and when I read them back, it doesn't do us justice, and it doesn't seem right to tell someone in that way. The words are robotic. Rehearsed. It's impossible to explain our joy and our love and our pain. But I wish I could. I wish I could tell people how I felt. How I still feel."

He reaches up, his fingers moving my hair behind my ear. He whispers, "Still?"

"Yes. Still." I'm quick to add, *"But I meant what I said earlier, Josh. We can't let this change us. I've built a life for myself in St. Louis. I've made friends and I'm doing well in class and on the school paper. I volunteer at a place I love, and I'm getting a lot out of all the therapy I do."*

"I'm happy."

"For the first time in a long time, I'm happy. Not as happy as I would be if I got to see you more often. But not as miserable as I would be if you gave up skating to be with me."

He smiles at that, his hand cupping my neck while his thumb gently strokes my throat.

"So if one night with you is all I get, I'll take it and carry it with me. And I'll cherish it all the days we're apart."

CHAPTER 31

JOSHUA

I wake up the next morning and without opening my eyes, without feeling for her next to me, I know she's gone. I know because she's taken half my heart with her. It's the same way I felt when I woke up the last time we did this. The last time we said goodbye without saying the actual words. The difference this time is that it doesn't hurt. Because when I reach under my mattress for the worn envelope, the edges frayed, the content evidence of everything we are—hope overpowers the ache, overpowers the longing. And even though she's gone physically, she's not gone forever. And the fleeting words I spoke the last time she did this still hold the truth. *She'll always belong to me.*

I pull out the envelope and flip it between my fingers, over and over, the weight of its content shifting like the weight of my heart between moments of Becca. My breath falters as I empty it, photographs spilling onto my chest. I pick up one, an image forever burned in my mind, and I scan over it, looking for a new meaning. I do this with all of them, one after another. Pictures of the wallpaper in her old room, a shovel in the dirt, dying flowers, Tommy's sandpit, porch steps, fried pickles, and birthday cakes. There are dozens of Tommy, of Tommy and her, Tommy and me, and a single one of all three of us. I stare at that one the longest. I always do. And I wait for my heart to slow, for the reminder to hit me... that I lost her once, but I won't lose her again. That I loved her once, but I'll make her love me twice. And when I build the courage, those thoughts infiltrating my entire existence, I pick up the letter, her handwriting scrawled in bright red ink:

"If you want to learn what someone fears losing, watch what they photograph."

- Unknown.

CHAPTER 32

BECCA

"I spent my *childhood Christmases staring out of my living room window watching kids playing with their new presents out in the street, all while dodging insults from my mother. Occasionally, I'd dodge the empty bottles she'd down during those insults.*

"I'd see the smiles on parents' faces as they held each other, their children's laughter bringing them more joy in that one day than I'd ever seen with my mother. It's not to say she wasn't a happy person. She was. Or, at least, that's how I saw her. She'd laugh when she was drinking, smile when she had her boyfriends over. But it seemed her ultimate happiness came from my misery. Even when she took her own life and attempted to take mine with it, she was laughing. It was sinister, but it was there. There was never any real joy, though. There was never a moment where I caught her looking at me the way those parents had—with love and adoration.

"I'd spent almost eighteen years of my life without ever really knowing what that look felt like. I lived in silence, blinded by darkness, and even though I'd been with guys before, physically, they never looked at me the way I'd hoped. The way I longed for.

"And then I met Josh—who looked at his son the way those parents on the streets had. I wanted so badly to be that kid that I found myself

envious of a three-year-old. But I had no reason to be, because in time, I'd know exactly what it felt like to be the object of someone's affection. To be loved. To be adored. To be the reason for someone's joy.

"We loved in ways that can't be explained, hurt in ways that can't be justified. We felt every possible emotion under the sun. Literally. I'll never be able to feel the sun on my skin, never be able to hear the sounds of spinning wheels against concrete, never feel the safety of someone else's touch—and not think of Josh Warden.

"My mother didn't give me a lot. In fact, she did everything possible to deny me the basics of life. I never knew what I was missing. Not until she took away my ability to speak. It wasn't until I felt Josh's love that I realized that even though I couldn't speak, it didn't mean I didn't have a voice."

Joey stares at me, his eyes wide in disbelief beneath his Santa hat.

I'd told Josh that I'd wanted to tell Joey about him, I just didn't have the words. But last night, as I was preparing my equipment for the family photos today, it all came to me. I wrote it down in my journal, and Cordy just repeated it word for word.

"I'm sorry about your mom, Becca," Joey says.

I smile, because even though I appreciate his words, I can see him trying to push down what he really wants to say.

"But holy shit! You and J-Ward!?" *And there it is.* "I don't believe you. No fucking way!"

I roll my eyes and type, *"You don't think your worshipped god would be into a girl like me?"*

He laughs as he picks up yet another plate donated by the fine families of Say Something. Every house we've stopped at for the morning appointments gave us a plate of leftover breakfast. Now we're sitting in a practically deserted park, me with my gear and him dressed as Santa, taking advantage of their generosity.

"Don't get me wrong," he says, chewing on a strip of bacon. "It's just... I mean... it's J-Ward! The guy's, like, the king of kings in the skate world. At least to me, and you—you've sat there and listened to me talk about him and this entire time you knew him? That's fucking gnarly, dude. But I kind of still don't believe you."

I hold the phone between us and send a text to Josh.

Becca: Hey.

His reply is instant.

Josh: Hey! I was just thinking about you. Merry Christmas! How are the family photos going?

I show Joey the response, but he shakes his head, his shaggy surfer blond hair falling over his eyes. "I'm suspect. That could be anyone. It could be your dad and you've just put him in your phone as Josh. Is this a prank? It's a pretty shady one if it is."

I roll my eyes.

He mocks it.

Becca: It's going well. I'm in a park with Joey taking a little break. I told him about you.
Josh: About me? Or us?

I hold the phone right in front of Joey's nose, my eyes wide in question. "See?" I mouth.

He scoffs. "That's nothing."

Sighing, I type:

Becca: Us.
Josh: Huh. So you finally found the words?
Becca: They're as close to worthy as I can get.

Josh: Can I see them?
Becca: One day. Maybe.
Josh: I'll take it. So... this Joey guy? Do I need to be worried?
Becca: lol. He's harmless. Trust. Besides, he has more of a boner for you than he does for me.

"Don't tell him that!" Joey yells.

Becca: He doesn't believe me anyway.

Josh sends through a picture of him, his goofy grin from ear to ear. He's sitting at Grams's kitchen table, probably having lunch with her. I show Joey the image, but he just shakes his head. "That could be taken from any online image search."

Becca: He's still suspect.
Josh: Give the kid your phone.

I hand it to Joey, who's practically bouncing with anticipation. A second later, the phone vibrates in his hand, alerting him to a video call. He hits answer, and swear, he actually squeals like a girl when Josh's face lights up the screen. "Dude!"

Josh smiles. "Yo. What's up?"

"Shut the fuck up right now. No way!"

Josh laughs as he walks outside, closing Grams's door behind him. "It's Joey, right?"

"Y-yeah, man. Holy shit!"

"Nice Santa costume."

Joey rips off the Santa hat and fake beard from around his neck. "Fuck!"

With a chuckle, Josh says, "It's all good, man. It's a cool thing you guys are doing." He walks across the driveway toward the garage and a moment later, I hear the door lift. "What size do you ride?"

"Um. A 7.75."

"Dude, I got plenty of those," Josh says, flipping the camera so it's pointing away from him. The screen fills with a bunch of different style boards. "Take your pick."

If possible, Joey's eyes fall out of his head. "Dude!"

"I have the new J-Ward signature one. You want that?" Josh asks.

"The one that hasn't been released yet?!" Joey yells.

I wish I could speak so I could get in his face and say *"I told you so!"* but I can't, so instead I just watch and listen to Josh acting in a way I've never seen before. The old Josh would've shied away from the attention like he did the first time he took me to the skate park. This Josh... I don't even know this one. But I think I *want* to. And that has to mean something.

Josh records himself signing the board. "I'll send it to Becs. You should have it soon. I gotta jet, though. Becca's grams is waiting on me." He waves, a cheesy smile on his face. Then he hangs up, leaving Joey with his mouth open, and me with a cocky grin.

"Holy shit, Becca! I just... Josh fucking Warden."

Before I get a chance to respond, I get another text.

Josh: I'll be in Oregon during your spring break. I'm going to buy you a plane ticket. I'll e-mail you the details.

Josh: In other words, I miss you and I really want to see you, Becs.

Josh: If you can make it, I'll be the happiest man on earth. If you can't, I'll cry myself to sleep.

Josh: No pressure, though.

PART III

CHAPTER 33

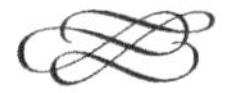

JOSHUA

"Twenty-one," Ry says, settling next to me on the plane to Dallas.

"What's twenty-one?"

"That's the number of days it takes to create a habit."

I shake my head and eye him sideways. Ry's the newest member of the team, plucked by Chris from a skate park somewhere in Cali. He's only eighteen and had never left the state until Chris knocked on his door, wooed his mother, and he's been with us ever since. That was three months ago. Now, he's attached himself to me, calling me his big bro. Not that I mind. He's more on my level than the other two guys. Maybe because he's young and new, and the fame and rewards of the skate world haven't ruined him yet.

We spend most nights on the road skating in random places while the others hit up bars and hit on girls.

"What habit?" I ask.

He points to the phone in my hand opened up to a picture of Becca pouting. She'd sent it to me New Year's Eve with the text "I miss you." I hadn't known what to make of it, or why she'd sent it, but I didn't care. I missed her, too, and I wished she was with me, or I with her, it didn't matter, and I told her that. We spent way too long, stayed up way too late, texting back and forth with promises to keep in touch. It was the only promise we made. Nothing about who we were to each other, or what we'd be the next time we were together. She's in my life and obviously thinking about me, and for the past two months that's been enough.

Ry says, pulling me from my thoughts, "If you don't talk to her or look at her for twenty-one days, she should be out of your system."

"Who says I want her out of my system?" I ask incredulously.

"Your face." He laughs once. "Who is she, anyway?"

"Becca!" Reece shouts, taking a seat opposite us. "One day, young Ry, you'll know all about Becca."

"She your girl?" Ry asks.

Reece answers before I can. "She'll always be his girl. Even if she has no idea she is."

~

Becca: How's Dallas?
Josh: Not as good as Oregon will be. You're still coming right?

The minutes feel like hours while I wait for her response.

Becca: I actually wanted to talk to you about that. I'm going to try my hardest to make it, but there's so much going on at the moment, I don't know if I can get away.
Josh: But it's spring break!
Becca: I know, but I have this huge paper due right after, and all the volunteers at Say

Something leave for break but the kids don't so...
Josh: Crushing my heart, Becs. But I understand.

I don't. Not really. I *should*, but I don't.

Becca: Are you mad?
Josh: No.
Becca: You're mad.
Josh: I'm not mad.

I'm a little mad.

Becca: You are.
Josh: I'm not really in the mood to start an argument I'm not gonna win.
Becca: Okay.

~

It's not that I want Becca out of my system. I just don't want her to infiltrate it. Which she has, and everyone's noticed. Even Ry. "Twenty-one days," he keeps telling me. So I try his stupid theory. Twenty-one days of no Becca.

I make it three.

The thing about Becca is simple. She's like walking into a warm house when you've been out in the cold. You don't realize how good it feels until you're surrounded by it. And when you head back out you know, in the back of your mind, that the warmth is still there and you crave it and miss it and want nothing more that to be enveloped by it. And yeah, I'm sure if you spend twenty-one long-ass, empty days in the cold, your body, your mind, grows accustomed to it just like I'd been in the year Becca and I had spent apart. But then she showed up just outside the Globe tour bus and I was reminded of the warmth, the comfort, and the longing kicked in and I wanted it. No. I *needed* it. Needed *her*. And so I stand on the balcony of some random hotel in Florida and take a picture of the night sky, moon out, stars surrounding it. I send it to her, along with the words:

Josh: You know that really cheesy thing people do when they're apart? They tell the other person to look at the stars and know that wherever they are, they're looking at the same ones?
Becca: Yeah? You want me to do that?
Josh: No. I want you to look at the stars and realize that there's a whole universe out there, and this world you and I live in is so tiny in comparison. But there's nothing—not a damn thing in the entire universe you could possibly ever say or do that would make me mad at you, Becs. I'm sorry if I made you think that.

An eternity passes before I get a reply.

Becca: Why have you been AWOL?
Josh: Because I've been in denial.
Becca: About?
Josh: About my feelings for you.

She replies with a picture of the night sky from her view.

Becca: There could be an entire universe out there, and you're right, we may be small in comparison. But what if you and Tommy make up the majority of my world? Does it really matter what else is out there?

Josh: Any update on tomorrow?
Becca: I'm really going to try. I'm going to pull an all-nighter, and make some calls to see if there's anyone who can cover my shifts but it's not looking good. I'm so sorry, Josh.
Josh: Just let me know either way, okay?
Becca: I promise.

I smile, nod, and make small talk with the fans, signing whatever they need while sitting at a table in the back of a new Check and Deck store in downtown Portland. At least that's where I am physically. Mentally, though? I'm nowhere.

Becca's plane should've taken off ten minutes ago with her hopefully on it. I haven't heard from her since we texted last night, and I didn't want to push her. So instead, I'm sitting here going out of my mind waiting for the news.

I pick up my phone, the ringer set to loud so I don't miss anything, and hope for some kind of miracle.

"Still nothing?" Nico, my teammate, asks. He's been with me the longest. Chris found him on YouTube skating in some abandoned warehouse in Puerto Rico. He set Nico and his family up in some mansion in California, the same area as Reece and Ry. So while they're all out there, I'm in North Carolina, and Becca's in St. Louis. Makes total sense, right?

As if right on cue, my phone alerts me to a message and I almost jump to read it.

Becca: I'm so sorry.

CHAPTER 34

BECCA

Seriously, I could watch Josh Warden forever. Even from outside the store, peeking through the window in between the gaps of the displays, it's enough to satisfy my longing. He signs whatever is placed in front of him, and smiles at his fans and female admirers. Okay, that last one I'm not too thrilled about, but whatever. It's still Josh, and I'm still close enough that I could smell him. Not that I am. That would be weird. The point is I'm here… he just doesn't know it yet.

The air conditioning pricks my skin when I step inside the store and my luggage gets caught in the doorway. I struggle aimlessly, my cheeks warming as I make a fool of myself. "I got it," someone says, holding the door open long enough for me to pull through my bag. I smile, thankful, only to realize it's Chris. "You finally made it," he says, pointing to someone who takes my suitcase and disappears. Chris leans in closer. "Does he know you're here?"

Chris had been the one to contact me a couple weeks ago, not knowing Josh had already invited me to Portland. But

Chris's invite came with a private plane and an extra four hours with Josh. I'd be stupid to say no, so I agreed, on the condition that we surprise Josh with it.

I shake my head and look over at Josh, my heart racing at the sight. He smiles at the two girls in front of him, but it's neither genuine nor forced. It's definitely not the way he smiles at Tommy, or at me, and that realization sets off something deep inside me. He quickly moves on to the next person in the line—a younger kid. He signs a board, a magazine, a shirt and the back of a phone, all with the same smile on his face, and gosh, he's beautiful.

Chris places something around my neck, pulling me from my daze, and I look down to see a lanyard with the tag: *Becca (Warden).*

Becca Parentheses Warden.

Becca *Warden*.

If I were ten, that name would be scribbled all over my notebook.

"You ready?" Chris asks.

After a nod from me, he leads me through the crowd with his hand on the small of my back while my heart picks up pace. We stop at the side of the table, where Josh is in the middle of talking to a fan. He glances up quickly when he feels our presence, but quickly goes back to the kid in front of him. He picks up a pen and starts signing the board, but he pauses halfway through, his eyes narrowing.

Then he looks up. Up. UP.

This time, nothing stops. Nothing. Not even him. His chair tips backward, his table forward, and the next thing I know, I'm wrapped tightly in his arms, my feet barely touching the floor while the world falls away around me.

CHAPTER 35

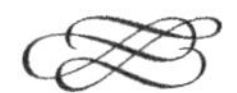

JOSHUA

warmth
wɔːmθ/
noun
1. the quality, state, or sensation of being warm; moderate heat.
2. enthusiasm, affection, or kindness.
3. **Becca**

I've done a lot of difficult things in my life. Raising Tommy on my own was one them. So is trying to balance my work with being a dad. But, sitting next to Becca for two hours, her scent invading my nostrils, driving me wild, and feeling her warmth next to me while wanting to throw her down on the table and make out with her face (What? She's hot!), and not being able to do so is pretty high up on the list. So is not punching every fan that looks twice at her. Occasionally, the roles get reversed, and it's a girl on the other side of the table. Some want shirts and posters signed, a few want body parts. That's when I really feel Becca's warmth—like lasers shooting from her eyes and into the side of my head. Kind of adorable, kind of hot, but mainly funny. Besides, she messed with my mind—told me she wouldn't be here—and now I get to enjoy messing with hers.

I sign what's in front of me: boards, shoes, stomachs, cleavage. Whatever. And take pictures with whoever wants them. Time ticks by slowly. So damn slowly I fight the urge to fake a sickness and leave with Becca. Go back to the hotel and you know… *talk.*

Stepping out through the storeroom doors and into the alley is like breathing in fresh, cool air for the first time in days. I take Becca's hand and pull her into me until there's no space between us, and I hold her. Memorize her. Find and lose myself in her. "I missed you," I tell her, squeezing her tighter.

She laughs. I don't hear it, but I feel her shoulders bounce and her breaths warming my chest. Too soon, the door opens, and my teammates join me. I introduce them to Becca just as the limo pulls up. Becca hops in first, and I follow, sitting closely next to her. I rest my arm behind her, and that's all I do because anything more could possibly get me arrested.

"So we finally get to meet *My Becca,*" Nico says once the car's in motion.

Becca looks up at me, her brow bunched. "My Becca?" she mouths.

I shrug. "Tommy talks a lot."

"My neck's all stiff," Reece says, rubbing the back of his neck, and tilting his head from side to side. "Or maybe it's just all the sexual tension in this car."

Ry attempts to stifle his laugh while I kick Reece's leg. He feigns hurt and points to Chris. "You see that? Write him up a warning!"

"Idiot," I murmur.

But Reece just leans forward, his eyes focused on Becca. "You're a lot hotter in person, My Becca."

I kick his leg again.

"Chris!" he shouts. "Josh kicked me!"

"You started it," I mumble.

Chris sighs. "Settle down, children."

My hand covers the handle of Becca's luggage while I roll it behind me, the other taking hers as we walk into the hotel lobby. "You want me to book you a separate room?" I ask, turning to her.

She nods.

I freeze.

Then she smirks.

"You're mean."

I hold her hand tighter and rush through the lobby toward the elevators, praying for the first moment alone. The second we're inside, I hit the button for the twentieth floor. I stare down at her, watching her bright green eyes lift to mine. "Hi," I say.

"Hi," she mouths.

After releasing her bag, I wait for the elevator doors to start closing before holding her face in my hands. But that's all I can do because the doors ping open again, and the rest of my team, plus Chris, step inside.

I drop my arms.

"Team cock-block to the rescue," Reece shouts.

Chris shakes his head. "Leave 'em alone."

Ry laughs.

Nico says, "I bet you can't wait to get her in your room, be alone, get down and nasty." He smirks at me, winks at Becs, then presses the buttons to every single floor between here and the twentieth.

"I hate you," I tell him.

Becca presses her face to my chest, hiding her laughter. I'm glad she thinks it's funny. I'm pissed.

Swear, an entire lifetime passes before we actually make it to our floor. I'm the first to step off, but not without a pocketful of condoms jokingly supplied by my so-called friends. I hustle Becca down the hall and into my room, making sure the door is closed, locked, secured, and then I grasp her hand when she starts to walk farther into the room. I gently push her against the wall just inside the door. "Where do you think you're going?"

She looks up slowly, her eyes meeting mine, her teeth working on her bottom lip.

I move in on her, smiling when her eyes widen. "You've been bad, Becs, messing with my head like that." I almost laugh when she rolls her eyes. Instead, I move closer until I'm flush against her. "You crushed my heart, and you know how fragile my heart is."

She smiles when she rises to her toes, her lips aiming for mine, but I don't let her have it. Not yet. I pull back just in time, and place my hands on her hips, pushing her away from me. "I'm mad at you."

Her eyes dance with amusement as her hands flatten on my stomach, beneath my shirt, and I almost lose it. *Almost.* Her touch is warm, *hot,* satisfying all my cravings, all my longing. I hold off, fighting the urges coursing through my veins. She raises her hands slowly, so damn slow I can feel the pulse in her fingertips as she makes her way up to my neck, taking my shirt with her. I try to think. Try to come up with a plan that will give me the control and right now—the way she's looking at me... I can't think of a single reason to stop her when she removes my shirt, wraps it around my neck, and then uses it to pull my mouth to hers.

She kisses me softly, slowly, as if we have all the time in the world. Her tongue darts out, tracing my lips, and—*knock knock.*

"Fuck off!"

Knock knock.

Frustrated, I sigh/grunt loudly, and reach for the door.

Reece quirks an eyebrow after peeking into the room. "Wow. It's been what? Two minutes and she's already got you on a tight leash?"

Becca pulls my shirt from around my neck and hands it to me.

"What do you want?" I ask, my tone clipped.

"Team meeting after the signing. Remember?"

Fuck. I'd agreed to have the meeting in my room because Becca wasn't supposed to arrive until later. Without an invitation, Reece enters the room, now joined by Ry, Nico and Chris, while I replace my shirt and hide my *excitement.* Becca grabs her laptop out of her bag and points to the door but Chris stops her by saying, "You need to be here, too."

I'm glad he says it because I was about two seconds away from throwing her over my shoulder, dropping her on the bed, and tying her down so she won't leave my side. I restrain myself, obviously. After taking her hand, I lead her to the bed where I sit next to her, my arm around her waist, annoyed and frustrated and *why the hell can't they just leave us alone?*

"You brought your camera, right?" Chris asks her.

Becca nods, a genuine smile crossing her lips.

"Good." He pulls out some papers from his folder, and hands them to her.

"An NDA?" I ask incredulously. "Really, Chris?"

He shakes his head. "Becca and I discussed her being the official photographer for the skate park tomorrow. Those are the release forms and payment contracts."

Becca reaches into her pocket, pulls out her phone, then types, her words relayed through the speakers, *"I don't want to be paid. I'm happy to do it."*

"Take Chris's money," Reece says.

"Yeah," agrees Nico. "Take it."

I look over her shoulder as she flips the pages, pausing when she sees the amount she'll be paid. *$300.* I glance at her just in time to see her eyes widen and her thumbs working franticly on her phone.

That's way too much! I can't accept—

She doesn't get a chance to play the message before I grab the phone and toss it across the room. I take a pen from the nightstand, add a zero at the end, and tell her, "Initial here." I point to new amount, followed by the blank space waiting for her signature. "Sign here."

She looks between Chris and I, but Chris gives her nothing. He'll pay her the three grand, even if it comes from me.

Becca shakes her head. "I can't," she mouths.

"It's called negotiation," Chris tells her. "And clearly Josh has been around Daniel too long."

"Daniel?" Becca mouths, raising her eyebrows.

"My manager."

She takes the notepad from the side table and writes: *I thought your mom was your manager?*

"I'll explain later."

"Is there a reason for this meeting?" Reece huffs.

"Yeah. Is there?" I ask, my question aimed at Chris while I tap on the paper to refocus Becca's attention. "Just sign it."

Becca does what I tell her, though clearly hesitant, before handing them back to Chris who simply says, "I'll pay you in cash tomorrow."

We spend the next fifteen minutes discussing the plan for tomorrow—a meet-and-greet/fun skate at a local skate park—and then the media and demo shoot agenda for the following day. All things I know about and all things I wish I could back out of because *Becca's here*. She's here and she's real, and the second the guys are out of my room, I let her know with my lips, my hands, my physical worship of her presence, just how much I appreciate that she is.

Being intimate with Becs on any given day is a blessing, but being with her after months spent apart is something else. I feel like I'm moving through a haze in a dreamlike state… like my hands grasping hers while she writhes beneath me is nothing more than a fantasy. In the past, I'd caught myself laughing, thinking about the way I'd be, the way I'd act when she was finally in this position. I'd expected her to be naked within seconds, and me finishing a few seconds after that, but that's not what's happening. Instead, we take our time, removing clothes one after the other, our breaths merging, warming our bodies until I've worked up a sweat and she's done the same. It's not until I reach for the condom in my wallet that she comes out of her daze "Pill," she mouths.

"*Bill*? I don't know who the fuck this Bill guy is but I'm Joshua Warden." I jokingly tap my knuckles on her forehead. "Remember me?"

She slaps my chest while silent laughter bubbles out of her.

"I miss you like this," I tell her, leaning up on my forearms, my fingers lacing through her hair.

She spreads her legs, welcoming me, and when the warmth of being inside her infiltrates my entire being, I remind her of how much I love her. How much I *need* her.

CHAPTER 36

BECCA

We spent the entire afternoon, evening, and night holed up in Josh's hotel room, only making contact with the outside world when we got hungry and ordered room service. His phone ringing wakes us the next morning. He mumbles an apology before shifting me off of him to reach for it in the pocket of his discarded jeans sitting on the floor. "It's Tommy," he says, his voice scratchy from sleep. "Video call."

I lift the covers over my bare breasts and try to get out of the bed, but he holds me to him, refusing to let me go. Tommy's face lights up the screen and the speakers crackle with his squeal. "My Becca! Nanni, look! My Becca's with Daddy!"

Josh chuckles while I hide my smile against his chest.

Tommy waves, his smile from ear to ear. "Hi, Becca!"

Josh runs his hand slowly up and down my arm while his mother comes into view on the phone. "Morning, Becca." She waves.

I smile and wave back.

Ella says, "Sorry for calling so early. I forgot the three-hour time difference. Tommy wants to tell you his new joke."

"Let's hear it, bud," Josh says.

"Ready?" Tommy asks, his blue eyes bright.

"Go for it."

"Why did the roll of toilet paper roll down the hill?"

"Why?" Josh asks.

"To get to the bottom." Tommy's cackle warms my heart. He adds, "What was it saying as it rolled down the hill?"

"What?" Josh replies.

Tommy throws his hands up. "Weeeeeeeeee!"

Josh shakes his head. "That's really funny," he tells his son, looking at him with love and adoration I no longer envied. "Hey, it's really early here, buddy. Becs and I need to get back to sleep, but I'll call you as soon as I finish breakfast, okay?"

"Okay, Daddy!"

"I love you."

"I love you, too, and I love Nanni and Ma'am and Mommy and Justin and Aunt Kimmy and Uncle Robby and Aunt Chloe and Uncle Hunt, and most of all, I love *My* Becca."

Josh smiles at him. "Bye bud," he says, before hanging up and throwing the phone across the room. He flips to his side, and wraps his arms and legs around me. A moment later, his eyes are closed and his breathing's even, and I try so hard to settle my mind so I can join him, but I can't. All I can think about is Tommy. I treasure his voice, his laughter, his excitement in seeing me.

"Becs," Josh murmurs. "Go back to sleep."

I press closer to him, letting him know I've heard him. But I can't go back to sleep. Not anymore.

He sighs when he flips onto his back, his forearm shielding his eyes. For a moment, I forget I'm naked and so is he, so I don't think twice about straddling his lap and pushing down on his shoulders. He links his fingers behind his head, the muscles in his arms and chest flexing with the movement, while I run my hands through his hair, knowing I'd give just about anything to be able to speak. To be able to tell him how happy he makes me. Even if it's just for the next two days… before I go back to a reality without him in it.

He sits up to switch on the lamp on the nightstand. Then he resumes his position, only now he has one hand behind his head, the other flattening against my stomach. "I like this view."

"I like it, too," I mouth.

His eyes narrow, his mind searching. "You lick the poo?"

"What?!" I mouth.

He laughs and sits all the way up, his hands on my waist and his gaze on my lips. "No. We should totally do this. I need to learn how to lip read. Say something else."

I mouth, "Something else."

Pressing his lips together, his eyes shift from my mouth to my eyes and back again. "Dumplings sell?"

I stifle my laugh. "You're the worst," I mouth.

He stares at me a long time. "Whores and squirt?"

Josh and I eat breakfast with his team, Chris, and Daniel, Josh's manager. I wait until we're back in his hotel room, skateboard parts and stickers strewn all over the floor, to ask him about his mother.

He takes a moment to answer, distracted by searching for a certain sticker to place on his board. "It was mutual. She thought that being my manager was ruining our relationship, and I agreed. Besides, the novelty of traveling wore off real quick for Tommy, and he said he'd rather stay home. Plus, she wants to be there so she can be around your grams. And, Tommy has to start kindergarten this year so Mom offered to home-school him for a while until things settled down for me. It kind of worked out well for everyone. Where the fuck are my Globe stickers?"

I get down on my knees and help him search for the right

stickers, while typing on my phone at the same time. *"You have to do this before every event?"*

"I normally do it the night before so I'm not rushing, but you know, I was a little distracted last night." He looks over at me, his bottom lip between his teeth and his gaze skimming my body.

I find the stickers with the Globe Shoes logo and hand them to him before sitting back on the bed and checking my camera gear. *"Are you nervous?"* Cordy asks for me.

"Not really." He sits next to me, and starts placing his sponsor's logos on the underside of his deck. "Are you?"

I'm quick to respond, glad I'm able to talk to him about it. *"A little. I've never really photographed action stuff before. I watched some videos on it when Chris asked me if I'd be interested. I'm scared one of your boards is going to fly right at my head!"*

Josh laughs. "I'll make sure the boys know where you are at all times."

I wait until he's done with his board and he's looking at me before I have Cordy say, *"You know there are pictures of us online from the signing yesterday?"*

"Yeah?" he asks, his eyebrows raised.

I nod. *"People are commenting, wondering who I am to you, and what my name is and stuff..."*

"So?"

I shrug. *"It's a little weird, no?"*

"Not really." He scratches the back of his head, and turns to me, his leg folded beneath him. "It's kind of part of my job, so I guess I'm used to it. People are nosy, and gossip is a marketing tool around here. But if you're not comfortable with it, I'll be sure not to play grab ass while we're out there today." I can tell he's half joking, half testing, waiting for a reaction... which I don't have, because I honestly don't know how I feel about any of it. It's not as if we've talked about what we are to each other, and I really don't want to be the center of anyone's gossip, true or not.

"We'll just play it cool today, all right?" he says, his tone calm. But I can hear the hurt in his voice, and I start to respond but he stands quickly. "It's no big deal, Becs. We can worry about it later."

The limo parks at the skate park built under some bridge. Outside, the crowd's formed, cheering loudly for a glimpse of their heroes. "Let's pray," Nico says.

I almost laugh, because praying seems so out of character for these guys. I wait for someone to crack a joke about it, but they don't. They just bow their heads and close their eyes, all while I look on in disbelief. Nico clears his throat, his accent full when he says, "Now I lay me down to sleep, I pray the Lord my soul to keep..."

Someone should probably tell them this is a bedtime prayer... not one used in hopes for luck before something important.

He continues, "...and if I die before I wake..."

The others join in sync, including Josh, "...I pray in heaven, I can skate."

The three-hour event flies by so fast I barely feel it. The first two hours were just the boys skating, showing off tricks, their love for their profession evident in their smiles and banter. During the last hour, the guys give the crowd the opportunity to earn giveaways—boards, shirts, sunglasses, and those stupid booty shorts. Reece suggests a wet T-shirt contest for those, to which—going by their hoots and hollers—the crowd agrees. Josh shuts it down real quick, eyeing me from across the way, obviously trying to tell me that it's not *at all* what goes on when he's on the road with the boys.

I shouldn't be worried, but I am. There's this constant tightening in my chest. It's there every time a girl calls his name, or when they smile at him in ways that makes it clear they want what I sometimes have… but the worst is when they speak.

They *speak.*

And I *don't.*

"Did you get some good shots?" Josh asks, his hand on my leg once we're back in the limo and away from prying, public eyes.

I nod, keep my head turned, and stare out the window, wishing for the same silence in my mind that's a constant from my lips.

As soon as we're back in the hotel room, he says, "You okay?"

With a shrug, I sit down on the edge of the bed and start removing my shoes.

He adds, "You haven't said a word since we got in the car."

My gaze snaps to his, my eyes questioning.

"You know what I mean," he says through a sigh. "Did something happen there?"

Nothing happened. But at the same time, it feels like everything's changed. *"Things have definitely changed, huh?"* Cordy says for me.

"What do you mean?" He leans against the desk on the other side of the room, his arms crossed, keeping his distance.

I chew my lip, my thumbs hovering over my phone as I choose my words wisely. *"You and me... we're not just a boy and girl playing house in your apartment anymore."*

"But we're still the same people, Becs."

I don't know if I agree with him, but still, I say, *"And you think it's enough?"*

He stares at me a long moment, his eyes narrowing more with each passing second. "What are we even talking about right now?"

"Nothing," I type quickly.

"Bullshit *nothing*." Josh pushes off the desk and squats in front of me. His eyes search mine, worried and confused. "What's going on? You overwhelmed or something?"

I shake my head, and after a loud exhale, I type, *"I get that this is your job. Your passion. And I know I'm being petty, but I just didn't expect all these girls around you all the time."*

He sighs, frustrated, but not at all surprised by my admission. "*That's* what this is about?" he says, standing quickly. He begins to pace, his hands locked behind his head. "We have two days together. This is our last night and you want to do this *now?*"

"I told you it was petty!" Cordy says. I wish she came with more than just a play button. Like a *whiny shout* one.

He stops pacing and turns to me. Shaking his head, he says, "It's just kind of rich that you're the one bringing this up. Especially when I've been faithful to you when you weren't even mine. When there was no faith left at your end, and you moved on with that other guy—"

"Aaron," I whisper. I don't know why I say it. Why out of all the things I could possible say it's *that.*

He tenses, his breath catching before his eyes drift shut and his fists clench. "I know his name. I just don't want to say it." He goes back to moving, pacing back and forth, all while I stay silent, my heart aching.

Sinking.

Breaking.

Josh rubs the back of his neck. "This is so dumb," he mumbles, turning away from me and toward the bathroom. "I'm going to shower." He removes his shirt, revealing the onset of bruises and scrapes on his back from today's skate session.

I'd seen him fall too many times to count, and he'd seemed momentarily frustrated, angry with himself, but he never once showed any sign of pain.

I stand quickly, drawn to him, my fingers reaching his back before the rest of me does.

He freezes in his spot, his shoulders sagging when my hand flattens on the sores. "It's nothing," he whispers.

After moving past him, I start to run the water in the oversized tub while he leans on the doorframe.

He watches me.

I watch the water.

We don't speak. Not when I turn the water off. Not when he strips naked and gets in the tub, then motions for me to join him. Not even when I sit opposite him, my soapy hands running slowly over the dark spots on his shoulders.

I wish I could take it back. Wish I'd never said anything. Because now the mood's turned dark, dull, taking away the shine from the rest of the time we've spent together. I run my finger over a scar on his right shoulder and finally make eye contact with him.

He swallows loudly. Then explains, his voice low, "I dislocated it one too many times. I had to have pins put in."

I nod while my hand moves down to his elbow, and I thumb the long scar I noticed while I was with him over winter break. "Last broken elbow. Bone popped out." His eyes are sad, just like mine. He lifts his hand, making the water cascade around us. "I have more scars than skin," he says, his lips curling at the corners. He reaches up, his thumb skimming the scar on my collarbone.

I freeze momentarily, my mind clouded by darkness.

At some point, I've expected him to ask about them, and I knew that I'd have to confront my past, but I also knew that no matter how much I thought about it, how many times I've played out this moment in my mind, I'd never be prepared. Never.

Josh presses his lips gently over the tough skin before pulling back and looking at me. First my eyes, then my lips, then down to my hands. His voice shakes when he asks, "You feel like sharing stories?"

I hesitate a beat, then dry my hands on a towel and reach for my phone on the counter. Josh pulls me closer to him, his hands on my hips and my legs wrapped around him until there's nothing left between us. *"Are you sure?"* Cordy asks for me.

He lifts his gaze. "Only if you are."

We take a moment, my pulse quickening and my mind racing while the air turns thick.

"It's going to hurt," I warn him. *"It'll probably hurt you to hear as much as it'll hurt me to tell you."*

"If you don't want to—"

"It happened when I was nine," I cut in. *"My mother was in a mood. More like a rage. She was cutting my hair and the end of the scissors dug right in."* I hold my head high, years of therapy helping to convince me that it's not my shame to carry.

Josh blows out a breath, my hair shifting with the force of it. Then he swallows loudly, his fingers moving up the middle of my back. I know what he's aiming for, and I'm not at all surprised he knows it's there. Like I said, he knows my body better than anyone. Better than myself. But he's never asked before, and he's asking *now*.

He taps the small lumps of skin between my shoulder blades. "Are these..." He can't even get the words out, so I do it for him.

"Cigarette burns. I was fourteen. She found out I had a boyfriend. The burns hurt as much as her knee pressed on my back." A sob fills my throat as I watch his eyes, my pain mirrored behind his

tears, his ache as strong as mine. His jaw tenses, fighting against the fear, the anger I can see building inside him.

I capture this moment, my gaze locked on his, and I memorize it, store it, treasure it as the first time in my life I'd felt a love greater than my own.

I wipe at my cheek as Josh's lips move to beneath my left eye, kissing the scar there. "And this one?"

"Are you sure you want to do this?"

"We can stop," he rushes out. "If you can't…"

After a shaky exhale, I type, *"She hit me with a pan, right before she dragged me by my hair, kicking, screaming and bleeding, toward her car. It happened just before the accident."*

He nods slowly, his glassy eyes never leaving mine. Then he kisses me, slow and soft, right on the long diagonal scar on the side of my neck. The scar that hurt the most. Not physically, but because of *why* it's there. Josh's voice cracks when he says, "I assumed it was from the seat belt in the accident, but then I found out you weren't wearing one so…"

I lick my lips, my mouth dry, and I can feel my pulse in my thumb, reminding me of its existence, of its need to be between my teeth so I can let the physical pain overpower the emotional one. I fight the urge, and instead, I use my thumb to type: *"It was from the accident. But not the seatbelt. She had a knife. She held it there."*

His eyes charge with rage, with hate, with all the things I've *tried* to feel toward the person who created the scars.

"She was dead a few minutes later," I tell him, like it somehow makes up for her actions.

Minutes pass while silence descends, and I wait for him to say something. *Anything*. When he finally finds his voice, the words he chooses surprises me. "Is she on your list of fears?"

Josh pulls me closer when my eyes widen in shock, his arms wrapping tight around me. "Your dad told me about it. I'm sorry. I didn't know if it was a huge secret or something. I just know that I was on it, and I mean, it has to be working for you… you conquered me, right?" His lips curve into a smile.

I nod slowly, my heart swelling at his words. *"Do you want to see it?"*

His smile is instant. "Only if you want to show me."

We dry off quickly, dress, and move hand in hand toward my bag where I pull out the piece of paper. It's way too worn, but too filled with memories to replace. I sit on the bed, waiting for him to do the same before I slowly unfold it.

He takes it from me, treating it just as carefully. I watch his eyes move from side to side, getting lower and lower down the list. He takes his time, his breaths shallow, his eyes narrowing at some that may seem confusing. "Ice cream?" he asks skeptically. "How is anyone afraid of ice cream?"

I type out the reason, feeling his breaths on my shoulder as he reads what I've written, and when I'm done, he stares right ahead, his mind lost, his anger brewing. "It's okay," I whisper.

Shaking his head, he slowly turns to me. "I think it's just… you've never really spoken to me about it so it's a little overwhelming…."

"I know," I mouth.

He clears his throat. "I wouldn't have cared," he says. Then quickly adds, "I mean, I would've cared about what happened to you, but you have to know that it wouldn't have changed the way I feel about you."

I bite my thumb gently, not knowing how to respond. I've thought about it a lot in the time we spent apart, mainly when I was cooped up in the "Personal Development" center back in North Carolina. It was a psychiatric hospital filled with patients suffering from severe depression. Some, like me *then*, had tried to find a way out, and some, like me *now*, were fighting the battle one day at a time. Cordy asks for me, *"What's that thing Chloe told you? Those words that are on the magnet?"*

"Choose to be happy, fire truck the rest?"

I nod. *"That's why I didn't tell you," I type. "Because while you chose happiness, I chose peace."*

"You chose peace," he repeats, his voice barely a whisper. He looks down at the list again. "So you've marked off all but one?"

I nod again.

He reads the last item aloud, *"Go back to the house of nightmares and face my demons."*

I don't react when he lifts his gaze to mine, so he goes back to the list, his fingers skimming the lines used to cross out each item. Then he moves to the dates marked next to each one. His throat bobs when he swallows, his finger paused over the fourth line. *Be intimate again.* He taps on the date, *December 23rd*, and exhales loudly, realization setting in. "You and me," he says.

I don't know if it's question or statement so I don't offer a response.

After a while, he breaks the silence. "So you were never with Aaron…?"

I wait for him to look at me before shaking my head.

"But you had feelings for him, right?"

I inhale deeply, knowing that lying to spare his feelings would only make things worse. Besides, I've bared all my truths, why stop now? *"I loved him."*

He sucks in a breath, his gaze shifting away from me. "So why didn't you ever…"

I tap on his arm, making him face me so I can see his reaction when I tell him, *"I loved him, but I didn't love him in a way that could justify sharing something that important with him. I saved that for you, Josh."*

He chews his lip, nodding slowly. "So you loved him the way I love Nat…" Again, neither a statement nor a question. "You worry about me cheating on you, Becs?" he asks, his eyes searching mine, while mine question his. "Why isn't that on your list?"

I push down the sob forming in my throat, just like I push

back the tears pricking behind my eyes. *"Because my fear isn't that you'll cheat on me."*

"Then what is it?"

I sit still, my thumbs paused over my phone as I let my thoughts consume me, let them own me and control me, until the words form and I allow them to fill what little space is left between us. *"My biggest fear is that you'll wake up one day, tired and miserable because you've spent yet another night consoling me, protecting me from my nightmares. You'll look at me and realize that I'm not the perfect girl you made up in your head. I'm not even close. I'm broken. Shattered."*

His breaths are harsh by the time I find the courage to look up at him. He seems lost, distant. He rubs his eyes—eyes worn and tired and miserable, just like I've imagined when I've pictured him in the way I just explained. He releases a breath and places The List carefully on the bed before turning his entire body to face me. He takes both my hands in his and says, "I get it, Becs. I didn't show you how I felt, how much you meant to me. But I'm here now, and I'm not letting you go until I give you everything I am." Each word is clear, concise, spoken with clarity and purpose. "And if it's still not enough, if you still won't believe me, then I'll keep trying. Over and over. Until you realize that you could have come to me shattered, broken, in an infinite of pieces, and I would've made you whole. I would have loved you. Every damaged piece of you. In all way and for always."

Tears escape from my eyes, wetting my cheeks. They fall onto our hands, the same time I fall into *him.* "I love you," I mouth.

He quirks an eyebrow. "Olive juice?"

CHAPTER 37

JOSHUA

The shower running wakes me the next morning. Becca's not in my arms, not beside me, but her bags are still here so I know she hasn't left. Through the curtains, I can see the sun's already up. I reach for my phone and curse when I see the time. It's almost noon, which means Becca's leaving in half an hour. She's going to visit Chaz for a couple of days before going back to St. Louis. The team has a day full of stupid interviews before we head off to… I don't even know where. The only thing I know is that I'm not ready to say goodbye, and so without thinking, I take a page from Tommy's book, get out of bed and rush to hide all her bags and clothes in the closet. I put her laptop and phone in the safe, set the code, and quickly get back into bed and pretend like nothing happened. I keep my back to the bathroom and my eyes closed when I hear the shower switch off. A moment later, the door opens.

Her footsteps sound around me, moving from one spot to another. I feel her next to the bed, her hand on my arm, slowly shaking. I don't budge. Okay, maybe I smile. And maybe she sees it because she playfully slaps my face. I open my eyes to see hers narrowed at me. She mouths something—I don't know what, but I'm pretty sure the word "where" and "fuck" are thrown in there.

"What's wrong?" I tease.

She throws her hands in the air while her lips move again, but they're moving way too fast, and even if I cared enough to try to read her lips, it'd be impossible. She's naked beneath her robe. I know, because when she leans over me to look beneath the blankets behind me, I get a glimpse of her bare breasts, and I chuckle. She smacks me on the back of my head when she straightens up, so I do the only thing I can think to do. I pull on the strap around her waist and undo her robe, giving me a perfect view of her naked form. She rolls her eyes, but I can see the amusement in them, and because I'm the luckiest fire trucking man on earth, I know she'll give in to me in three…

She removes her robe completely.

Two…

She reaches for my phone and types away.

One…

She shows it to me. *We have ten minutes.*

I throw the covers off me and pull her down until she's lying on top of me, her body flush against mine. "Have you learned nothing, Becs? I only need ten seconds."

Fifteen minutes later we're satisfied, but we're still in bed, still naked, still delaying the inevitable. "I don't want you to go," I tell her, my lips meeting the skin just below her belly button.

One of her hands finds my hair while the other types away on my phone.

"I don't want to leave you, either."

"So don't."

"Josh."

My mouth moves from her stomach to her hips and I kiss the bones sticking out beneath her perfectly smooth, dark skin. "You've lost a little weight since I've seen you last. Make sure you eat, okay?"

"I'm just busy," the phone says for her.

I glance up at her. "Well, make time. You can't be beating yourself up physically. It's not healthy. Three meals a day, Becs. Make sure you drink lots of water, eat all your fruit and vegetables."

She tilts her head and smiles down at me. *"You like me."*

I make my way up her body so I can *see* her. See *my* emerald eyes clear of pain and despair, see her raven dark hair splayed across the pillow, see her lips… lips I've craved and now tasted, and I wonder how it's going to be possible for my heart to function when she won't be around to make it beat. Make it live. Make it ache in a way that lets me know that living is just breathing, but living with *her* means living with purpose. With awareness. With love.

Her smile turns to a frown as her eyes search mine. "I love you," she mouths, and I convince myself that it's enough. It has to be.

"You're coming home for summer break, right?" I ask.

Moments of silence pass before the phone says, *"St. Louis is my home."*

I sigh. "So that's a no?"

She removes her hands from around my neck and brings them between us so she can type with both hands.

"I wanted to tell you in person but it never felt like the right time. I got offered this amazing paid internship on a statewide online newspaper and I'd be stupid not to take it."

I drop my head, my forehead meeting the pillow beside her.

"But I've already told them that I want some time off."

I lean up quickly, my eyes snapping to hers. "When? Give me the dates!" I take my phone from her and open up my calendar.

Now we're both holding the phone while she swipes at the screen, looking for the date. Her hands freeze, her eyes cast downward, and it's all I need to see for the disappointment to kick in. She taps on the dates and brings up my schedule in Hong Kong, then opens the Notes app:

I checked your website for your tour dates and it had nothing for these dates! I can't change them. I had to fight for them as it was!

"I know. Hong Kong host this gnarly yearly event and they don't announce a venue or the competitors until two weeks before. It's invite only, and it's Nico's first one. I promised I'd go."

She pouts, looking as dejected as I feel.

I kiss her softly. "I'll make it work, okay? I'll find a way."

CHAPTER 38

BECCA

I look out the window while the cab driver speaks. "You visiting family?" he asks, watching me through the rear view mirror. "Where you coming from?"

I point to my throat and shake my head, then refocus on the trees that line the streets and the rays of sunlight filtering through the leaves. I wind down my window and inhale deeply, feeling the spring sun against my cheeks. Then I close my eyes and rest my head against the seat. I recall everything I felt the first time this happened. The fear of uncertainty had wreaked havoc on my mind and I was so afraid of the woman sitting next to me, a woman I would later call Grams. She spoke to me softly, gently, like she knew how I felt but understood me anyway. Now, I'm feeling it all over again... afraid and uncertain, only this time it's because I have no idea how she'll see me, or if she'll see me at all.

The house is eerily quiet when I get here. Maybe because I'm used to seeing Josh and Tommy outside, hearing their laughter mixed with Grams's, or maybe because Grams isn't in the kitchen or on the couch reading a book. Maybe it's because I feel like an outsider, and it feels strange that I just used a key to let myself in. I carry my luggage up to the guest room, glancing quickly inside Grams's old, now empty, bedroom, and then into my old, now Sadie's, room. I drop my bags just inside the room, and decide it's best to wait for Sadie and my grandmother outside. Being in the house brings out the fear, brings out the uncertainty. I start down the stairs, and that's when I hear the front door open and my grandmother's voice. "I know, Joshua," she says, clearly on the phone. "She should be here very soon. Oh, I'm so excited to see her. Did you lovebirds have a good time together?" ... "That's great! Is she just as beautiful as ever?"

I make it known by the loudness of my steps that I'm here and that I'm waiting. I think she sees me before I see her because I'm greeted with a squeal, followed by a whimper as she covers her mouth. Her eyes are already filled with tears, just like mine. Slowly, she stands up from her wheelchair and moves toward me. "I have to go, Joshua. My Becca's home."

JOURNAL

It's amazing—that one simple word can mean so much.
MY.
In most cases, my in front of your own name may seem wrong, like you're nothing but a mere possession.
But it my case, it's the opposite.
It means I belong, I'm loved, and I'm wanted.
And when you spend the first eighteen years of your life alone and discarded, searching for someone to claim you as theirs, my means everything.
My is the air in my lungs.
The light battling my darkness.
The hero fighting my villains.

CHAPTER 39

BECCA

Grams feels so thin, so weak, so frail beneath my touch. I'm almost too scared to hug her back. Josh had sent me updates, along with pictures, but none of them could've prepared me for the woman standing in front of me. We only spend five minutes together, her asking me questions and me typing out answers, before it becomes clear she's struggling to stay awake. Sadie notices too and tells her it's time for bed and that the walk they'd been on when I got here would've tired her out.

Grams doesn't fight her, only nods and points to the bathroom. Sadie helps her walk there, and I watch, helpless and confused when I see Sadie go in with her. Maybe Josh was holding out on me, not wanting to give me the truth to spare me the pain of how bad things truly are with her. My mind switches from *This is the new normal* to *Maybe she's just having a bad day* over and over in the few minutes it takes for them to finish their business in that tiny room.

Sadie gets her settled in her bed, and only now do I realize that it's not *her* bed, not the bed that was here the last time I was, and not the bed I found myself crawling into when the pain, the suffering, the longing became too much. Now, it's the same type they had in her hospital room, the same type I've spent countless nights in after feeling the wrath of my mother post "episode."

I hold Grams's hand until she falls asleep, which doesn't take long. Then, as morbid as it sounds, I grab my camera from upstairs and take pictures of Grams in her peaceful state. There's so much a lens catches that the eye doesn't, and I plan on spending the entire night searching for those things. I want to study the expression on her face, the wrinkles that trace the outline of her lips. I want to compare the two of us and find similarities. It's clear my eyes came from my dad, which means that he most likely got them from his. Grams's eyes are a dark brown. Almost black. It should be impossible that so much light, so much hope, can come from such darkness.

When I'm done, I take my camera back upstairs, but before I look at the images, I send a text to Josh.

Becca: How come you didn't tell me how bad things were with Grams?

Josh: Because they're not...?

Becca: She's in a hospital bed, Josh. She needs help going to the bathroom. You never mentioned those things.

Josh: I guess I just didn't see it as such a big deal because they were progressive. It's not like it happened overnight. I'm sorry. I should've told you. She was really excited to see you. Did she recognize you?

Becca: Yeah.

Josh: So that's a good thing, right?

Becca: I guess, but I feel like I should be doing more. You're taking on so much of this and it isn't fair to you. I want to be here with her. I think I'm going to drop out and move in.

I don't know why I said it, but before I get a chance to rethink it, I've already hit send. Truth is, I was toying with the idea even before I saw Grams. Spending that time with Josh was like a slow, sweet form of torture. I know it's dumb, wrong, stupid, pathetic—all the possible words to describe a girl who'd give up everything just to be closer to the boy she loves… and I'm not going to do it. Like I said, I was just toying with the idea.

Right?

Right.

Josh: Shut up, idiot.

I smile at his response, half amused and half relieved.

Becca: What? I could be serious?!
Josh: Even if you were, I wouldn't let you.
Becca: Why not?
Josh: For a plethora of reasons.
Becca: Give me two.
Josh: Reason one… It's not as if it's *just* college in St. Louis. You have friends there. You have Say Something. You have the school paper. Internships. And most importantly, you have all your therapy there. You can't just up and move and forget all that exists.

Wow. Seems like I'm not the only one who's thought about it.

Josh: Reason two: I love you and I won't let you.
Becca: I love you, too.
Josh: You won't be saying that in ten years when I'm retired and have a beer gut and receding

hairline and mangled bones and scarred skin and walk with a limp because I've snapped my ankle eleventy-three billion times.

Becca: I'll be saying it always, Josh, even if you're not around to hear it.

Josh: You do insane things to my heart, Becca Owens.

Warming at his response, I lie down on the bed, the lack of sleep from the past few days catching up with me.

Becca: What am I supposed to do about Grams?
Josh: You hope for a better tomorrow.
Becca: And if it doesn't come?
Josh: Then you cherish a greater yesterday.

Sadie knocking on my door jerks me awake the next morning. I rush to answer it, panic pumping through my veins. "Hey," she says, smiling wide. "Josh is on TV. Thought you might want to watch him."

Relieved, I shrug on a sweater and make my way downstairs where Grams is sitting up in her bed glued to the television. "There he is," she says, pointing to the screen. "There's my Joshua. Isn't he handsome, Sadie?" she calls out, glancing at me quickly. Her face falls and she looks behind me. "Who are you? Where's Sadie?"

"I'm here," Sadie answers, walking into the room with two coffees in hand. She hands me one before sitting on an armchair on the other side of the bed.

Grams is still looking at me, her head cocked, gaze blank. It's not until Josh's voice fills the room that she tears her eyes away from me. Josh and his teammates all take up spots on a large couch, a huge widescreen television behind them showing a highlight clip of them skating. "Sorry," Josh says, phone in hand.

"You texting?" the male host asks.

"Yeah. I apologize. This is really rude of me." Josh shoves the phone in his pocket while his team laughs.

"I bet it's a girl," the female host says.

"Or twenty," replies the male one.

The woman on the screen giggles.

The guy adds, "What's that like for you? Fame and no-doubt fortune, plus that adorable son of yours... Boys want to *be* you, and the girls... well, you must have them hounding at you."

Reece chuckles.

"Just one girl," Josh says, shaking his head. "And she *barely* tolerates me. Believe me."

Grams laughs, a sound that brings back memories of easy summer days. "He's talking about Becca," she mumbles. "All he has to do is see the way Becca looks at him. She adores him. Stupid boy."

Yeah. Stupid boy.

Sadie matches Grams's laugh, but her eyes are on me.

I take a chance and hold Grams's hand. Her eyes snap to mine. "Sweetheart," she practically squeals. "When did you get here?"

Sadie tells me that Tommy will be around later that evening so I have the day to spend with Grams if I want to. She also tells me that today is a good day. Grams woke up somewhat alert and with more energy than she normally does, which means she'll want to go for a walk through the park—the same park the police found her in the night all this started for her. It's only two blocks away, but Grams needs a lot of help, and can't be out long because of her deteriorating immune system. Normally, Sadie drives there and pushes Grams's wheelchair from one end of the park to the other and back again.

We go the park with Grams huddled under layers of blankets. I push her chair while Sadie follows a few steps behind with a paper bag full of groceries. Apparently, Grams has been doing this most of her life since she moved into her house—going to the park and handing out food to the few homeless. Strange I wasn't made aware of it during the almost eight or so months I spent with her, but then again, she'd disappear for hours at a time, telling me she had errands to run, and I chose not to tag along, finding it more important to dwell on my past or, later, spend time with Tommy. It dawns on me that I know very little about my grandmother. Besides the fact she goes to church and had my father at sixteen, I don't really know her at all. And now, it might be too late to ask.

"Stop, Sadie," Grams says. I don't correct her. She points over at a couple of people sitting in front of a bush, their few possessions in a garbage bag settled next to them. Grams waves and shouts, "Good morning, Johnny!"

I wheel her over to them while Johnny smiles at her. "Our angel of hope," he sings.

Sadie hands them a loaf of bread, a large bottle of water, and jars of peanut butter and jelly. Grams spends a good fifteen minutes with them, talking about anything and everything. She asks the same questions a couple of times, but the couple continue to smile, repeating the same words already spoken. They seem to understand Grams's illness. Heck, they probably understand it more than I do. And if what Sadie said is right—that Grams has been doing this a while—they probably see her decline as "progressive" just like Josh said. The couple pushes aside the worn-out blanket covering their legs so they can stand and hug Grams goodbye, and when they do I notice the plastic bags surrounding their feet. Grams must see it, too, because she gasps. "What happened to your shoes?" she says, her voice laced with sympathy.

Johnny shrugs. "No big deal, angel," he says, waving a hand in front of him. "Someone obviously needed them more than we do."

My heart tightens at his words.

The lady with Johnny must see my reaction because she smiles and pats my arm. "It's okay, sweetie," she coos.

I pull my phone out of my pocket, type out a message and have Cordy say, *"Grams... you know who has a garage full of shoes?"*

CHAPTER 40

BECCA

Grams goes back to sleep after our outing, and I go back to my room. I'm in the middle of editing the photographs I'd taken last night and earlier today when I hear a knock on my door that has my breath halting and my stomach flipping. The knocking sounds again, fast and light, letting me know exactly who it is even before I answer it.

Tommy's grin is all consuming. I fall to my knees, my arms wide and ready for him. He barrels into me, holding my neck tight to his chest as he sways from side to side. "I missed you," he whispers, and I swear, my heart physically expands, escapes from my chest and falls right into his little hands.

He pulls back, his eyes on mine. "Nanni's at Dad's making dinner. You want to come over and play with me?"

I nod, standing slowly and taking his hand.

"We have to be really quiet. Ma'am's sleeping."

"Okay," I mouth.

"Follow me." Tommy releases my hand so he can tiptoe down the stairs, using the rail to help him. As soon as he's off the steps, he lays flat on his stomach and looks up at me, holding a finger to his mouth. After I nod, he waves for me to join him on the floor, and I do, because who the hell can say no to a Warden boy?

As silently as possible, we army crawl past the kitchen, into the living room, and toward the front door. Tommy points to the doorknob above us, and I reach up and turn it as slowly as possible. Once outside Tommy says, his voice back to normal, "Ma'am sleeps a lot now. She doesn't play like she used to." He picks up a skateboard leaning against the house, flies down the porch steps, jumps on the board and kicks, then pushes, off the ground. He rolls the ten feet toward the bottom of the apartment stairs before jumping off and turning back to me. "You coming?" he asks.

I realize I'm still standing on the porch, too fascinated with watching him that I haven't even began to move. I put one foot in front of the other, my movements slow, my fascination increasing. Tommy waits at the bottom of the stairs, holding the skateboard under his arm. He's wearing a backwards cap, a gray Globe shirt, dark skinny jeans and a pair of Globe shoes that look way too big for his feet.

He looks so much like Josh it's scary.

"What's wrong?" he asks.

I shake my head, and he starts to move again.

He even climbs the stairs like Josh.

Opens the front door like Josh.

Slips off his shoes like Josh.

Throws his skateboard on the couch like Josh.

"He's changed a lot the last couple of months," Ella says, catching me staring at her grandson. "He thinks he's all grown up." She wipes her hands on a dishtowel as she walks toward me. As soon as she's close enough, she hugs me gently.

There's something safe, yet completely unfamiliar about being in her arms. My stomach flips as she looks down at me, her eyes seeming to hold a secret only she knows. "It's so good to see you," she says, pulling back and settling her hand on my cheek. "Did you have a good time with Josh?"

I nod, afraid to make eye contact in case she can somehow see *my* secrets.

"And you liked Portland?"

Another nod.

"Are you hungry?"

I chew my lip and glance at her quickly. Then offer another nod.

"Becs and I are going to play in my room," Tommy says, taking my hand and dragging me away.

Even his room has changed.

There are no longer posters of trains and Pixar characters covering his walls. In fact, there's nothing on his walls but the chipped blue paint Josh told me Tommy had picked out himself just before his second birthday.

Tommy sits on his bed, leans against the wall and starts tapping on his iPad. He's not actually doing anything, just tapping away, opening and closing apps. "Daddy loves you, right? That's why he asked you to meet him in Poland."

With a smile, I have Cordy say, *"Portland?"*

"Daddy didn't ask me," he says through a sigh. His eyes lift, eyes full of sadness and confusion. "I don't think daddy loves me anymore. Not like he used to."

My mouth opens, a thousand words spinning in my mind. "No," I mouth, shaking my head and sitting next to him. *"Your daddy loves you so much,"* Cordy says for me.

Tommy shrugs. "Mommy's coming home soon, and her and Justin are getting married, so he'll be my new daddy like last time."

A knock on Tommy's door saves me from responding.

"Dinner's ready," Ella says.

"Little trees?" Tommy asks.

Ella laughs. "Yes, little trees. And carrot stick logs and—"

"Pea sea!" Tommy jumps off the bed, and pulls me up by my hand, his heartbreaking confession already forgotten. "You want to be a T-Rex with me?"

~

Going by Tommy's expression, I'm the best damn vegetable artist in the world, something I can now add to my list of small achievements. Our vegetable land goes beyond his plate, onto the table, through the bowl of fruit in the middle, and ends on a cookie tray. I make little cavemen from tater tots joined together with tiny slices of carrots, and even make their clothes from green beans. I realize the food's cold, but I don't care, and neither does Tommy. "It's past his bedtime," Ella says, but I can see she's enjoying this as much as we are.

"Five more minutes," Tommy tells her, his tongue out, concentrating on placing the peas in a pile to create a wave in his "Pea sea."

Fifteen minutes later, we're all standing around the table (Tommy on a chair) with our hands close to our chests pretending to be T-Rexes. "Ready?" Tommy whispers.

Ella and I nod.

"Free. Two. Ready. Set. One. Go!"

Swear there's nothing funnier than watching Tommy demolish an entire table of vegetables with only his mouth and tiny little T-Rex arms.

Wait.

I was wrong.

There's nothing funnier than watching *Ella* do the same thing.

"Come on, Becs!" Tommy yells, an entire caveman in his mouth.

"Neh Mecs!" Ella struggles to say, green beans and carrots falling form her lips.

In another world, another life, being with Josh and Tommy, even with Ella—belonging to a world I'd once desperately longed for—this would've been enough.

Maybe it still is.

I listen to Tommy's cackle mixing with Ella's giggles, and I take a mental photograph of the moment and store it safe in my heart, and I make a promise to myself to keep it there... even if I lose it all, I'll cherish this moment as *a greater yesterday.*

With Tommy showered and clear of any food scraps, we crawl into his bed together so I can spend what little time I have here with him. Tomorrow morning, I'll be gone again.

We start to video call Josh from Tommy's iPad while Tommy tells me, "Daddy doesn't answer too much."

But Josh does answer this time—from what looks to be a crowded restaurant. Josh smiles when he sees us, two days' worth of growth covering his jawline, his hair scruffy as always. "I was hoping you'd call," he shouts, moving through the crowd until he finds a quieter spot. "You guys having fun?"

"Yep," Tommy shouts. "Daddy, want to hear my new joke?"

"Go for it, buddy."

"How do you make a tissue dance?"

"How?"

Tommy picks his nose then shows it to Josh. "Put a little boogy in it."

"Dude, that's gross."

"But funny, right?" Tommy says, his body shifting with his laughter.

"And gross."

"Becs made the best vegetable land!"

"She did, huh?" Josh says, eyes wide in mock surprise. "I guess I'm gonna have to step up my game when I get home."

Tommy shrugs. "Becca can just stay here, and then you don't have to come home at all."

"What?" Josh's smile drops, uncertainty clouding his features. "You don't want to see me?"

Another shrug for Tommy.

I can see the thousand questions fleeting through Josh's mind, but before he gets a chance to respond, someone calls out his name. For a split second, Josh looks away from the camera, jerks his head at whomever, and then comes back to us. "I'll be home soon, okay?"

"That's what you said last time," Tommy says, but his voice is low, masking his hurt and I don't think Josh hears it, or sees it, because he simply says, "I'll call you later, bud." And just like that, he's gone.

Tommy stares at the blank screen. The longer he does, the more painful it becomes. Frustrated, he throws the iPad across the room, and crosses his arms over his chest. "Will you read me a story?" he murmurs, a scowl etched on his features.

It takes a moment for the shock of his actions to pass, and when it does, I nod slowly and select a book from the shelf built into his bed. I pull out my phone and start to type exactly what's written in the book. Tommy's hand covers my phone, his grip as tight as the tick in his precious little jaw. "I said *read* me a story."

Shaking my head, I keep my eyes on his and, with a struggle, pull my phone from his grasp to type, *"But you know I can't speak. Right, Tommy?"*

Arms crossed again, Tommy yells, "Yes you *can*!" He holds up three fingers between us. "See? Three fingers. That means we *talk*. One means we don't. Two means we whisper. Three means talk. Now *talk*!"

"Tommy," I mouth, tears pricking my eyes. He snatches my phone and throws it across the room, creating a dent in his wall.

My jaw drops, and I look back at him—at nothing but the anger simmering in his eyes.

He inhales through his nose.

Exhales the same way.

"I *hate* you!" he screams.

I cover my head.

Ella enters the room. "What's going on?"

"Becca won't read me my book!" Tommy yells, standing in front of me. "I *hate* her."

"Tommy!"

I wipe at my tears, tears that came on so quickly I had no idea they were there until I tasted them on my lips.

"You're a stupid head!" Tommy yells.

I force myself to look at him.

"You're never around, and when you are you won't even talk to me! Daddy's never home! Mommy's never home!"

"Tommy!" Ella says.

"Nanni, No!"

I find my feet and aim for the door, my heart a shattered mess in the hands of a little boy who'd declared me *his* Becca.

I feel like an outsider again, looking out through the gaps of the curtains from a room that's no longer mine, in a house that's no longer mine, and a world that will never *be* mine.

"Becca," Ella says, grasping my forearm. "Please stay. We need to talk."

I can't talk, I want to yell. But I can't. So instead, I nod and make myself useful, cleaning up the mess I'd helped create in the kitchen. I try to ignore the ache in my chest, the doubts in my mind, but they're there. They're there and they won't go away. And no matter how hard I scrub on the counter, my tears blurring my vision and my breaths strained, they're fucking there.

Ella's hand lands on my arm, and I flinch. I quickly wipe my tears, turning away from her to hide my pain. "Tommy's asleep," she says, her voice soft. "His little outburst wore him out."

I nod, still refusing to look at her.

"He didn't mean what he said," she says, gripping my hand to stop me from scrubbing. With gentle hands, she forces me to face her. "He's dealing with a lot of changes in his life and he's been lashing out at everyone." Her words are faded, lost amongst the pulse drumming in my ears.

I stare ahead, unable to respond.

It's not until she raises both her hands that I seem to refocus. She smiles, right before she *signs*, "Are you okay?"

My eyes snap to hers—to clear, dark eyes filled with hope and understanding.

"How…" I mouth.

She points to my hands, encouraging me with a nod.

I sign, "You know ASL?"

"J O S H," she signs. Then says, "He tried to learn on YouTube but it was hard because he had no one to tell him if he was doing it right, so he asked if we could take classes together. We go once a week over at the community college… but because of his travel, he doesn't get to go much and so I try to teach him what he's missed out on." Her hands move again, signing, "I hope I'm doing it right."

"You are," I sign back.

Ella nods, her gentle smile reaching her eyes as she leans against the counter. Then she says, "Josh is so happy you're back in his life, Becca. It's like he'd just been going through the motions, you know? After his dad passed away, it was like he was doing everything because he felt like he needed to, for Henry… but then you came back around, and it's as if he found his purpose again. His joy." She pauses a beat before adding, "I hope I'm not coming on too strong, or making you want to run and hide. I know it's only been a couple of months since you've reconnected, but you've both been through so much. You care about each other so deeply. Tommy wouldn't be in Josh's life the way he is if it wasn't for you." Ella moves around the kitchen and reaches into a cupboard where Josh stores what little alcohol he keeps. She pulls out a large album and rests it on the counter, flipping the cover to reveal a newspaper cut out —a picture I'd taken freshman year when I first started on the paper.

Confused, I stare at the image, stare at the text that goes with it, and then stare at the highlight of my name beneath the picture. I swallow the lump in my throat and turn the page, and then another, each one a different article. Toward the back of the book, there are less images and more of my human interest stories. Ella moves next to me, her arm brushing mine. "When he found out you were on the paper," she says, "he went on the online message board over at WU and asked for someone to send them to him. He even got them to send the older editions so he had the full collection. He didn't want to subscribe in case you somehow found out about it."

I keep my gaze on the album, my heart beating wildly for a boy who has no idea that even from a distance, even through his secrets, he's finding a way to heal me. "Why are you showing me?" I sign.

Her response is instant. "Because I want you to know how much you mean to him." She points to Tommy's room. "Tommy's a lot like Josh. They're quick to act. Quick to speak. They don't think, they just *do*. They can be arrogant and stubborn and they get that from my late husband. But the things Josh holds dearest to him are the things he won't share. He's probably never told you what it felt like to hold Tommy in his arms for the first time, or what it was like for him when you accepted him *and* Tommy into your life. He wears his pain on his sleeves, and hides his joys in his heart, because he's so damn terrified of losing them. And maybe that's why you clash sometimes, because you're the opposite, Becca. You only share your joy, while you hide your pain. And, maybe, if you can both find a way to balance that, you'll find your *coast*."

CHAPTER 41

JOSHUA

Becca goes home the next morning.

And after a lengthy and somewhat confusing conversation with my mother, so do I. Because at some point between the comps and media tours and the demo shoots, I'd unknowingly lost focus of my reason for doing what I was doing it in the first place. None of it was supposed to take my time away from Tommy, but it had. Without me realizing, Tommy had come second to all those things, and I hadn't known the effect it had on him until now. I just hope I'm not too late to make up for it.

The earliest flight I could book had me landing an hour after Becca left. Not that it mattered. I'm not here for her. I'm here for Tommy.

Mom's standing in the kitchen when I open the door to my apartment. Her hands settle on her hips, her eyes scanning my body for any new injuries. She opens her mouth, but I hold a finger to my lips, cutting her off. I mouth, "Tommy?"

With a smile, she points to his room, and as quietly as possible, I set my gear by the door and head straight for him. The door's open, but his back is to me, headphones too large for his head covering his ears. He's on his iPad, and when I come close enough, I can see he's on YouTube, watching videos of *me*. My heart dips in my chest, but just as quickly, it rises, swells, beats to the rhythm of whatever pride he must still hold that I'm his dad, and that he's my son, and there's a bond that no amount of time spent apart could ever diminish.

I tap his shoulder and step back when he turns around, his eyes wide and smile all-consuming. "Daddy. I didn't know you was here!" he yells, ripping his headphones off his head as he stands. He jumps the few steps separating us and lands right in my arms, and for a second, he's just like the kid I left behind on the first trip I made without him—three years old and needing me as much as I needed him.

I don't exactly know why I get the sudden urge to cry, or why his laughter makes that urge stronger, but I miss him. I hadn't realized how much I've missed him until this exact moment. Maybe it was the threat of another man taking my place in his life, like Mom had said, or maybe I just missed being Josh, the dad, and not J-Ward, the skater.

Whatever it is, it's not really relevant anymore.

"Are you leaving again soon like last time?" he says, pulling back so he can hold my head in his hands, his palms pressing into my cheeks.

I shake my head. "No, bud."

He reveals his perfect teeth behind his grin. "Remember last time, you said we would build a fort. Ma'am said you could. In her yard! Remember that? Like last time?" He shouts every word, each one with more excitement than the last.

"Yeah, I remember that," I say, placing him back on the floor. I settle my hands on my knees and bend down so we're eye-to-eye. "You think we should do it?"

Tommy taps his chin with his finger. "How long would it take?"

"A few days. Two if we get Uncle Rob to help."

Tommy frowns. "And if we don't get Uncle Rob to help, and it's just you and me, maybe it would take one whole entire week. Like, a infinity of minutes! And then you don't has to go to work for a whole infinity."

"Just you and me?" I ask.

"Yeah. Like last time!"

It takes a week to build a fort, which, technically, I could've built in a day. But Tommy and I took our time planning the build, talking about it, gathering the supplies, and on the fourth day, we finally got to building it, just him and me, like he wanted… like I didn't know I *needed*. I'd missed so much in my absence that spending that time with him was like re-getting to know him. The more I looked at him, spoke to him, watched him from afar, the clearer it became that he was getting to be more like me. When I told Becca about it on one of our late-night chats via a computer screen, she mentioned that she thought the same thing, and that maybe it was his way of trying to be close to me, or maybe his way of trying to get my attention, my approval, something I never want my son to be searching for. Still, it made sense, and that just made it harder for me to think about my future plans and my stupidly hectic schedule—a schedule that would keep us apart. So the night before I was meant to leave, I told Chris I wanted out. He told me I was stupid. I was. But, he did offer to go through my schedule and cut back where he could. Summer was the busiest time for us, and he couldn't do much with what I had going, but after the summer, he'd look at cutting back. He offered twenty percent, I said seventy. He said I had sponsors and relationships to maintain—ones that had been with me from the beginning and it would be unfair to disappear off the face of the earth. A valid point. We negotiated and ended up on fifty.

So with that knowledge, I spent the final night sleeping under the stars of a newly built fort in a two-person sleeping bag with my son. "Did you know My Becca was home?" he says, turning to his side, his hands clasped together beneath his cheek.

I match his position and face him. "I did know that. Did you have fun with her?"

He nods, his eyes wide.

"And how was Ma'am?"

"She was good. She kept thinking I was you."

"Oh yeah?"

"Her and Becca stole a bunch of your shoes."

"They *what?*"

He cackles with laughter, making me do the same. Once he's settled, he grabs the flashlight from beside him, switches it on, and aims it at the ceiling. "Daddy, look," he whispers, pointing up. "It looks like a boobie."

"You're crazy, bud."

"Crazy like the chicken who crossed the road because did you know the car hit it?"

I shake my head and make a tsking sound with my tongue. "What a crazy chicken."

He laughs again, and I listen to the sound that gives me hope, gives me purpose. "Hey, buddy. I wanted to talk to you about something."

His eyes move to mine, then to the fort door, then to the boobie-light on the ceiling. "Uh oh."

"No. It's not bad." At least, I hope it's not. "I just wanted to talk to you about your mom and Justin."

"Okay."

"Are you excited about the wedding? You have a lot of

responsibility. You're going to be the ring bearer, and that means you have to protect their wedding rings with your life."

"I know." He says, moving the boobie-light around in circles. "They told me already last time."

I clear my throat and push down the ache in my chest. "Have you thought about what you're going to call Justin once they're married?"

Tommy stares at me, his gaze searching, before blinking once, twice, and on the third time I look away, because the question in his eyes makes me question myself.

"He's just… *Justin*," Tommy says slowly, as if I'm the child in this situation.

I'm so damn afraid, so nervous it's making me stutter. "S-so… you're not—not going to call him dad?" I ask, facing him again.

Tommy places the flashlight between us, the glow casting a shadow over his face. He faces me, his eyes right on mine. "I like Justin. He's cool," he says. "But he's not my dad, *Dad*."

I exhale, relieved. "How did you grow up so fast?"

"I'm six. I am grown up." Tommy shrugs. "Daddy?"

"Yeah, buddy?"

He moves the flashlight behind him and shuffles closer until his arm is over my chest. "I like my fort. Thank you for making it for me," he says through a yawn. "But I didn't really need it. I just wanted you to *see* me."

CHAPTER 42

JOSHUA

The guys and I were supposed to meet up a few days before we left for Hong Kong to promote the event. We only had a day home from a trip to Mexico before heading off to tour again. It was on that one day home when I got a phone call from Chris. He groaned into the phone, his words echoing around him. "Promo trip's canceled," he mumbled. Then puked into what I assume was a toilet. "We'll meet for the flight to Hong Kong."

"Are you good?"

"Not at all."

Turns out that on a night I chose to stay in and spend a couple of hours video chatting/messaging with Becca while in Mexico, the guys decided to try their luck at some local food stands. Apparently, it didn't turn out well.

For them.

For me, it was a sign.

I packed my bags, and Tommy's, too. Then I called Mom, told her to pack hers, said goodbye to Chazarae who had no idea what day or year it was. I told her I loved her and that I'd be back soon, and a few hours later, the three of us were boarding a plane to St. Louis.

I guess I probably should've notified Becca at some point between Chris's phone call and the boarding of the flight that I was coming to see her, but it was rare that I got a couple days off to do whatever *I* wanted, and I wanted *her*. Even if it were for the few hours I'd get to see her between work at her internship and shifts at Say Something. Even if it meant being her personal chauffeur to those things and kissing her goodnight at her door, it didn't matter. I just wanted to see her. Be near her. Do bad, *bad* things to her.

Okay, so the whole long distance thing was starting to wear me down. There's only so much a guy can take. Becca and I tried to make some form of contact at least once a day, but with both our schedules, it became almost impossible. I'd wait three hours for a response, only to be dragged away for a few hours, and then she'd be busy, and so it goes, on and on, until a day passes, or two. And when we finally *can* be at one place for more than an hour, we sit and talk and we discuss how badly it sucks that we can't be together, and we make up stupid fantasy lives where nothing and no one else exists but her and me. It's as satisfying as it is depressing because it's exactly what I said; *a fantasy*.

Then a few days ago, she randomly sent a text that read, "*You should just move here. Lol.*"

That stupid "lol" distracted me for way too long, and I thought way too much about it. So much so that I found myself looking up houses near her. Houses I thought *she'd* like. Until a single thought infiltrated my mind, and I slammed my laptop shut and called myself stupid. Because *Chazarae.*

I couldn't leave Chaz.

I tried to reason that moving wouldn't be such a big deal and that she'd want to be near Becca, too. You know, on the days she actually remembered who Becca was. Besides, she had in-home care. It's not like I'd be taking her out of a special home to be with us.

Right?

Wrong.

I'd be taking her away from *her* home, and that thought alone had me shutting down yet another fantasy my mind had unknowingly created.

~

It's dark by the time I find myself standing on Becca's porch, memories of the last time I did this freezing me to my spot. I take a mental scan of my surroundings: the single car in the driveway, the dim flickering of the TV on inside, and then I work up whatever courage I need and knock on the damn door.

I step back as soon as it opens, and Martin appears, eyes narrowed in confusion before a grin appears. "What are you doing here, Warden?" Swear, he actually sees the relaxing of my shoulders when he says those words because he chuckles, deep and gruff.

"I came to surprise Becs," I tell him.

He nods, a hand going in his front pocket while the other opens the door wider for me. "She's not home, but you're welcome to wait for her."

I enter their house for the first time and pull out my phone to send a text to Mom, letting her know I'll be back at the hotel later. She replies quickly, telling me she didn't expect me at all that night, and by the time I shove the phone back in my pocket and look up, Martin's standing in front of me with a beer in each hand. I take one and accept his offered gesture for me to sit on the couch.

I glance around his house—at the kitchen attached to a living room and a bunch of doors I assume lead to bedrooms and bathrooms. It's bigger than my apartment, but much smaller than Chaz's. "Becca's at work," Martin says, sitting next to me.

"At the paper?" I look at my watch. It's almost ten. "Still?"

"I take it she didn't tell you?" Martin grimaces.

"Tell me what?"

CHAPTER 43

BECCA

I freeze just inside the doorway and look over at my dad, who's sitting on the couch next to Josh, both of them grinning like fools. And then something takes over me. This burst of elation that I hadn't felt since some punk skater gave me my very own skateboard with a single note, a single question, asking me to be his. I drop my bags, my keys, my need to look pretty in front of Josh, and I charge at him. He stands just in time to catch me, his arms wrapping around my waist, lifting me off my feet. "Surprise," he murmurs against my neck, his laughter mixing with Dad's.

I pull back and grab his face in my hands, and then I kiss him. His mouth, his cheeks, his chin, his nose, his everything, over and over.

"I think she's happy to see you," Dad says.

Josh settles me carefully on my feet and sits back down. I sit sideways on his lap, my arms around his neck, refusing to let him go. I try to contain my smile, but nothing in the world can prevent it from splitting my face in two. My cheeks sting from the unfamiliar pressure, and for some reason, I'm bouncing. I grab Josh's face again and get him to look at me. "Why?" I mouth.

"I had some free time." He shrugs. "There's nowhere else I'd rather be."

I look over at Dad. "Did you know?" I sign.

"No. It was a last minute thing," Josh answers for him.

My eyes snap to his, my smile somehow getting wider. I knew he was learning ASL, but I wanted to wait until he was ready to bring it up. His grin matches mine and I squeeze him tighter, my legs kicking out in front of me.

"I miss you so much," I sign.

"Why do you think I'm here?" he signs back.

I press a hand to my chest, trying to relieve the ache his actions brought on.

His eyes focus on my hands when I sign, "How long are you here?"

"Two nights," he says.

My fingers move again. "T O M M—"

"He's here. We can see him tomorrow," he says, tapping my leg. "Tonight, I just wanted you to myself."

I squeal. It's silent, but it's there. And Josh knows exactly how I feel because he chuckles. Dad stands, pulling my attention away from Josh. "Are you staying the night?" Dad asks him.

"If that's okay with you?"

Dad nods. "I'll get the couch ready for you."

My jaw drops, my eyes narrowed at him, causing him to laugh. "I'm just playin', sweetheart. I'll see you in the morning."

Josh and I wait until he's in his room, the door closed after him before facing each other. "So," he says.

It should be physically impossible to smile as much as I am.

He lowers his voice, his breath warming my neck. "I've always wondered what your room looks like in person."

Standing up, I take his hand and lead him to my room. I

shut and lock the door behind us and when I turn around, he's standing close. Almost too close. He smirks, looking at me in a way I've seen many times before. I know what he's thinking. I'm thinking it, too.

We're in so much trouble.

"I like your room," he says.

He hasn't even looked at my room.

Lying, I sign, "I have my period."

He squints, his lips pressed tight. "I don't know that last one. Spell it for me?"

"P E R I O—"

"Shit," he cuts in. But recovers quickly. "I mean, that's cool. It's not like that's the reason why I came to see you."

I push on his chest until the back of his legs hit my bed and he falls back, landing on the mattress.

Josh's eyes widen as I start to strip out of the stupid coveralls work makes me wear. He leans up on his elbows, his eyes taking in every movement, every inch of skin I reveal until I'm standing in front of him in nothing but my underwear. He sits up completely—his hands finding my hips, fingers dipping into the band of my panties and twisting them, pulling the fabric against my center, making my eyes drift shut in pleasure. He says, his voice husky, "I thought you said you…"

"I lied," I sign, opening my eyes when I feel his tongue sweeping my navel.

He glances at the door.

I click my fingers to get his attention. "It's locked," I sign.

He smiles. "You're in so much trouble."

I watch him from the doorway of my bathroom… watch the muscles in his back outlined by the dim light of the lamp on my nightstand. He's facing away from me, his head moving, eyes scanning the wall of pictures and articles of him I'd found online. They sit above my desk where I normally sit when we video chat. He's had no idea they'd existed until now. I'd started collecting them the day after his return at SK8F8, but I'd kept them hidden, just like my true feelings for him. It wasn't until our time together during spring break that I was finally ready to admit to myself that those feelings weren't going away.

They never had.

He turns when he must hear me approaching, his carefree smile making me weak. "Stalk much?" he says, arm around my shoulders, pulling me flush against his side.

I nod, my thumb between my teeth, slightly embarrassed about what he might be thinking. But then I remember what his mom had shown me and I forget my insecurities and get lost in his embrace. With warm lips, he kisses my forehead. "I'm kind of stupidly crazy about you, Becs. Just so you know. And if I thought for a second that it wouldn't make you mad, I'd shout it from the rooftops."

I grasp his hand and lead him to my bed, where we settle on our sides, our eyes locked, searching, consuming each other's presence, knowing our time is limited. It always is. "Can I ask you something?" he asks, lazily playing with a strand of my hair.

I blink once.

"Why do you smell like ketchup?"

I laugh into his chest and reach over him for the phone on my nightstand. I have no idea how I'd even begin to sign the answer. *I work at a ketchup factory, watching the bottles go by on a conveyer belt and making sure they all have that little aluminum cover that keeps them fresh on the shelves.*

He reads my note more than once and asks, "How did I not know this?"

Chewing my lip, I type: *Because I didn't want you to know.*

You'd make it into something it's not and it would become a bigger deal than it really is.

His mouth opens. Closes. And opens again. "So what... you're doing that as well as the internship and the hours at Say Something?"

I nod.

"Why? Do you need money for something? I have money, Becs. Lots of it. You shouldn't have to be spending your summer working two jobs and—what do you even need the money for? College? Equipment? You've booked your tickets to see your Grams, right? Because if you need it for that, I can cover you."

"Stop!" I mouth. I set my phone under the pillow and stare up at the ceiling, frustration building in my chest. This is *exactly* why I didn't tell him.

"I'm sorry." He leans up on his elbow. "I just don't get it."

"Get what?" I sign.

After shifting my hair away from my eyes, he says, his voice barely audible, "You're my girl, Becs. Why won't you let me take care of you?"

His words hang in the air, more like a statement than a question, and I let them repeat in my mind, over and over, until I come up with an answer that's both satisfying and true. I grab my phone and wait for his eyes to switch from mine to my hands before typing, *You being here, being on the other end of the phone, that's you taking care of me. I don't want or need anything else. But if it ever comes to that, and it might, I promise I'll ask you. I don't want your money to define our relationship. I don't want to be the poor college student depending on her rich boyfriend. I just want you, Josh. All I've ever wanted is to love you, and for you to love me, and that's it. That can't be enough?*

His defeated eyes move to mine, before his head lowers, his mouth soft and *safe* as he brushes across my lips. "Promise you'll ask if you need it."

"Promise," I mouth, and switch the app on my phone to have Cordy say, *"Now let's get some sleep. We have a big day tomorrow. I'm skipping group therapy and taking you to Say Something. We have a huge charity shave, and then I want to have your mom and Tommy here for a late lunch before you and I go out for dinner and drinks with some people from my paper. I'm going to show you off to everyone, and you better be on your best behavior, Warden."*

He laughs, his head dipping, causing strands of his hair to brush against my chest. "So we should probably get all the naughty stuff out of the way now, right?"

"How naughty are you thinking?"

"How thin are these walls?"

CHAPTER 44

JOSHUA

I jerk awake with Becca's arms thrashing wildly, hitting me from all angles. I try to grasp her hands but it's too dark, and before I can switch on a light, before I can think, it all stops. I wait for her next move, not wanting to spook her in case it sets something off. She sits up quickly, her feet landing on the floor with a thud, and reaches for her phone. I try to settle the pounding in my chest while I rub my eyes, adjusting to the dark.

Her door rattles, catching my attention, but it doesn't open.

"Unlock the door, sweetheart," Martin says. His voice seems calm—too calm. But Becca doesn't move.

I get up quickly, unlock and open the door for him, not knowing what else to do.

He doesn't acknowledge me, just goes straight to her and squats down to her level, taking her hands in his. I assume she alerted him, that's why she reached for her phone, and I wonder how often this happens. Because it seems *too* routine.

My heart breaks at the sight of her, and at the silence that surrounds us. "It was a bad one, huh?" Martin says.

Becca nods, her shoulders shaking with her sob and *why the fuck am I just standing here?*

"You need to breathe, Becca. Deep breaths," he soothes.

It should be me. Why didn't she turn to me?

Martin eyes me quickly before refocusing on Becca. "Remember what Dawn said—that the nightmares appear when you find yourself truly happy. Think of what's making you happy, Becca."

Becca nods again while wiping her eyes across her forearm. Martin catches my stare and motions for me to join him. It takes a moment for me to come to, for the shock and semi-disappointment to dissipate.

I put one foot in front of the other and hope that my presence isn't the cause of her misery.

"Josh is here," Martin says, patting her hands. "Do you remember that?"

Becca blinks.

Once.

Twice.

Then she looks up at me. Moments pass. Moments of heartache. Eventually, she smiles, and I feel the air in my lungs for the first time since she woke. She takes my hand and places my palm on her cheek, letting it soak in her tears. She looks so young, so dejected. I wait for her to say something. *Anything.* Because in the haze of everything that's happening, I forgot for a second—just one—that she can't *say* anything. But she moves… back into bed, scooting to one side, making room for me to lie with her. Without hesitation, she nestles into the crook of my arm, her hand on my chest, her legs tangled with mine.

Martin nods at me as he moves to the door where he stills, one hand on the knob, the other rubbing his nape. I can see the battle in his eyes, unable to decide whether to close the door and give us some privacy, or leave it open so he has peace of mind.

"Leave it," I whisper, making the choice for him.

He nods, the relief easing out of his shoulders. He's gone a moment later, but he doesn't go back to bed. Instead, I hear him in the kitchen, his footsteps moving, fridge door opening, coffee pot churning, and I know that, just like me, he won't sleep. Not until we know our girl is no longer in pain. That the suffering is gone. That her past won't take away from the joy of the present. At least for one night.

I focus on Becca, on stroking her hair and feeling the heat of her breaths on my chest, and I push aside all other emotions and remember how badly I wanted this. How badly I craved and missed this exact feeling. Every night away from her, in whichever hotel room I'd find myself in, I'd close my eyes and think about this, and during the months after Dad's passing, it was the only thing that kept me going… this one thought… this one moment of calm and clarity.

Minutes pass until an entire hour ticks by and I spend that time switching between staring at the ceiling, staring at her, and listening to Martin in the kitchen. Slowly and carefully, I untangle her arms and legs from around me, making sure she's still asleep before shrugging on my jeans and joining him.

"Coffee?" Martin asks, his voice low.

I nod and sit at the table, exhausted and overwhelmed.

"Couldn't get back to sleep, huh?" he says, placing a mug in front of me.

I shake my head and rub my face. "Does that happen a lot?"

"Not as much as it used to. The last one was when she was at her grandmother's during spring break." He sits down, kicking out his legs to the side. "Her therapist says it happens whenever she feels as though she's truly happy. It's like her subconscious's way of trying to make her believe that she doesn't deserve it." He takes a sip of his drink. "It's messed up.

Even in her death, her mother still finds ways to haunt that little girl."

I almost tell him that Becca's not a little girl, but I see her through a father's eyes and I understand.

"To be honest," he adds, "with you showing up the way you did, I was almost expecting it to happen."

"You did?" I ask, looking up at him through my lashes.

"For her, true happiness means you, Warden."

We sit together—two grown-ass men who once despised each other—and we find an even ground through the one thing that connects us. *Becca.*

We talk, not just about her, but about everything. I ask him about his work, he asks about mine. I thank him for cashing the blank check I gave him, even though it wasn't anywhere near as much as I'd hoped he'd go for. He tells me what all the money went toward, as if I'd want to know. I don't. I just want to make sure she's taken care of. And the longer we sit, the more I get to know him, the clearer it becomes that with or without that money, Martin would have found a way. He would've moved mountains to take care of her, even if the strength it took to do so was eighteen years in the making.

We take turns making excuses to check on Becca, who seems to be back to sleeping deeply, peacefully. The sun begins to rise, the birds make it known it's morning, and on my third coffee, Martin receives a phone call that has him standing quickly and heading right for Becca's room.

I follow, of course, and watch as he nudges her awake with a hand on her shoulder. "Becca, wake up."

She stirs slowly, her beautiful eyes clear of tears, and looks up at him. "Where's Josh?" she signs.

I move toward her. "I'm here."

Her dad says, "Lexy just called. She wants to see us. Get ready."

Becca shoots out of bed and goes to her bathroom. A moment later, her shower turns on.

"Who's Lexy?" I ask Martin.

"Her voice therapist. You coming?"

"Y-yeah," I mumble, picking up my discarded clothes scattered all over the floor along with Becca's bra and panties. I pick up her underwear and quickly shove them in my pocket, hoping he doesn't see them.

But he does, because he cocks an eyebrow and points to my pocket. "Souvenirs?"

Becca sits in the middle of her dad's truck, bouncing in her seat, while Martin drives. I sit on the other side of her, staring out the window, trying to forget the shame of this morning.

"It has to be good news, right?" the car speakers sound, relaying the message from her phone. She calls it Cordy... because her vocal cords are whack. She finds it ironic. I find it kind of morbid, but whatever.

"I don't want you getting your hopes up, Becca," Martin says.

"Hopes up for what?" I chime in.

Becca takes my hand, neither of them answering me. She types on her phone, *"Make sure you tell your mom and Tommy about coming over."*

"Over where?" Martin asks.

"I invited them for a late lunch at our house."

"Oh no," Martin murmurs. "Tell them to wear something with lots of pockets to hide the inedible scraps Becca calls food."

~

There's a skip in Becca's step while we make our way up to a large building. Going by the signs on the door, I assume it's filled with medical suites. She walks through the foyer, my arm gripped tightly to her chest and when we reach the elevators, she presses the button that has the doors opening. Once inside, she hits the button for the third floor, her smile uncontainable when she looks up at me.

She's so damn beautiful.

And I'm so damn lucky to have her.

I squeeze her hand. "Olive juice," I mouth.

Her smile widens. "So much," she mouths back.

~

Becca introduces me to Lexy and I shake her hand, call her ma'am, tell her it's an absolute pleasure to meet her and that Becca's told me great things about her, even though I know almost nothing about her besides the fact that she's her voice therapist. (A voice therapist for someone who has no voice... now *that's* ironic.) But, Becca said I had to be on my best behavior, so that's what I'm doing.

We sit in her office, an office filled with medical degrees and diagrams of mouths and throats and chests and a bunch of other gadgets I also know almost nothing about.

Again, Becca sits in the middle—still bouncing with excitement—her dad on one side and me on the other and we sit in silence, waiting for Lexy to pull out a file and sit behind her desk.

We wait.

And wait some more.

Finally, Lexy looks up from the desk and speaks. "I called

you this morning because I didn't want you waiting any longer, and with the news I have, I didn't want to have to tell you over the phone." Her demeanor is the opposite of Becca's from earlier and we must all see that, because the air turns thick and Becca's no longer bouncing.

"So what does that mean?" Martin says.

My head's spinning, a million scenarios running through my mind. What the hell *does* it mean?

Lexy leans on her forearms, the folder now open in front of her. "Doctor Schmidt looked over your file and your medical history. And while I did the same and thought that you'd be the perfect candidate for the operation,"—*what operation?*—"he was unable to give us the outcome we all wanted. I'm so sorry, Becca. The operation's not suitable for someone in your position. There's just too much damage that's irreversible."

Operation.

Damage.

Irreversible.

That's basically all I got from her speech.

Becca inhales deeply and squares her shoulders. "It's okay," she signs, but it's not.

It's not okay at all. She's fighting the disappointment. Fighting the *tears*. "We all knew that the operation wasn't a sure thing, right?"

What fucking operation?

Martin clears his throat. "So that's it? There's no alternative? No second opinion?"

Oh, we'll get a second opinion!

Lexy closes the folder and leans back in her chair. "Dr. Schmidt is the most advanced doctor in his field. But I don't want you to be discouraged, Becca. There can be so many developments. So many things can change and you're young. That's a good thing."

Becca nods and plants the fakest of all fake smiles on her face. Her hands rise, her fingers moving. "It's not so bad," she signs. "At least now I can quit my crappy job."

CHAPTER 45

BECCA

"I'm good," Cordy says for me.

It's the third time I've tapped the *speak* button since we got back in the car ten minutes ago. I haven't needed to change the response once, and I don't know why Dad keeps asking. I said everything I needed to say in that office.

It was never a sure thing.

I'm *not* disappointed.

I just *am.*

Josh blindly reaches for my hand and squeezes it once, but he won't look at me. Apparently what's on the other side of his window is more fascinating.

"I'm good," Cordy says again, the two words echoing through the small, unbreathable space.

I almost push Josh out of the car when we finally pull into the driveway, needing the fresh air in my lungs more than I need Dad's questions, more than I need Josh's support. Without a word, Dad goes into the house while Josh and I stand in the driveway.

"Do you want to talk about it?" he asks, his eyes holding a tinge of gold against the morning sun.

"There's nothing to talk about. It is what it is," I sign.

Josh sighs. "I'm sorry," he almost hesitates to say. "Your hands were going too fast… I couldn't…"

"Don't worry," I sign.

"No." He steps forward and tugs on my top. "Just try again. Just go slower this time."

Shaking my head, I reach in my pocket for my phone, and have Cordy do my talking, *"I said, let's talk about it later. I've got a long day ahead and I need to go to the store to get things for lunch. We can meet at Say Something at eleven. Okay?"*

"I can go to the store with you," he says quickly. "We can pick up Mom and Tommy on the way to the center."

I press my lips tight and wrap my arms around his neck, rising to my toes so I can kiss him. "I'm good," I mouth.

He grasps my hips and gently creates space between us. "I just feel like we need to talk about this."

Seriously. What's there to talk about? He might be disappointed that he's in love with a girl who can never speak again, but I'd already come to terms with my fate long before this stupid operation even came up.

It is what it is.

I am who I am.

And, "I'm good," I mouth again, peeling his hands off me. I sign, "I'll see you at eleven. You know where it is?"

He nods.

I kiss him again. "Olive juice," I mouth.

He sighs. "So damn much, Becs."

Josh: Are you here? We just parked.

I leave dad inside the Say Something warehouse, manning the popcorn machine, and meet Josh and his mother in the parking lot. No sign of Tommy. Ella greets me with a hug. "You look adorable," she says, and I force a smile because I can't see Tommy. Can't hear him. And if he's not here, I don't know that I could handle it emotionally. My heart's thumping in my chest, my eyes searching their car—a different car than the one Josh left my house in. I look over at Josh, whose goofy grin makes me smile for real. He points to the back door. "He wanted you to get him out of the car."

I practically rip it open, and the moment I do, my heart fills with a joy only Tommy's giggle can create. "Did you think I wasn't here?" he shouts.

I nod, hold a hand to my chest and roll my eyes at him.

He laughs harder. "I tricked you."

After unbuckling him from his car seat, I help him down from the giant SUV. He stands in front of me, trucker cap on backward, Globe shirt, skinny jeans, Globe shoes, and… *pierced ear*? I gasp, silent, and reach out and fiddle with it.

Tommy giggles. "Gnarly, right? Nico and I got it done together in Dallas. Daddy wouldn't let me get a tattoo, though."

I look over at Josh, my eyes wide.

He just shakes his head. "Don't get me started."

"Hey Becs!" Tommy says, and I give all the attention in all the world back to him. He lifts his hands, his little fingers moving in front him. He *signs*, "M Y B E C C A"

My jaw drops, along with my stomach and I cover my mouth and I cry. Then I laugh. And I cry and laugh some more. And yeah, I look crazy, but it feels like everything is hitting me at once.

Josh consoles me.

So does his mother.

And Tommy looks on as if he's done something wrong, which he hasn't. So I take him in my arms and lift him in the air and I hold him. I hold him and I hold him and I hold him and I'm never, ever letting him go.

I'd spent the morning in a daze, not wanting to come to terms with a loss. Because as much as I didn't want to admit it to anyone, especially to myself, Lexy's news felt just like that—a loss. But all it takes to redefine that word and all the feelings that come with it is a single boy's laughter, and *a sign*.

His signing meant everything.

Changes everything.

I carry Tommy, who's already half my size, on my hip and wrap my free arm around Josh's waist. Then I lead them all toward Say Something—a *safe place*.

Only it's not *my* safe place.

My safe place isn't a *place*.

It's bright brown eyes and shaggy dark hair atop identical smiles. It's the sound of laughter, of the spinning of four wheels on concrete. It's touches of ease, of comfort.

My safe place is the knowledge that when I fall, *they* will help me fly. Help me soar. Help me *coast*.

For the day, Say Something has been converted to a party, of sorts. A hair shaving party to raise money for a little girl named Vanessa. She'd been one of our kids for a while, moving from one foster home to another. Recently, she'd been diagnosed with leukemia, and because of the costs and time involved in her care, her last foster parents were unable to accommodate her. Without a second thought, Sandra took her in and now she kind of belongs to everyone at Say Something. At only eight, Vanessa, or Nessa as she liked to be called, is wise beyond her years and stupidly adorable. Before she lost most of her hair, people said we could be sisters… only she had big, bright brown eyes and I had green. Or emerald, as Josh would say.

The moment we step inside, Tommy's instantly squirming out of my arms and wanting to play. I set him on his feet and before I can do anything else, he's running toward the bounce house. "I got him," Ella says, her pace much slower as she goes after him.

Josh puts his arm around my shoulders. "So this is it, huh?" he says, looking around. He's never admitted to the large donation that I'm sure came from him, and I've never asked, but the new paint on the walls, the new computers, and the new carpet he's taking in all exist because of him. Because of his heart.

"I want you to meet someone," I sign.

"I'm on my best behavior," he jokes. "Lead the way."

It only takes a minute to find Joey—it's hard to miss a guy dressed as a clown, giant red shoes and wild, orange wig. His back is turned when I reach him. I push down the excitement at seeing Joey's reaction to his hero—*the* Josh Warden—being here, and tap his shoulder. He glances at me quickly, says, "Hey Becca," then continues to make a mess of a balloon animal.

"This is that Joey kid? The Santa?" Josh murmurs in my ear.

I nod.

Now Josh taps his shoulder.

Joey turns, his eyes widening when he sees Josh. He falls back a step, and then another, and another, until he's on his back on the floor with a dozen kids (and me) all laughing at him. "Joey fallded," one kid yells through a fit of laughter.

Josh releases me to offer Joey his hand. "Hey, man. It's good to meet you in person."

Joey takes Josh's hand, and when he's on his feet again, he glares at me. "I hate you," he says.

"Hate's a bad word!" Zac, one of the boys, yells. His eyes narrow at Joey, right before he goes for the junk punch.

I laugh harder.

Josh, being a guy and knowing what a junk punch must feel like, glares at me just like Joey had. He places a hand on Joey's shoulder and bends at the knees so he's eye-to-eye with a hunched over Joey. "You good?"

"Oomph."

"Who are you?" Zac asks Josh.

"I'm Josh." He points to me. "I'm Becca's boyfriend."

"No!" Zac yells. "*I'm* Becca's boyfriend!"

"Umm..." Josh looks to me, his eyes pleading.

"Fight for me," I sign. Joking, of course.

He looks down at Zac, his throat bobbing with his swallow. He covers his junk, just in case. "I've known her longer," is all he can comes up with.

"I know you are. You said you are. But what am I?" Zac sings, his hips swinging from side to side.

"You—you're..." I wish I was recording this so I could upload it to YouTube and have the world witness Josh, a man, trying to find verbal retaliations against a nine-year-old. Josh smiles wide, an insult coming to him. "You're a butt sniffer!"

Okay.

Zac's eyes narrow as they move to Josh's protected junk. "Well, I'm rubber and you're glue, what you say bounces off me and sticks to you. You butt sniffer!"

Josh stands to full height. "You can have her," he says, sticking out his tongue at Zac. "She has smelly farts!"

The kids cackle with laughter while I turn beet red.

Josh points to me. "Becca the stink bottom!"

We spend the next hour going from person to person while I introduce them to Josh. They all know about him from what I've told them in the past, and they're all as happy to meet Josh as Josh seems to be to meet them. He plays with the kids and speaks with the adults, charming the crap out of everyone. And I love him for it. I love that he is who he is, but he still has the time and the genuine interest to listen to Sandra tell him all about the strange noise coming from her basement.

We catch up with Tommy at the Play-Doh table sitting next to Vanessa, telling her all about a teleporter he plans on building. "It's going to deliver ice cream machines to all the houses."

Nessa smiles at him.

"Do you like ice cream?" he says, thumping his fist down on a slab of Play-Doh.

"I guess," Nessa says, shrugging.

"Is it your birthday?"

Nessa's lips purse before she says, "No. Why?"

"This party's for you, right?"

Nessa shrugs again. "It's not really a party. It's so people can give me money so I don't have to be sick anymore."

"What's wrong with you?" Tommy asks, fist frozen in the air as he turns to her.

"That's not nice, Tommy," Josh cuts in. "You shouldn't ask people those things. Apologize to Nessa."

"It's okay," she says, taking Tommy's pile of Play-Doh and adding it to hers. "I have leukemia." It comes out as "wookemia."

"But you're so pretty," Tommy tells her.

I smile into Josh's arm while Nessa's cheeks darken. "Fanks."

"Your hair's pretty."

A frown pulls on Nessa's lips. "It's not my real hair. It's a wig."

Tommy finally lowers his arm. "Oh."

Nessa turns to him, her voice soft. "I like your earring."

"Thanks!" Tommy smiles brightly at her. "Can I see you without the wig?"

"Tommy!" Josh whisper yells.

Tommy's eyes snap to his. "What?"

Nessa removes the wig and hands it to Tommy. There's very little hair left on her head from the chemo she's endured.

Tommy tilts his head, taking in Nessa in all her shy but beautiful glory. "My Aunt Chloe got sick and lost her hair," Tommy tells her. "She had cancer."

Nessa nods, her eyes cast downward. "That's what I have."

Tommy places the wig on his head, causing Nessa to giggle into her sleeve. "Do I look good?" he asks her, tugging on the ends.

Nessa giggles. "You look like a girl."

"Your smile is pretty, too," Tommy says. "And I don't think you need the wig. You're pretty without it." Wow. Kid's got game.

I don't realize Nessa's made a heart from the Play-Doh until she hands it to Tommy. "You're nice to me," she tells him.

Tommy takes it from her, as carefully as he can, and stares at it a long time. Then he looks up. "Hey. You want to be my girl?"

"Oh God," Josh mumbles.

"Okay!" Nessa yells.

And just like that, they walk away, hand-in-hand.

"What the hell just happened?" Josh mumbles. "He tells her she's pretty and now they're what? Dating? Is he dating? He's six! He can't be—oh no." He turns to me, his eyes wide. "I have approximately ten years before... shit, Becca. I'm not ready for this."

"Relax," I sign, rolling my eyes at him. "He's just crushing on a girl."

"Yep. I'm going to be a grandpa."

Tommy ends up taking a photo with Nessa, and with the help of Ella, he uploads it to his Instagram with a link to both Nessa's and Say Something's GoFundMe pages. It takes no more than five minutes for Nessa's page to raise ten thousand dollars, the amount Tommy had asked for in order for him to shave his hair. Comments flood both his Instagram and the GoFundMe page from people stating they would double their donations if his dad would do it, too. Which, of course, Josh does.

Later, in the parking lot, a newly cropped Josh asks Tommy where he learned his smooth moves with the ladies, to which Tommy responds, shrugging, "Nico taught me." He ticks off each item with his finger. "Tell a girl she's pretty. Say something about her hair, her smile, *her ass,* and she's all yours."

A total of one hundred and twenty thousand dollars is raised that day, all thanks to a little boy wanting to take care of his girl.

CHAPTER 46

JOSHUA

Lunch with Becca and her dad goes smoothly. Martin and my mother make up most of the conversation with music that was popular "in their day," while Tommy shows Becca what all he's learned with ASL.

Mom managed to get an online tutor for him who video chats with us once a week. He's a specialist, working mainly with sudden hearing-impaired children, so it works really well for Tommy. Once Tommy starts to get really comfortable with reading and spelling, he'll probably end up knowing more than I do.

Watching Tommy have to say goodbye to Becca sucks, to say the least. Becca and I are meeting her friends tonight and I have to leave early in the morning, so that doesn't leave much time for them. "But why can't I stay here with you?" Tommy asks. Over and over. Becca hugs him, seeming as disappointed as Tommy is. I can see her questioning her choices, wondering if it's possible to change her plans, but her determination wins out and she promises Tommy that she'll be all his in just two days. She even promises to have a sleepover with him in the fort, something I have a feeling won't go down too well once she realizes just how open it is. She hates anything small that flies. With a passion. To the point where she'll give you radio-silent treatment for an entire week if you place an innocent dead moth on her pillow.

I learned that the hard way.

Tommy and my mother leave with just enough time for Becca to make herself prettier, if that's possible. She showers, gets dressed, and dabs on what little make up she wears while I sit on the edge of her bed and watch, because I can't *not.* "Is this a fancy thing? Because I didn't bring a change of clothes. I don't really do well with fancy. It's either casual or full tux with me."

She quirks an eyebrow and covers her wrist with a gajillion bracelets. Then signs, the metal of her bangles clanking against each other, "You've worn a full…" she pauses… her hands frozen. Then she spells out, "T U X?"

"I have," I answer defensively. "Once. At my uncle Rob's wedding."

She rolls her eyes. "How are they?" she signs.

"My aunt and uncle?"

She nods, moving toward me, her hips swaying, before sitting sideways on my lap. She signs, "I like them."

"Well, my uncle's gone a little crazy and my aunt's the size of a house." Becca's eyes widen, causing me to chuckle. "Three rounds of IVF later, she's finally pregnant. They're going to name him Josh."

"Shut up," she mouths.

"I'm kidding. About the Josh thing. But she really is pregnant. She's due in a couple weeks."

Grinning, she signs, "That's great."

"You should come down for a weekend once they have him. They'd really like that. They ask about you all the time." I kiss her shoulder, exposed from the extremely tight tank top she's wearing. "I'll organize it when I'm home and get C-Lo and Hunter to come down, too. They've been wanting to catch up with you ever since we got back together."

There's something peaceful about Becca's smile. Like, without truly knowing her past, you can tell that it's something to be cherished. Something that can only be created by moments worthy of them, and going by the way she's looking at me, perfect teeth displayed behind a more than perfect smile, she makes me feel worthy of it. Of her. And so I kiss her, and kiss her some more, tasting her strawberry lip-gloss against my tongue and I know I'm probably ruining her efforts to look prettier but she doesn't seem to mind. At least until my hand moves to her stomach, and beneath her top, and up, up, up to her breasts and that's when she puts an end to my wandering mind.

She grasps my forearm and pulls away from my still half-open lips, her eyes opening slowly as if it's taken all her will to do so. "Let's go," she mouths.

I grunt, causing her to laugh silently.

I call for a car and five minutes later, it shows up. Chris set us all up an account with a nationwide car service so we don't catch cabs. It's for security, he says, but I think it has more to do with the fact that pictures (which I'm sure a cab driver had taken) of Nico receiving um... pleasure... in the back of a cab once surfaced. Nico thought it was amazing. So did the other guys. I thought it was funny. Nico's grandmother—a crazy old Puerto Rican lady who always seems to be holding something she can use as a weapon—did *not* find the amazement or humor in it.

She beat his ass pretty bad—though he'd never admit it—and promised to paddle the boat that would take him back home, all while cursing the entire United States of America.

Poor fucking Nico.

. . .

We arrive at the sports bar & grill soon after the car collects us. Becca told me earlier that it's where a lot of the students from her college hang out. She said we were meeting up with a *few* of her friends. A *few* is a table of fifteen. "The girl of the hour," some guy shouts, standing up and moving toward us as soon as we come into view. He hugs her and she hugs him back, and they seem to do this for a long time. Much longer than I'm comfortable with. *Best behavior, Warden.*

"You didn't tell me you were bringing someone," he says, his eyes scanning me from head to toe. I do the same, mentally calculating the outcome should push come to shove. He offers me his hand. "You must be Josh?"

Men are such dicks, and I say that as a man who two seconds ago was ready to throw down over some guy hugging his girl.

He says, "I'm Pete. I'm the editor on the school paper."

"I'm Josh... but you knew that already."

He rolls his eyes. "Yeah. Becca's slightly obsessed with you."

Becca shoves his shoulder.

And in less than a second he goes from "imminent threat" to "one of the guys." As I said, men are dicks.

He leads us to the table, introducing me to everyone there, as well as what their roles are on the paper. I'm surprised by how many of them are still here even though it's summer break. Once I'm seated, they explain that many of them get local summer jobs and/or internships just like Becca has. In the back of my mind, I recount Pete's statement. *The girl of the hour.*

Soon enough, meals are ordered, eaten and drinks are flowing and that thought passes. Becca sits, listening to her friends talk, our hands linked under the table. They discuss things I know nothing about, but Becca does, because she laughs with them and although silent, the impact on my heart is the same. I'd be lying if I said I didn't miss it—her voice, and the sound of her laughter and the occasional snort that came with it.

Pete stands, clanking his fork against his beer bottle, gaining my attention. "I want to make a toast to Becca," he announces, waving the fork in the air. Becca grasps my arm, using it to hide her face. "If only half the population could see the world through your lens."

The rest of the table applaud and cheer for Becca. I turn to her, pull my arm away and ask, "What's going on?"

"She didn't tell you?" Pete asks, and I go back to hating him.

"That's so Becca," shouts a girl at the other end of the table.

"It's not a big deal," Becca signs.

I shake my head, trying not to let my annoyance take precedence over whatever the hell it is we're supposed to be celebrating.

"Your girl Becca here..." Pete says, pointing his bottle at her, "wrote an article and attached a photograph with it that now has"—he looks over at the That's-So-Becca girl—"how many retweets now?"

The girl looks at her phone, a huge grin splitting her face in two. "6,438!" she yells.

"It's the most in WU history," Pete tells me, sitting back down. "It's had so much exposure that it caught the attention of one of the board members from Fine House Awards. He wanted to buy it from her, but she refused to sell it, so instead, he nominated her for debut artist of the year!"

It must've happened recently because I have all the newer editions of the paper at home. I just haven't had a chance to go through them. "That's amazing," I tell Becs. Part excited, part angry, part annoyed that they all seem to know more about my girlfriend than I do.

She rolls her eyes and holds her phone between us, using the Notes app to type, I assume so the others don't hear. *It's just a nomination. I'm not even a finalist.*

"Still, Becs. That's huge. Why didn't you tell me?"

I was going to, but it happened the same day you told me you moved up a world rank and I don't know...

She shrugs.

It just wasn't as exciting.

I shake my head, my eyes narrowed at her. "I want to see the picture."

She smiles now, her eyes lighting up with it. She reaches into my pocket and grabs my phone. Her thumbs work to enter my pin, open the Twitter app, find the WU account and follow it. Then she hands it to me.

On the screen is a black and white photograph of Chazarae with a couple, sitting on the grass, a single blanket covering their legs. Chazarae sits in the middle, a man on one side and a woman on the other, both wearing woolen caps pulled low on their brows and layers upon layers of sweaters and jackets. The weariness in their eyes mixed with the slight dirt on their jaws along with the plastic bags piled next to them makes them appear homeless, and knowing Chazarae, they probably are. The picture's taken from beyond their feet. Chazarae, barefoot, feet angled, heels together and toes apart. On either side of her, the couple wear new, bright white sneakers with the familiar Globe logo on the soles. But it's none of those things that have my breath catching and my eyes fixed on the image. It's the fact that Chaz is laughing, carefree and full of life. She's laughing so hard, her head's thrown back with the force of it. I hadn't seen her smile like that in a long time, and I wonder for a moment how long ago the picture was taken. But her hair's short so I know it's recent, because Sadie had called a few months back and told me she'd found Chaz in the kitchen, eyes blank, cutting off her hair because of the spiders living inside it. She was having a bad day, obviously. A *black* day. But this image captures the Chaz I know, the Chaz she *is.* The Chaz she wakes up every day trying to find. The ache builds in my chest caused by pity and relief that she was able to be herself, even for the few minutes it had taken for Becca to capture the moment, capture Chaz in all her perfect glory. Beneath the image is the caption:

Photo Credit: Instagram – ViewsOfEmeralds.

Title: True Angels Fly Without Wings.

I blow out a heavy breath. And then another. And another. All while I blink back my emotions. Push back my tears.

"Do you like it?" she signs, her hands low so I can see them.

I look up at her, my bottom lip between my teeth to stop the trembling. "It's beautiful, Becs. You captured your grams…" The lump in my throat prevents me from saying anything more, but she knows what I mean, because she nods, her hands cupping my face, thumbs swiping at my closed lids, removing the tears caught in my lashes.

When I open my eyes, she's smiling at me. Her hands leave me to sign, "Have you seen that couple before?"

I shake my head. "Never."

She switches to her phone again, knowing what she wants to tell me might be too advanced for my sign language skills. *I took it when I was with her during spring break. They're a homeless couple from the park. Did you know she goes there often to hand out food?*

I nod. "She's always done it. Tommy and I have gone with her a few times, but not for a while."

We stole a bunch of shoes and clothes from your garage and spent the day handing them out on the streets and in shelters. Sorry. I meant to tell you... She chews her lip, peeking up at me, waiting for my reaction.

I laugh once. "I don't care."

She seems to relax. *So you really like it?*

"I really do, Becs."

Good. I want to make Grams proud. And you, too. I know how much she means to you.

"Becs..."

She curls her hand around my neck and pulls my face to her bare shoulder, letting me use it to wipe the stupid tears away. I can handle most things life throws at me, but not this. Not the life He seemed to have chosen for Chaz. "It's not fair," I murmur, forgetting for a moment we may possibly have an audience.

Becca presses her lips to mine, soft and warm, and she leaves them there. Not kissing. Not really doing anything but letting me know she heard me.

I'm the first to pull away, eyes scanning the table to find fifteen sets of eyes watching us. I clear my throat and sit up higher, throwing an arm around Becca's shoulders. "We should celebrate," I mumble.

I order a round of tequila shots for everyone. Followed by another. Then four more. Until we're *that* table at the restaurant. Young, drunk, and obnoxiously loud.

"Are you any good?" Pete yells across the table, his eyes glazed from the alcohol.

"Good?" I ask, leaning forward so I can hear him. "At what in particular?"

He rolls his eyes. "At skateboarding! Are you good?"

I rear back a little, confused by his question. Becca settles her hand on her stomach to ease the ache of her continuous laughter.

The guy next to me, I have no idea what his name is. Let's call him... *Bob*. So Bob yells, "He's a pro skater, asshole. Of course he's good!"

Ah, so Becca did tell them about me. I was beginning to wonder if anyone besides Pete knew about me or if I was just Becca Owens's boyfriend from out of town. Not that I'd care.

"I skated once," Pete tells me. "Figure skating. On ice."

The table erupts with laughter.

The That's-So-Becca girl—*Fuck, I should really learn their names*—yells, "Not at all the same thing, douche hole!"

"I want to see you skate!" Pete yells, waving a finger between us.

"You can just type in my name on YouTube," I tell him.

He repeats my words mockingly, and maybe I should be offended, but the laughter around me has me guessing this is just Pete being Pete.

The waitress approaches, asking if we'd like to order anything else. I lean in close to Becca and ask, "Are we here for the rest of the night?"

She rubs my newly shaved head. I don't know why. She's been doing it all night. Then she signs, "We normally close out the place."

I order a few pitchers of beer for the table and another round of shots. "Actually, just leave the tequila bottle here," I tell the waitress.

She scoffs. "The manager's going to want you to pay for your meals and drinks and keep a card at the bar before I can get you anything else."

In unison, everyone at the table moans as they reach for their wallets.

"I got it," I shout.

Becca grasps my arm. "Sure?" she mouths.

I hand the waitress my card. She stares at the black American Express I just handed her, cocks an eyebrow, and then looks at me. "Yeah, I'm going to need to see some ID."

I give her my license, used to the treatment.

"I'll be right back," she says, spinning on her heels.

"So you actually make money from this 'pro skater' gig, huh?" Pete says, using his fingers to emphasize *pro skater.*

"You're an idiot," Bob tells him. "He's like any other pro-athlete, but instead of major team endorsements, he earns individual ones. Globe, Red Bull, Oakley, Primitive, they all pay him to wear their brands and promote their products."

I face him, my eyebrows raised.

He shrugs. "I write the sports column. It's just general knowledge, right? It's not like I stalk you in particular."

"Fucking lies!" the That's-So-Becca girl calls.

Becca slams one hand on the table, her eyes filled with tears from laughter. She knocks over her drink in the process, and instantly frowns at it. I lean down, my lips to her ear. "You're a hot mess, Owens."

"You should teach me to skateboard," Pete shouts.

I find it hilarious that everyone's yelling.

He adds, "Skateboarders get all the hot chicks!"

My eyes snap to Becs, who's still silently laughing. She signs, "He's drunk. And I'm almost positive he's gay."

I cackle with laughter at her response, while the waitress returns with the beers and bottle of tequila and places them on the table. "We'll keep your card at the bar, just grab it from me when you leave," she says, squeezing my shoulder.

Becca's hands are on my head again.

"What did Becca sign?" Pete yells.

So much yelling.

All the phones on the table go off at once. Everyone picks theirs up quickly, their eyes scanning. Then they all laugh loudly. Bob even goes to high-five Becs.

"What just happened?" I shout.

Bob sits back down and shows me his phone and the group message with everyone at the table.

Becca: If that waitress bitch touches my boyfriend again I will cut her. And just so we're clear, when I say "cut her" I mean, I will throw down and declare war on her ass. I don't care if he has a black card or not, I can

> go from Sweet-B to Trailer-Park in less than a second!

I turn to Becca, my grin wide. "Sweet-B?"

She crosses her arms. "I'm serious," she mouths.

"Sweet-B to Trailer Park!" Pete shouts. "That's fucking gold."

We drink to Becca, again, and so the night goes. Sixteen college students and me, all sitting at a table, alcohol flowing, conversation loud, laughter constant, and for tonight—just one night—I'm nothing more than Becca Owens's boyfriend from out of town. And it's perfect.

Almost *too* perfect.

CHAPTER 47

BECCA

"What the hell are we doing, Becs? You're going to get my ass thrown in jail and I can't go to jail. It's in my contract and ooh, my mamma will be sooo mad," Josh says, his words slurred as I slip the key into the entrance of Say Something.

He's drunk, clearly, which—in theory—is bad timing to bring him here and tell him what I want to say, but he's leaving in a few hours, and I need to get it out, so here we are.

I take his hand and lead him through the dim light of the Say Something warehouse and to the bottom of the staircase that leads to the rooftop. "Who first?" I sign.

He tilts his head, confused. Then he nods once. "You're pretty. And you have pretty hair and pretty eyes and a pretty ass so you should go first, so I can watch your pretty ass."

Surprisingly, we make it to the top without any casualties. Especially considering we spent the entire climb with both of his hands on my ass.

I pick up the battery-operated lantern I keep in the metal box by the door and move to the middle of the rooftop. Tugging his hand, I sit on the ground, my legs crossed, waiting for him to do the same.

"Seriously, Becs, it's almost four in the morning. What are we doing here?"

"I wanted to talk," I sign.

His face scrunches and he rubs his jaw. "We couldn't do that from the comfort and warmth of your bed?"

I shake my head. "Josh," I sign. "I feel like I owe you an explanation… about the operation and everything that happened this morning."

He clears his throat as he scoots closer to me, his knees touching mine. "Okay, babe," he says, his tone sobering. "Go ahead. I'm listening."

I point to my phone, knowing I'll struggle signing it.

Nodding, he places his hands on my knees and keeps his eyes locked on mine.

After taking a breath, I activate Cordy and gather my courage. *"The truth is, after what happened with Tommy last time I was there, I tried really hard not to let it affect me, but it did. And I kind of lost my way a little bit."*

"You know he didn't mean what he said, right?" Josh says, his voice low. "He was angry at me and he took it out on you."

I shrug. *"It doesn't really matter why it happened. It did. And as much as I didn't want it to—it hurt. Not so much that he said those things, but it was more the realization that I could never read him a bedtime story like he wanted, or that I could never sing with him, or talk properly to him. I thought about our future—not just you and me, but all three of us—and I somehow convinced myself that it wasn't fair to have to put that burden on either of you."*

I hit speak and watch Josh as he takes in every relayed word. He's no longer looking at me, though, he's looking down at his lap. He doesn't speak, so I continue, *"But I was selfish. I wanted him in my life as much as I wanted you and I wasn't willing to give it up without a fight. So I spoke to Lexy and asked if there was anything I could do. She told me about Dr. Schmidt, a doctor in Germany—a surgeon who specializes in his field. He comes to the*

States twice a year and operates on four patients who are prime candidates for what he does. Lexy thought I would be suitable, so she passed on my medical history...

"If I could have had the operation, it would've been a couple months from now. That's why I got that job, but it wouldn't have been enough, and I don't know why, but I feel like you should know that I would've gone to you, Josh. I would've asked you for the money. If it came down to it... that's how badly I wanted it."

I wipe at the tears building and attempt to push down the ache tugging at my chest. Without looking at him for a response, I add, *"I don't deal well with disappointment. I shut down and I pretend like it doesn't exist. That's part of the reason I pushed you away this morning, because I knew you'd want to talk about it. I knew you'd try to come up with your own ways to fix the problem, because that's who you are. You like to fix things, and I knew you'd do anything to save me."*

"Maybe it's my pride. I don't know. But it's just like your money. I don't want it to define us. I don't want you to have to take care of me. I don't want you to always be the hero, and for me to always be the girl who needs saving."

"Becca, it's not about that," he says quickly. "It's about me loving you."

"I know that. You've shown me that. You and Tommy both. And that's why I wanted to talk to you about all this. When I saw him today and he showed me that he'd been learning sign language, he took that fear, that disappointment I'd been drowning in, and he made them disappear.

"I can't even begin to describe in words how much it means to me that you've all found a way to make me feel like this impairment isn't an impairment at all. You've made me feel like I'm part of something, and that my inability to speak is something I'll never have to worry about. You've made me feel accepted, something I struggle with daily, but more than that... you've given me hope, Josh."

His hands tighten on my knees, letting me know he's heard me.

I sniff back a sob. *"You've given me so much hope. And I don't think I even realized that that's what I've been searching for this whole time. Walking away from that hospital room and away from you was the hardest thing I've ever had to do."*

I let my emotions control me a moment, struggling to see through my tears. Josh stays silent, knowing there's more, knowing I'm about to give him *everything.*

"I left because I thought I needed to grow, needed to find myself, and I did. To an extent. But I never felt whole, never felt complete, not until I had you and Tommy again, and I know that's pathetic—"

"It's not," he interrupts.

"But it's the truth," Cordy says over him.

I look up at him. He's shaking his head. "You had every right to leave me, Becs. I said and did horrible things—"

"You were hurting. I should've been there for you."

"You didn't cause my hurt, though. *I* caused yours."

The alarm on my phone sounds and I stand quickly. "Get up," I sign.

He stands, his eyes narrowed in confusion.

"Stand still."

"Okay?"

I sign. "Don't move." Then I shove my phone in my pocket, link my fingers with his and I wait.

Right on cue, the train's whistle blows, echoing through the night. A moment later, the all-too-familiar sound of the birds cawing fills my ears. Josh tries to move, but I grasp his hands tighter and mouth, "Don't move."

He nods, but there's a fear in his eyes that has my lips twitching with a smile.

The birds grow louder, now mixing with the sound of their flapping wings.

I close my eyes, waiting for *the* moment.

The air changes, rushes of wind prickling my skin, and I know they're close.

"Becca..." Josh says. "They're coming right for—"

He doesn't get a chance to finish before the birds swarm, flying between us and around us, their wings brushing against our bodies but never right at us. It lasts only a few seconds, five at most, and then it's silent again.

Like a true athlete, Josh soaks in the adrenaline and stands unmoving, waiting for it to pass. "Holy shit!" he breathes out. "What the fuck was that?"

Grinning, I pull out my phone again. *"Cool, huh?"*

He shakes his head while sucking in a huge breath. "You do this a lot, I take it?"

I nod.

"Why?" he asks.

Cordy says for me, *"Because it teaches me that if I stand tall, brave and unwilling to back down, then the chaos, the destruction—it can't attack me. It can't touch me. It makes me feel invincible."*

He laughs a disbelieving laugh and pulls me into his arms. "You're some kind of phenomenal, Becca Owens," he murmurs, kissing the top of my head.

I squeeze my hands between us so I can type, *"This is my second favorite place in the entire world."*

"Oh yeah? Where's your first?"

"Right here. In your arms."

We sit and watch the sunrise from the rooftop, his legs on either side of mine, his arms around me, cocooning me, unknowingly protecting me.

"You know what the dictionary definition of *coast* is, Becs?"

I shake my head and face him.

"It's where the land meets the sea." He presses his lips to my temple. "What if you were the land, and I were the sea? What if the coast we'd been searching for was *us* all along... living and existing together...?"

We count down the minutes until we have to live and exist apart again. But something's changed between us, something that confirms my *hope*. That regardless of how far apart we might be physically, there's something that holds us together, keeps us close, keeps us *us.*

All three of us.

~

The car ride home is spent in silence, our embrace the only thing we need to communicate how we feel. No goodbyes. No see-you-laters. No unspoken promises.

"You know," I sign, turning to him when I reach my front door. "If you wanted to shout it from the rooftops—about you and me—I might not be as mad as you think."

He smiles at that, kisses me once, and makes his way down the porch steps and into the waiting car.

I walk through the house as quietly as possible, even though I'm sure Dad's awake, waiting for me to arrive safely. I crawl into bed, letting the exhaustion take over me. I'm almost asleep when my phone chimes in my back pocket, alerting me of a notification. A few seconds later, the alerts are constant, vibrating against my butt. I pull out my phone and with one eye open, I tap on the screen. It's an Instagram post from Josh that he'd tagged me in—a picture he'd taken the first night he spent here. I'm lying in the crook of his arm, half my face hidden in his chest. I'd been shy, I remember, because I'd just walked out of the bathroom naked after making love for the second time. Even though the blanket's pulled up to my chin, you can tell that we're naked, and going by the flush in our cheeks, it's obvious what we'd been doing. I should be mad that of all the pictures he'd taken of us, he'd chosen this one. But I'm not. I'm almost proud, and that pride turns to pure joy when I read the caption beneath it:

My Heart.
My World.
My Coast.
My Becca.

~

Josh: Two things. And please don't be mad.
Becca: About that Instagram post? I'm not mad.
Josh: No. I mean, it's good you're not mad about that but that's not what I wanted to tell you.
Becca: Oh no.
Josh: Where's your car?
Becca: Dad likes for me to keep it in the garage. Why?
Josh: Oh.
Becca: Why?!
Josh: Because when you told me you had a job and you wouldn't tell me why, I assumed it was because you were saving for a car. So I kind of maybe ordered you one online while you were sleeping. It's being delivered today.
Becca: What?! You can't just "order me a car"!!!
Josh: Clearly I can, because I did. Also, I accidentally stole your bra and panties. Please don't tell your dad.

CHAPTER 48

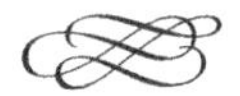

JOSHUA

"Wake up, white boy," Nico says, slapping my face. "Funny. Your hair *still* looks stupid today."

"Fuck off."

"Wheels up in three hours."

"It's like the ass-crack of dawn. Who the hell flies a plane this early?"

"Maybe if you'd gotten some sleep instead of chatting with your girl all night, you'd be well-rested like me."

"How long is this flight again?"

"Fifteen hours," he sings.

"Fuck."

"We're flying commercial, too. And Chris could only get four seats in first class, so you're in coach."

"When the hell was that decided?"

"In Mexico when you were in the hotel room chatting with your girl."

"Ugh."

"Ugh all you want, but that's what happens when you decide not to take part in team activities."

"Catching food poisoning and spending the next few days hugging a toilet bowl is team development now?"

He shakes his head at me. "Just get your ass dressed and meet us outside. My grandma's driving us to the airport."

"She finally got her U.S license?" I ask, slipping on a shirt.

"Nope."

~

Becca: I'm about to get on the plane. By the time I land, you'll be in the air. Sigh. I miss you, Skater Boy.

Josh: I'm going to video call you as soon as I land. I don't have the mental capacity or mathematical knowhow to work out what time it will be for you so I won't be mad if you don't answer. Give your grams a kiss for me. I love you.

Becca: In all ways. For always.

~

It's easy to jump to conclusions, to let your worst fears take hold of you and not think logically. Especially when you get off a fifteen-hour flight, switch on your phone and get a message from your mom saying that you needed to call her right away.

"Josh," she says, her voice a whisper.

"What's going on, Ma?" I ask, trying to work through the crowd at Hong Kong International while not losing sight of my teammates. "Is it Tommy? Is he okay? Becca? Chaz?"

"Josh," she says again.

"Just say it, Mom."

She sobs into the phone, making me freeze in my spot. I drop my luggage, causing someone to trip over it. People move around me, shoving me from side to side and all I can do is stand there, listening to my mother cry. "Mom?"

"Tommy's fine. But there's been an accident, sweetheart, and you need to come home."

PART IV

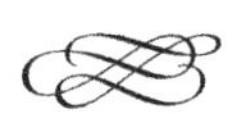

JOURNAL

Darkness seeps in my veins like acid poured in my soul until grief is my only burden.

I have no concept of time.
Of lights and shadows.
Of sounds and silence.
There's only pain.
Too afraid to sleep,
Yet too afraid to breathe.
I lie on the floor.
In her room.
Right where her bed used to be.
I stare at the ceiling.
Unblinking.
Unthinking.
Unexisting.
I block out the voices in my head.
The constant humming of voices downstairs.
The car rounded the corner too fast, they said.
But I know.
I saw it in her eyes.

Right before she walked in front of it.
I saw her.
I saw it all.
I wish her God had taken my sight instead of my voice.
Because then I wouldn't have to see it.
Over and over.
And maybe, I could've begged her to stop.
Just... stop.

CHAPTER 49

BECCA

"I hate you the most, Becca."

I wake up gasping for air and blinking back tears… tears caused by the nightmare. It's light out, the curtains are wide open, and I try to recall when I did that. I didn't. I fell asleep where I lay, forced numbness on my mind. Voices sound, filtering from downstairs, but none of them belong to the one person I want to hear. "He caught the company jet from LAX," I hear Josh's mom say. "He should touch down within an hour." I don't know how long I've slept. I don't know what time it is. What day it is. All I know is the nightmare is still there, infiltrating my mind, just like it has many times, only this time I don't treat it as a dream. I treat it as a memory. As a sign. And with false determination, I pick myself slowly up off the floor and make my way to Grams's bathroom. I shower, get lost in the heat of the water, and make sure to clear my face of the tears that have lived there. I need to do this, I convince myself. I need to *be* this.

For *him*.

Both Ella and Josh's uncle Robby are standing in the kitchen, no Tommy in sight. "Hey sweetheart," Ella says, approaching me slowly. I raise my hands between us, not wanting to be touched. "Josh will be home soon," she says, her voice cracking, signs of rejection and hurt hidden in her fake smile. "Are you hungry? I can fix you something? You haven't left that room for"—she looks at her watch—"too long."

"I'm not hungry," I sign.

"I'm really sorry, Becca. About everything," Rob says, moving around the kitchen counter. He doesn't make a move to touch me.

"You look really nice," says Ella.

I look over at her—at the lack of make-up revealing the dark circles around her eyes.

"Is that a new dress?"

I realize her voice isn't husky from her emotions. That, unlike me, she hasn't been able to sleep at all. I wonder if that makes me a horrible person. Maybe I don't know how to mourn. How to grieve. I didn't shed a tear when my mother died. Not even at her funeral.

"It's Josh's favorite," I sign. "I thought it would be nice for him to see me in it when he comes home." Strange that I can cry thinking about Josh—hoping that I can take some of his anger and pain away with a stupid dress, but I can't seem to feel anything when it comes to losing my grandmother—a woman who took me in when no one else could.

"He'll love it," Ella says.

"I think..." I begin to sign, but pause, my hands freezing mid-movement. The memories hit me again, like physical punches to the gut, making me weak. Blinking hard, I attempt to push them away and continue, "Josh doesn't handle bad news very well. He might get physical. Or say and do things that are hurtful but he doesn't mean them. He's just... hurting. And I think it's really important we stay strong and be there for him. Okay?"

Ella stares at me a long time before switching her gaze to

Robby, who has no idea what all I just said. "Okay," she says. "We'll be strong. For *Josh*."

I nod, quickly swiping at the tears on my cheeks. "I'm going to wait for him outside. On the porch steps. He loves the porch steps..." I contain my sob, just long enough to add, "It's where we fell in love."

But the porch steps are only half of what they used to be, and it's not the same.

Nothing's the same.

It never will be.

I pick wildly at the bolts that keep the stupid ramp in place until the tips of my fingers begin to throb. And then I use my entire hand, trying in vain to loosen them so I can remove the ramp because it doesn't fucking belong here. Grams hated it here! My thumb catches on a spike of metal on the bolt, and I do it again and again, wanting to feel the pain, waiting to feel the numbness it will soon create.

I angrily swat a hand off my shoulder, not bothering to see who it is. I just want them to leave me alone so I can get this damn bolt off and move to the next so I can get back *our* steps.

Voices.

So many voices.

I blink hard, trying to rid the voices, but they're everywhere.

Behind me.

Above me.

Inside me.

Grams likes the quiet.

She doesn't need all these damn voices.

"Shut up! Shut up! Shut up!" I yell. No one hears. They never do. "Grams is resting, dammit! Shut. Up!"

The bolts are red now, covered in my blood. Blood I didn't know was there.

"Becca?" Ella says.

"Shut up, shut up, shut up, shut up."

A hand covers mine, stopping me from my task, and I flinch against his touch. But then I realize it's safe. His touch is *safe.* I look up to see dark and wary eyes watching me. "It needs to go, Josh," I sign. "These are our steps and they're not the same with this stupid ramp here. These are our steps and this is Grams's house!" I wipe my face on my forearm, letting my tears and sweat soak through my skin. "Someone's going to take her house and our steps, and it won't be the same! It won't be the same, Josh! It won't!" I pick at the bolts again, my tears falling, seeping into the grains of the timber.

"Becca..." he whispers, his breaths heavy. "I won't let anything happen to the house, okay? I promise. Just please stop. You're hurting yourself." He yanks on my hands, but I keep them in place. "Please, baby." He cups my jaw with one hand, his thumb swiping at my cheek, while the other hand takes both of mine and holds them to his chest. His gaze shifts behind me, and he nods once. The loud blaring of a drill fills my ears, and I cringe at the sound. "Stop!" I yell, but it's silent. Still, Josh sees it, *sees me,* and his eyes narrow in question. "Grams is resting."

CHAPTER 50

JOSHUA

I'd given Chris the news and parted ways with the rest of the team at the airport. I'd spent five hours there waiting for the next available flight, sitting on my phone, trying to research all the ways a person can suffer from grief. I wanted to be ready for anything when I got home. I'd been through this with Tommy before, and while his and my father's relationship was short lived, they were still close. I didn't want to compare which loss would be greater for him, and I definitely didn't want to assume. He was older now, and a lot more in tune with what went on in the world. I'd be there for him, but I'd let him grieve in his own way.

Becca, though—I had no idea what to expect with Becca. I didn't even know what to search to find out.

How does a person with a history of depression deal with death?

How does a person with a history of abuse handle grief?

What to expect when someone with a mental history loses a loved one?

How to be there for someone who's lost a grandparent.

The list went on and on, and it did nothing to clear my head and lessen my assumptions, but it did help deflect from my own feelings—feelings I wasn't ready to recognize.

Not yet.

I waited until I was on the plane, until we were in the air and the meals had been served, and the cabin lights were dimmed to pull the thin blanket the airline provided over my head so I could shield the other passengers from my cries. I let the memories flood me, let it all sink in, and I let it *hurt.* Because I know better than anyone that it's not worth losing control of your actions, control of yourself, just to hold it all inside and one day explode, destroying everything that mattered to you. I sobbed into the blanket, curled into myself, my body shaking with the force, until I had no tears left to cry. And at some point—I don't know how, I don't know why—I just stopped.

Just... *stopped.*

And I sat up in my seat, lifted the window shade and looked out at the wide-open sky and the pillows of clouds I seemed to be floating on. They were pink—the same shade of pink as the roses that lined Chaz's porch—and this strange calm washed through me.

I'd never believed in God.

I'd prayed to one, but never truly believed that a higher power existed.

I'd joke in the past that Chaz was the only God I knew, the only saving grace I'd ever need.

And as I stared out the window in awe of how vast the world was, my beliefs didn't change.

Chaz was the only higher power I needed to know, and it wasn't Google who was going to help me get through this, who was going to help me process this new normal with Becca. It was Chaz's guidance and the knowledge that I wouldn't have felt peace in my heart, in my soul, if Chaz wasn't the one offering it. Because she felt it, too—at peace—in a world above the clouds where her mind was as clear as her memories.

Becca sits on my closed toilet seat while I tend to her bleeding fingers. She's smiling. I don't know why she's smiling, but I smile back because I don't know what else to do or what to think or how to feel.

"Do you like my dress?" she signs once I've applied the last bandage.

I stare at her, conflicted. A part of me wants to be just like her—to carry on as if nothing's happened—but another part of me wants to shake her, make her wake up and deal with this. Mourn and grieve, and do all the things she should be doing. But then her emerald eyes lift to mine, clear of pain, of heartache, and I almost want to wait until Tommy gets here and sit them both down and treat her like I would him.

Tommy... he's gone through way too much change in his six years.

"Do you?" she signs, her eyes wide, waiting for my response.

I push away all other thoughts. "I love your dress, baby."

Her smile widens. "It's your favorite."

Grief can cause insanity, I tell myself. "I know. Thank you for wearing it."

"Can we eat ice cream?"

"What?" I ask, tired and confused. I step back when she stands up.

"I C E C R E A M," she spells out.

"I know what you said, but I don't..." *I don't know why you said it, Becca.* "I don't think I have any."

She nods, her lips pressed tight. "My dad will get me ice cream." She walks out of the room on a mission to get to her phone.

Slowly, I follow after her. "When is your dad getting here?" I ask her back.

She stops mid movement, her shoulders lifting with each inhaled breath. Then she turns, her head cocked to the side. "I don't know," she signs slowly. "When did you call him?"

"I didn't, Becs." I approach her with careful, heavy steps. "Did you?"

She looks at me a beat, as if coming to terms with her actions. Then her head moves from side to side and she steps away from me. Her hands come up between us, shielding her from me. Tears fill her eyes, and a moment later she's on the floor, her hands covering her head, her body rocking back and forth like she'd done in the past when a nightmare had taken her down to the depths of her hell. Only this isn't a nightmare. It's real. And it's happening right now.

"Becca." I rush to her but I don't dare touch her. I know enough not to.

For minutes, she stays that way, her cries silent, and her thumb between her teeth. Finally, she looks up, her eyes void of any emotion. She looks *through* me, her hands raised, shaking as she signs, "She's dead. Dead. Dead. Dead. Dead. Dead. Dead—"

I cover her hands to stop her from repeating the word, and I use my chest to cover her face, cover her pain. Then I find the strength to pull away and I kiss her. I kiss her, I kiss her, I kiss her, until the trembling stops and she kisses me back, her hands desperate as they wander over me. We stand together, our lips locked and movements frantic as we strip out of our clothes and make our way to the bedroom where we both know that we need the physical pleasure to take away at least some of the torment. And with tear-soaked eyes, and broken hearts, we do what we can to protect our broken, shattered souls.

CHAPTER 51

BECCA

---

crazy

'kreɪzi/

informal

adjective

1. mad, especially as manifested in wild or aggressive behavior.

My grandmother loved summer storms. From the very little, yet random things I knew about her, that was one of them.

One night during the summer I stayed with her, she jerked me awake just so we could stand out in the rain and listen to the thunder and watch the lightning turn the world white. *"Some people believe that storms are God's way of showing us his anger,"* she'd shouted. *"But I don't believe it. God can never truly be angry. It's just his way of reminding us that we exist, not just in ourselves, but as an entire race. That's why the heavens open, Becca. So we can celebrate life together."* She danced in the rain that night, her bare feet stomping, splashing water around her while her laughter outweighed the claps of thunder.

I'd stayed on the porch, protected by the roof, completely mesmerized by her movements, her words. *Just her*.

I never got the chance to dance in the rain with her.

Never got the chance to celebrate life.

But I am now.

I spin in circles, my feet splashing, my head tilted back letting the rain pour down on me. Thunder cracks, and I flinch. But then silent laughter bursts out of me and I widen my spins, my arms slicing through the air, through the heavy sheets of raindrops.

My therapist says I control who I am and who I want to be. My mother was crazy. So was my grandmother. But my mother was crazy in the evilest form, while my grandmother was a million different shades of it in all the best possible ways.

If I got to choose which brand of crazy I'd end up being, I'd choose to be like Grams.

"What the hell are you doing, Becca?" Josh shouts, standing just outside his apartment door. He's wearing nothing but boxer briefs, exactly the way I'd left him in bed a couple of hours ago. He squints down at me through the darkness of the night. Another clap of thunder, followed by a flash of lightning. "Jesus Christ, you're going to get yourself killed!"

I don't know why he's yelling at me. I'm just celebrating Grams's life like she'd have wanted. I sign up at him, "Dance with me!"

He charges down his stairs, only slowing his steps when he's a few feet away from me. He's so beautiful, so graceful.

"Becca, it's too dangerous to be out here," he says, his voice laced with pity.

A gush of wind almost knocks me off my feet, but he holds me steady, saving me.

He's always saving me.

Always taking care of me.

"I love you," I sign.

"I love you, too, Becs. But we need to get inside."

"Just dance with me," I sign, pouting up at him. "One dance."

He shakes his head.

I swing my camera behind my back, the strap spinning around my neck, and wrap my arms around his waist. Settling my hand on his chest, I let the wind control our movements. We sway together, awkward in our soaked embrace. But it's perfect. Because it's him and it's me, and we're dancing in the rain, doing what Grams would be doing. Until he grasps my shoulders and gently pushes me away. "I'm going to get sick, Becs. I can't afford to get sick right now."

I shove his chest. "So leave!" I sign and point to his door. "Go!" I turn my back on him and face the flowers lining the fence. Then I lift my camera, switching it on as I do. I bring the viewfinder to my eye and press down on the shutter. The shutter never sounds. I pull away and check the battery icon, but nothing shows on the screen. I switch it off and on again, my bandaged thumb slipping against the switch. I try again. And again. Nothing works.

Josh is standing beside me now, his gaze switching from the camera to me. "Why won't it work?" I sign.

He sighs.

"I wanted to take some photographs for Grams," I tell him. "Summer storms are her favorite. Like this dress is your favorite." I point to my dress. "Do you like it?"

"I love your dress, babe. I already told you that."

"You did?" I sign.

His lips form a line as he nods once. Slow. Careful.

I frown and look down at my camera again. "Why won't my camera work?" I sign.

Josh steps to me, his arms going around my shoulders. He brings my face into his bare chest while thunder cracks and lighting turns the world bright. "In all ways. For always," he murmurs, but I don't think he's talking to me.

~

Josh helps me into his apartment, into his bathroom, and into the shower. He watches me, but not the same way he did in Portland. His eyes don't wander my body. They don't wander at all. They stare at my eyes, and they question. They question who I am, who he is, and who we are together, and whether it's possible that his declaration to love me unconditionally is actually possible. I know that's what he's thinking, because I think it, too.

The shower acts like a cold one, the sprays of water blanketing me with the realization of what I'd done and the way I'd acted. Maybe I'm my own brand of crazy. And maybe after watching me Josh realized that. And as I step out of the shower and into his waiting hands—hands holding a towel he uses to dry me—I decide to give him the only truth, the only secret I've kept to myself. Not just because he deserves to know, but because after everything I've caused him to experience, he deserves an *out*.

I tap his shoulder and wait for him to look at me. "I can't have your children, Josh," I sign.

He freezes, his towel-covered hands on my leg. "What?"

I grab my phone off the counter. *"Physically, I probably can. I just don't want to."* I keep my features even, not willing to reveal any sign of the heartache it causes to tell him this. I don't want him to know it hurts. I just want him to *know*.

Josh stands to full height, his breath leaving him. "Why not?"

I choose my words carefully, wanting to give him the truth, and not cloud the facts with my emotions. *"I did this study in sociology in high school. Nature vs. Nurture. My research paper was on what would make a mother an abusive alcoholic. If it was how she was raised or what she was around. She had a perfect adult life, really. A decent job, decent social life. But she used to always tell me about her dad's drinking. How he hit her mother in front of her. She told me that right afterward, they'd have sex in front of her to show her that that's what love was. You fight and you love. I'm not saying it's an excuse for what she did to me. I'm just saying I don't want it to be an excuse for what I might possibly do to my children."*

"Becca." He shakes his head, his eyes disbelieving. "You can't live your life like that."

I ignore his statement and add, *"It doesn't hurt to think about anymore. It used to. Then I met Tommy and saw how you were with him and I thought, at some point, if I didn't physically have a child, then I didn't have to worry about treating them the way my mother had, or the way her parents had treated her. But if I had my own..."* I trail off, shrinking beneath his penetrating gaze. *"We could still be a nice little family. You, me, and Tommy. But that's all we'd ever be. Just the three of us. And if that's not enough for you, I would understand, Josh. I wouldn't stop you from walking away like I once did. You earned that right. And I'd let you go. Because it's not fair that you should have to love me broken, especially when I can never make you whole."*

CHAPTER 52

JOSHUA

Becca's crazy.

And I know it's wrong for me to say that, but if she thinks that her completely unselfish decision to not want to bear any children is going to make me leave her then yeah, she's fucking crazy.

I'd never leave her.

Sure, I've thought about what our children would look like; bright emerald eyes behind a sea of raven dark bangs. She'd be a girl, of course, because why the hell wouldn't I want two versions of Becca in my life? And, yes, I appreciate her telling me how she truly felt. But did it change the way I feel about her? Not one bit.

"Will you come to bed with me?" I ask. "And *stay* in bed with me? I've spent too many nights away from you, woken up too many times and not had you there. Just stay and *be with me*, Becs. That's all I want. Now and forever."

JOURNAL

My dad arrived at the same time Tommy came home.

The same time Sadie decided to pack her bags and leave the house.

If she'd been around this entire time, I didn't notice her.

I don't notice a lot of things.

I live in my own world, trapped in my own head.

Days pass.

Dad makes me eat.

Makes me shower.

Makes me sleep.

There are no summer storms.

And the storm that came took away her roses.

Now they're dead.

Just like her.

And I don't even have a camera to capture it.

To capture beauty in the face of death.

I should have captured her beauty.

I should've—

CHAPTER 53

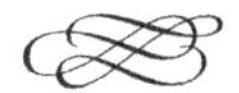

JOSHUA

"She's just not responding at all," Martin says, his words as rushed as our footsteps.

I practically crash through the front door, past the living room and into the kitchen where Martin said Becca had been for the past two hours.

I'd spent the past few days with Tommy, who'd taken the news better than I thought, and meeting with my mom to organize the funeral tomorrow and all the other things I needed to do as Chazarae's power of attorney. Mom mentioned she was surprised at how well I'd taken Chaz's death. I was purposely keeping too busy to feel *anything*. At least that's what I told her. I'll never tell her the truth. I'll never tell anyone. Besides, how do you tell someone that you truly believe a person who had so much to offer alive was better off dead? She was no longer that person we all wanted to believe she was. By the end, she'd lost the fight to fake it, and now—she no longer had to.

I'd checked in on Becca often since her dad got here, even had her stay with me at night. She'd been bad, but never like this. Never so out of it that she couldn't acknowledge my presence.

She's sitting on the floor, her knees raised close to her chest, wearing one of my t-shirts—a shirt so big she uses it to cover her legs. She's not crying, but her eyes are glazed, not with tears, but with complete and utter misery.

Her hands are on her head, her eyes staring at nothing in front of her.

It hurts to swallow.

About as much as it hurts to see her like this.

Completely *empty.*

I step toward her, careful not to spook her, and that's when I focus on the hundreds of pictures littered around her. Pictures of Chazarae, some of them together, some of her alone. Some I've seen before, most I haven't.

Martin says, "She was up all night on her computer, and I heard the printer running but I didn't…" He rubs his eyes—eyes tired and defeated.

"Becca." I squat in front of her. "Baby, what are you doing?"

She doesn't react. Not in the slightest.

"Daddy?" Tommy says from behind me.

My eyes drift shut. He shouldn't be here. I told him to stay in bed.

"Is my Becca okay?" he asks, standing next to me, his hand on my shoulder.

He's not wearing a top. Just pajama bottoms.

"Becca's very sad, buddy," I tell him.

Tommy nods, and then copies my position. Only he settles a hand on her knee, and I almost cringe, fearing her response. I know not to touch her when she's like this. He doesn't. But the response isn't what I was expecting. For the first time, her eyes move. First to Tommy, then to me, and even through her daze, through the tangled web of emotions that brought her here, sitting in the corner of the kitchen surrounded by painful memories, I can see the apology in her eyes. See the regret she feels that Tommy has to see her like this.

Her lips move, but her words are silent. Quickly, but carefully, I move Tommy out of the way and shift closer to her. "What is it, baby?"

"I want," she mouths, rocking back and forth.

"You want…? What do you want?"

"I want," she repeats, tears filling her eyes. She blinks once. Hard. And the tears fall, fast and free, giant droplets of withheld emotions streak down her cheeks and fall with purpose. "I want," she says again, rocking faster, crying harder. She points to one of the many photographs on the floor.

Tommy's the first to reach for it, the first to see the image of a woman with curly blonde hair, wearing a blue dress, carrying a toddler on her hip… a toddler with raven dark hair and eyes the color of emeralds…

"Is this your mamma?" Tommy asks.

Becca nods slowly, a silent sob filtering from her mouth and wrapping around my heart, taking away its pulse, its reason. It's hope.

Tommy whispers, "You want your mamma?"

Becca nods again, covering her head as if to cover her shame that of all the things she could want, she could need, it's the one person who tried to take it all away.

"Sometimes when I'm sad, I want my mamma, too," Tommy says, his innocence defying all logic. "But most of the time, I want my daddy."

Becca looks up, her eyes right on his, and her chest rapidly rising and falling with her breaths.

"Do you want me to sleep in your bed with you?" Tommy asks. "I can cuddle you. That's what my daddy does when I'm sad."

Becca nods again, her cries still silent, and takes Tommy's offered hand to help her up. He keeps a hold of her hand all the way up the stairs and to her room.

"You raised some kid there, Warden," Martin says.

I blink, coming to terms with everything that's happened. I pick up the photograph Becca had pointed to. "This is her mom?" I ask him.

"That's Rebecca."

I don't know why I feel the need to take the picture and shove it in my pocket, but I do.

I make my way upstairs and toward Becca's room where I stand in the doorway and watch Tommy sitting against the headboard, patting his lap. "You can lie your head here, and I can stroke it. If you want me to. That's what Daddy does when I'm sad, too."

Becca lies on her side, her head on his lap, and he does exactly what he said he'd do. Becca cries. He doesn't see it, but I do, because she's looking right at me. She mouths, "I'm sorry." And I shake my head at her. She has nothing to be sorry for.

"It's okay, Daddy," Tommy says, and my eyes meet his. "I got this. I'll take care of *our* Becca."

I move to the side, away from his view, but I don't leave. Instead, I listen. I listen to him singing—a song Chazarae used to sing to him when she was still capable of having him spend the night. "Somewhere over the rainbow…" he sings, "…way up high…"

I lean against the wall, my son's voice the soundtrack of our grief, our mourning, and I break. A thousand times over. I slide down the wall, my pain, my heartache, all of it consuming me, and I wonder how it's possible that a six-year-old is the one to keep it together. To keep *us* together. "Don't worry, Becs," he says, the song now over.

I sniff back another sob and wipe my face with my sleeve.

"My Pa's in heaven, too. He'll take care of Ma'am. Even if she's yelling at him to stop being so grumpy, and he's yelling at her to stop being so loopy. They'll take care of each other. And they'll take care of *us*."

coast
kəʊst/
noun
the part of the land adjoining or near the sea.

If I am the land,
and Josh is the sea,
Tommy is the shore that completes us.

CHAPTER 54

BECCA

"You look so handsome," I sign slowly, hoping Tommy will understand.

"I look…?" he asks.

I spell out, "S T U D," and smile up at him as I fix his tie.

He sounds out the word a couple times, before yelling, "Stud! I look like a stud?"

My grin widens.

"You guys ready?" Josh asks, entering Tommy's room, dressed as he is.

"What about Daddy?" Tommy asks. "Does he look like a stud, too?"

I stand and take Tommy's hand and lead him toward his dad. I kiss Josh quickly, and press my hand to his chest. "Stud," I mouth.

He smiles down at me. "Let's go celebrate your Grams's life."

We hold the service at Grams's church, of course.

They suggested we make it an open service. Because of everything my grandmother had contributed to the community, a lot of people would want to attend. Josh's mother, however, suggested we keep it closed, keep it intimate, especially because of his status. It was hard to gauge who exactly would show up. We didn't want media, and with how open Josh had been about his relationship with my grandmother, we were afraid it might take away from the reason we were there. But Josh disagreed with her and was adamant about it, so he hired security to keep the media out so that the doors of the church could remain open for everyone. No judgments. No questions. It was clear Grams had touched a lot of people in her life, and it wasn't fair to her for me and Josh to be the ones to decide who could and couldn't pay their respects.

Tommy sits between us. My dad next to me, and Ella, Robby and a heavily pregnant Kim, Nat and her fiancé Justin, Blake and Chloe and their families taking up the rest of the pew on the other side of Josh.

Josh's team had flown back from Hong Kong without attending the event, and going by the look of surprise on Josh's face, he wasn't aware of their decision. They sit behind us at the front of the church, along with their families and many others from Josh's work life.

Members from Grams's church take up one side of the room, we take up the other. Soon, the church begins to fill, murmured voices and condolences filtering through the air.

I sit with my gaze lowered, with Tommy's little hand in mine, his finger tracing circles in my palm—another thing Josh does for him when he's sad.

The service starts, the priest says a few words, and so do her friends and other members of the church. Ella speaks, too, her words covering everything Josh and I feel. And soon, but nowhere near soon enough, it's all over. I breathe, relieved that I was able to make it through without breaking down. We stand in unison, Josh leading the way, me in one hand, Tommy in the other, and we hold our heads high as we walk down the aisle and toward the church doors. There's no space in the room left unoccupied. Groups of people stand against the walls, against the corners, anywhere they can to pay their respects to a woman who created a legacy. As we reach the doors, doors ajar from the people trying to pile into the room, I hear a tiny voice call Tommy's name. We all stop and turn to the sound.

"Nessa," Tommy shouts, letting go of Josh's hand. He runs back a few steps and slows just in time to not crash into her. "What are you doing here?"

"We came for Becca," she says simply, pointing down the row. Members of Say Something—volunteers, kids, parents take up the entire row and the one after it. I cover my mouth with my hand, shocked and confused, and the confusion doubles when I see Pete and the rest of the team from the paper. I turn to Josh, now standing beside me, "How?" I mouth, allowing a single sob to escape. "Why?"

Josh shrugs as he points a couple rows down toward Dawn and Lexy and even Aaron. "They all wanted to be here, Becs. For you."

I move to Dawn first, allowing her to hug me. She's been such a huge part of my life for so long and I'd taken that for granted. She's here. For me. "You're going to get through this," she whispers in my ear.

"I know," I mouth, believing her more than ever before.

I will get through it.

For Grams.

For Josh.

For Tommy.

"You need to look outside," Dawn says, smiling genuinely at me.

My feet falter, my steps slow as I make my way back to the

entrance, Josh doing what he can to keep me upright. It's all too much. I'm on the verge of falling apart, of shattering in his arms, of becoming nothing more than a thousand pieces he'll have to work to make whole again.

The crowd at the doors part, allowing Josh and I to walk through.

We freeze when we see it.

Just like time does.

People stand on the steps of the church, litter through to the sidewalk and onto the road, far beyond where my eyes can see.

Hundreds of people stand…

…beneath a sea of red balloons.

Next to me, Josh grabs one from Grams's crazy friend Mavis and hands it to me, then takes one for himself.

Mavis clears her throat and leans in to whisper, "Your grandmother told me this is how she wanted to be remembered. Up there,"—she points to the sky—"she wanted to give everyone she came across a red balloon."

"Why?" I mouth, looking up for an answer.

I release the first balloon, then watch as a couple join them, followed by dozens, until the sky is filled with nothing but red.

People clap.

People cheer.

People chant my grandmother's name.

Mavis laughs, her arms waving in the air as if to work up the crowd. "Your grams was a thousand shades of crazy, Becca," she shouts. "And we loved every single one."

"He finally went down," Josh says through a sigh, walking into his bedroom while tugging at his tie.

I sit with my legs crossed in the middle of the bed, already changed out of my black dress and into one of his t-shirts. "I can't believe he's not exhausted," I sign.

Josh sits on the edge of the bed, his shoulders hunched. "I know." He removes his tie completely and unceremoniously dumps it on the floor. Then he just stares at it. Moments pass before he turns to me. "I'm so beat."

I scoot on my knees until I'm next to him and start to undo the buttons on his shirtsleeve.

"It's going to be strange," he mumbles, his free hand stroking my leg, "coming home and not racing up her porch steps, excited to see her." He rubs his eyes, not to rid the tears, but to fight the exhaustion. Inhaling deeply, he stands up and starts stripping out of his clothes until he's standing in his boxers. I watch, because there's too much beauty in his presence to look away. *I seriously could watch him forever.* But I don't have forever. I have the next two days until I go back home and back to the internship, back to double sessions with Dawn three days a week. And Josh goes back to work, all while the world continues to spin with one less wonder in its population.

I move to the top of the bed, lean against the headboard, and pat my lap, returning the smile he offers me before he lies down, his head where I wanted it, his eyes on me.

I stroke his hair with one hand and type on the phone with the other.

"Did you pay for all those people to come from St. Louis?"

Josh shakes his head slowly. "Does it matter?"

He did pay, but he's also right. It doesn't matter at all.

"Will you tell me about her?" I ask.

His brow creases. "About your Grams?"

I nod, still stroking his hair. *"I feel like I don't know her... not like I should. And by the time I realized that and wanted to ask, it was too late. She'd didn't really know herself anymore."*

He stares blankly at the ceiling. "What do you want to know?"

"Anything, really," I have Cordy say. *"Like, what did she do for work?"*

His head lifts a little, as if surprised by my question. "She was a nurse," he says after a beat.

"Really?" I mouth.

"You didn't know that?"

I shake my head, trying to imagine Grams in a life before my time. *"Tell me more."*

Josh's lips curl at the corners. "You know what..." he says, sitting up. "I can do one better."

After slipping on a pair of shorts and handing me a pair, Josh checks in on Tommy, and then leads me down his apartment stairs and toward his garage.

He starts moving boxes around, and I do the same, though I have no idea what I'm looking for. "So I was in here the other day and remembered what you said—about handing out the clothes and shoes at the shelter." He drops one on the floor and turns to me, his hands on his hips.

"Sorry. We got a little carried away," I sign.

He shakes his head. "No, I was actually thinking that we should do that. My mom—she runs the charity side of the business—the Henry Warden Foundation—maybe we could make it a thing, you know? We could do something under Chaz's name. Maybe get some sponsors involved."

"Grams would love that," I sign. "And I'd love to be a part of it... if your mom's okay with it."

"Oh man, my mom would flip if you joined her on it." He kicks a box out of the way so he can get to me. "My mom loves you, Becs. She loves you as if you were her own. You know that, right?"

I didn't know that. Not until he said it. But then again, I'm not really sure what a mother's love is supposed to feel like. Still, I find myself smiling up at him with yet another lump in my throat.

"You're so cute." He pats the mess of hair on my head. Then he spins on his heels and continues to search through boxes while I stand there, wondering if I'm worthy of his mother's love.

"Here it is," he says, pulling me from my thoughts. After grabbing the cardboard box from the highest shelf and placing it carefully on top of a pile of shoeboxes, he points to it. "Open it."

I bite down on my lip as I lift the flaps, one after the other, treating it like treasure.

Albums.

Photo albums.

A whole pile of them.

All dated.

"Maybe you can find more about her in those," he says, his voice quiet.

I pick up the first one and flip the solid red cover with 1986 scrawled on the top. The first picture is of Grams with two other women. She would've been in her mid-thirties. They're sitting on a bench, all in the same nurse's uniform.

"I told her I'd convert them to digital and store them in the Cloud for her—in case there was ever a fire or something," Josh says, and I look up at him. He shrugs, his eyes distant. "I guess I never got around to it." After a beat, he clears his throat, his gaze moving to mine. "Maybe you can make a timeline of her life from all of them. Plus, we have the Internet, maybe we can find more there?"

Josh falls asleep on his stomach, his hand resting on my leg while I sit up in his bed, surrounded by pictures of my grandmother captured in moments that make me question life.

CHAPTER 55

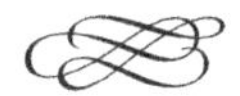

JOSHUA

FOUR MONTHS LATER.

"It was hell," Becca signs. "Remind me to never go shopping with Dad again."

I smile at the sight of her through my computer screen.

She rolls her eyes, a trait that annoys me on most people but is hot on her. Crazy, I know, but it's those damn eyes. "How much did he try to get off this time?" I ask.

"Half," she signs, throwing in another eye roll. "I was so embarrassed."

"He's just trying to get a good deal. I still don't know why you won't just let me buy you a new camera. You're a photography student, babe. How are you even managing classes right now?"

"I'm borrowing equipment, and that's kind of the reason I called."

"It is?" I ask, grinning from ear to ear. "You're going to let me buy it?"

"I have enough money saved for the body and a couple

lenses, but…" She pouts into the screen. "I can pay you back in a couple weeks."

I lean forward so I can reach the keyboard, and send her my Amazon account and password. "Just get whatever you need and save your money," I tell her. "And don't worry. I'll find ways for you to pay me back."

"You're dirty," she signs, her nose scrunched in disgust.

"No!" I shake my head quickly. "I don't know where your mind went, but I was thinking more along the lines of giving me some of those pieces you're selling on Instagram."

"Oh," she mouths, her gaze lowering.

"Filthy girl."

Shrugging, she looks back up, her emerald eyes bright against the screen's reflection. "I could do other things, too. I miss you… in that way. Touching you and making you—"

"Stop!" I almost shout. "Ry and Chris are in the room."

She laughs, silent but there. "They can't hear me, idiot!"

"Oh yeah." I'd gotten so used to communicating via ASL that sometimes I forget others don't hear or understand her. Still, I find myself leaning closer, using my arms to shield the screen, before saying, "Making me what?"

She licks her lips. God, I miss her lips.

"Wait. I have to ask you something else," she signs.

"Okay. But first tell me what you were going to say," I rush out. "Make me what?"

"Make you come, dickhead!" Ry shouts. "Touching you and making you come!"

Chris laughs.

Becca's eyes widen. "How?" she mouths.

Ry gets up and into the shot, his hands moving faster than mine do. He speaks as he signs, "My best friend's deaf. I've signed almost all my life. And by the way, your conversations are lame."

"Get the fuck out of here," I tell Ry, pushing him toward the door. He chuckles to himself as he gathers his shit from my room. A moment later, the door closes.

"Did you not know?" Becca signs, her eyes huge.

"Swear it, babe. I had no idea. What were you going to ask?"

She points down to her keyboard, and I nod, adjusting the program so I can see what she's typing.

Remember the Fine House Award I got nominated for?

"Of course I remember."

I made it to the finals.

A slow smile spreads across my face. "That's awesome, baby. I'm so happy for you. You deserve it."

Thank you.

"So what now? We wait to see if you've won?"

She bites down on her lip, preventing her grin from fully forming. *I did win.*

"Shut up!" I shout. "That's amazing! I knew you would!" My words are rushed and loud and now Chris is behind me, looking at the screen, wondering what the hell is happening. "I'm so fucking proud of you, Becs. Holy shit!" I can see her laughing at my reaction, but I don't care. I'm excited. Maybe too excited. But she deserves this so much and it's about fucking time she had something good happen to her.

She type: *So I guess there's this fancy dinner coming up where they hand me an award and pass over one of those huge checks and I make a "speech" and I know it's really late notice because it's happening in two weeks, and this might possibly be the longest run-on sentence in the history of the world, but it would mean a lot to me if you were able to make it as my date. I just really want you there but I understand if you can't because you have so much going on right now.*

I sit higher. "What's the date?"

It's two Fridays from now.

Chris is already on his phone, no doubt checking his

calendar and when his gaze lifts and his eyes meet mine, I know it's not good.

"Can I call you back real quick?" I ask Becca. "I just need to go over some stuff with Chris."

"Okay," she signs. Then types: *If you can't make it, I understand. Honestly. I don't want you to feel bad.*

"I'll call you back."

As soon as my laptop's shut, Chris says, "It's the Teen Choice Awards. You're presenting an award. You have to be there."

I grunt in frustration, and look up at him, hoping he can see the plea in my eyes. "I know that I've asked a lot from you lately, especially with the whole Chaz thing—"

"Don't do that, Josh. Don't use her to guilt me—"

"I'm not," I say, my hands up between us. "It's just that I need to make this happen. For Becca. And for me. Chris,"—I grasp his shirt so he knows how serious I am—"It's time…"

CHAPTER 56

BECCA

I stare at the picture of my grandmother, her head tilted back, her hands and forearms covered in white silk gloves, one of them holding the hand of a mystery man as they pause their dancing so the photograph can be taken. The year on the album had her at twenty-two in this picture. Around the same age as me. The dress she wore was black, high collar, flowy skirt, white buttons down the middle. It was simple and elegant and beautiful, just like her. I found the dress in a box in the back of the closet—it's condition as perfect as it was in the picture.

Both the dress and the gloves look better on her than they do on me, but I don't mind. The point isn't to look good, it's to remember that she's with me, tonight and all the nights after.

"The speech is perfect," Dad says, walking into my room with his brand new tux, the sleeves and pant leg a tad short, but it's hard to find something for his stature that doesn't come with a tailor-made price tag.

I take the piece of paper from him and fold it, placing it in my purse, along with the photograph of grams, before standing from my desk chair and going to him. "You look so handsome,"

I sign. I pat down the collar of his jacket. "Thank you for leaving work early and coming tonight. It means so much."

"I wouldn't miss this for the world," he says, his voice soft and sweet, a complete contrast to his usual tone. "Besides, I missed all your special nights. All those dances and proms… so I'm going to make you dance with me. I hope you know that."

"A: I didn't go to any dances and proms and B: I don't think there'll be any dancing tonight."

He scoffs. "Just because there's no dance floor or music, doesn't mean we can't dance, Becca."

My eyes snap to his, my heart skipping a beat. He's definitely my grandmother's son.

"Did I say something?" he asks.

I shake my head. "You just reminded me of Grams, that's all."

Before he gets a chance to respond, there's a knock on the door that causes my panic to spike.

"That must be Prince Charming," Dad says, cracking his knuckles. "Time for a beat down."

I narrow my eyes at him and sign, "Stop. He's still so afraid of you."

"Me? Why?" he asks, looking down at me with his nose in the air. "I'm harmless."

I roll my eyes and pat down my dress. "How do I look?" I sign.

He turns serious. "You look beautiful, Becca. He's lucky to have you."

~

Josh stares at me.

I stare at him.

He blows out a breath.

I inhale one.

"You…" he says, and stares some more.

"What?" I mouth.

"…do insane things to my heart, Becca Owens."

"You're not so bad yourself," I sign.

He runs his hand through his hair, still in the middle of the awkward grow out stage from when he shaved it. "I tried. Not that it matters. No one will be looking at me when you're on my arm." He reaches into his pocket. "I got you something."

"Why? You didn't have to!"

"It's nothing really. Actually, it's stupid cheesy," he says, revealing a dark green velvet bag. He empties the content into his palm and then hands it to me. It's a ring, similar to the one he gave me on my eighteenth birthday, only this one reads: *I shoot like an award winner.*

I kiss him a little too passionately considering my dad's now standing behind me, but I don't care. I love my stupid cheesy ring and I love Josh. It's been four whole months, and I miss him.

With a chuckle, Josh breaks the kiss and nods over my shoulder at Dad. "You guys ready to go?" he asks, pointing to the limo waiting at the curb.

Dad rubs his hands together. "I've never been in a limo," he says, marching down the steps. "Is there champagne?"

The event is held at a fancy hotel in the fancy part of downtown and the room is filled with fancy people who speak fancy words while consuming a fancy dinner. I'd asked Josh if he could purchase Sandra a ticket to the event, along with Dad's, knowing they weren't able to afford them, because like I said, the event is fancy. I needed Sandra here so she could relay my speech. Sure, I could've written it in a way that Dad or Josh could translate for me, but I knew how much it meant to them to see me up on that stage and to celebrate my achievement together.

There's a slideshow of the award winners' work displayed on a huge projector screen up on the stage. There are only five awards, and that means only five images, and Josh and Dad make a show of applauding every single time Grams shows up on the screen.

Every.

Single.

Time.

It becomes a game to them, something the people sharing our table seem to find amusing. "That's my girlfriend's," Josh says to anyone who will listen. "That's my daughter's," Dad says, doing the same. And so the game continues and the night goes on and I watch in awe at the two men in my life who seem to have found a common ground. There's no longer detest in my father's eyes when he looks at Josh, and no longer fear in Josh's when he looks at my dad. Now, there's just an underlying respect and the knowledge that at the end of the day, they both want the same thing. They want to take care of me. They want to save me. And after everything that's happened, I realize that it's not so bad to let them do those things. As Dad once told me: It may be hard to ask for help, but that doesn't mean I can't accept it when it's offered. Then he made a speech about bruised apples that made absolutely no sense.

Soon enough, the meals are over and silence descends as the president of Fine House takes the stage. I'd been given a program of the night, so I know that my award will be given last. I don't know what I'd prefer. I sit through the speeches, one after the other, my knee bouncing and my palms sweating.

"You got this, babe," Josh says, his hand on my knee under the table.

"I'm nervous," I sign. "How do you do this all the time? Comps and media and photo-shoots?"

He chuckles. "You don't want to know what I do."

"I do!" I sign, nodding frantically. "Tell me."

He leans in close, his lips skimming my ear. "I picture you naked."

I rear back. "That helps?"

"No," he says seriously. "I just like doing it. *A lot.*"

"Becca Owens!" the speaker on stage announces.

My eyes go huge.

Josh stands, his applause as loud as my dad's. "Get it, baby," Josh says.

Swear, I've never been so self-aware of the way I walk until this very moment. Every step is like walking in quick sand, and if Sandra wasn't next to me, encouraging me to move forward, then I'd have run back into Josh's arms. He wouldn't let me, though. He'd probably throw me over his shoulder and make me stand on that stage while Dad cheered him on.

Good Lord, it's hot.

Why is it so hot?

Why are the lights so bright?

How did I get on stage?

"You ready?" Sandra asks.

I nod. Then, "Oh my God," I mouth. I sign to Sandra, "My speech is in my purse at the table." Before I finish signing the last word, Josh is already jogging toward me, my purse held tightly in his grasp. He jumps on stage, ignoring the steps on either side of it. "Here you go, baby," he says, handing me the purse and kissing my cheek. Then he faces the audience. "She's my girlfriend," he says, his shoulders square. The room fills with light chuckles. "Isn't she cute when she's nervous?"

I wait until he's off the stage before getting the speech from my purse and unfolding the paper. I look over at Josh and my dad, the only two people in the room who are on their feet. Josh taps his nose, and then his chest, his cheesy grin causing me to do the same. I nod at Sandra who translates my signed message into the microphone, "That was my boyfriend. Isn't he cute when he's saving me?"

The laughter that comes eases some of the tension, and I refocus on my task, on the words scrawled in front of me. I look over at Josh and my dad one more time, both of them smiling, the pride in their eyes giving me the encouragement I need.

~

"I fell in love with photography when I was fourteen, when a simple image I'd taken had captured my breath and captured my heart. I remember sitting there, looking at the screen, at this one image, and knowing for certain that life had so much more to offer than what we all chose to see through shielded eyes and shielded minds. It became my task—to capture moments that made me question the world, question my life, question everything.

After seventeen years of living a life in fear, in darkness, I thought I'd accept my fate.

By eighteen, I began to question it again.

Because it was at that point that I met my grandmother, the woman in the center of this photograph. My grandmother believed in fate, believed in faith and in God, and even though she believed in His purpose, that didn't mean she didn't question it. And that, in turn, made me see things through her lens. Through her eyes. Eyes that have experienced sadness and loss and joy and elation.

My grandmother was a nurse.

A teacher.

A green thumb.

An artist.

A hell raiser.

And a poet.

But above all those things, my grandmother loved.

This was the last photograph I took of her before she passed away.

Before she was laid to rest and there was nothing left to question. But she taught me better than that. So on the night she passed, I stared at this image, stared at her tiny hands, stared at her smile, stared at her dark, soul-filled eyes. It wasn't the first time I'd thought about it—how it should be impossible that so much light, so much hope, could come from such darkness...

...but here I stand, proof that anything is possible."

CHAPTER 57

BECCA

"Becca, I love you. A lot. And your speech was phenomenal. Truly. And this night is all about you," Josh says, "*All. About. You.* But seriously, I can't go on that roof again. I just can't. And you may love me less, and you might see me as less of a man, but for real, I had nightmares for days after the last time. Those damn birds were everywhere. And in my dreams—Becca!"—he tugs on my hand as I lead him up the staircase and toward the rooftop of Say Something—"In my dreams, they were crows and they were eating my eyeballs while I was still alive!"

My head throws back with laughter. "No birds this time," I sign.

"Promise me."

I laugh harder.

"Becca, I'm serious! Promise me!"

"I promise," I mouth.

I grab the lantern as well as a blanket I'd prepared earlier and walk to the middle of the rooftop, Josh following closely behind me. After laying the blanket down, I sit on it, pulling Josh's tuxedo jacket tighter around me. It's colder now than it was the last time we were here, and though I haven't been up here since, I thought it'd be the perfect place to talk to him about something that's been on my mind since Grams passed and I realized that life's too damn short not to be living it to the fullest.

"That really was a great speech, Becs," he says. "And in case I haven't told you, I'm really proud of you."

"You've told me," I sign. "But I love hearing it."

"Good. So what's up?"

"Nothing." I shrug.

"Liar," he says, poking my knee. "I can tell you want to talk. I know you."

"You think you 'see' me, huh?" I sign.

"Yeah." He nods, looking directly in my eyes, wistfulness in his stare as if my eyes hold all his memories of us. Maybe for him, they do. His smile holds all of mine. "I *see* you, Becs."

I sit up straighter, yanking up my sleeves so he can see my hands clearer. "I do want to talk to you."

"Okay…"

I sign, "I realized after the internship over the summer that I was going down—"

"Okay, stop," he cuts in, covering my hands. "I'm sorry, I can't… maybe go a little slower or…"

I reach for my phone.

"No, we can try signing, it's just…"

"It's okay," I mouth.

"I'm really sorry, babe. It's just hard for me to try to find the time to practice and learn—"

I wave my hand between us. "Stop it," I mouth. Then kiss him quickly. "You've already learned so much in so little time," I sign. Then have Cordy say, *"I love and appreciate it, but some things are easier for me to type anyway."*

He nods, but he's still unsure.

"Seriously, Josh. Even I would've struggled with signing."

He nods again. "Go ahead."

"So..."

"So...?" he asks.

"Okay. Here goes..."

"Uh oh."

"It's not bad."

"Then why am I nervous?" he says. "You're making me nervous. Just say it."

I blow out a breath.

"You know what?" He moves behind me until I'm settled between his legs and his arms are around my waist. He rests his chin on my shoulder and says, "Just type it and I'll watch. This way you can't delete anything without me seeing."

I kiss his cheek and refocus on my phone. *What I wanted to say was that after the internship over the summer, I realized that I was going down the wrong path...*

"Yeah? Too much journalism and not enough photography, right?"

I nod.

"I was wondering if you'd think that."

You did?

"You just didn't seem happy when I asked you about it, that's all."

You do see me!

He squeezes me once. "Of course I do. So where's your head at now?

I'm not really sure. I just know that I want to photograph anything and everything. I don't want to have to write about it, though. I want the photograph to speak for itself, you know? And I don't want to just do it here. I want to do it all over the world.

"Okay..." he says slowly. "So... what does that mean? You quit college?"

No, I type quickly. *I can't quit. And I don't want to. For the same reason I couldn't stay in North Carolina with you. I feel like I've been through too much to get here, and I deserve this. And I want to finish. Not just for me, but for Grams, too, because she would've wanted that.*

"So what's the plan?"

I glance at him, trying to hide my smile, my enthusiasm evident.

Well, I was thinking how good it would be to travel the world once I graduate. I have the rest of this year and next, but after that, I'd definitely want to do it. How stunning would it be to see all the different architecture and lifestyles and meet people from all different walks of life? I mean, even for a year, it would be amazing.

"A whole year?" he asks, his voice soft.

I nod and type: *Then I realized something...*

"What's that?"

My amazing boyfriend travels for a living...

Josh's entire body tenses, and he smiles against my shoulder. "He does, huh?"

And he has money to support my artistic dream...

He chuckles lightly, "He sounds like a great dude."

He's the best! I spin around until I'm sitting opposite him, my excitement evident. "So, Josh Warden," I sign, grinning widely at him. "Will you save me? Take care of me?"

His weight slams into me, then lifts as he eases me onto my back, his eyes holding mine, while his smile brings me back to the first hotel room we ever stayed in, the first time he made me his, all those years ago. He kisses me gently, his lips warm against the frigid air. "I would love nothing more than to be your hero, Becca Owens."

CHAPTER 58

BECCA

I awaken the next morning to a cold and empty bed. Outside my bedroom door, I hear movement, shuffled steps and the television blasting. I reach for my phone on the nightstand, wondering where the hell my boyfriend is. There are no messages on my phone, so I send him one.

Becca: Way to make a girl feel special, Warden.
Josh: Had errands to run.
Becca: What's her name?
Josh: Why? You gonna go all trailer-park on her?
Becca: If the situation fits.

He sends through a picture of him and Tommy holding random sticks.

Josh: I promised I'd take him to the park to throw sticks at people rollerblading.
Becca: Why?!
Josh: Because rollerblading is for losers. Duh.

Becca: I do not want to partake in those activities at all.

Josh: You were a rollerblader, huh? Loser.

Becca: When can I see him?

Josh: Tommy?

Becca: No, the stick.

Josh: You're such a cranky pants when you wake up. Go out and have a coffee with your old man. My mom organized a lunch date for all of us. He has the address and time to meet up.

Becca: K.

Josh: Becs.

Becca ?

Josh: I may have accidentally stolen your underwear again.

~

Dad already had plans to go golfing with a couple of his friends he met at a bar. Their names are Paul and Howard. One is a finance investor and the other works at a gas station. One is married. One is divorced with two kids. His kid's names are Sasha and Sarah. Why he told me all this random information, I have no idea. A simple "No thank you" to my lunch invitation would've sufficed.

I get in my new car, the one Josh had bought me—a small economical Ford—tap in the address he'd given my dad into my phone and wait for it to calculate my route. Ten minutes later, I'm slowing to a stop on a dirt road with no cafes or restaurants in sight.

Becca: I'm here, but I think you gave me the wrong address.

Josh: What are you looking at right now?

Becca: Nothing really. There's a fence and some trees.
Josh: Is the fence green?
Becca: Yes.
Josh: Drive up the driveway and park at the bend of the arch just by the front door.
Becca: Is this someone's house?
Josh: Just go. Tommy's waiting, he's excited to see you.

With that image in mind, I put the car back in gear, and steer into and up the long driveway, parking where Josh told me to. There are no other cars in sight, but I figure there might be a valet inside who'll move it later.

Becca: Okay. I'm here. Do I just go inside? Is it fancy? I'm not dressed for fancy.
Josh: Just hurry up. We're waiting, and I'm starving!!!!!!!!!!!!!!!!!!!!

I calculate twelve steps to get to the front door of what looks (at least to me) to be a mansion. I push down on the handle slowly and peek inside. The place is empty. And I'm not talking empty of people, I'm talking *empty.*

No furniture, nothing on the walls, *nothing.*

Nothing but dozens of pictures littered on the floor.

I squint, trying to make them out, and gasp when I realize they're pictures of Grams, of me, of Josh, and of Tommy. I step inside and pick one up, my heart racing, my hand going to my mouth. With shaky hands and tear-filled eyes, I pick up another, and then another, following the trail from the foyer, through the living room, into the kitchen and out the back patio where more pictures await. I breathe for what seems like the first time since I opened the door, letting the cold air hit my lungs, reminding me that I'm alive, though I'm pretty sure I left my heart beating somewhere by the front door. I glance down by my feet and take in the next image before picking it up. It's of Grams and Tommy sitting on the steps leading to Josh's apartment. He's handing her flowers, clearly picked from her garden, and she's smiling… the kind of smile that took hold of the atmosphere and made everything as bright and happy as she felt. I follow the photographs down the patio steps and into the soft dewy grass. I keep my head lowered, picking up every single picture and studying them a moment before going to the next. The farther I move, the pictures begin to change. Josh and Tommy together. Me and Josh together. Me and Tommy together. Until I get to one of all three of us, and I pick it up and stare at it the longest. It's one Josh had taken on his phone from the sand-stealing night at the beach. The night of the first kiss, of the first shared feelings we'd kept secret, simmering just below the surface. Tommy looks so young. We all do. My gaze moves, searching for the next picture, but there isn't one there, and when I see what's in place of it, my breath catches, and everything stops.

Everything.

Josh and Tommy stand side by side, in matching gray suits… beneath the arbor Josh had made my grandmother for her sixty-fifth birthday. I swallow forcefully and let the tears fall as I look at the arbor, and at them, then at our parents standing beside them. Then something strange happens. Something I can't explain. A force pushes me forward, like hands on my back, urging me toward them, and I move… one foot in front of the other, my hand still covering my mouth. I exhale a shaky breath and stop a few feet away, knowing, but not really believing that all this is happening and it's happening to *me*. I'm a sobbing mess by the time Josh takes my left hand in his. "Hi," he whispers.

"Love," I whisper back, because it's the only thing I can say, the only thing I feel.

He smiles, but beneath that, I can see the nerves, the fear, and I want to assure him that he has nothing to be fearful of, but he hasn't yet asked and maybe I'm wrong… Maybe I'm jumping to conclusions. But then he pulls out a ring from the pocket of his slacks, a giant square emerald surrounded by diamonds. He clears his throat and takes a deep breath, his eyes glazed and his voice soft when he says, "Remember that night when I told you I wanted you back, and I asked you for a sign that you felt the same way?"

I nod quickly and wipe the tears from my eyes because I want to *see* everything. I want to *see* him.

"Do you remember kissing me?"

I nod again.

"I went out the next day and got you this ring because I knew…"

I can't breathe. I can't think. I can't *anything*.

"…I knew we'd eventually be here. I've been carrying it around with me ever since, waiting for the right time…"

I look over at my dad, a man who stepped up and took me in, no questions asked. Then I look over at Ella, a woman who loves me as her own. And then to Tommy… *my best friend*.

"Now, Daddy?" he asks, pulling out a plastic, green ring from his pocket.

Josh's eyes penetrate mine, searching, questioning, reminiscing. Then he smiles, allowing me to drown in the joy of our memories "Now, Buddy."

In sync, they get down on one knee, each holding one of my hands.

I force time to stand still so my mind—my heart—can capture the moment.

Josh places the ring on the tip of my finger, and the words

leave his mouth, each one spoken with purpose, with clarity, with confidence. "Coast with *us*, Emerald Eyes?"

EPILOGUE

BECCA

The house with the green fence and the long arch driveway was ours. Josh said he'd been in town for a whole week prior to my awards night, dealing with realtors and finding us the perfect space. And it was perfect. A little on the big side, but Josh said it was the only house he could find that had everything he wanted: a basement apartment for my dad to stay in when he was home from work so he didn't have to pay rent for his old house, a small cottage for his mom at the back of the property by the pond. Yes, a pond! He didn't want to leave his mom alone in North Carolina, and having her with us meant she could be close to Tommy and help out when he was traveling—which he did a lot less of. He didn't want me carrying the weight or the so-called burden of taking care of Tommy once I was done with classes and work, and he still wanted me to enjoy being a college student, drinking at the bar with my friends until the early hours of the morning. I appreciated that, as much as I appreciated him.

Tommy enrolled at the local elementary school and started attending actual classes with actual kids, meaning he had an actual routine to live by. It was hard on him at first, not being the center of attention and mixing with kids his own age, but after a while, he settled in, and a few months later, Natalie and Justin bought their first house as newlyweds only four blocks away. They wanted to be close to Tommy, and Tommy—he couldn't be happier.

Ella, though—she was going out of her mind with boredom. Even though she worked at Say Something, running the art therapy classes with me, and managing the sales of my work through Views Of Emeralds, she still couldn't find enough things to occupy her time. So one night, we sat down, just her and me, while Tommy was spending the weekend with his mother, and decided to start the Walk For Chaz Charity, a sub-section of the Henry Warden Foundation. After a few glasses of what we declared "Jesus Juice," we had a plan set out. So, every four months for the past two years, we collect donations from Josh's sponsors and hand them out to the less fortunate. We have one branch here, one in North Carolina run by Josh's aunt Kim—Josh's old garage apartment being the headquarters. We decided to lease out Grams's house and give the profits to her church. Josh and I found the perfect tenant. A seventeen-year-old single father who stepped up to take care of his daughter. Josh has never admitted it, and I'll never ask, but I highly doubt our "tenant" has ever paid rent for that house. Still, the church seems to get a check once a month from Grams's estate—an estate she left in Tommy's name for when he turns twenty-one. We also have a branch in California, the heart of the skate scene, run by Nico's crazy grandmother who, by the way, loves the "Jesus Juice" as much as my Grams did.

After a year of living in the house, Josh built an indoor skate park on our land, because... why not, right? And because he wasn't traveling as much, he spent his days in there training while I was in class, and Tommy was at school.

College, classes, homework, tests, finals—all of it sucked. Bad. Especially since I had big plans after graduation and I kind of just wanted it to be over. It wasn't only the year of travel and adventure that Josh, Chris, and I had mapped out—plans that included Tommy coming with us as much as possible—but there was also that small little detail called *the wedding.*

Josh and I married a week after I graduated—a small ceremony on an island in Hawaii where Grams had grown up. We invited our family and a few close friends that included Sandra and Pete and Josh's teammates, plus Chris and Josh's manager and of course, Blake and Chloe. Tommy invited Nessa, his "long time" girlfriend who was, by then, cancer free.

I'd never really thought about my wedding day. Not in detail. Dawn, my therapist, who I still see, along with Lexy, my voice therapist, suggested that maybe I didn't give myself the false hope because I didn't believe I'd be around to see it. Maybe they were right. No, I'm sure they were.

The day went by so fast I barely remember it, but I do remember one thing—Josh and Tommy waiting for me at the end of the aisle—an aisle made of sand and rose petals. They wore identical outfits, identical smiles, and identical hopes for our future.

It was fitting, right? That we'd spent years apart, searching for the *coast*… and ended up marrying on one.

Traveling with five guys plus Tommy was not as fun as it sounded. Swear, by the end of the first trip, I was able to differentiate the smell of each individual's fart. Dudes are gross. Seriously. But that's the only real complaint I had about that entire year. I got to see so much of the world, got to experience so many different places and people and food… oh my God, the food! I think, by the time the year was over, even the guys began to appreciate the things they'd been taking for granted. They saw things through my lens, so to speak. And that first year with my husband, my husband, my husband—sorry, I just like saying *my husband*—brought us even closer. We learned things about ourselves, about each other, about *us*. Josh was wrong when he said that he loved me once, and that he'd make me love him twice, because during that time together, I fell in love with him over and over.

In all ways.

For always.

I guess maybe that's why I chose to stop taking the birth control pills as soon as we got home from our last major trip. In my heart, I knew that even though being Josh Warden's wife felt like a fantasy, and being Tommy's stepmom was a dream, I wanted more. And I knew that if I'd find myself falling because of my wants, they'd be there to pick me up, to help me walk. To help me soar. To help me coast.

Six months after that decision, I waited impatiently at the airport for him to arrive home from a short trip to Denver and drove him straight to the rooftop of Say Something. I didn't have to tell him, didn't even have to lift my hands. He already knew. Because he knows me. He *sees* me.

I clasp my necklace with my sweaty palm, allowing the five rings—the two Josh had given me, plus my engagement, my wedding, and the plastic ring from Tommy—to dig into my hand. I focus on that pain, and that pain alone, and try to ignore the one between my legs.

"You're doing so good, baby," Josh says, kissing my sweaty forehead and trying to remove his hand from my death grip.

"Kick off the stirrups if you need to, Becca," my midwife, Dianna, says, "and when I tell you to, you're going to need to push."

"Kick, push," Josh murmurs, smiling against my cheek.

The pain triples, and I squeeze Josh's hand harder. "Okay, push, Becca!" Dianna yells.

Tears fill my eyes, but I do as she says. I kick, and push, and on my third attempt, the pain disappears as if it was never there. Josh breathes out, his lips to mine, "Olive Juice, baby. So much."

Delirious and confused, I look between my legs at the tiny human we'd created. "Is it okay?" I sign to Josh, trying to catch my breath.

"*She...*" Dianna—familiar with ASL—says, smiling up at me.

The room fills with tiny, innocent cries that have Josh moving toward our daughter. "She's perfect," he says. "Baby, she's *so* perfect."

I reach out for them, my tears flowing fast and free, and by the time I have my baby girl in my arms, I'm consumed with relief, with overwhelming elation, and with unconditional love for her and her daddy. I place my finger in her tiny hand and she grasps on to it like it's been done so many times before.

She's so tiny, so pure, and so beyond perfection I find it hard to breathe.

"She's got your nose," Josh whispers.

"Let me know when you're ready," Dianna says. "Tommy's waiting just outside."

I didn't make a birth plan, knowing that it was unlikely we'd actually stick to it. The one and only thing I wanted was for

Tommy to be with us as soon as possible. I wanted him to be the first to see her, to hold her, to love her.

I *hope* he loves her.

I hope he doesn't feel like he's going to be replaced by her.

I hope he knows that I love him as my own.

"I'm ready now," I sign.

Dianna nods and makes her way to the door. "You can come in, sweetheart," she whispers.

I sit up in the bed when Tommy peers in the room. "Is it ready?" he asks.

"You got a little sister, bud," Josh tells him, while I wave for him to join us.

Tommy grins wide, a nervous giggle bubbling out of him. "Can I hold her?"

"You have to be really careful," Josh says, making a spot on the bed for him.

Tommy sits, his legs crossed and his arms ready for me to place her gently there. "She's so little and cute," he whispers, looking up at me. Josh navigates Tommy's hands so he's holding the back of her head in place.

"She likes you," I sign to Tommy.

Tommy giggles again. "She has to like me, I'm her big brother." He looks down at her. "Did you hear that, Chazarae?" he says, knowing our plans to name her after Grams if she was a girl. "I'm Tommy. I'm your big brother. And I'm going to take care of you, and love you, and be there for you always. And I'm never going to let anybody or anything ever hurt you. Ever." He rocks her slowly from side to side, his boyish voice filling the air. "Somewhere, over the rainbow..."

For the first time, Baby Chazarae's eyes open, seeming to lock on Tommy's. Tommy stops singing and smiles down at her. "She has your eyes, Becs."

I smile and kiss her tiny button nose. Then I look up at Josh, who sniffs once and rubs his eyes. "Thank you," he says, his hand taking mine. "Thank you for giving me you, for giving me our daughter. You're going to be an amazing mother, Becs. I don't ever want you to doubt that."

Tommy looks up now, his eyes narrowed at me. "Why would you doubt that?" he asks me. "You've been my mother for years…" He glances at Josh, a mixture of confusion and innocence. "Right, Dad?"

"That's right, bud," Josh answers, his voice soft.

And as I look down at our daughter in the arms of her big brother, any ounce of doubt, of fear, leave me in a rush and I know that they're right. I can *feel* it.

A mother's intuition.

"Can you get my purse?" I sign to Josh. "And Dad… can you get him?"

After Josh pokes his head out the door, Dad enters the room, his eyes trailing my body making sure I'm okay. When he sees Tommy and baby Chaz next to me, a slow smile forms, a build-up of emotions. "You okay, sweetheart?" he asks.

I nod, my eyelids heavy.

Josh returns with my purse and I reach inside for my wallet, for the piece of worn paper that'd been neglected for years. I unfold it, not wanting it to rip, and I scan *The List*—the list of *fears*. I let the memories flood me, each conquered fear… each captured moment. But none of them compare to this one.

Not even close.

I look up at my dad and remember the promise I'd made him make… that he'd be with me when I crossed off each fear. Then I pick up the pen from the side table and pause a moment, re-reading the only item left unmarked.

Go back to the house of nightmares and face my demons.

Slowly, I move the pen from left to right, each letter, then word, marked for eternity. Tommy's voice continues to fill the room, his words a perfect melody for his perfect baby sister.

"You went home?" Dad asks.

I shake my head.

Josh whispers, sitting down next to me, "Then, how? Why?"

I offer him a smile, along with my tears, and then my lips move, my heavy breath creating the whispered words, "Because I no longer fear it."

ALSO BY JAY MCLEAN

Sign up to Jay McLean's Newsletter

Visit Jay McLean's Website

See all Jay McLean books on Amazon & Kindle Unlimited

See Jay McLean on Goodreads

Jay McLean books on BookBub

ABOUT THE AUTHOR

Jay McLean is an international best-selling author and full-time reader, writer of New Adult and Young Adult romance, and skilled procrastinator. When she's not doing any of those things, she can be found running after her three boys, investing way too much time on True Crime Documentaries and binge-watching reality TV.

She writes what she loves to read, which are books that can make her laugh, make her hurt and make her feel.

Jay lives in the suburbs of Melbourne, Australia, in her dream home where music is loud and laughter is louder.

Connect With Jay

www.jaymcleanauthor.com

jay@jaymcleanauthor.com

Made in the USA
Las Vegas, NV
14 November 2024